MW01505193

SHADOWRUN:
THE COMPLETE FRAME JOB

EDITED BY JOHN HELFERS

This is a work of fiction. Names, characters, places and incidents either are the products of the author's imagination or are used fictitiously, and any resemblance to actual persons, living or dead, business establishments, events or locales is entirely coincidental. The publisher does not have any control over and does not assume any responsibility for author or third-party Web sites or their content.

If you purchased this book without a cover you should be aware that this book is stolen property. It was reported as "unsold and destroyed" to the publisher and neither the author nor the publisher has received any payment for this "stripped book."

The scanning, uploading and distribution of this book via the Internet or via any other means without the permission of the publisher is illegal and punishable by law. Please purchase only authorized electronic editions, and do not participate in or encourage electronic piracy of copyrighted materials. Your support of the authors' rights is appreciated.

SHADOWRUN: THE COMPLETE FRAME JOB
Cover art by Derek Poole
Design by Matt Heerdt and David Kerber

©2019 The Topps Company, Inc. All Rights Reserved. Shadowrun & Matrix are registered trademarks and/or trademarks of The Topps Company, Inc., in the United States and/or other countries. Catalyst Game Labs and the Catalyst Game Labs logo are trademarks of InMediaRes Productions LLC. No part of this work may be reproduced, stored in a retrieval system, or transmitted in any form or by any means, without the prior permission in writing of the Copyright Owner, nor be otherwise circulated in any form other than that in which it is published.

Published by Catalyst Game Labs,
an imprint of InMediaRes Productions, LLC
7108 S. Pheasant Ridge Dr. • Spokane, WA 99224

CONTENTS

INTRODUCTION

Or Meet Your Editor, Mr. Johnson

JOHN HELFERS

I've been editing fiction for Catalyst Game Labs for several years now, and I like to think I'm more than pretty decent at it. But even though I've commissioned dozens of stories and novels, some projects still require a bit more of a hands-on approach due to their unique nature. And along with that uniqueness often comes a deadline that is just as immovable as anything else in publishing.

Just like the one for this introduction was. How was I supposed to write about overseeing the creation of six interlinked novellas set in the new backdrop of the next edition of *Shadowrun*, and featuring the new characters from the Beginner Box Set and take you through how that all came about?

While I was staring at my computer screen, trying to get the words flowing, the core idea hit me: for all intents and purposes, a tie-in fiction editor is a lot like a Mr. Johnson in the Sixth World.

Exactly like one, in fact.

I receive my assignment from the corp: It all started when the CGL overlords (well, one of them) Randall Bills started a thread (or perhaps an e-mail) about how to tie our fiction line into the upcoming release of the next edition of the *Shadowrun* RPG. He came up with the idea to do five interwoven novellas, each centered around one of the new characters that make up the SR team. I assured him that this was a great idea (it was), but (because I'm apparently some kind of masochist) it really should be *six* interwoven novellas—five for the characters, and one more to tie up the actual run itself. And of course I could commission six original (!) novellas, all featuring a team of runners out to score some kind of major run on a corp, and have the first one ready to publish in about 45 days from initial concept (!!), with the next five to follow in two-week intervals leading up to the launch of the new *Shadowrun* edition this August.

When I realized what I had gotten myself into, I hyperventilated for a minute, then set to assembling my shadowrunning (shadow-writing?) team, pulling together the group of writers I would hire to handle this trickier-than-usual job. Commissioning six *Shadowrun* novellas is easy; commissioning six novellas whose plot paths cross over one another and weave in and out as the overall story progresses is a very different item. I needed to find writers I not only could trust were familiar with the *Shadowrun* universe, but who were also solid writers that would play well with the rest of the group. If we didn't have cohesion as each writer turned in their separate plot for the others to tie their stories into, the whole project could fall apart.

Fortunately, I've been editing this IP long enough that I know several excellent writers who can turn in wonderful stories on relatively short notice. I also had contacts on the sourcebook side of SR, and Line Developer Jason Hardy put me in touch with a couple writers who had been working hard on the core rulebook, were experienced in writing *Shadowrun* fiction, and who were also free (and willing) to tackle this project in the limited time frame it required.

So, relatively quickly, I assembled my team: game designer and writer Dylan Birtolo; two *Shadowrun, Sixth World* writers, Brooke Chang and CZ Wright; professional game guy and *Shadowrun* enthusiast Bryan CP Steele; former *BattleTech* and *BattleCorps* editor, and current *Shadowrun* and *BattleTech* freelance writer Jason Schmetzer; and to wrap the whole thing up into a nice neat ending, the same Jason M. Hardy (because he didn't have enough to do with overseeing the creation of the new edition in the first place) who gave me his author list in the first place. Once again, no good deed goes unpunished.

I brought the team together on our online Basecamp project managing site, gave them their assignment, and turned them loose. I pretty much let them loose on figuring out the who, when, where, why, and how the overall plot would go down while I kept tabs on how things were progressing and weighed in on ideas and answered questions when needed. The authors all came together nicely, and soon the ideas were flowing fast and furious.

I took the results of each section of the overall mission and made sure they work for the parameters I'd been assigned: The novella manuscripts started hitting my inbox, and that's when I really got to work in editing and shaping each piece to make sure they fit our vision of what the overarching story was going to be. I'm pleased to say that everyone delivered stellar work, and each new incoming piece cleared the high bar of their predecessors.

Okay, so there was no posturing for respect on the mean streets or last-minute double-crosses among the writers (good thing, too) or betrayals from the corp itself—the closest thing to any obstacles

I encountered was that some of the authors needed a few more days to complete their stories (and one time cover art was delayed, necessitating a rescheduling of the publication of one novella). Frag, I even work on a computer for 99 percent of the time, so I don't even get so much as a paper cut nowadays.

The team I put together worked like a well-oiled machine that gave me the results I wanted, and the final product is a great introduction to the exciting world of *Shadowrun, Sixth World*. I completed my assignment, making my corp happy and allowing a very talented group of writers to show all the *Shadowrun* fans, both old and new, what they can do. In short, I executed like a true Mr. Johnson.

But now, as I re-read this, maybe editing tie-in work isn't all that hazardous, and perhaps I'm stretching that editor-as-Mr. Johnson analogy a bit too far...

Nah...

YU

DYLAN BIRTOLO

The crowd at The Sports Bar let out a communal cheer as the Sonics sank a basket that all but sealed the win. The display at the bottom of the screens updated to show the home team leading by four points with only twelve seconds left. Nothing short of a miracle—or magical interference—would let the Kings come back.

"*Eish*, I can't believe you're gonna win this one." The dwarf woman shook her head, her mohawk swaying with the motion and causing the lights of the bar to make her face tattoos shimmer. Her nose wrinkled, but a smile at the corners of her mouth betrayed her true feelings over the loss.

"Come on Z, you should know better than to bet against the home team." Yu flashed a charming grin that had convinced more than one woman to abandon her better judgment and accompany the elf to his private room. He'd learned to cultivate and appreciate his talents—not that he'd ever consider using them on a member of his team. They were family. He reached up to brush imaginary dust from the sleeve of his suit jacket. One never knew when it would be important to look good.

"One would also think you'd learn by now not to put all your eggs in one basket." He emphasized the last word, eliciting a groan and a heavy eyeroll from his companion as she pushed herself up from the table and walked to the bar. Yu laughed at his own joke, leaning back until the front two legs of the chair lifted from the ground. He rested his weight on the tips of his toes, trying to balance the chair as he waited for Zipfile to return.

As he hovered around that edge, he reached into his pocket and retrieved a burned-out BTL chip. Tapping the useless piece of tech with his thumb, he scanned the bar, taking in the diverse crowd both in terms of metatype and social standing. Sports had a way of bringing folks together, even when they supported bitter rivals.

His gaze drifted over the chip in his hand and he froze, as if noticing it for the first time. What had been wayward spinning turned into slow shifting to catch the changes in light coming from the multitude of screens. His arm ached, and he reached up to rub his shoulder, even though his logical mind knew the wound—and the flesh it had damaged—had been removed long ago. That injury had resulted in his brand new cyberarm, which in most cases functioned better than his original one. But this one came with aches he knew he'd never be rid of.

"Nice chip you got there. Shame it's burned out. Wishing you could go back to fabricated bliss?"

The whisper came from behind his right shoulder, and only Yu's years of training allowed him to keep his composure. Nonetheless, he snapped his arm down, tucking the BTL chip away and out of sight. It was not something meant for others to see under any circumstances. And on the practical level, it was highly illegal, not that anyone in this establishment would consider pulling in Knight Errant.

Keeping his face pointed away from the speaker, Yu tried to glance at the newcomer out of the corner of his eye. The man was human, dressed in clothes that had been nice once, but were spoiled from too many nights exposed to the elements, their wrinkles giving them away as slept in. His hair was short and scraggly, and while he tried to maintain a calm demeanor, after a couple of seconds his eyes flicked to the side, jumping at some motion or shadow. His talents as a salesman were street worthy at best.

"What are you proposing?" Yu asked, keeping his voice low and tucking his chin to direct his voice at the stranger.

"I saw what you had. If you want some fresh ones, take a trip of your wildest dreams, I can make that happen. Fresh stuff, straight off the boats, not like anything you'd've seen. Well, you might, since it's, like, from your homeland."

Yu resisted the warring urges to roll his eyes and strike the man in the throat. The muscles across his shoulders tightened, but that served as the only indicator of his true feelings.

"Meet me outside in five, around the north side of the bar," he replied.

Without another word, the man wandered off, weaving toward the exit. He kept his hands in his pockets and his head pointed down at the floor, but Yu made out the subtle shifts as the unsolicited dealer veered away from anyone who got too close. He recognized the motions and reactions, falling back into old habits of judging the man to gauge whether or not he'd be useful. This one would not meet the standards of his Triad back home. He'd be considered a threat, a vulnerability.

Not that it mattered anymore, but old habits died hard. Of course, not being back home meant he could deal with the BTL dealer as he saw fit. If there was an opportunity to find out more information about this shipment, he might be able to do some real damage to the industry. He wasn't naïve enough to think he could make much of a wave, but any ripples were victories.

His thoughts captivated him so much, he didn't notice Zipfile coming back to the table until she placed a heavy mug in front of him. Shaking his head, he plastered a smile on his face with practiced ease.

"What's in your head?" she asked, lifting her own mug and taking a big swallow.

"Nothing. Just distracted." He saluted her with the beer and took a swallow, not even tasting the cold liquid as it slid down his throat. His mind was too focused on other matters, like watching the clock to see how many minutes had passed. If the dealer went to the meeting location right away, he'd be expecting Yu to show up in three more minutes. If Yu waited too long, the man might get nervous and leave, or at least have his guard up. It would be better to get the drop on him earlier than later.

"Want to bet on the next game? Should be starting in about a half-hour, and it's not like I've got anywhere to be."

"I have something I need to take care of."

"AR drone race, then? Want to check it out? Starts down near the Needle at ten, and lasts until the Knights show up." Zipfile leaned forward, betraying her excitement for the upcoming event.

"Another time." Yu brought his mug up and chugged the last half of the glass, setting it onto the table as he stood up. "I'll catch up with you later."

Zipfile reached out and placed her hand on top of Yu's arm before he could step away. She tilted her head to look up at him with a questioning glance. "What's going on?"

Yu appreciated that she didn't bother to question whether or not something was wrong. She knew him better than that, but this was something he didn't want her to get involved in. Not if he could help it.

"I'm fine." He reached out and eased her hand off, putting it back on the table between them and pressing down in a subtle gesture to leave him be. "I'm just not feeling well, and want to get home."

The lie tumbled with ease from his lips, and he doubted she believed it, but time was running out. He needed to get in position soon if he wanted to get the drop on the dealer before the fool's guard went up. He should've given himself more time.

Yu stepped away, turning his shoulder so he didn't have to look at the dwarf if she offered a rebuttal. She didn't, and he turned his full attention to the upcoming task. He navigated easily through the crowd, sliding through like a rivulet of water always finds a trail downhill, and took the back exit, a fire door with the alarm long-since disabled. Regular patrons frequented this entrance, especially on busy championship nights.

The night air had a refreshing chill compared to the room behind him. There was a hint of moisture too, a welcome change from the sweat and booze permeating every atom inside The Sports Bar. As soon as the door closed behind him, the raucous conversation and celebration faded into a dull hum. Around the corner, passing cars splashed through puddles from the morning's rainfall.

For the moment, Yu had the small street to himself. He didn't count the raccoons sniffing around the piled trash bags as intruders on his solitude. Walking to his left, he approached the corner leading to the north side of the building. When he reached the edge, he hugged the wall, peeking around the edge to scout out the area. He might not be the best thief in town, but his skills still ranked higher than most at not being seen.

The BTL dealer stood against the wall, facing the main street and the corner leading to the front of the building. His weight shifted from one foot to the other in jumpy, jittery movements rather than the subtle swaying of someone who had one too many drinks. After a few seconds, his head whipped around, but he didn't appear to see Yu staring at him from the shadows. The dealer looked at his hand, then back toward the front entrance.

Sliding out from around the corner, Yu slipped forward, his feet gliding over the cement as he moved with almost unnatural grace. He navigated around a couple of puddles, making sure not to splash and alert his prey to his arrival until it was too late.

The man never turned until Yu reached out and grabbed his shoulder. He tugged hard, yanking the man backward and making him stumble back in an attempt to regain his balance. In response, Yu swept out the dealer's rear foot right before it touched the ground, making him fall onto his back with a yelp of surprise. Yu followed him down, dropping his knee so it pressed against the side of the man's throat and turned his face away.

"Please! Don't hurt me! You can have 'em!" The dealer reached toward his jacket pocket with a shaking hand.

Yu didn't let him get that far. Experience taught him not to let anyone, especially terrified targets, grab something unseen. He reached out and smacked the man's wrist with the back of his hand while leaning forward and putting more weight on his knee. The target got his meaning well enough and froze, not even trying to look up through the corner of his vision to look at his assailant.

"You said you dealt in BTL's, that you had a fresh collection off the boats?"

The dealer tried to nod as best as he could with the elf's knee wedged up against his jaw.

"Do you know where the shipment is?"

"I can't tell you."

"Listen, *cat tau*, right now I'm the one you should be afraid of. I'm the one who literally has your face pressed up against the stones. I'm the one who could break every bone in your hand one by one if I wanted to."

To accentuate his threat, Yu reached down and grabbed one of the dealer's fingers, bending it back as far as it would go without snapping. His victim cried out, but silenced when Yu pressed harder with his knee. The tortured scream faded into a whimper. Yu released the man's finger, but kept his hand nearby as a reminder.

"It was being loaded into a warehouse down in West Seattle. It's probably still there. Takes a few days to move it out to distribution. They're just sitting in boxes off the boat. But you can't get in. They've got guards and drek, take you out if you don't got proper business there. I can get you in. Say you're there for a deal. You could buy as much as you want."

Reaching down, Yu patted the man's clothes, searching for his commlink. When he found it, he fished it out and tossed it to the ground near his prisoner's hand. "Show me."

The captive man did as instructed, pulling up a map without moving the rest of his arm. A green dot marked the warehouse, and the map offered directions from their current location.

Yu squinted and pulled up the warehouse on his own commlink, using his DNI to keep his hands free to deal with the criminal if necessary.

"Want me to take you there? I'll show you the best trips ever, stuff you can't even imagine. A trip out of this world."

Yu's face lost all emotion, becoming laser-focused on the dealer underneath him. He thrust his entire weight down into his knee, using the motion to snap the dealer's neck. He stood up and turned away, closing his eyes and lowering his head, not wanting to look at the fresh corpse. His hands clenched into fists and shook at his sides, but he forced himself to take a deep breath.

After a few seconds, he shook out his arms and straightened his jacket. He walked out of the street, never turning to see the body behind him. At this point, it was just another casualty of the illicit BTL trade.

It took several blocks before Yu found himself capable of pasting on his trademark smile and nodding to others in an attempt to elicit a smile or a lifted eyebrow. He leaned against the wall of a late-night café with a steady stream of customers and pulled up the map on his commlink, turning it over to satellite view and getting as good a look at the warehouse as possible with public tools.

As far as he could tell, it looked like a normal warehouse along a string of such buildings in the industry district of West Seattle. Nothing about it stood out from the other warehouses along the strip, and it didn't have any labels or signage he could see from these limited viewpoints. If he wanted to find out anything, he'd need some help.

<Hey Z, sorry for ditching you at the bar. I need a favor if you've got a few minutes. Figure it shouldn't take you too long.>

<Somehow, I'm not surprised. Run into some trouble with your personal business you had to take care of? You could've saved some time if you'd brought me in the beginning, you know.>

<What can I say? I have a flair for the mysterious. Can't have you knowing everything about me. After all, what fun would that be? My secret rendezvous are part of my charm—they give me that extra bit of flair. I realize you don't have as much experience, but trust me when I say the women love it. The men, too.>

Yu imagined the growl from Zipfile as she read his message and composed her reply. It turned the corner of his mouth up.

<Enough. Just tell me what you need.>

<There's a warehouse. I'll send you the address. I need to know who owns it.>

<I'll dig around and let you know what I come up with. I assume this is part of your personal matter, and you're not coming back to the bar?>

<Not tonight. I need to check on something.>

That portion of the business taken care of, Yu called for a ride to take him down to West Seattle. In normal circumstances, he might be worried about leaving such an obvious and easy-to-follow trail, but he hadn't been on a job in a couple of weeks, and they didn't have anything coming up soon, either.

Yu got out of the car a couple of blocks away from the row of warehouses, walking the rest of the way to his destination. Along the way, he slipped into the shadows out of habit. He didn't make his stealth obvious. Rather than hug building walls and cling to the darkness, he picked a path that strayed toward the darkest areas. In his experience, such behavior would prevent people from noticing his presence unless they were on guard, and sometimes not even then.

A breeze picked up, carrying the heavy salt odor from the Sound, combining it with a mixture of rust and grease he associated with heavy machinery. Even from here, Yu saw large cranes arcing up over the top of the buildings, devices for unloading giant crates of cargo. Down here, Seattle gave the impression of being a port in ways the center of downtown did not.

As he approached his destination, Yu slowed his pace and made sure no one stood on the streets before turning the last couple of corners. He still gave the impression of someone walking rather than skulking. If anyone noticed him, the worst thing he could do was draw attention by looking like he was trying to hide. But a hesitant step here, a thoughtful pause there, these things helped to keep him from walking into someone's line of sight.

The object of his interest came into view, and he kept it at the edge of his vision as he strolled down the street. From here, he gained little information about it that he didn't already know, which amounted to it being a warehouse. Lights shone from the windows, and shadows danced along the walls as people inside moved about. The entire structure sat behind a chain link fence with barbed wire looped around the top. A soft buzzing pervaded the air, the familiar noise of drones flying nearby. He hadn't seen any yet, but he couldn't mistake the sound.

This side of the fence had a gate with a guard sitting at his station, his head propped up on his fist. He wore a uniform, but it didn't have any logos or branding, suspicious in its own right. Usually the security corps wanted to advertise their jobs, a way to showcase their dependability.

Yu considered his options. He could bluff his way past the guard, but doing so without knowing anything about the warehouse might prove too difficult. But he didn't need to get in there himself. All he needed as a glimpse through the windows to see what lurked inside. And he did have a camera drone from Emu. He'd never be able to pilot it as well as she did, but this job should be easy enough.

Continuing his circuit, he turned the next corner, making sure the warehouse was no longer in line of sight. To be extra careful, he went a full block over, using the intervening building as cover. Better safe than sorry, especially since he didn't have the backup of his team. He could reach out to Emu and ask for her help, but she'd want to know what he was doing out here, and he didn't know if he wanted to share those details yet. Their family still felt new, fragile, and he didn't want to do anything to risk fracturing it.

Pulling out the small camera drone, he connected it to his commlink and turned it on. It hummed to life and he saw through its camera. Taking control of the device, it flew up over the building and he saw the entire district spilled out before him and stretching to the water beyond, lights from the city reflecting off the dark surface. He didn't waste time savoring the view, and instead flew forward, heading for one of the warehouse windows.

The drone shot forward, and Yu stopped it short, worried it would break through the glass. The sudden shift in momentum rocked his entire view and the drone pulled back as he overcompensated. Struggling with the controls and cursing in Cantonese under his breath, he managed to ease the drone up to the window to peer through the glass.

In that moment, the effort made it all seem worthwhile.

Several people walked around, all armed with automatic weapons carried in plain view. A few stood at the edge of walkways on the second level, looking down on the cargo below. There had to be at least twenty crates inside, most of them sealed and stamped with a combination of letters and numbers that meant nothing to Yu. One of the crates stood open in the center of the room, with two men and one woman looking over the contents. Zooming in with the camera, Yu saw what captured their attention. BTL chips.

There had to be hundreds of them in that crate alone. This was no minor operation, but rather a major link in the BTL supply chain into Seattle. Yu licked his lips before chewing on his bottom one. The value of the cargo explained the sheer amount of firepower present in the room.

All of a sudden, his view rocked so hard he jerked himself out of the drone controls. The sounds of gunfire echoed around the buildings to him. That answered the question of whether the drones around the warehouse were armed or not. Now he'd have to face Emu's wrath for getting one of her drones destroyed. At least he had some answers. It looked like the cargo had just arrived at the warehouse, which meant he had a few days to do something.

But what could he possibly do? Even if he told the team and pulled them into this, it was too big for them to handle alone. And considering how strapped they were for nuyen, hiring an outside support team was out of the question. He could tell the Triads, but they'd wouldn't act unless it was in their own best interests. He couldn't think of a legitimate way that taking out this operation would benefit them, which brought him back to square one.

He puzzled over this problem on his way back home. A possible solution came to him in the form of a message from Zipfile.

<I tracked down the owner of the warehouse—at least I think I did. I expected all those warehouses to be owned by Federated Boeing, but congratulations, you managed to find a strip of privately-owned buildings in that maze of warehouses and shipping containers. According to the records I found, four of those buildings in a row are owned by Rip Current Sea Lanes. They're a tiny corp, possibly owned by someone else. I'll keep checking. They lease out the storage units you found. Here's the thing. The warehouse you asked about? It doesn't have a lease. Right now, it should be empty.>

<It's anything but empty right now,> he responded. <I was there checking it out. The area's swarming with activity. Don't suppose you got an address for the owners? Might be interested to see what they say about someone squatting in one of their warehouses.>

<Eish, who do you think you're talking to? You know I've got it. I'll send it your way. Do you want backup?>

<No need. This will be strictly above the books. I'll even go during the day, when there aren't any shadows, to show my good intentions.>

<*That doesn't even make sense! There's tons of shadows during the day. That was bad, even for you, and that's saying something.*>

Yu chuckled and spent the rest of the trip lost in his thoughts as a plan formed in his mind...or at least the next steps.

The following morning, Yu took his time getting breakfast before heading out to the address Zipfile had provided. She checked in with him once again to see if he wanted backup, but again he turned down her offer. He saw no reason to be worried about making a polite business call during the middle of the day. Showing up with an entourage or having them waiting in the wings would be more suspicious than showing up alone. He could've contacted Rude, and claimed the man was a bodyguard. They'd played that part before, and it was more than half-true. What was it Brother Lee used to say? *"The best lies are based on truth."*

At the thought of his former mentor, Yu's hand strayed to the burned-out BTL chip in his pocket. His fingers tightened around it through the fabric until its sharp edges bit into his skin. Letting go, he smoothed his pants, making sure not to leave any trace of the gesture.

The trip to Rip Current Sea Lanes passed without incident. The office building was as unimpressive as the corporation's rating, not even worth being looked at by the Corporate Court. It was a simple one-story building nestled between a towering corporate skyscraper and a family restaurant.

Stepping through the front door, Yu recognized the façade for what it was. True, the paint was peeling in a couple of places and the walls looked thin, barely a step above a temporary office situated on a construction site. However, there were other clues. Micro cameras situated around the corners of the room in such a way to prevent any blind spots. A heavy-duty maglock system attached to the door leading to the back offices.

It left Yu with the impression of a building designed to look far more amateurish than it actually was.

The receptionist at the front desk was a young elf woman, offering him a beaming smile that lit up her face, either that or it was the small lights just under her skin near the corner of her eyes. She tilted her head to a practiced angle, giving off the impression of someone who not only completed finishing school, but excelled at it.

"Welcome to Rip Current Shipping Lanes. How can I help you?" Her voice had a perfect sing-song quality that only came with months of practicing tone fluctuation. In short, she was a master of her craft, and far too experienced to be working at a no-name company in the middle of nowhere.

Yu offered her a polite bow, then reached up to run his fingers through his dark hair, making the trained motion look natural and using it to draw her attention. She wasn't the only one skilled in such subtle manipulations.

"Greetings, young miss. I came here hoping to speak with someone about renting a warehouse down in West Seattle. You came highly recommended from a friend of mine." He raised his first two fingers as he dropped his chin in mock apology. "Of course, I can't divulge the identity of my associate. I am sure you understand the need for such discretion. But rest assured, they speak very highly of your services and consideration."

"Of course. Give me just a moment." She rose and headed toward the back room, but hesitated when she got to the door and glanced back to give Yu an appreciative look, taking in his entire body. He pretended not to notice, even though he savored the reaction.

She swiped an access card and entered the back room, leaving him alone in the false front. But the cameras squashed any temptation to give anything more than a passing glance. He stood in front of a framed display of a map of downtown Seattle from the late 20th century.

The heavy *clack* of the door captured his attention and made him turn. The receptionist stood in the doorway, holding the door open for him.

"Mr. Miller is willing to meet with you. He's behind the second door on the left."

Yu nodded to her. "Thank you. I appreciate you getting me in on such short notice."

He walked down the hall, looking at his surroundings without turning his head or slowing his steps. Stepping through the door was like stepping into a different building. Whereas the front gave off a shoddy impression of a company barely managing to survive, the back hall could've passed for the entrance to a clean room, including fluorescent lights and sliding doors filled with frosted glass. The polished floor tiles made his dress shoes *clack* with every step. Easier to notice someone trying to sneak around in this setting.

The second door on the left stood open, and a large human sat behind a desk with an AR display floating over the surface. With a gesture in the air, he slid the display to the side and pointed to one of the office chairs in front of him. He wore a tailored suit that had to cost more nuyen than most people made in an entire year. His solid gray hair was slicked back, without even a trace of the original color.

"Won't you please come in and have a seat, mister...?"

"Chen." Yu offered the pseudonym as he stepped forward and extended his hand. Mr. Miller took it and gave it a firm shake. His grip was strong enough that Yu appreciated having a cyberarm.

"Please take a seat. Melanie tells me you wanted to inquire as to the availability of one of my warehouses? We are a small business, but we find it helps to keep things moving."

"You might say that you run a tight ship?" Yu offered as he took a seat.

If Mr. Miller noticed the joke, he didn't appreciate it. "Yes, quite. However, part of the reason we are able to function underneath the shadow of some of the other corporate giants in the district is because we are very discerning with our clientele. I would need to know much more about you and the potential business you offer before I could offer a mutually beneficial proposal."

"I can appreciate that. You have your own reputation to be concerned about, as I have mine. I am well familiar with the power of reputation. In the right hands, it's almost as powerful as information."

Mr. Miller paused and stared at Yu, locking gazes and trying to make the smaller man squirm. It was a tactic Yu was very familiar with from his years of experience. He sat in his chair, as relaxed as possible, and remained calm without looking away. After the space of a few breaths, Mr. Miller broke the gaze to turn and pull up something in his AR display.

"As you can see, we have a perfect record throughout our entire tenure of business, more than twenty years. At the time we had only one warehouse, but our operation has grown to encompass four buildings, each of which is capable of storing at least 350 cubic meters of goods for as long as your contract holds. We provide our own security forces at no extra charge, and are authorized to insure your goods, provided they abide with all import regulations, of course. We're not responsible for any misunderstandings with authorities of the law."

"Do you currently have any open contracts with any clients, are all of your warehouses available?"

"You must realize I am not at liberty to divulge such information. The discretion of my clients demands my silence to avoid any potential unpleasantness. I'm sure you can understand."

"I do, and I was not trying to get you to give away any corporate secrets." Yu looked up at the ceiling behind Mr. Miller as if searching for thought while he gestured in the air making small circles with his free hand. "I have a special shipment arriving soon, one that will require multiple storage solutions. I was hoping to use a single contractor for all of my needs, and I'm afraid I would need all of your warehouses to do it."

Mr. Miller steepled his hands in front of his face and rested his chin against them as he narrowed his eyes. When he spoke, his words were slow and deliberate.

"That would require a substantial investment on your part, Mr. Chen. And you have yet to inform me what your business is. I'm sure we could handle such a request, but I would need to be assured of your reputation."

"I find it surprising you'd speak about reputation when you don't even know what's going on in your own warehouses. Either that, or you tend to make promises you can't keep."

Before Mr. Miller had an opportunity to respond, Yu pulled up an edited clip from the drone footage of the night before. It showed part of the flight toward the warehouse, and while it wasn't professional, the shaky footage gave unmistakable proof of activity.

"Where did you get this?" Mr. Miller asked.

"Irrelevant. What I can tell you is that this footage was taken last night at what you claimed to be an empty and available warehouse. It seems like someone is squatting in your property. So, my question would be which element of your reputation is at risk, your honesty or your security?"

Yu hoped that by keeping Mr. Miller on the defensive, the man wouldn't pry too much into his paper-thin story. He didn't have credentials or anything to back up his claim, but he knew how to navigate a verbal minefield. The question was whether or not the corporation knew about the BTL dealers. He hoped Mr. Miller's reaction would give him the evidence he needed, one way or another.

Mr. Miller lowered his hands and leaned back in his chair. The index finger on his right hand tapped against the opposite finger as he hesitated before responding. "I will need to check with my associates, but I have no record of this warehouse being in use. It would appear that this is an unsanctioned situation which we will deal with appropriately."

"How do you plan to deal with it?" Yu asked, leaning forward in his chair. He caught the motion and stilled himself, hoping the reaction might pass unnoticed.

The predatory grin of the man across from him showed the futility of his hope. "It seems you are more interested in the perpetrators and this specific warehouse than you are in actually concluding business. Given the nature of your call and the evidence you provided, it also seems safe to venture a guess as to your true vocation. You work with certain elements of society who prefer not to be seen or noticed, do you not?"

Mr. Miller lifted up a hand to quell any response Yu might have offered. "There is no need to respond. But for our conversation to continue, I suppose it would be more prudent for you to address me as Mr. Johnson, would it not?"

Yu sat up straighter in his chair, legs tightening in anticipation of a hasty retreat. He didn't see any armed guards in the building, and no automatic sentries. The sprint to the front office should take no more than a few seconds if he needed a quick exit. Alternatively, there was the door at the far end of the hall. But he had no way of know if it would be locked or where it would go. And both of those exits required him to get out of this room with only one exit.

Despite his thoughts, other than the straightening of his spine, he forced himself to appear at ease. Showing fear would give his new associate too much power in this negotiation. Besides, he had been in far worse situations.

"Very well, Mr. Johnson. What is it I can do for you? If you didn't have business for me, I expect you would've called security and had me escorted out of this office by now."

Mr. Johnson chuckled, leaning forward to slap his palm on the desk before pointing a finger at Yu.

"I like you. You've got courage mixed with a healthy amount of foolishness. Not only that, but you're observant, paying attention to your surroundings and calculating ramifications of actions as easily as breathing. In a different situation, I would consider offering you a role as a wageslave. But my instincts tell me you'd balk at such a prospect."

Yu didn't respond, waiting for the Johnson to continue.

"Very well. I expected as much. Your observations once again prove accurate, I do have something requiring the attention of someone in your line of work. I trust you have suitable references?"

"Ms. Myth speaks highly of our skills," Yu provided.

Mr. Johnson nodded, an indicator that he knew the name. Ms. Myth made it a point to spread her reputation amongst those who hired runners—it was her job, after all. But she didn't usually bother with single nation companies. If this Johnson knew her by reputation, he had to be more connected than he appeared on the surface. Perhaps his job here was as much a false image as the front room of the office.

"I will have my assistant perform an inquiry to verify your reputation. While we await the results of that check, tell me, what is your interest in my warehouse? And don't insult us both by claiming to be a philanthropist with only my best interests at heart." Mr. Johnson interacted with his AR screen while he spoke, fingers flying through the air. The view changed to a private one, but Yu didn't need to see the display to recognize the motions.

"Let's call it professional business. It would serve my interests if the business transpiring there stopped before it had a chance to finish."

Mr. Johnson stopped interacting with his AR display and turned to give Yu his full attention. He brought his hands back to the familiar steeple and tapped his index finger a couple of times.

Yu continued, "I'm sure someone with your influence could arrange to have such a business shut down with prejudice. I mean, it wouldn't do to have your reputation soiled by the illegal activity transpiring within."

Mr. Johnson raised an eyebrow. "Is that a threat?"

Yu held up his hands in with his palms facing out in a surrendering gesture. "Not at all. I point it out merely to alert you to the potential threat if someone with less discretion happened to come across the business. I know the value of silence. As you pointed out, I have experience working in the darkness. You don't work in that business long without knowing how to keep your mouth shut."

Something must have alerted the Johnson, as he turned to the side and stared at the empty air. Yu's legs tensed as he expected security to come bursting through the door. He hadn't heard anything, but didn't know how well the door muffled sounds. Through it all, he maintained an outward veneer of calm, knowing the value of appearance during negotiations. It would take more than a couple of potential goons to get him to jump.

When Mr. Johnson turned back to face him, he relaxed his shoulders and sat back. "It seems we have much to discuss. Your reputation checks out, and I believe you have the skills and expertise necessary for my little venture. I offer an exchange of services. You do me this favor, and I will arrange to have your competition removed from the warehouse, with excessive force, of course."

Mr. Johnson waved his hand in the air as if chasing away a fly. "And of course, I'll provide a nominal fee for your trouble as well. I know your type is not often spurred into action without the promise of nuyen."

Yu knew better than to respond to the emotional barb. "What is this venture of yours?"

"A simple matter, something I'm sure your team is more than capable of completing. I have a file I need uploaded to a server. A trivial task."

"If it were trivial, you wouldn't need my team to get it done. Earlier you didn't want me to insult you. I would expect the same consideration."

Mr. Johnson dipped his head, conceding the point. "This file needs to be installed on an offline server, one I cannot gain access to without drawing undue attention."

"The target?"

"Telestrian Industries on Denny Way."

Now it was Yu's turn to pause and take a moment to consider the options. Telestrian Industries was a large enough company to give him pause. The job wasn't above his team's abilities, but it wasn't a milk run either.

"Why would a single national company want to target an AA giant? Seems like swinging a bit outside your weight class, don't you think? A difference like that is worth a premium charge. You don't know how intense the security is in companies like that. It's not a simple matter of passing a few maglocks."

"I'm sure by now you've determined that we are more than we appear. Rest assured, I have intimate familiarity of the lengths such corporations will go to in order to protect their investments."

"Anyone can make claims. Give you felt the need to verify my reputation, I trust you can understand the need for me to verify yours. I need something more than your assurances."

As way of response, the Johnson summoned an AR display in the space between them. It didn't take long for Yu to discern its meaning. It looked like a hierarchical org chart, with many branching lines descending from a common node at the top. At the bottom of one of the leaves of the tree sat Rip Current Shipping Lanes. At the top sat an all-too-familiar name: *Renraku.*

Just seeing the name of the AAA corporation made his chest tighten, and Yu hoped his outward appearance didn't betray his reaction to the revelation. Assuming it was true. Then again, claiming to speak for a Triple-A corp was a risky endeavor. They tended to not look kindly on charlatans, and had the authority to make sure most thought better of the attempt—if they even survived it in the first place.

Working for a Triple-A corp came with considerable risks, but also considerable benefits as well. It put to ease any doubts he had about the Johnson's ability to handle the threat at the warehouse. Even with the firepower they had on display, it was nothing compared to what a company like Renraku could bring to bear. If he wanted them taken care of, this was the opportunity to guarantee it.

"I need to run this by my team. It will take a few days to scout the location..." Yu said.

"I will not move against the criminals using my facilities until you complete your end of the bargain. I do wonder, however, how long it will take them to deliver their merchandise through the appropriate channels."

The Johnson's interruption halted Yu's train of thought. Even though he knew it was another attempt to goad him, the statement was nonetheless accurate. His team didn't have the luxury of taking their time before accepting and carrying out this run, not if he wanted to make sure Renraku handled the BTL dealers. The nuyen was secondary; dealing with the threat was the primary reason to take this job.

But he needed something to mollify his team. "How much nuyen are you offering?"

"This is a low profile run, and we are arranging for alternate forms of payment. I believe with those factors considered, five thousand would be a fair price. All payable up front. Consider the business with the warehouse to be your second half of the payment. Are we agreed?"

Yu considered asking for more nuyen, but decided not to push his luck. He needed that warehouse taken care of, and this seemed like the best possible course of action to accomplish his goals. He had walked in without a plan, and walked out with a greater prize than he thought imaginable. Not to mention, it never hurt to get in the good graces of those with power and influence.

"We are agreed, Mr. Johnson."

The Johnson reached into a drawer of his desk and pulled out a portable drive, commlink, and certified credstick, laying all of them on the table. He slid back in his chair, out of reach as Yu stood up to claim the items. Mr. Johnson had already turned back to his AR display, turning to the side and dismissing Yu with the unspoken gesture.

The runner took the items and left, flashing a smile at the receptionist on his way out of the building.

<*Team, we need to meet up. I have a job for us, but it needs to be done soon, today if possible. Before you all start hollering, I know it's short notice. I'll explain when we meet.*>

Catching a lift downtown, he got out a block away from the safehouse. Old habits died hard. He never took a car directly to the apartment they used as a base of operations. The rideshare programs claimed their logs were secure, but he had personally retrieved logs from more secure facilities than he could remember. The wiser course of action involved getting out a few blocks away and enjoying the walk while keeping an eye out for shadows.

He got up to their apartment without incident, confident that no one had followed him. The middle of the day often made it harder to spot a tail, since the streets were full of people going about their daily lives. Mainly wageslaves on their lunch breaks or running errands. Down here Knight Errant and sometimes corporate security took regular patrols to make sure the sidewalks remained clear of "undesirables."

When he got to the apartment, he saw he was the last to arrive. Zipfile sat at the breakfast bar, zoned out in the Matrix, judging by her glazed expression. Rude, the big burly troll, sat on the couch in the center, both arms stretched out to either side, taking up the entire seat himself. His stained trench coat looked to have been through a war zone, and quite possibly could have been.

Frostburn stood near one of the windows on the far side, gazing out at the city skyline, taking advantage of their twelfth-floor view. Her eyes flicked to Yu when he entered, giving him her attention without turning away. Emu sat in the center of the floor, various bits of drones and other machinery Yu couldn't identify scattered around her as she picked apart the guts of what he guessed was three machines at the same time.

Rude spoke first. "What's the job and why so short, elfy-pants? Ain't like ya to pick up somethin' without talkin' it to death first."

With his words, the rest of the team turned to face him, their questions evident. Frostburn had her lips pressed together, and Rude looked bored. The other two members of the team seemed curious, waiting for Yu to explain.

"It's a simple run, doesn't pay much, but comes with some special benefits. Not the least of which is getting in good with someone who could give us lots of work down the road. Bigger jobs, and well worth the investment of effort."

"Get to the point and stop tryin' to butter us up with yer fancy talk."

Yu nodded, conceding the point. He needed to be more direct, even if he didn't want to share all the details. "Five thousand nuyen in advance, with the option for a bonus. A simple B&E job where all we have to do is upload a file to an offline server. Should be easy nuyen."

Zipfile held up her hand, and Yu tossed her the portable drive.

While she looked into it, Rude shook his head. "Chump change. Not worth it. We pull bigger paydays'n that without even tryin'. Ain't worth the trouble."

"You need to keep in mind who we'll be working for, and what it will mean for our future. This may be a small job, but it's in the big leagues. Consider it an investment in things to come."

Rude wrinkled his nose, but it was Frostburn who spoke. "Who's the client?"

"Renraku."

Everyone stilled when he said the name, even Zipfile. She paused in her digital examination and looked over at Yu, who cleared his throat. "Like I said, this is it. This is the big leagues. The job may be small, but the cred we'll get is worth more than just the payment."

"Dealing with a corp like that, nothing's simple. And if it seems simple, then you're not seeing the whole picture." Frostburn shook her head. "I don't like this. How'd you find this job? Did this come through Ms. Myth? Why the urgency on the timeline?"

"I was following a lead for some personal business, and found the Johnson masquerading as the CEO of a smaller company. You know how I work. We got to talking, and he decided to throw some work our way. When I pushed him, that's when he admitted who his real employer was. But by then, the deal was already made."

Yu took a deep breath. "Look, if you're not comfortable with the job, I understand. It's a bit of an odd one, for sure. But when the opportunity presented itself, I didn't want to let it slip by. This is a case of being in the right place at the right time, and I think we should move on it. The job's easy enough that I'm confident I could take it on myself, keep any of you from being at risk. I'll just work my way in, install the file, and get out without them being any the wiser."

"And take the entire pay?" Rude scoffed.

"No, I'd still split it. We're a team."

"Works fer me," Rude leaned back and tilted his head back until the couch groaned.

"We're not going to let you go there alone, that's foolish," Frostburn said. "Even if the job is as easy as you claim, something might go wrong. Like you said, we're a team. We're not leaving you on your own, right, Rude?"

The troll responded with a grunt, which was the extent of his support when he didn't agree with a course of action.

Yu looked over at Emu to see what she thought. She shrugged. "Like you said, the job seems easy enough, but that makes me nervous. The short timeline does too. But if it'll get us in good with one of the AAAs, it might be worth it. Certainly sounds like something we could handle."

"Thanks, Emu."

"I still need to talk to you about wrecking my drone," she growled.

"Right." Yu turned toward Zipfile, making a mental note to come back to that at some point. She tossed the drive back to him and he snatched it out of the air, tucking it into a pocket in a blink.

"Didn't open the file in case it's some kind of virus, but the install package is pretty standard. Just plug it in and it should auto execute. Nothing fancy I could find in my brief scan."

<*This deal connected to the warehouse?*> Her private message came to his commlink as she spoke.

<*Yes. I need to deal with something there, and this seems like the best way to take care of it. That's why the payment is so low.*>

<*You know I won't pry, but I'll just say you should share it with the team. We'll all be more likely to have your back if you just come clean about it. Well, maybe not Rude, but the rest of us...*>

<*I'll keep it under advisement. And Z... Thanks.*>

"I say we go for it," Zipfile said with a shrug. "It's a risk, but everything we do is. This particular one just might have dividends that pay off down the line."

"What's your plan?" Frostburn asked. She stepped away from the window and shoved Rude's arm off the back of the couch so she could perch on the edge.

"If Zipfile can drum up some credentials for one of my SINs, I walk in the front door as an employee during the morning rush tomorrow. Security will be too swamped to run a thorough check on everyone, so I should be able to get in relatively easily. They're not expecting an intrusion, so they won't be on high alert. Once inside, I a terminal in the offline server, plug the drive in, and then walk out the front door. How long will I need?"

"A couple of seconds. The package on the drive isn't large, so it should be near-instantaneous. And drumming up some credentials might be doable. Who's the target?"

"Telestrian Industries."

Zipfile jumped into the Matrix while the rest of the team, except for Rude, watched her. When she spoke, her eyes still had the distant-view quality indicating her dual presence in the Matrix as well as the room. "I can work something up for you by the morning shift. It won't open any security for you, but it'll get you through the front door."

"That's all I need."

Rude was still clocking Yu with his cybereyes. "I don't care what ya think, or how smooth ya think it's gonna go. I'm still comin' along and waitin' in case ya need an alternate exit. Yer gonna get killed one of these days if I'm not watchin' yer back."

"I wouldn't have it any other way. If we're all in agreement about this, I suggest we use the rest of the night to get as much info as we can. We don't have a lot of time to prep for this one, but there's some special circumstances in play for why it needs to be done on such a short timeline."

The team quieted down as they went to work, finding ways to get whatever they could about the target. Emu took Rude for a scouting mission while Frostburn retreated to her room to perform her own version of scouting. Zipfile sunk deeper into her digital world, leaving Yu alone in the main room of the apartment.

He reached out to Billy Shen to see if his Triad contact had any insight into Telestrian or connections he could take advantage of, but came up empty. He considered telling Billy about the BTL shipment, but thought it would be better and more valuable to share the info after the problem had been dealt with.

Reaching out to a few other people he knew resulted in similar results, leaving Yu with nothing to do while he waited for others to finish their reconnaissance. He moved to his room and sat on the edge of the bed, lifting his heels and bouncing his knees. After a few seconds, he got up and paced the room from one end to the other. When that failed to provide relief, he dropped into a fighting stance and practiced shadow boxing, fighting imaginary opponents that assaulted him in his imagination. He picked up speed, the motions turning into a blur as he snapped from one position into another, lashing out at his mental adversaries and imagining them reacting to the blows. Soon his clothes stuck to his body when he moved, but it did not slow his assault.

At one point, he flopped onto the bed, staring up at the ceiling and taking deep breaths. Sometimes this was the worst part of the job, the waiting. Sometimes it was worse than others. His hand strayed to his pocket and he removed the BTL chip, staring at it as he lifted it over his head and tumbled it across his fingers. Every scorched line was etched into his memory as much as the silicon, but he couldn't help examining it again and again.

Thrusting it back into his pocket, he rolled over and scrambled to the bedside table. Jerking the drawer open, he reached inside and grabbed a couple of pills rattling around, popping them into his mouth without bothering to see what they were. In the end, it didn't matter. Only the end effect was important.

Rolling onto his back, he stared at the ceiling once again, his breathing ragged and heavy. As he recovered from his exertions, the colored lines of light in the ceiling began to swirl, mixing and turning around before his eyes. His breathing slowed as he studied the designs that formed with the mixing of the colors. His arms splayed out to either side, he smiled as he lost himself in the hallucination. He caught the odor of lavender on the air, along with a touch of ginger. The odor made his mouth water and he licked his lips, but otherwise didn't move from the bed.

His trip ended with him drifting off to sleep, despite the early hour. When he woke, he still had several hours until daylight. His clothes stuck to him and he could smell his own sweat caked onto his body. Considering he needed to be on the job soon, he set to getting himself cleaned up and presentable. It wouldn't do to show up in a wrinkled, sweat-stained suit. His mission depended on blending in and not drawing any undue attention which might result in security forces reviewing his credentials. Whatever Zipfile could concoct would not stand up to heavy scrutiny. She was good, but no one was that good on such a short timeline. The burden of success rested largely on his shoulders.

As he showered, Yu went over the plan in his mind, rehearsing possible scenarios to prepare for any number of ways it could go wrong. At least if it did, he was the only one at risk. He didn't want to expose his team to the dangers of this run, especially since the main reason for accepting it was his personal vendetta. He'd used lots of pretty words to convince the team, but deep down he wouldn't lie to himself. He promised he would never do that. And being honest, this job was about the BTL dealers.

After getting dressed, Yu reviewed the information the team had gathered. Walking out into the main room, he saw Emu passed out on the couch with her drone pieces and tools scattered on the floor in front of her. She never stopped working on her machines.

Nobody had found anything out of the ordinary. Telestrian Industries appeared to be much like any number of other corporations, struggling to increase their influence and bottom line in an attempt to gain greater power and a more impressive rating. To them, their workers were cogs in the machine, and most cogs looked like any other. That simple fact was why their relatively straightforward plan might work. There were lots of ways to not be seen, and sometimes the best involved walking through the front doors in plain sight.

By 0500, Yu was fed and ready to head over to Telestrian headquarters. While some enthusiastic wageslaves eager to prove their worth would be up at that hour, most would wait at least until the sun came up. And the larger the crowd, the easier it would be for him to blend in.

To keep from getting too restless, he passed the time reviewing the latest basketball news. He had missed a couple of championship games, and they held his interest long enough for Emu to wake up.

She yawned and stretched, her shoulders popping loud enough for Yu to hear them in the kitchen. "How long have you been up?" she asked.

"A few hours. Been catching up on some games. Have any trouble last night?"

Emu shook her head and reached up to tousle her hair with both hands. "Nope. Pretty standard internal security. Got a couple of guards on the lower level, some scanners, and lots of cameras. Didn't see anything on the outside or pick up on any drones. As long as you don't hit any snags on the inside, it might be as easy as you think. Worried the file might trip an alarm though. Who knows what it does?"

Yu shrugged. "Not any different than anything else we do. Need to take chances somewhere, and the payoff's too good to pass this one up?"

Emu scoffed. "You call 5k good?"

Yu sighed and slumped a bit, leaning on the breakfast bar. "There's more than just the nuyen."

Emu got up and walked over, standing across from Yu and staring at this face. "What else is there?" She grinned. "You get into trouble sleeping with the wrong girl who turned out to be the Johnson's daughter?"

Despite the jab, Yu didn't smile and bite back like he knew Emu expected. He frowned and turned away, rummaging in the fridge for something, even though he wasn't hungry. When he turned back, Emu stood in the same position, the joking grin faded from her face.

"Door's open if you want to chat about it. In the interim, I'll give you a lift. Rude said he'd break our legs if we left without him, and I'm never quite sure if he's kidding or not."

Yu put both hands on the edge of the counter, using them to brace himself. His fingers tightened on the cool surface until they squeaked as his skin stuck while sliding. For her part, Emu stood silent and waited for him to speak. He looked up, scanning to see if any of the others entered the room, but they had the space to themselves for the moment.

"You know that BTL chip I carry around?"

Emu nodded.

"It's from someone important to me. He tripped out on it and went crazy. I..." he swallowed. "It killed him. I was there when it happened. There's a reason I won't touch BTLs, even with all the other stuff I do. They're just bad."

He left out the part where he was the one who had had to kill Brother Lee, and that his cyberarm was a daily reminder of the incident, even more so than the burned-out chip he carried. He wasn't ready to share those details yet. Giving them a voice would make the memories more real, and he had a job to do.

"I found a warehouse full of next-gen BTLs, ones straight off the boat and better than anything you'd find over here. Sitting in a warehouse behind more firepower than we can deal with, otherwise I'd want to take them out myself. *Ham gaa caan* those pricks. They've got it coming, and deserve worse."

Yu took a deep breath before continuing. "The Johnson said he'll take out the dealers once we do this job for him. We need to get it done before they get a chance to move their cargo."

Emu said nothing, but after a brief pause reached out and put one of her hands on his and gave a comforting squeeze.

"Don't tell the others, 'kay? Don't want to deal with Rude's 'yer getting too emotional, elfy-pants' shit." Yu dropped his voice and puffed up his chest as he imitated the troll, making Emu grin. The impression injected some much-needed levity into the scene, and his own smile was genuine as he pushed the memories into the back of his mind where they belonged. After all, he had work to do and he needed focus.

It took a few hours for the others to wake up and check in. Frostburn and Zipfile both left, but Rude crashed in the safehouse for the night, and Yu knew better than to wake the troll. If he could be difficult when rested, Yu didn't want to tempt fate by disturbing the troll's limited sleep. The solid *thump* of the troll's feet hitting the floor let him know when it was time to finish getting ready.

Looking over his wardrobe, Yu debated how to try and pass himself off to security. In normal situations, they would have taken the time to acquire an old uniform or fabricate one. But with their limited timetable, he'd need to use what he had available. Passing himself off as a maintenance worker was too risky, given they didn't know who serviced the Telestrian Headquarters. Such a mistake would make him recognizable as an imposter even with a passing glance.

The limited information they had indicated the office in Seattle involved biotech research. The company itself occupied most of the building on Denny Way, with only a few small businesses occupying the ground floor, mostly in the food industry. Passing as a member of one of those companies would be easier, but wouldn't get him access to the terminals he needed to reach.

Which meant his best option was to pose as a manager of some sort and pull up any techno jargon he could about recent Telestrian products and public research. Of course, Zipfile had anticipated this need and prepared plenty of files for him to review and commit to memory as best he could. Putting on one of his higher-end suits, he got to work studying the materials to back up his story.

He continued reviewing the information, quizzing himself and listening to presentations to make sure to get the pronunciation correct for complicated medical terminology. Rude pounded on his door once, hard enough to make Yu question its stability.

The three of them left for Telestrian HQ. The sun had risen by now, and the streets were crowded with people anxious to get to their jobs before their corporate overlords penalized them for tardiness. Yu didn't understand how people could put up with it every morning. At least when he committed himself to the Triad or to his team, it was for a family. Corporations viewed their subordinates as pieces of machinery, simple cogs to get the job done. What value did they gain from such a relationship?

In the end, Yu got out a block and a half from the building, joining the heavy tide of people walking on the sidewalk. It seemed easier than waiting for the cars to move along. Plus, it afforded him the benefit of Emu's car not being seen when he entered the building. The fewer risks they took, the better. He had every faith in his ability to succeed without a problem, but a little extra caution never hurt.

Yu turned with the stream of people diverting from the main river and approached the front doors of the Telestrian building. It stretched thirty-six stories into the sky. Sunlight glinted off the mirrored windows, making him squint even without looking up. It gave him an excuse to drop his head as he stepped through the doorway, taking advantage of the environmental effect to limit his exposure to cameras which might run facial recognition software.

The main floor of the building was mostly open space, with several shops ringing the perimeter. A sniff rewarded him with a pleasant whiff of fresh-baked pastries and hot soykaf. Several vendors already had long lines, all of which followed a strict protocol of winding back and forth on themselves, even without the aid of guide ropes.

Most of the workers strode across the center of the building to the secure access point on the far side, manned by a couple of bored-looking security guards. They both stood at their post, but one of them had the glassy-eyed stare of someone distracted by the thoughts in their head. The other guard, a troll woman, waved her hand in a slow perpetual circle as she directed scanned employees through to the elevators.

As Yu stepped up, he prayed the fake SIN would pass the scanner test, knowing there was little he could do about it now. If something went wrong, he might be able to talk his way out of it, but until that happened, he didn't so much as acknowledge the guards' presence. Doing so would make him stand out from the rest of the horde as they prepared to chain themselves to their desks for the day.

And then he stood on the other side, heading toward the elevators. The troll continued her ceaseless wave, and he wasn't even sure the other guard so much as blinked. The easy part was done, now he needed to find a terminal that would give him access.

<Any luck figuring out where I need to go?>

He sent the message to the entire team, even though he knew Zipfile was the one reviewing the floor plans and piecing together the data from their brief information gathering. He would be willing to bet she had stayed up throughout the entire night trying to form a full 3D model of the building.

<Try the 23rd floor,> she replied. <They've got a large power draw on that level, but their labs are all located above level 30. I can't find any information about offices on that level, so it might be server farms.>

Yu stepped into the elevator and timed his button press to coincide with another rider's. It was a simple matter of jostling into position at the right time. If the elevator locked out certain floors until credentials were scanned, the timing let him bypass the security measure.

None of the other people in the elevator got off on the 23rd floor, leaving him standing in an empty hallway covered in sickly gray carpet. He noticed the flat panel beside him, even though it should be flush with the outside of the building. No windows meant they wanted to prevent an easy access point. The bright lights on this floor chased away any thought of shadows, meaning skulking about would not be an option. Yu strained to listen, but only caught the faint *ding* of one of the elevators as it opened on a nearby floor.

Summoning all the confidence he could muster, Yu strode down the hallway. If he couldn't hide, the best thing to do would be pretend like he belonged there.

The pathway split up ahead and he glanced in each direction, seeing doors opening off to either side, but no signs. He walked up to the nearest door and opened it, peering inside to see an empty office.

<Any info on this floor yet? There's lots of doors, so it looks like plenty of offices. No name plaques or anything though. They appear empty.>

Zipfile's response came back within seconds.

<*Still nothing, just a skeleton outline. It's like that entire level was wiped from the floor plan. With what I'm looking at, the entire floor should be one giant studio.*>

<*I guarantee you that's not the case. I'm looking at ten offices, and that's just in this hallway. None on the interior wall though. I wonder if...*>

A soft creak interrupted his message, sounding like rubber squished underneath a heavy weight. Yu grabbed the handle of the door next to him and ducked inside, easing it closed with as much speed as he could manage without making a noise.

Once it latched shut, he slid across the wall to the far corner, where the darkness was thickest. At least this office didn't have windows either, making it almost pitch black. The only light leaked through from underneath the door.

<*Yu? Is there a problem?*>

Zipfile was the first to ask a question, but Rude's message came through right after.

<*Need me to cause a distraction?*>

<*No, I'm fine for now. Just looks like this floor might not be abandoned.*>

The footsteps grew closer, approaching the door. They were soft and muffled through the wall, but unmistakable. Yu crouched down, coiling his legs and getting ready to spring if need be.

When the footsteps continued past without any hesitation, Yu remained in position, counting to five before allowing himself to skulk back to the door. He pressed his ear against it, listening for some trace of the patrol, but hearing nothing.

Yu opened the door, turning his face away from the crack and letting the light in so his eyes could adjust. Then he peered through. He caught a glimpse of a human-sized person in uniform turning a corner. He didn't get to see much, but he did notice the guard carried some sort of rifle. Yu slipped into the hall, closing the door behind him to leave it as he found it.

<*Guards patrolling the floor with heavy weapons. Heavier than what the goons at the front gates carried. Something important's on this floor, no doubt.*>

Yu didn't wait for a response before continuing down the hall.

<*Might be a secret lab. Based on what you've said, I'd guess it's somewhere in the interior. I'd bet they remodeled the floor and kept the outside offices because they still needed the hall space. Try to find a path toward the center of the building. I'll see if I can access their security system and check for any power draws or cameras on the level.*>

He turned toward the center of the building as Zipfile had suggested, working away from the perimeter. These halls lacked the large number of doors lining the hall, presenting him with a blank wall that gave little, if any place to hide.

Yu steered away from the long hallways, searching for an alternate route that wouldn't leave him exposed for as long. Given the general atmosphere of the floor, talking his way out of a situation could prove difficult if someone saw him.

The next corner he turned down had small alcoves spaced out along the length of the passage. Yu decided to go this way, his feet gliding across the carpet without making a sound. He paid extra attention to any possible noises, straining to catch any advance warning of the patrols. A cough came from up ahead, and Yu ducked into the nearest alcove, pressing himself into the corner. Forcing himself to take slow breaths in through his nose, he stayed in control and calmed his heart rate. The fingers of his cyberarm curled into a tight fist as he waited for the guard to come into view. He didn't want to force a conflict, but if he got caught, he might not have much choice.

The footsteps grew louder as the guard got closer. He noticed a few details, like a soft scuff of the feet across the fabric of the carpet. The guard had a rapid-fire cough, and tried to clear their throat. Time seemed to slow down with each step. The first thing to come around the corner was the barrel of a rifle, followed by hands covered in armored gloves.

The security guard came into view, the human woman staring straight ahead as she marched forward in measured steps. Her gaze didn't shift as she continued on her route. Yu stayed in the alcove, remaining out of sight and not wanting to move until he counted out her steps and assumed she must've reached the next corner. Only then did he peek out, looking to the end of the hall.

When he saw it was empty, he didn't hesitate to leave the alcove and continue on his path toward the only door he could see. Taking time to relish his luck did nothing to help accomplish his goal. If anything, it would hinder it. And this was business.

Yu picked up his pace, moving as fast as he dared. Years of training had him easing his weight onto each foot and rolling off the ball in a smooth motion. His knees were bent, taking long strides as he ate up the distance to the door.

When he reached it, he saw it was locked with a maglock. Removing a maglock passkey from his jacket, he swiped it through the lock. The lock turned green, and a solid *click* let him know his luck continued to hold. Yu opened the door and slipped inside, easing it shut behind him to maintain his stealth.

"*Diu,*" he swore.

The room he found himself in was gigantic. It had to take up at least a quarter of the entire floor. In here were row after row of server racks, fans spinning in a pervasive hum that drowned out all other sounds. Lights flickered from the computers, creating dancing shadows throughout the cavernous space. He couldn't be sure, but if he had to guess, the cushioned floor underneath him was some part of the cooling system. And possibly the security system.

The dim lights did not provide an excellent view of his surroundings, but he made out a few cameras mounted up along the seam where the wall met the ceiling. They were in plain view, with no attempt made to hide them. Whoever designed the security for this room wanted to make sure any trespassers knew the trouble they would find themselves in. Some part of his brain wondered how many of the cameras were functional, and how often anyone watched the feed. Was it true security or were the obvious cameras just a plant, hiding the true threat?

<Zipfile, got any lead on the cameras yet? Looks like they don't want folks poking round here too much.>

<Not yet. I've got some stuff for a couple of the floors with more public access, but that entire floor is sealed off like it doesn't exist. I could try to get a hardline in the building if you need.>

Yu shook his head, even though his companion couldn't see the gesture. *<Don't risk it. I'm almost done, and I think there's enough gaps in their coverage to let me slip on through.>*

He'd been watching the cameras, and his statement was not simply an attempt to keep the others safe. The limited light would help him slip along the perimeter. Although he'd want to take it slow in case they had motion sensors. But that wasn't anything he hadn't dealt with before.

<You think it matters where I plug this drive in?>

<Not really. Odds are they're all connected in their private network. If the Johnson didn't specify, I can't imagine it'll matter much. Just stick it in anywhere you can.>

Rude was the next one to chime in. *<Really? That's how ya say it?>*

Yu focused on the situation in front of him, checking on the cameras' field of view. He inched along the wall, not wanting to go for the first couple of racks, which had a camera centered on them. It took several minutes before he stood across from a rack he felt comfortable approaching.

Crouching low, his knees ached as he crept toward the computer hardware. The lower his profile, the better his chances of getting away unseen. He had to grip the rack frame for balance and to relieve some of the pressure on his legs. Feeling around with his fingers in the shadows, he found a port he could attach the drive to. He connected it, staying in position as he waited for the device to finish doing its electronic magic.

<How long do I have to wait?>

Before he received a response, the lights on the computer in front of him blinked wildly and some hardware inside it whined in protest. His hand hovered over the drive as he debated whether to jerk it free.

The lights in the entire room turned on, making Yu wince at the sudden flood of brightness. He snatched the drive free and leaped back to the wall, trying to stay hidden.

He headed for the door, a bit faster than when he entered the room. Just before he reached it, he heard the maglock slide open and saw the handle turn.

Yu jumped forward, getting behind the door as it opened. When he saw the barrel of a gun sticking out around the edge, he placed both hands on the door and slammed it on the intruder.

The door smacked into the corpsec guard on the other side, eliciting a grunt from the woman as she got knocked into the frame of the door. Yu swung around the door and beat the barrel of the gun aside with his wrist as he stepped forward and put his foot on top of the guard's. Having her pinned in that position, his left hand snaked out, striking the woman in the neck just below her jaw.

She tucked her shoulder and pulled away from the blow, absorbing some of the shock and turning a debilitating blow into an uncomfortable sparring injury. To her credit, she didn't try to bring her gun to bear in the close quarters combat. She dropped it, letting it clatter against the floor as she jerked a knife free from an arm holster. She swung the weapon at Yu, forcing him to knock it aside with his regular arm.

The impact stung up to his shoulder and had little effect on the attack. If he hadn't twisted to the side, he would've gotten stabbed. She had to be chromed up underneath her corpsec uniform. She continued her assault, her arm picking up speed and her series of quick slashes forcing Yu to retreat into the room.

He couldn't let the fight continue. She could notify security any second, assuming she hadn't already. He feigned a stumble, luring the guard into trying a heavy stab. He fell faster, dropping under the strike and grabbing her wrist in his cyberarm as he approached the ground. His fingers tightened, applying more pressure than any normal limb could take. He yanked down at the same time, adding all of his strength to the weight of his falling body.

The guard lurched forward, unable to support them both from her compromised position. Yu used that moment to swing his legs around and snap his foot into the side of her forward knee. It caved, and she crashed to the ground. Yu rolled out of the way, keeping his hand on her wrist to make sure he didn't find the knife in his side.

The guard cried out, the sound making Yu hiss in frustration. He reached out and grabbed her head, picking it up and slamming it into the ground to stun her. As her head rolled from one side to the other, he dragged her back into the server room by her wrist, yanking off her commlink and shortwave radio. If she had body mods, there was nothing he could do to restrain her, at least not on short notice. The best he could do was get distance on her.

He slammed the door shut, not caring about the noise it created now, and smashed the maglock a couple of times with his fist, hoping it might at least slow her down.

<I need those elevators, ready to go now. Might be coming out hot.>

<I don't see any alarms in the system. If any bells are going off, they must only be on that floor. You might not be coming out hot after all.>

The update from Zipfile reinforced Yu's need to get off the floor with as much speed as he could manage. He sprinted around the corners, following the path he took with unerring accuracy. If he ran into another security force, there was no way he'd get away without a fight. He found himself missing the comforting weight of his handgun. Usually he hated the weapon and saw it as a last resort, but right now he couldn't think of any better way to describe his situation.

Seeing the elevators around the next corner made him bust into a full-blown sprint. As he reached the doors, he doubled over and took several breaths as much from exertion as from fear. As he stood there, he realized there was no elevator call button or scanner to request access. The elevator doors stood next to a flat, featureless wall.

<About that elevator? I need options.>

He shook his head at his own stupidity. He should've checked this when he'd gotten off the elevator in the first place.

<I can't put in a request for the 23rd floor. They've got it locked down. I don't know how long it will take to bust through. I'm guessing you need to request the elevator from the front desk.>

Rude chimed in with his standard solution. *<Need me to turn a wall into a door?>*

<You could do that, or he could take the stairs. If you can get down a floor, then catching an elevator shouldn't be a problem at all. I've got the cameras on the other floors and can keep you from being seen.>

Yu took a deep breath and ran down the hall again, heading toward the stairwell as directed by Zipfile. Even if they didn't have a blueprint of this floor, it wasn't like stairs could magically change location for one floor alone. The question was what type of security might be on that door.

"Freeze!" a deep voice shouted from down the hall, right before the heavy rattle of gunfire. Corpsec wasn't waiting to see if he responded to the command.

Yu stumbled forward and swerved to the side, skinning his elbow as he slipped rounding a corner to get out of the path of the bullets.

Judging solely by the tone of voice, this was a new adversary. It didn't matter if the earlier guard had sent out an alert, this one had had more than enough time to do so. It was only a matter of time before the entire security force would be coming after him. So much for a quick job and getting out before anyone noticed he was there. Now Yu needed to improvise, and do so without endangering his allies. They didn't have enough information to come in with guns blazing. The risk would be too great. He needed to at least mitigate their risk before calling them in.

Not to mention he'd never hear the end of it.

At least the corpsec guard couldn't keep up with his pace. That additional armor came at a cost, and Yu pressed his advantage as much as he could, sprinting until his lungs burned with each heavy panting breath. He ducked around every corner he came to, making sure his path kept him going in the general direction of the stairwell. He didn't want to take too meandering of a path because seconds mattered.

When he reached the door, luck swung once again, this time turning in his favor. The door was locked, but had an emergency release on this side. It seemed like all of those mandated safety regulations had a positive side to them as far as runners were concerned.

He slammed his shoulder into it, bursting through and rushing to the stairs. As he put his hands on the railing and prepped to jump down to the next landing, he hesitated.

<You said you have all the cameras?>

<Yeah, I do. I'll make you a ghost once you get off that floor.>

<I'm going up.>

Logic and fear both said to go down, which meant that would be where they expected him to go. If he couldn't be picked up on camera, then he might blend in by going upstairs. It might be unconventional, but it also just might work.

Yu leaped up the stairs, taking four at a time until he had climbed two stories. He stood on the landing, taking short but deep, explosive breaths to calm down. Once he could take normal breaths and didn't feel new beads of sweat forming along the sides of his face, he opened the door and stepped into the hall beyond.

A couple of wageslaves in the area looked up from their displays when he stepped out of the stairwell into their cramped office area. They went back to their tasks, continuing to work for their corporate overlords and attempting to keep from falling behind. Yu understood their dedication and fear, having seen it plenty of times in the past with those who worked for the Triads. If they didn't perform, they would be let go. And if that happened, finding another corporate job would be impossible. Their previous employer would guarantee it.

Yu kept his eyes pointed forward, putting a slight scowl on his face. Very few people wanted to interrupt a manager who looked irritated and overworked. That was a sure way to get more tasks put in your inbox, and that was the best-case scenario. The entire corporate environment was one of fear, something Yu knew how to manipulate to his advantage.

As he walked through the floor, he soaked in as many details as he could, looking for eye twitches, nervous ticks, sudden intakes of breath. Anything that might indicate reason for alarm. But it looked like Zipfile's assumption was correct. The news of his interference had not appeared to reach the employees on this level.

<Heading to the elevators now. Planning on taking them down to the ground floor and walking out of here.>

<Take your time, but don't dilly-dally. If I keep the cameras looping for too long, someone's bound to notice. Also, corpsec's running around the 22nd and 21st floor, as well as sweeping the stairwell. I'm putting a ghost on the 21st floor, hoping to keep them running around chasing their tails for a while.>

Yu lengthened his stride, increasing his pace without looking like he rushed through the aisles. He almost bumped into a dwarf carrying a stack of papers. With a spin, he avoided impact and snarled in Cantonese. The dwarf muttered an apology, backing out of his way even after he passed. The trick was to growl and snap at people dressed worse than you were. Clothes served as a measure of status, provided one knew how to read the subtle language of fashion.

"—Did you hear about what's going on?" Yu caught a snippet of conversation as one wageslave leaned over a divider and talked to his neighbor. "I just heard from Shane on 21. He said corpsec's locking down the entire floor."

Yu's jaw clenched, but he forced himself to keep his steady pace on his way to the elevators. The news spread like wildfire, radiating out from the source in waves. He managed to stay ahead of it, but heard the rumors following behind him. If it had already spread to this floor, it was a safe bet that soon the entire building would hear about it. And once that happened, he imagined it wouldn't be long before Telestrian saw no reason not to spread his face around as well.

When he reached the elevator and pressed the button, every ounce of him wanted to fidget. But he tapped into the calm spirit he had learned standing in front of criminal syndicates as a child. It took more than this to rattle his nerves enough for others to see it. His insides may have been jumping around like crazy, but he saw no reason to give that information to any observers.

The doors opened, and he expected to be staring down an elevator full of corpsec. Instead he saw a few scientists and business officials. Yu nodded briefly in acknowledgment, keeping the scowl on his face and stepping in before jamming the button for the ground floor, even though someone had already pressed it. It helped to maintain his image and discourage others from engaging him in conversation. Everything in life was an act.

The elevator began dropping, and Yu couldn't help clenching his fist as they passed the 21st floor, but didn't slow down. He dared to hope this might work. They stopped a couple of times to let on passengers and let others off, but it wasn't long before the doors opened onto the ground floor.

Yu stepped out first, getting ahead of the other travelers. He passed through the security station. The guards had their attention focused outward still, not looking at the people exiting the building. Yu passed through and walked into the largest cluster of people, blending into the crowd and then working toward the exit, avoiding the large open area in the center.

It took a few minutes, but when he stepped out of the building, his pace was easy and he didn't feel a need to look over his shoulder. Emu's vehicle sat next to the curb up at the end of the block. Yu walked over and climbed inside, Emu easing into traffic as soon as the door closed.

Rude twisted around in his seat, an impressive and uncomfortable feat considering his size. "I'm impressed, elfy-pants. Thought I was gonna have to go in and save your ass."

"I know you find it hard to believe, but I can take care of myself, no matter what Frostburn says sometimes." Yu smirked, then winced when a flash of pain lanced through his side.

He reached down and probed it with his fingers, feeling a tear in his clothes along with some wetness. He didn't need to look at it to know the moisture seeping into his clothes was blood. One of the bullets must have caught him. He assumed his adrenaline kept him from being aware of the injury.

It was a good thing he wore a dark suit to hide it from the wageslaves. Otherwise, no amount of posturing would've gotten him through that floor without incident.

"Don't suppose you have a patch? Looks like I've gone and found religion." When Rude furrowed his brow together, Yu brought his fingers around, showing the blood. "You know, because I'm so hole-y?"

Rude growled and shook his head, the scowl on his face making it seem like he wanted to put more holes in his companion. He fished around in a pouch and grabbed a patch, hurling it at Yu before turning around and facing front.

Yu grabbed the patch and applied it, the drugs seeping into his system about the same time he became aware of the pain. It dulled the edge of it and kept his mind sharp.

"So you completed the job. What next?" Emu asked.

"Next we head back to the safehouse, and I contact the Johnson and let him know the job is done and arrange for final payment."

He looked in the rearview mirror, making eye contact with Emu and sharing their unspoken agreement. He knew she had kept his secret about that payment. As much as he didn't want to share the information, it was a relief to share the burden with someone he trusted.

"Sounds like a plan," Rude rumbled. "I like gettin' paid to do nothin'."

As they reconvened at the safehouse, Yu went to his private room to contact the Johnson. He needed some measure of privacy to finish the last step of negotiations.

Mr. Johnson picked up at the first ping. "Is it done?" he asked, cutting right to the root of the matter. The connection was audio only.

"Yes. Delivered the package just a few minutes ago. I trust you've put things in place for the final payment?"

"Of course. Once I verify the contents of the package delivery, I will put in the final call. I trust you would like to observe the final result?"

Yu hesitated. He hadn't considered this before. Some part of him wanted to watch the BTL dealers get taken out. It would be helpful to guarantee they were removed once and for all. Otherwise, the Johnson could easily claim to have taken care of the problem and not do anything at all. How would Yu confirm what happened? If anything, the corp would do whatever it could to prevent such an incident from becoming public knowledge. It reflected poorly on their business, and reputation was one of the most valuable currencies to a corporation.

But if he were honest with himself, he couldn't deny that part of him wanted to watch for the satisfaction of watching them being dispatched and their illicit cargo torched. When it came down to it, it wasn't a choice.

"Yes. I need to verify the completion of the deal, just like you. Otherwise, how can we trust each other and continue to do business?" He didn't know if the Johnson believed his excuse. It sounded probable, but in the end, he didn't care.

"Very well. Assuming successful package delivery, then I will arrange for the incident to be carried out at 2100 hours this evening. The later hour increases the chances of a greater presence. I would prefer to teach the perpetrators a lesson, and not just confiscate the cargo. After all, there is our reputation to consider."

"A pleasure doing business with you." Yu cut the connection and collapsed on the bed. It looked like the entire plan had gone off without a hitch. Whatever the package was, it had been delivered, and was no longer his problem. Let the corporations play their games. The more they stabbed at each other, the more work for him and his teammates, and the more opportunity for the Triad to benefit. And if he could indulge his personal vendetta in the process, why not?

Sitting up, he transferred twenty-five hundred nuyen from his personal account into their group account. It would hurt, but he had the savings to spare right now. And this way they wouldn't ask questions. For the moment, only Emu knew his secret, and he preferred to keep it that way.

Walking out into the main room, the other members of the team turned to him.

Yu flashed an easy grin at them. "Good job, team. We got a bit of a bonus. Not much, but I worked my magic and a little something is better than nothing. We'll give it an even split, and I'll let one of you pick the next job. Who knows, maybe know we'll get one of the big ones. Client said he was happy with our work. It doesn't hurt to have a name like Renraku willing to back us."

The team nodded their assent and went back to their personal business and conversations. The job was finished, now was the time to relax before the inevitable looking for more work. Part of the price for being a shadowrunner.

Zipfile came up to Yu. "I'm going to head down to The Sports Bar again tonight. Want to come along and see if you can win another round?"

Yu shook his head. "Maybe another time. I need to see if Emu's willing to shuttle me around for a bit. Plus, I have to buy her dinner or something, makeup for wrecking one of her drones."

"Suit yourself!"

Frostburn retreated to her room, and Rude left without telling anyone where he was going, leaving the two of them alone for the moment.

"You need a lift to the warehouse, don't you?"

"How'd you guess?"

"Figured you'd want to make sure the Johnson kept his end of the bargain. I don't like this. I don't like you going out alone and not having backup. You know what Johnsons are like, always looking for a chance to double-cross. This is the final payment you're going out to pick up. How many times has that gone sour?"

"Only twice."

Emu frowned. "And three more times where it might've if Rude hadn't been there."

"I get your point, but this is different. The Johnson doesn't know where I'll be. I'll be in the shadows far away, keeping an eye on things. As far as he's concerned, our business is done, and we have no reason to contact each other."

"If you say so. I'm just letting you know I don't like it."

"Does that mean you won't give me a lift?"

Emu tilted her head down so she could glare at him through her eyebrows. "And leave you to take a rideshare that's gonna dump you and jet, or give you reason to go seducing some poor woman just so you can use her car? No thanks. I've seen you drive."

The hours passed with painful slowness, and Yu considered letting time slip by a bit faster with a dip into his stash, but his righteous rage kept him from doing so. He wanted to be focused when the BTL dealers were dispatched, and didn't want to risk still being high when that time came. Instead, he went to the Vigilant Iron Schooling House, using the hours to train until he worked up a heavy sweat, and then trained some more. After several sparring matches, he cleaned up and went back to the safehouse.

The ride over to West Seattle was quiet. Yu tumbled over his own thoughts, analyzing them to the point where he didn't even register Emu's presence. She kept silent, giving him the opportunity to self-reflect.

When they got nearby, she pulled over to the side of the road a few blocks away. "You know, I can dispatch a drone, and you don't even need to get close."

He assumed an offer like this was coming, and shook his head. "I appreciate it, but this is something I want to see myself. And I'd rather do it alone, if you don't mind."

"Of course. I'll be here waiting to take you back when it's done."

Yu climbed out and walked down the street toward the warehouses owned by Rip Current Shipping Lanes. The ocean smell and cool breeze helped to keep him focused as he walked, cutting through his tumbling thoughts and making him pay attention to his surroundings. Now that he knew what to look for, he recognized the activity around the warehouse, even when it was still several buildings away. He looked around for a good vantage point.

The best possible spot to get a view and guarantee he was out of the way would be the roof of one of these buildings. Yu entered an alley across the street from the warehouse, and looked at the wall in front of him. It wouldn't be easy, but he had enough experience climbing that he could make use of the uneven masonry of the brick building. There were windows on each floor, with thick sills he could balance on.

The climb was slow, but he arrived with plenty of time to spare. Yu reached the top and pulled himself over the edge, lying down on the roof of an office building.

Staying low, he crawled to the front edge of the building, pulling himself up just high enough so he could see the warehouse across the way. Two people in unmarked uniforms stood at the gate, and from this angle, Yu saw the armed drones circling around the building. This reaffirmed his decision that it was far too much for his team to handle alone.

Now he sat and waited to see if Mr. Johnson would fulfill his obligations. There wasn't much Yu could do if he decided to pull out. Since the package had already been delivered, he had nothing Mr.

Johnson wanted any more. The worst he could do was spread the news through the runner community. But doing so would require sharing far more information with the public than he wanted.

Minutes ticked by, each one had Yu checking the clock at least five times before it rolled over. 2100 came and went, but nothing happened.

At 2104, when Yu's legs itched and he longed to get up and pace just to keep his limbs loose, he caught movement at the edge of his vision. Turning, he saw several Knight Errant vehicles lining up in the street.

These weren't the standard cars used by officers attempting to patrol the streets and keep them safe, using a loose definition of safety by anyone's terms. These were the armored vans carrying multiple officers in full battle gear. Seemed like Mr. Johnson, true to form, didn't want to get his hands dirty while dealing with the problem. Yu didn't care who dealt with it, as long as the BTL dealers were eliminated. He gripped the corner of the roof as he watched, one of his feet tapping as he watched the enforcement corp get into position.

And then the chaos started.

There were no sirens, no flashing lights, no booming voice telling the criminals to surrender. Instead, the caravan drove forward in a spearhead formation, slamming through the fence, with one of the vans aimed straight at the guard manning the station. He brought his weapon up and fired a few shots, the rapid explosions echoing through the air. They were followed by the high-pitched ring of bullets bouncing off an armored shell in a shower of sparks. And then there was the *crunch* as the vehicle rolled over the man.

The wheels hadn't even stopped when the back doors flew open and the Knights rolled out with military precession. These weren't the standard rank and file either, these were the elite members, well-trained to do their job. They covered each other as they circled around the warehouse in tight formations, shooting at the building. From his vantage point, the gunfire made his ears ring as the two forces exchanged shots.

A large explosion lit the night as a grenade went off near one of the vans, sending a few of the Knights scrambling and rolling across the cement. One of them didn't get up again.

The sudden burst of light made Yu turn his face away from the blast in time to see the roof access door to the office building open.

He sprang to his feet and rushed toward the doorway as a large troll in Knight Errant riot gear stepped out and began coming toward him. The troll looked toward the warehouse, his gun coming around as he did. Yu already had his pistol out and trained on the target. He fired as he circled around toward the door, not expecting the bullets to do any lasting damage, but hoping they served as a distraction.

His plan worked and the troll stepped back, bringing an arm up to cover his face. Most of the bullets bounced off or sank into his armor, but at least one cut along his bicep where the protection wasn't quite as thick. Yu ran out of bullets, but reached the doorway as his weapon clicked empty. He jumped through, hoping to clear the first set of stairs and head down toward the exit.

But slamming into the ork coming up the stairwell was like jumping into a rock wall—and just as forgiving. As he tumbled to the ground, Yu had enough presence of mind to kick out, knocking the rifle out of the ork's hand, robbing her of an easy kill.

If the disarm bothered her, she didn't seem concerned. She reached down and grabbed Yu by the front of his jacket. He twisted free from one hand, but the other had too solid of a grip. She lifted him up from the ground and slammed him into the wall, cracking the back of his head against it, and knocking his pistol loose as well. Her tusked face blurred from the impact, but he felt her lift him to slam him into the wall again.

Yu lifted his feet behind him, using them to cushion the blow, then sprang forward as she pulled him back. The sudden shift in momentum let him flip over her head into the open air between the looping switch-backed stairs. She held on, stopping his flight short and yanking her into the railing so it caught her in the side. The impact knocked the air out of her lungs even through her protective clothing, but she held on with a growl.

As he struggled to tear himself free—and drop four stories to the ground far below, which somehow seemed like a better option to his dazed mind—the troll stomped into the stairwell, an ugly sneer on his face. He reached out to help the ork subdue the criminal, and Yu knew his life would be forfeit if those meaty fingers curled around one of his limbs.

Not seeing much in the way of options, Yu straightened his fingers into a knife hand and slammed them up into the bottom of the ork's armpit. The blow made her let go, the nerve acting on reflex despite all her training. And Yu fell away from both of them.

He reached out to catch himself on the next railing, but missed the timing. His wrist slammed against the metal bar, and he thought he heard a *crunch* of bone. The impact knocked him out of the center and he tumbled toward the opposite side, catching himself on the railing by draping both of his arms across it and letting the metal bar slam into his rib cage.

For several seconds, Yu struggled simply to breathe.

His foot slipped as he clambered over the rail, and it took three tries before he collapsed on the stairs on the other side. Compared to his other injuries, slamming into the cement steps didn't even register. The gunfire from above as the ork opened fire did, however.

Through his pain, a voice in his head reminded him that his life was over if he didn't move.

At first, sliding down the steps was the best he could manage. Once he got to the next landing, he slid over to the wall and used it to prop himself up. As much as he wanted to take a moment to catch his breath, he doubted the pursuing Knight Errant officers would be willing to grant him that luxury. Yu shuffled forward, almost toppling over when he reached the next set of steps.

He took stock of his injuries as his lucidity came trickling back. His wrist felt broken, as well as possibly a couple of ribs. But his legs and lungs still worked, and they were what he needed most right now. Fighting was out of the question. He doubted he'd stand much of a chance against these two if he were fresh. In his current state, it would be suicide, even if they didn't have guns.

To make matters worse, he heard voices shouting from the floors beneath him. He didn't let it slow his pace. Whatever was down there couldn't be any worse than what was pounding after him from behind, firing off the occasional shot that cracked into the cement around him. It might be just as bad, but he saw no reason not to keep running.

As he finished another flight of stairs, he saw a body on the landing. The corpse wore a Knight Errant uniform, but judging by the amount of blood pooling around it, wouldn't be getting up any time soon.

Yu didn't stop to take a closer look. He rushed past the body and continued toward the exit, hoping for a miracle. The miracle came as he passed two more bodies on the ground floor, slumped on either side of the front entrance. This wasn't a coincidence. This was a death trap. Somehow they knew to storm this building, and had done so with the same military efficiency they used against the BTL dealers. The nearby explosions and sounds of veritable warfare continued, but if anyone looked in his direction, they were too preoccupied with their own battle to stop him.

Emu rushed up, tires screeching against the pavement as she slid to a stop in front of the entrance of the building. Yu tried to get to her car, but his leg collapsed under him as something bit through his calf. The ork had reached the bottom floor and opened fire, catching him before he managed to reach the vehicle. She leaped down the last few steps to land on the ground floor proper and get a better angle.

Two drones buzzed to life from the back of Emu's vehicle and zipped forward, guns rattling as they opened fire into the building. The ork ducked back and dove behind the stairway, but left a trail of blood in the process. Yu didn't know if she was dead or not, and didn't want to wait around to find out. Not to mention wait for the troll. The drones continued firing, alternating to maintain cover fire but conserve ammo.

A giant roar ripped through the sky as at least 300 kgs of muscle and rage crashed to the sidewalk from the roof. The ground shook and the cement cracked underneath the Knight Errant officer. He reached out and grabbed a drone, hurling it against the wall in a flash of sparks. It sputtered on the ground a few times before he stomped on it, stilling it.

Yu pushed himself up to his feet and held out his good arm in front of him in a fighting stance. The troll didn't hesitate, grabbing the arm and pulling Yu toward him. He hoisted the elf high overhead before tossing him to the ground behind him.

Halfway through his trajectory, Yu reached out and pulled the pin from one of the standard issue grenades attached to the troll's belt.

The other drone turned to fire on the troll, but retreated down the street while shooting. The Knight lumbered after it, moving at speeds no non-augmented meta could manage. Yu ignored the pain in his ribs and rolled over on his side, ducking behind Emu's car for some measure of protection.

The grenade went off, and what was left of the troll dropped to the ground and didn't move except for a few post-mortem twitches.

Yu pulled himself to the rear door of Emu's car. It opened for him and he crawled inside. It lurched forward before he got his entire body inside. When his head reached the far door, he rolled onto his back and took a deep breath. Halfway through he coughed from the pain, a reaction that made fire lance through his chest at multiple angles at once.

"Don't die back there after bleeding all over my seats. You also owe me another drone, and a detailing job after this!" Emu sped out of the district, slowing down once she reached the highway, but not daring to stop. "You alive back there?"

Yu took half the breath he did before, taking his time and making sure not to push it too far. He took measure of how much he could breathe without kicking off the pain.

"You were right... It was a setup."

"Did you at least get what you wanted?"

Yu thought back to the destruction at the warehouse. The Knight Errant troops would eliminate the dealers, and the cargo had a high chance of being destroyed in the process. If it wasn't, he didn't know what the Knights would do about it. But at the least, they'd removed some portion of the threat from the streets of Seattle. And there were a handful fewer BTL dealers left in the world. These were all good things.

"Wasn't...worth it." Yu managed between his short gulps of air. Talking took effort, but it helped distract from the pain threatening to push him into subconsciousness.

As he started to drop into the darkness, a thought jolted through him providing all the wakefulness of a shot of epinephrine.

"The others! Are they okay?"

"What do you mean?"

"They knew to look for me."

<*Zipfile, Frostburn, Rude, check in. The Johnson tried to burn us, are you okay?*>

Zipfile was the first to respond. <*I'm fine. What do you mean the Johnson tried to burn us, how do you know?*>

<*Emu and I just got attacked.*> Yu winced as Emu turned a sharp corner, the momentum reminding him of his precarious condition. <*I think the Johnson might be tying up loose ends.*>

He waited for a few seconds before sending another message. <*Frostburn? Rude? Are you there?*>

<*Easy, elfy-pants, I'm here. Just hadda finish a little business of my own. Made sure everything's nice and tidy after yer little sneak-and-peek. Ya don't think I'd be lettin' ya fall to a couple of KE goons, do ya?*>

A couple of pieces slotted into place. <*Thanks, Rude. I owe you.*>

<*More like ten or twelve by now. I stopped countin'.*>

<*What about Frostburn? Anyone heard anything?*>

The silence coming across their private channel was answer enough, and made Yu curl up as best he could despite his pain. If anything had happened to her because of this job he'd taken... He couldn't finish the thought. His face paled even more, and his hands shook. His good arm reached down to his pocket, feeling for the BTL chip he carried, squeezing it tight in his palm.

<*I'm here. There's been a complication, which is why there was a bit of a delay in my reply.*>

<*Puk gaai! Thank whatever gods you believe in that you're okay. What happened? What's going on?*>

<*Our safehouse received some unexpected guests. I happened to be in my room when they made a forced entry, and managed to escape. But let's say their entrance was none too friendly. That safe house is now anything but. Not to mention it's been shot to hell, literally.*>

Yu collapsed into the seat, eliciting a groan as his ribs protested the motion. But it didn't matter. The team—his family—was safe for now. That was the important part. But it would take work to stay that way.

<*This has to be the Johnson. It's the only job we've taken in a few weeks, and the timing fits too well. He knew where we'd be and set us up. We've all dealt with double-crosses before, but usually that's just to get out of a payment. This reeks of something more. This is making sure no one involved with the job is left alive to talk about it. This also means we have to assume no place we use or that's connected with any of our names is safe.*>

A moment of silence filled the channel. Yu continued, the encroaching darkness approaching with more speed than Emu on a racetrack. <*We need to get together and figure out our plan of action. Somewhere safe we haven't used in a while, where no one will think to look for us. Either that, or we all scatter to the winds to wait for this to blow over and take our chances.>*

Despite suggesting the option, Yu couldn't help but hold his breath. He needed to put the option out there, especially since he was the one who had dragged them into this mess. But he hoped they wouldn't take it. Not because he was concerned for his own safety, but because he wanted to help protect the other members of his team, and make up for the trouble he brought to their doorstep.

It was the least he could do for his family.

<Fuck that. They wanna hit us, I say we hit 'em harder. Just tell me where ta start shootin'.>

The rest of the team agreed with Rude's sentiment, and Yu lost the strength to resist the temporary relief of passing out. He dimly remembered the team discussing where to meet and how to move forward as the darkness claimed his awareness.

EMU
BROOKE CHANG

Emu glared through her rear-view mirror at the bleeding, half-conscious elf in the back seat as her Commodore sport sedan rocketed across Harbor Island. "Next time you want to arrange a meet that might get crashed by the cops, let me pick the location."

Yu didn't respond, and after a moment, Emu realized he'd stopped trying to sit up. Muttering a curse, she made sure the data cable plugged into the dash was secure, then activated the vehicle control rig implanted in her brain—a process riggers called "jumping in."

The Commodore's controls disappeared, and an eyeblink later, Emu felt the wind rushing over the car's exterior as though it were her own skin. The control rig translated Commodore's sensors into 360-degree vision, and the bullet holes in its chassis into something resembling a particularly bad bruise—painful, but not enough to impair her function.

Behind the Commodore, the armored Ares Roadmaster trucks Knight Errant had sent to the meeting-turned-ambush weren't bothering to give chase; they must have known there was no way they could catch a sport sedan with a head start, especially not one driven by a woman who could control a vehicle with her thoughts.

Unfortunately, the Roadmasters weren't Emu's biggest problem; that distinction fell to whatever support units Knight Errant's High Threat Response team had called in. If she was lucky, the support would be a couple of those annoying little wheeled pursuit drones; fast enough to catch her, but not sturdy enough to weather the guns the Commodore sported.

Then bullets started pounding the asphalt around Emu, and it quickly became clear that she was not, in fact, lucky. An upward glance through the Commodore's sensors confirmed her fears: Knight

Errant's support was a helicopter. A Northrup Wasp, to be precise, a security model that would have no trouble keeping up with her car, and that typically carried a light machine gun in its underslung weapon mount. The Commodore had enough armor to stand up to the odd pistol round, or maybe a low-powered rifle, but it wouldn't stand a chance against a weapon like that.

Emu sighed. Being a rigger wasn't just about being a fantastic driver or pilot: it was also about knowing the best way to get to wherever you wanted to go. If she couldn't outrun or out-fight her pursuers, she'd have to get creative.

A sharp turn of her wheels sent the Commodore drifting around a corner and beneath an elevated section of freeway, earning Emu a few precious seconds out of the helicopter's line of fire. She used the moment to punch a destination into her navigation system, purely to check the distance—no self-respecting rigger relied on a nav system for directions—then grimaced at the answer: *one kilometer*. Barely worth a mention on a normal day, but with an injured teammate in the backseat and a hostile helicopter overhead, it felt a lot longer.

And now, she was out of cover.

Emu opened up the throttle and threw the Commodore into another hard turn as the Wasp opened fire again. Rounds from its machine-gun sent plumes of dirt and asphalt chips into the air as they struck the road where the car's engine block would've been if Emu had kept going straight. Ignoring the panicked honk from a food truck she cut off as she skidded into a nearby parking lot, Emu weaved the Commodore between obstacles so fast that the vehicle careened from side to side, bouncing first on its left wheels, then on its right pair like a kid playing hopscotch bounced from leg to leg. *Seven hundred meters.*

The Wasp laid down another fusillade of machine-gun fire, and the control rig implanted in Emu's brain translated the impact of each round against the car's roof into the sensation of hammer-blows against her back. The rigger spun the sports car into a bootleg turn and raced in the other direction, forcing the Wasp to overshoot, then zig-zagged again to put herself back on course—and promptly saw stars when the Commodore's nose went straight through a steel grille fence. The impact made her feel a little bit like a charging ram, but Emu didn't have the luxury of waiting until she'd shaken it off. *Five hundred meters.*

The Commodore lurched forward when it hit open space, and Emu felt a bone-rattling shake as her tires hit a set of train tracks. Plumes of dirt and gravel kicked up around her as the helicopter's machine gun tried to track the car's erratic movements, and she felt a hard punch to the shoulder when a bullet knocked off the Commodore's driver's-side mirror. *Two hundred meters.*

Emu opened the Commodore's throttle to the max and kept her course as straight as she could, trying to pick up enough speed to jump a second set of train tracks—and when the Wasp shot off her other side mirror, the rigger knew she was out of time.

She twisted her wheels hard once more, and felt a jarring *crunch* as her tires hit steel...then started breathing again as the Commodore sailed through the air and plowed through a chain-link fence before spinning in a half-donut and skidding to a halt.

The Wasp's machine-gun fire stopped just as abruptly, mere centimeters away from the fence Emu had just knocked over—the one proudly displaying the logo of Mitsuhama Computer Technologies, the largest megacorporation in the world—and one entirely outside Knight Errant's jurisdiction. As far as the law was concerned, the meter or two between Emu and the space where the fence had stood might as well have been the Pacific Ocean.

Resisting the urge to give the police helicopter a "frag you" honk—Mitsuhama had their own corporate security forces, which were undoubtedly on the way to investigate why their fence had been knocked down, and the noise would draw them right to her—Emu spun the Commodore around and took off into the rail yard, leaving the Wasp to fume impotently at her escape.

The Knight Errant pilot must have been *really* angry at not catching their prey, because it took an hour of hiding in a disused warehouse at the rail yard before the salty bastard finally left. The delay gave Emu enough time to dig her medkit out of the Commodore's trunk and treat the worst of Yu's injuries. Miraculously, the Wasp's strafing attack hadn't hit either of the runners—although it *had* left holes in the Commodore's roof, torn up the rear seat cushions, and blown the cabin ceiling light to pieces.

When the coast was clear, she pointed the Commodore south to a large storage unit deep in Auburn's industrial area. Zipfile had rented the unit under a fake SIN as a *backup*-backup rally point when the team had first gotten together.

When Emu and Yu arrived at the storage facility, Frostburn and Zipfile were already there—the mage pacing, the decker motionless on a cheap inflatable mattress in the back corner, probably fooling around in the Matrix.

Frostburn's head snapped toward the door when she heard the new arrivals, her tone more gruff than usual. "What the frag happened?"

Yu lit a cigarette, then shook his head. "Johnson set us up. Are you alright? Where's Rude?" He looked around the room, as though there was furniture big enough for the troll to hide behind.

"Not answering his commlink. Zip's trying to reach him."

"*Puk gaai!*" Yu forced himself to take a deep breath as he ran his cyberhand through his hair. "I'm sorry, this is my fault."

"Yeah, it is." Frostburn's jaw tightened. "Why were you so keen on taking this job in the first place? The real reason, not that 'for the exposure' bulldrek you fed us before."

Yu cursed under his breath and turned away from Frostburn and Emu, taking a huge drag from his cigarette to calm his nerves—at least until his busted ribs must have started protesting, causing the elf to grunt and clutch his side. "I found the Johnson when I was tracking down a BTL dealer—he owned the warehouse where the chips were being stored. He claimed he had no idea his renters were using the place to smuggle *gong cung*, and offered to shut them down if I took this job against Telestrian. Everything else happened exactly the way I said before, including the part about the Johnson working for Renraku."

"Why would you want to take down a beetle dealer? I thought all you Triad boys moved chips," Frostburn said.

The elf turned stone-faced at the question, but Emu saw a hint of anger in his eyes at Frostburn's implication. "It's personal."

Frostburn wasn't deterred; on the contrary, she stepped toward Yu, shaking an accusatory finger in his face. "You know what else is personal? My family being in danger because I decided to be a team player and help you with your stupid fraggin' run. How long do you think it'll take Renraku to run my SIN and figure out where my parents live, huh? Or my brother, or my sister and her daughter? If they found our safehouses this fast, what makes you think they wouldn't—"

"That's *enough!*" Emu's voice boomed as she stepped between her quarreling teammates. "Frostburn, Yu's not the one who called Knight Errant on us. Don't blame him for something that's Renraku's fault. And Yu, I know we don't generally pry into each other's pasts, but if what happened then is going to be a problem in the present, the rest of us need to know about it." Not that Emu didn't already know the reasons for Yu's aversion to Better-Than-Life chips, but it wasn't her story to tell.

A long silence ensued while Yu paced back and forth, taking sullen drags from his cigarette until he tossed the butt out the open door and shoved his good hand into his pocket, sighing heavily. "My brother got hooked on chips when I was a teenager. Eventually, it killed him. That good enough?" Even the perpetual youthfulness of his elven heritage couldn't erase the weight of years in Yu's face.

"Yeah." Frostburn looked as weary as Yu as the tension drained out of the air. After a moment, the ork lifted her chin at the splint on Yu's non-cybernetic wrist. "What'd you do to yourself?"

"I fell down the stairs." Yu rolled his eyes at Frostburn's skeptical glare. "No, seriously. When the Knight Errant goons showed up and started chasing me, I had to fight them off, and fell down the stairs as I was getting away."

Frostburn waved at the chair and table on one side of the storage unit. "Sit down, I'll fix you up." Yu did, and Frostburn placed a hand on his shoulder and squeezed her eyes shut.

"Thanks Frostb—*hrk!*" Yu clutched his side and almost doubled over in pain, and even Emu winced at the audible *pop* as his ribs shifted back into place. "Enjoying this, aren't you?"

"Maybe a little." Frostburn sighed as her spell ended. "We need a plan for how we're going to fight back. Renraku's not like the no-name corps we're used to working for. They're way out of our league."

"We already know who the Johnson is," Yu said, rubbing his still-tender ribs. "Or at least who he's pretending to be: the CEO of Rip Current Sea Lanes. It's not like he—"

"Ag, that *domkop!*" The outburst prompted the rest of the team to turn at Zipfile as she sat up on the couch, rubbing her eyes. "Why can't he just answer his 'link like—oh, hey guys." She belatedly waved to the new arrivals.

Emu waved back with her cigarette, but her expression was all frowns. "Did you manage to track Rude down?"

The dwarf shook her head. "I tried tracing his commlink, but wherever he is, the Matrix coverage is too shoddy for me to me to stay connected. His biomonitor says he's alive, but that's all I can tell."

"Don't worry about Rude, he's probably just holed up somewhere in the Underground. It's not like Renraku will find him down there," Frostburn said.

After a moment, Yu continued. "Anyway, like I was saying: if Johnson's cover ID is the CEO of even a small corp, he can't just vanish into thin air. There'll be trails we can follow to find him, either by Zipfile chasing him down on the Matrix, or one of us just walking into the office and asking for him."

"That's kind of stupid of them, isn't it? Why hire runners through a Johnson that's so easy to find?" Emu asked.

"Sounds like they want to be found," Frostburn mused.

"If they do, we'll make them regret it. In the meantime, if they already hit one of our safehouses, this place probably isn't 'safe' either," Yu pointed out. "We can use one of the Octagon's crash pads for a few days, until we can arrange something more long-term."

Emu nodded. "I'll work on finding us another safehouse, then. Hopefully the owner won't charge us too much if it gets shot up." She didn't sound optimistic about that. "How soon can you talk to your Triad mates?"

"I wasn't going to bother. Billy's even harder to get a hold of than Rude," Yu said. "It's at the Guangdong Palace in Tacoma, by the docks. The crash pad entrance is around the back."

Frostburn grunted an acknowledgment. "I'll meet you there after I check on my family and try to find Johnson." The mage stalked out the door.

With the impromptu team meeting at an end, Emu, Yu, and Zipfile retrieved the gear they'd stashed in the storage unit and loaded it into their respective vehicles, then set off for Tacoma.

By day, and a large part of the night, Guangdong Palace billed itself as the largest Chinese buffet in the Seattle Metroplex. Emu had no idea whether that was true, but she decided if there had been a competition for the largest Asian massage parlor in the Metroplex, Guangdong Palace would've won first prize.

The ground floor of the building seemed to have been set up as a legitimate (if poorly-patronized) Chinese restaurant, but the entire second story of the building had been set aside for "relaxation massages" offered mostly by attractive young women, with a few young men thrown in for good measure.

More relevant to Emu was the staircase that led from the brothel down to a granny flat in the building's basement, which would serve as the team's safehouse until she found somewhere better—or until Yu's Triad bosses found out he'd let his shadowrunner friends use the place without having asked permission. After seeing the suite's two dorm-style rooms and common area, Emu wanted to ask Yu if the Triads would be open to letting the team pay to just stay there instead; as safehouses went, you could do a lot worse than semi-private rooms in the basement of a restaurant guarded by a crime syndicate.

Unfortunately, the elf had already zonked out in their shared bedroom by the time the idea popped into her head, so the rigger had to settle for bugging a contact of hers: a Knight Errant dispatcher chronically stuck on the night shift. Emu knew her contact would've been on duty during the ambush at the Harbor Island warehouse, so she dug his commcode out of her commlink's contact list and put a call through.

A few moments later, a man's voice answered. *"Draper."*

"Steve? Hey, it's Natalie," Emu said, giving the name on her fake SIN, and trying to sound like she hadn't been shot at an hour ago.

There was a pause before the man responded. *"Hey, Nat. What's up?"*

"I was just thinking it's been a while since we've caught up, and was wondering if you'd like to have breakfast after work. My shout." Emu might not have been a slick talker like Yu, but she knew how to stay on a contact's good side, and everyone likes free food.

"Uh, sure. Meet you at Grounds around seven?"

"Perfect. See you then." That would give Emu the chance to sleep before the meeting—except that instead of passing out, she spent hours staring at the ceiling, jumping at every noise. The close call at the warehouse had left her too wound up to rest, no matter how many times she told herself that she was safe among Yu's fellow Triad members, and the tension robbed what little sleep she did get of any restorative value. At least Draper's suggestion to meet at a coffee shop meant she wouldn't have to stop for caffeine on the way.

Of Seattle's many, *many* coffee shops, Grounds for Appeal was easily Emu's favorite. The cafe was owned by a retired lawyer, whose taste in soykaf—and real coffee, for those who could afford to pay ten times as much for the luxury—was thankfully better than his taste in puns. The morning rush hadn't quite started yet when Emu shuffled through the door. "Morning, Jamie."

"Morning, Natalie!" Emu would never cease to be amazed at how coffee shop employees could be so chipper at such ungodly hours of the day. "Extra-large black and a cheesymite?"

"Please." Another fantastic benefit to Grounds for Appeal was that it was catered by the much-beloved Pink Door bakery and bar, which made it one of the few places in the Metroplex to stock the quintessentially Australian cheesymite scrolls, or "buns," as they called them in Seattle.

Emu sent a mental command to her commlink, transferring enough nuyen to cover the bill and a generous tip. A moment later, the crinkle of wax paper and the scent of wake-up juice brought Emu back from the edge of dozing off. "And here you go." Jamie set the coffee and pastry on the counter in front of her.

"You're a lady and a gentleman, mate." Which of those Jamie was tended to vary by the week, if not the day, so Emu figured it was better to cover all the bases.

With caffeine and sustenance in hand, the rigger set off in search of a table that offered some degree of privacy. Draper showed up around quarter after seven, which was early by his standards; like most megacorps, Knight Errant considered their employees' regular work schedules to be minimums, not standards. Emu joined the dispatcher at the counter so she could make good on her offer to pay, then led him to the table she'd chosen once he'd collected his order.

"Well, well," Draper said, after his first gulp of soykaf. "How can I risk my job for you today?"

Emu raised an eyebrow. "Risk your job? You should've said something sooner, mate. What happened?"

The Knight Errant officer shook his head. "It's fine. I'm not in trouble or anything, it's just the usual office politics bulldrek."

"Ah." Emu paused for a beat to give him the chance to continue. When he didn't, she did. "I'm trying to find out who called in for an HTR team at a warehouse on Harbor Island last night."

"What's your interest?" The dispatcher had clearly been keeping up with his corporate-security training about challenging people who ask suspicious questions.

"I was supposed to meet someone there. They never showed, but HTR did, and I'd love to know who tipped them off."

"Oh, no. No way." Draper shook his head emphatically. "I can't just give up the name of a 911 caller or patrol officer. If you pay them a visit, someone's gonna ask how you knew to find them, and my name will be all over the audit trail. I could go to jail for that. Hell, if they're looking for you, I shouldn't even be here." He stood from the table and turned to leave.

Emu half-jumped out of her chair and grabbed Draper's wrist to stop him. "Steve, please—just hear me out. I'm only asking because my life is in danger."

When he looked back, Emu let last night's leftover stress and worry show on her face. Draper was silent for a moment, and the rigger heard her heart pounding in her ears as he studied her expression to gauge whether the emotion she displayed was real.

Finally, he nodded and sat down, and Emu started breathing again. She took a gulp of soykaf to try and calm her nerves, wishing the coffee shop allowed smoking inside. "Someone who claimed to work for Renraku hired me to do a job for them," she said. "I won't get into the details, but I did it, then arranged to meet with the Renraku bloke and collect my pay. Instead, five minutes after I show up, Knight Errant swarms the place and starts shooting everything in sight."

Draper sighed. "And what do you expect me to do, file an excessive force complaint?"

"No, of course not. All I'm saying is that the person who called you guys in isn't innocent, either. That's why I came to you," Emu said. "Your bosses aren't going to care if criminals go after each other, and I promise I'm not trying to settle a score with Knight Errant. I just want to find out who wants me dead so I can make them back off before their hitmen catch up with me."

"Okay, okay. I'll pull the report at work tonight, but if anyone asks me about it, I'm not covering for you. I've gotta look after myself, too," Draper warned.

"I wouldn't expect you to. Thank you, Steve. You might've just saved my life." Emu withdrew a certified credstick from her pocket and slid it across the table. "The rest when you've got the name. Just let me know where you'd like to meet."

"Yeah." Draper slid the credstick into his pocket and stood. "I'd better go. Wife'll be wondering why I'm not home already."

Emu winced. "Ooh. Maybe don't tell her you were with another woman."

"Nah, I'll just say I was meeting someone who wanted to bribe me for confidential info from work." Draper rolled his eyes, then waved over his shoulder as he left.

Seattle's housing market had never been friendly, but for a shadowrunner trying to find a safehouse on a moment's notice, it was downright brutal. Emu talked to four different fixers before she found a place that would house all five members of the team—she was still holding out hope that Frostburn and Rude would show up—and after seeing what Lenny was charging, she wondered if it wouldn't be cheaper to just pay Renraku off instead.

Still, the converted farmhouse near the Snohomish River was remote enough that even her own finely-tuned sense of direction had trouble finding it, which made security a lot easier; there was so little traffic in the area that the team could assume that everyone who showed up had done so on purpose, and that anyone who did so and wasn't them was hostile. It also had enough sleeping pods—morbidly nicknamed "coffins," the kind used in "coffin hotels"—to house the entire team.

With the safehouse squared away, Emu's next task was to replace the drones that she'd lost during the debacle at the warehouse, and to repair the damage that Knight Errant's helicopter had inflicted on the Commodore, preferably without anyone asking how it had ended up with bullet holes in the roof. That meant a trip up to Gio's Garage, a fine establishment in Everett that had a lucrative second life as a chop shop for the Ciarniello Mafia. When Emu wasn't running the shadows, she helped out around the shop, partly in exchange for them letting her use the space and tools to work on her own vehicles, and partly to work off a rather large debt she'd incurred with the Ciarniello Family shortly after arriving in Seattle.

That debt, Emu realized, added yet another complication to the situation with Renraku. If the megacorp had been able to locate one of the team's safehouses, it wouldn't be much trouble for them to figure out that Emu spent time at Gio's—and if her dealings with Renraku caused any trouble for the Mafia, she would take the blame, not the corp. Emu really couldn't afford any more headaches at the moment, so she resolved to try to stop the trouble before it started.

Every war has its demilitarized zones, and in the long-running syndicate war between the Mafia and the Yakuza, Casino Corner filled that role. Until recently, the entire area had been controlled by the Ciarniello Family, and the Golden Roll and White Pine were still the heart of their power in Everett. The *Mafiosi* were happy to display that power, too, when it wouldn't risk an open conflict that would drive customers away. Emu had barely gotten ten steps inside the White Pine when she saw a pair of no-neck thugs in ill-fitting suits shaking down a gambler who was pleading for more time to pay—an unwelcome reminder of what would happen to her if she didn't make some kind of deal.

Two more ambulatory walls stood to either side of the door that led to the casino's back rooms. One of them held a hand up when Emu approached. "This area's off-limits."

"Is Tommy here? Tell him Emu needs to talk to him about her loan payment."

The doorman didn't quite conceal his sigh as he let his eyes un-focus over Emu's shoulder, a sure sign he was using a commlink through direct neural interface. After a moment, his attention re-focused on Emu, and he waved for her to follow him.

A few minutes later, she found herself in an office in the bowels of the casino. The man behind the desk was young, probably not much older than Emu herself, and the image of the "young mobster" stereotype: one too many shirt buttons undone to show off the gold chains, grin shining as bright as the reflection of the overhead lights off his slicked-back jet-black hair.

"Heya, sweetheart." Tomaso di Stefano—or as most people called him, Tommy D—was one of the Ciarniello family's made men. To Emu, he was also a bizarre cross between a gossipy relative and a collection agent.

"Hi, Tommy. Looks like you're moving up in the world." Emu looked around the office. Last time she'd been here, he was still hanging out in the staff room.

The mobster's grin flashed as bright as his gold chains and gleaming hair. "Didn't you hear? It's Capo Tommy now. The Yaks whacked my old boss a few weeks ago, and the Don said he liked my 'entrepreneurial spirit.' No more runnin' around breakin' kneecaps for ol' Tommy, only friendly conversations."

Which just meant he had guys who'd break kneecaps for him, Emu knew. "Congratulations."

"Thanks, sweetheart. Now, what can I do for you? The boys out front said somethin' about your loan." The mobster gestured to the chair across from him.

Emu sat down, taking a deep yet inconspicuous breath. "I probably won't be around Gio's much for the next little while. There's some fallout happening from a job that I did, and I need to lie low for a while."

Tommy whistled and shook his head. "Tough break, but a deal's a deal. We agreed that you'd help out at the chop shop instead of making your entire loan payment in cash. If I went around changing deals every time they were a pain in the ass to keep, I'd be out of business."

"Come on, Tommy. It's not like I knew this was going to happen. Hell, I'm trying to help you out by making sure my personal stuff doesn't interfere with your business." Which was technically true.

The mobster ran a hand over his face. "Alright, look. If I cut you a break, the Don'll hear about it and I'll be in deep drek—unless I can say it's payment for some work you did for me. I got some goods down in a warehouse in Redmond. Bring 'em back here, and I'll call us even for this month. Deal?"

Emu's brow furrowed. "What's the catch? If it was just a courier job, you could send your own people." Tommy wasn't a bad guy as *Mafiosi* went, but he was cut from the same cloth as his boss—a man with financial instincts so sharp, the Seattle Mafia had nicknamed him "Numbers." She knew full well that if Tommy was willing to make a deal, it was because it benefited him somehow, which meant the run he was offering might be way over her head.

"The warehouse belongs to the..." Tommy frowned. "What the frag are they called, again? Shigedas? Kanagas? The Yaks. They stole some goods from us, and Don Ciarniello wants 'em reclaimed."

"What kind of 'goods', exactly?"

Tommy shook his head. "You don't need to worry about that."

"I do about some things. Like how big a vehicle I'll need, and whether your mysterious goods will break or explode if I hit a pothole." Emu folded her arms across her chest.

"Steel case with a blue stripe on it, small enough to fit in the trunk of a car, and it won't break or blow up. The RFID tags say SpinGlobal. Good enough?" The mobster gave her a pointed look, eyebrows raised, like he was starting to lose his patience.

"Fine. Send me the address. How soon would you like this done?"

"Is today an option?" Tommy grinned.

Emu shook her head. "I won't know that until I've seen the place, but I'll assume you mean 'as fast as possible'."

"Good guess. Here's the address." Chuckling at his little rhyme, the mobster tapped the surface of his desk, and a GPS tag popped up in Emu's AR field.

"I'll let you know when I have it." Emu stood to leave, wincing as Tommy bellowed for the doorman—who'd been left out in the hall—to show her out.

Back at the team's brand-new, unreasonably expensive safehouse, Emu grumbled to herself as she started planning her newest assignment. The Yakuza warehouse was located in a part of Redmond called the Bargain Basement, the largest open-air black market in the

Seattle Metroplex. The good news was that it was a relatively nice part of Redmond—not that that meant much when the worst part was literally a melted-down nuclear plant. The bad news was that the warehouse was still far enough outside Redmond's "business district" to fall squarely within gang territory. Groups like the Crimson Crush and First Nations liked to raid warehouses for supplies, both to use and sell for profit, so the Yakuza would be expecting an attack.

What they weren't expecting, Emu hoped, was the Lockheed Optic-X was circling overhead. She'd sent the drone off to surveil the site, taking advantage of its stealth systems to study the Yakuza's security arrangements without being spotted. Even hundreds of meters above its target, the Optic-X's sensors were good enough to make out the guards' facial features. Emu didn't have a facial-recognition database she could use to ID them, but she did confirm there were eight different people guarding the warehouse. Every guard had a katana strapped to their hip—because of course they did—and most of them carried the Shin Chou Kyogo submachine gun favored by Japanacorp security forces. The Yaks had also put concrete barricades up around the front and sides of the building, to give them cover when the shooting started and prevent any raiders from breaking in by ramming through the loading bay doors.

Emu sighed and took a drag from her cigarette. Rude was the tactically-minded one, not her. She'd learned bits and pieces by osmosis while the team planned their runs, but right now, she mainly remembered enough to know that she was in over her head. Her drones could pack plenty of punch when they had to, but assaulting a syndicate warehouse was a little much for her to handle alone. Rude's guns and Frostburn's magic might've turned the odds in her favor, but the tuskers still weren't answering the team's calls. At the rate things were going, Emu figured, she and the others might have to delay the heist to form a search party.

She had just gone back to planning the raid on the Yakuza when a bright red warning ARO flashed across her vision: something had set off the perimeter sensors she'd set up outside the safehouse. When Emu went to check the camera feeds, though, nothing was there—which did absolutely nothing to put her mind at ease. Had Renraku's assassins already found her? Emu swore and sent a stream of commands through her rigger control console, ordering her small swarm of Hornet surveillance drones to circle the house as she drew her Ares Crusader from its holster at her waist.

"Uh, everything okay?" Emu nearly had a heart attack when she heard the person speak, and thanks to the reaction enhancers implanted in her spinal column, had a bead on Yu before the elf got his hands up. "Whoa, easy, it's just me!"

"Fragsake, make more noise next time!" The rigger holstered her gun before she accidentally shot her teammate—though if she'd had gel rounds loaded, she might've done so out of spite.

"Yeah, that's what *he* said." Yu gave Emu a lopsided grin as he lowered his hands and looked around. "So, does this mean we literally bought the farm? For what Lenny's charging, we might as well have made a down payment."

Emu groaned at Yu's quips and flopped back down on the couch. "Have you heard from Rude or Frostburn yet?"

"Not yet. I asked Myth to see if Coydog would help track them down magically, but at this rate...well, if Coydog's as good as Myth says she is, we'll know soon enough."

"I guess. Oh, hey, would you mind helping me with something? The Ciarniellos want me to break into a Yakuza warehouse and steal some goods for them." Emu sent the warehouse's GPS coordinates to Yu's commlink.

He frowned. "You're working for the Mob now?"

"Not like, *working for* them. I just couldn't pay them this month because of how much this cost." Emu gestured to the space around them. "One of their guys offered to let me do this job instead of coming up with the cred."

"Aha." Yu furrowed his brow. "I'll have to talk to my bosses at the Octagon. The Hung Gwan might not want me involved in something like this."

"Why would your Triad bosses say no? Wouldn't they be happy with you hitting a rival syndicate?"

Yu rubbed the back of his neck. "It's complicated. If I go with you and something happens to me, my Triad brothers are sworn to avenge it, but we can't afford to get in the middle of a war between the Mafia and the Yakuza. The bosses don't like taking risks if they don't have to, and the rest of us took oaths to obey them, whether we like it or not." The elf's sour look made it clear to Emu that he didn't, in fact, like it.

"No worries, mate. We'll figure something out—" Another perimeter alarm popped up in Emu's AR field. The rigger reached for her gun again, but relaxed when she saw a familiar figure on the security feed. "Looks like Zipfile's here."

"And you're not pulling a gun on her? I don't know whether I should be flattered or offended."

Emu glared at the elf. "She doesn't give me a heart attack from sneaking past the perimeter sensors just to prove she can. And for the record, you tripped one of the ultrasound scanners."

Yu grinned. "See, now you know it works."

Just then, the safehouse door swung open to reveal the errant dwarf, carrying an armload of Stuffer Shack bags. "Here, guys. This should last us until a few minutes after Rude shows up." She hefted the bag on to the kitchen table, then rummaged around inside it for a soybar.

Yu snorted and grabbed his own soybar, then glanced at his AR clock. "*Aiya*, I should try to get some sleep before tonight."

"What's tonight?" Emu lit another cigarette, then went to stand beside a window when Zipfile started coughing.

"Myth called someone she knows at Renraku who hires for their runs in Seattle. I'm supposed to meet him at the Nikko later."

Emu frowned. "No luck with the secretary?"

"Not anything relevant. Apparently, 'Mr. Miller' called her this morning to say he wasn't feeling well, and would be working from home for the rest of the week, so Ghost only knows where he is now. Anyway, thanks for the food, Zip." Yu waved with his half-eaten soybar, then sauntered off to the side room that served as the safehouse's sleeping area.

Emu blew a lungful of smoke out the window, then left her cigarette in an ashtray while she grabbed a Buzz Cola from the pile of foodstuffs. "Hey, Zippo, could you help me with something?"

"As long as it doesn't involve running over someone's cat with a drone." The dwarf grinned, and Emu regretted—not for the first time—ever telling her that story.

"No, I can handle that on my own, thanks. I had to take a job for the Ciarniello Family to pay their bloody loan shark, though. It's a heist at a Yak warehouse in Redmond."

"A heist? Good thing we've got a thief then, yeah? I'm sure Yu will love it," Zipfile said.

Emu winced. "Uh, yeah, about that. He said he couldn't help. Something about getting in drek with his Triad higher-ups for getting them into a mob war."

"Seriously? *Eish*, that guy...probably just doesn't want to make his boyfriend angry." Zipfile ran a hand over her head. "Ehh, don't worry, you and I can still do it. How big is this thing they want you to steal? We could just run in and grab it urban brawl-style, yeah?"

"Sure, the two of us can just run in and steal it out from under a bunch of Yak goons." The rigger laughed, but her mirth faded when she saw the puzzled expression on Zipfile's face. "Wait—you're serious?"

Zipfile shrugged between bites of soybar. "Why not? I'll be in the van anyway, and if the cargo was valuable enough for bleeding-edge security they wouldn't be keeping it in Redmond, yeah?"

"That's crazy, mate."

"Crazy enough to work." The dwarf smirked. "You got a better idea?"

Emu gave Zipfile a sideways glance. "You've been spending too much time with Gentry."

Zipfile made a face at the mention of Ms. Myth's *other* go-to decker and urban brawl enthusiast. "Hey, my legs might be shorter than everyone else's, but I'm a smaller target, too. The Luxembourg Miners are almost all dwarfs, and they were in the Teuton Cup!"

"Alright, you've convinced me." Emu raised her hands in defeat, then sent Zipfile the warehouse's GPS coordinates. "The item we need is a metallic case tagged with SpinGlobal RFIDs. They wouldn't tell me what was inside it, just that it's somewhere in that warehouse and that they want it back as soon as possible."

"Good for them, but we have to find it first." Zipfile studied the feed from the Optic-X. "Eight guys...that's not too bad. Just need a big enough distraction to keep them all busy while we sneak in. Your drones can do that, yeah?"

"Yeah." The rigger chewed on her lower lip as she mentally sifted through the specs of all of her drones." We might even be able to take a few of them out ahead of time..."

Noticing Zipfile's surprised expression, Emu explained, and after a moment, the dwarf nodded. The two women spent the next few hours bouncing ideas back and forth, building on each other's suggestions until they'd come up with a plan.

With the Mafia assignment in hand for the moment, Emu turned her attention back to the larger threat: Renraku. An old teammate of Emu's had dealt with the Japanacorp before, acting as deniable hired muscle all over the Pacific, including a couple jobs in Seattle. Maybe the rigger's old comrade was connected well enough to dig up something useful. It was a long shot, but Emu didn't exactly have a wealth of options at this point.

Yu and Zipfile were off doing their respective things, so Emu flopped on to the safehouse couch and made a call. The ARO expanded to fit the video feed from the other end of the call, a sharper-than-life view of...a wall.

A rustling sound filled Emu's ears, and a voice followed several seconds later. *"Do you know what time it is?"*

"Time for you to invest in a datajack instead of using your commlink with your bloody hands." The rigger shook her head.

"Wha–Emu?" The wall promptly spun to reveal a woman blinking sleep away. *"Not like you to call this early."*

"It's noon, Lyara."

"That's what I said."

Emu rolled her eyes. "Look, I'm in a bind and I really need your help." The admission made her wince a little.

Lyara snorted. *"Again? 'Lyara, come rescue me from these Mafia thugs whose gun shipment I stole.' 'Lyara, help me deal with these bikies who're slotted that I ran over their cat.'* You should be glad I don't charge you for it."

Lyara was a mercenary, or as the suits in Melbourne liked to call it, a "security consultant." It was through Lyara's merc company that Emu had first stepped into the shadows, piloting recon and combat drones alongside the soldiers, though she'd shifted to being more of a vehicle rigger in the years since.

Emu sighed. "This time's not like that, Ly. A Johnson tried to have my team killed after a frame-up job—and it wasn't the usual 'try to kill us instead of paying us' bulldrek, either. They tracked my teammates down before the run was even finished, bombed one of our safehouses, everything. And you know full well the cat was a bastet, and I only ran it over because it jammed my wireless before I could stop the Doberman." At the time, they'd both gotten a good laugh out of the idea of a Matrix-attuned cat being chased by a drone named after a dog.

"Ugh... alright, I don't know what you expect me to do from here, but I'll help however I can."

"I'm trying to find some dirt on this slot from Renraku that'll make him back off." Emu sent the picture Yu had given her through the Matrix feed. "You still know people there, right?"

"Depends. Will you make it worth my time?"

"I thought you said you weren't charging me for it."

"Nah, mate, it's just a favor for a favor. I tried to order some merch from a place in Seattle, but the shipping's brutal. Could you pick something up and chuck it in the post for me?"

Emu raised an eyebrow. "You want me to hit the bottle-o while I'm out, too?"

"Nah, you've got shit taste in beer." Lyara grinned.

"Uh, it's called having standards? What am I picking up for you, and where?"

"It's a place called Powerline. Let me look up the address—"

"Don't bother, I know where it is."

The merc's eyes shot up. *"Oh, do you? Did moving to Seattle broaden your horizons in more ways than one?"* She rubbed her chin thoughtfully.

"No, it's— One of the guys on my team goes there sometimes. He asked me to give him a ride once, that's all." Emu felt her cheeks burning.

"So you're giving rides at fetish clubs now? You really have changed." Lyara grinned again, this time with mischief in her eyes. *"As for what I'm getting—"*

"Never mind, I don't want to know, I'm not list-en-ing," Emu said, covering her ears. "Just tell me whether it'll fit in the boot."

"It can be difficult to judge whether a package of a certain size will fit in the boot. Being able to tell at a glance is a matter of experience," the merc replied, deadpan.

"Lyara!" Emu's attempt to speak collapsed into sputtering, and she hid her face in her hands, not that it made much difference when the conversation was being pumped directly into her brain by DNI.

Lyara burst into a fit of cackles. *"I can't help it, you're so easy to get worked up!"*

Emu sulked. "You're a terrible person."

"I mean, were you expecting something else?" Lyara's grin stayed plastered across her face.

"Ugh, never mind...just tell me which fake SIN you used after you order it. Now, could we *please* get back to dealing with the Renraku thing before it literally kills me?"

"Yes, yes, I'll talk to my contacts and see if they know who that bloke is and how you can get him off your back. It'll probably be exy as fuck, though, just to warn you," Lyara said.

Emu sighed. "How much?" All the little extra expenses—not to mention the big ones—were adding up faster than Emu could bring the nuyen in.

"Last time I bought paydata like this from him, it was..." Lyara frowned and rubbed her forehead. *"Probably a couple grand? Assuming he already has it. If he has to hire someone to find it for him, it might be a lot more."*

"Great... Call him up, I guess. If I can't afford it, I can't afford it."

"No worries, mate. Can I go back to bed, or would you like me to stay up and torture you more?"

Emu snorted. "Night, Lyara."

Emu had rarely felt more self-conscious in her life.

From the first moment a visitor stepped inside, Powerline made its nature clear: it was a fetish club, catering to nearly anything its patrons could dream up, and probably a few things that hadn't occurred to them before. People of all persuasions and interests were mingling and chatting, undoubtedly—in Emu's mind, anyway—planning what sort of unspeakable acts they'd perform on each other later. Of the patrons Emu could see, every one of them was wearing some sort of fetish-related outfit, leaving the rigger to stick out like a sore thumb in her street clothes. The irony of the "normal" one being the outsider here wasn't lost on her.

Really, it wasn't even the fetish gear and public displays of far-more-than-affection that bothered Emu—it was the inquisitive looks she got from the patrons. *What's someone like* you *doing here?* They were the same looks she'd gotten as a girl, living in corporate housing with her father, where they were the only kooris around. Most of her father's colleagues and their families were white Australian or Japanese, a few were Chinese or Indian, and every single one of them had given her the same look. *What's someone like you doing here?* A few of them had even said it (and less pleasant things) aloud, as though Emu's obvious Kuringgai heritage meant she was destined to spend her life being a *koradji* out woop woop with her mother and half-siblings. Never mind that her mother's family had treated her like an outsider because she'd grown up half in a corporate housing facility and half in the bush, and that was before she'd polluted her body with cyberware by getting a control rig...

Emu shook her head to snap out of her reverie. *Just get it over with and you can leave,* she reminded herself. There was something like a reception desk not far from the front entrance, so Emu headed that way, silently thanking whatever power controlled the universe there was no line-up.

The man staffing the desk looked up when Emu approached, offering her a bright cheery smile. "Welcome to Powerline, honey! How can we delight you today?"

"How are ya, mate? I'm just here to pick up a package. Should be under Kylie Foster?" Emu glanced at an AR window she'd opened, reading off the confirmation number Lyara had sent her.

"Let's see..." The clerk fiddled with his terminal for a moment. "Ahh, here it is. Just a sec, and I'll go get that for you."

Emu mumbled a thank you, then passed the time by wondering how she'd gotten more comfortable with getting shot at by megacorp agents than being around people who were open about their kinks. At least the curious glances had mostly stopped, although there was one Japanese bloke—a drug dealer, Emu noted, after seeing a few of his deals take place—who seemed to have taken an unusual interest in her, while also trying not to look like he was watching. The elaborate tattoos on the dealer's arms marked him as a Yakuza member, but Emu didn't know enough about the Japanese syndicates to tell whether the man was part of the same group that controlled the warehouse, or even if she *could* determine that kind of thing from a Yakuza soldier's ink. She settled for keeping her hand close to her concealed Crusader and wishing she was somewhere else.

A few tense minutes later, Emu spotted the desk clerk returning—and struggled not to facepalm at the suitcase-sized box he carried.

"Here you go, honey," he said, dropping the parcel on the desk with a dull *thump.* "That'll be six hundred nuyen."

"Uh, sure." The rigger managed not to choke in surprise at the price as she waved her hand at an ARO marked "Pay Here" floating above the desk and transferred the required amount. *Six hundred? What the frag did she buy?* "Do I need to do anything else?"

"Nope, you're all set. If you're ever interested in finding more partners, though, you should definitely stop by sometime. With a range of tastes like yours, I'm sure a few people here could pick up some new tricks," the clerk said, gesturing to the box.

Emu's cheeks started to burn. "No no, these aren't mine—I'm picking them up for a friend."

"Oh, I see. Well, then tell your friend *they* should visit us," the clerk said, with a raised eyebrow and a knowing look in their eye, like he heard that excuse all the time—which, to be fair, he probably did.

For a moment, Emu considered trying to explain that no, the assortment of adult merchandise actually *was* for a friend, but another glance at the interested-not-interested drug dealer convinced her to cut her losses. "Thanks, mate." The rigger gave the clerk a friendly smile as she hefted the box, then strolled out of the club.

As soon as she stepped outside, Emu mentally commanded one of her Hornets to watch the door of the club. The drone buzzed away, and Emu kept one eye on its video feed as she stuffed Lyara's shipment into the Commodore's boot—or trunk, as people called it in Seattle. Thankfully, nobody else emerged from the building before she got everything loaded up. She paused just long enough to recover the Hornet on her way out of the parking lot, then made for the open road.

For people willing to rely on GridGuide and allow their cars' built-in autopilot to drive—that is to say, most people—the trip from Bellevue to the marina at Mukilteo Park would be a chance to play Matrix games or catch a quick nap. Like most riggers, though, Emu wouldn't be caught dead letting anyone else drive, especially an autopilot program. Luckily, her rabid insistence on controlling her own vehicle meant she was already watching the road when the staccato whine of a pack of motorcycles approached from behind her. A glance through the Commodore's rear sensors, filtered through the vehicle control rig implanted in her skull, revealed that the offending bikes were painted in garish red and orange: the colors of the 405 Hellhounds motorcycle gang.

Emu cursed. The Commodore—GMC's answer to Hyundai's better-known Shin-Hyung—was hugely popular among street racers. That made the sport sedans and their drivers equally popular as targets for the 405 Hellhounds' initiation rituals, something Emu had learned the hard way the first time she'd driven "their" stretch of road. Traffic was light enough at this time of day that the freeway was relatively empty, and thanks to her previous run-ins with them, Emu knew the Hellhounds wouldn't see the bog-standard Americars and Bulldogs nearby as more tempting targets.

As if on cue, half a dozen Thundercloud Contrail racing bikes closed in on Emu's Commodore. The Hellhounds whooped and hollered, whipping their bike chains against the sides of the car as they roared past, scraping gashes out of the paint and leaving gouges in the reinforced windows. For Emu, the feedback translated through her control rig made each strike felt like she was being slapped: no lasting damage, but painful as hell. After the first pass, the Hellhounds spread out, causing panicked honking from other drivers when they briefly drove the wrong way down the freeway, before coming around for another run at the rigger.

Fine, Emu thought. She really didn't need the extra hassle of scrapping with a go-gang right now, but if she couldn't avoid this fight, she was damn well going to win it.

She gunned the Commodore's engine—an action that her control rig translated into feeling like she'd taken off at a run, rather than the sedate jog she'd been maintaining—using the go-gangers' brief about-face to open as much distance as possible between them. The rigger knew the Hellhounds' bikes were quicker and more agile than she was, and she was determined to use them chasing her to her advantage for as long as she could. Just as Emu had hoped, the bloodthirsty go-gangers were eager to catch up with her, rushing at the Commodore in a virtually straight line.

Then the big, beefy Mossberg shotgun mounted in the Commodore's rear made its presence known when it blew out the closest Mirage's front wheel and turned the Hellhound riding it into a pile of shouting disbelief and road rash.

The others spread out and stomped on their accelerators, closing the distance even as they tried to avoid Emu's line of fire, but not before two more slugs from the Commodore's shotgun turned another go-ganger's torso into a ruined mess.

Through the Commodore's rear sensors, Emu saw the four remaining go-gangers toss their bike chains aside and draw guns, returning her fire as they closed in around the Commodore. Several bullets chewed holes through the car's rear bumper and windshield, which her control rig converted to a series of hard punches against her lower back.

Growling in pain and irritation, Emu skidded almost to a stop, prompting a furious honk from a driver who was forced to swerve around her. The Hellhounds shot forward thanks to the sudden difference in speed, and she grinned ferally as she flipped the Commodore's *other* Mossberg over to burst-fire mode. *Let's see how you fraggers like getting shot in the arse!*

The shotgun kicked, and the two go-gangers nearest Emu discovered that they liked it even less than the rigger had, tumbling from their bikes at speed as the Mossberg's slugs drilled into their backs. Realizing that the odds were very much against them and steadily getting worse, the remaining two Hellhounds wisely decided to quit before they got any further behind.

Emu was perfectly happy to let the remaining Hellhounds go, using the break in the action to put as much distance as possible between her and the scene of the firefight. The 405 was busy enough that someone had undoubtedly called Knight Errant to report the battle, and she knew the best way to keep them off her back was to make herself unprofitable to track down; the pawns might be a law-enforcement corp, but they were still a corp, and just as prone to thinking with their bottom line as any other.

To Emu's great relief, the rest of the drive to meet her smuggler contact was uneventful. She skirted the heavy police presence at the marina proper, instead heading north to Edgewater Beach and its long-disused pier.

The smuggler she was meeting, Jericho, made regular runs between Seattle and Melbourne. Emu knew better than to ask how a one-man operation got past the various border patrols, not to mention making trips across the Pacific. Likewise, Jericho didn't comment on how the box Emu handed him had a couple of obvious bullet holes in it, beyond offering to patch them up with speed tape. Emu readily agreed, and once she'd paid the smuggler's fees—which, somehow, was cheaper than the legitimate shipping companies, despite offering better service—she headed back to her car.

As Emu sped away from the docks, swearing she'd never haul Lyara's "personal items" again, she drafted a message by DNI. *<just dropped your package off, you owe me 700 dollarydoos>*

<ur a dollarydoo>, Lyara replied a few moments later, followed by a nuyen transfer pop-up. *<heard from taco shower, will get you a price today>*

Emu blinked, at the message. *<wtf is a taco shower>*

<Taco shower. Talk a sour. Tickle sewer.>

<wat>, Emu texted back, even more confused than before.

<dfa;'lskadjg TAKAZAWA, fn commlink voice recog>

Emu burst out laughing as comprehension dawned. *<sure it was... enjoy your new toys, don't mind the bullet holes>*

<wait wat bullet holes>, Lyara asked a split-second later.

Emu started to compose a reply, but deleted it. *She'll find out soon enough*, the rigger decided as she turned the Commodore down the freeway.

A day and a half after their breakfast meet, Emu heard back from Draper. The dispatcher had refused to discuss what he'd found by commlink, so they'd agreed to meet at the same place they'd first run into each other: Black's Junk Yard, an auto-parts and scrap dealership in Puyallup, just before the shop closed for the night.

Emu had opted to show up early, as much to browse the shop's stock as anything; for a rigger, wandering around a place like Black's was like being in a kid in a candy store. The other best thing about Black's was Hardpoint. The dwarf was Emu's counterpart on the first team Ms. Myth had put together, and he'd become something of a mentor to her since she arrived in Seattle. Hardpoint used the workshop at Black's sometimes, and the pair usually ended up talking shop if he happened to be there when Emu stopped by—and this time, he was.

"*Hisashiburi ne, Haadopointo-senpai.*" Emu waved as she entered the shop and sauntered toward the work area where the dwarf rigger was hanging out. She'd picked up a bit of Japanese when she was a kid, and after learning that Hardpoint spoke the language, she'd gotten into the habit of practicing it with him so she didn't forget it.

"Hm?" Hardpoint looked up from the workbench. "Ahh, *hisashiburi. Ogenki desu ka?*"

"*Genki da yo! Senpai wa-*at is *that?*" Emu's eyebrows shot up when she saw what Hardpoint was working on—a model of drone she'd never seen before.

Hardpoint chuckled. "Oh, this? You've heard about Ares' new stealth close air support drone, the Black Sky? That's Mitsuhama's refinement, the *Shingetsu*." He gestured to the craft with his torque wrench.

"She's a beaut," Emu said, full of admiration—and no small share of jealousy. "How does she fly? Have you taken her out yet?"

"Just a brief test flight to see how well the handling's dialed in. It's slightly less than twice as fast as a Roto-Drone with the same payload, and approximately thirty-three percent more maneuverable."

"Mmm." Emu craned her neck to get a better look, and stepped as close as she dared, though she was careful not to get any closer than Hardpoint himself. A rigger's workspace is hallowed ground, and she knew better than to impose on someone else's. "So, most important question." She grinned.

Hardpoint cracked a grin of his own. "No, I haven't decided what I'm going to arm it with yet. But at its optimal engagement range, a Barrett anti-materiel rifle is probably the most effective choice, or possibly a missile launcher. There's no reason to get any closer than that."

"Good point." The door chime went off, and Emu looked over to see Draper entering the shop. "Oh, here's my contact. I'll let you get back to work."

"Take care." The dwarf went back to tinkering.

Emu waved Draper over to the other end of the shop, out of Hardpoint's earshot; she knew her fellow rigger *probably* wouldn't eavesdrop, but better safe than sorry. "How's it going, mate?"

"Good, good." The words didn't match the dispatcher's wearied expression. "I found your guy: Haruki Satou. GPS places the commlink on Harbor Island when it was called in. Here's the full report." Draper gestured in mid-air, and an icon representing a file appeared in Emu's AR field.

"That's great." For the first time since the ambush at the warehouse, Emu felt her shoulders relax a little. She withdrew a credstick from her pocket and handed it to Draper. "Second half, as promised. Let me know if you ever need something I can help with."

Draper nodded and pocketed the credstick. "I will. So uh, you gonna go after this guy?"

"Depends on what else I learn about him. I won't say I'm not tempted, but there could be consequences if I push too hard," Emu said.

"Yeah, I'll bet. You've got a team and stuff though, right?"

Emu raised an eyebrow. "You're full of questions today."

"I am? I'm, uh, I'm just a curious guy, I guess." Draper's plastic smile was as unconvincing as his too-stiff attempt at a casual shrug.

"In that case, I'll let you know how it turns out. I'd better run for now, though. Don't work too hard, alright?" Emu noted the disappointment on Draper's face when she excused herself, but to her relief, he didn't try to stop her from leaving. Outside, the rigger circled to the alley behind the junkyard, walking back to her car as quickly as she could without looking like she was in a rush.

Like many riggers' cars, the Commodore had a smuggling compartment inside its trunk. Emu's was lined with a Faraday cage to prevent any Matrix transmissions from getting in or out—all it took was one RFID tag transmitting its signal at the wrong time to blow an entire run—and once she'd retrieved a backup Meta Link from the cabin, she shut her real commlink off and tossed it into the smuggling compartment, then called Zipfile.

"*Yeah?*" The dwarf's frowning face appeared in Emu's AR field. "*Emu? Why are you calling from a different commcode than normal?*"

"I think Renraku flipped one of my contacts," Emu said. "The police dispatcher. I asked him if he could look up some info that would help us find the Renraku Johnson. When I met him just now, he started asking me about what I planned to do about it, and whether I worked with a team."

Zipfile's eyes went wide. "*Oh, drek.*"

"Too right. The file he gave me went through my main commlink, so I chucked it in the smuggling compartment in case it had a worm or something."

"Good thinking. I'll scrub it when you get back to the safehouse," the decker said.

"Thanks, mate. See you soon." Emu ended the call and shoved the replacement commlink in her pocket as she closed the Commodore's boot with a *thump.*

At least, she assumed there was a *thump.* She didn't actually hear it, because someone chose that moment to try to kill her.

The world lurched, spinning downward like Emu had slipped on the Puyallup ash, but something was stopping her from falling, like she was leaning against the edge of a table. She couldn't breathe. Couldn't speak. She clawed at her throat, swung her arms behind her as rational thought gave way to sheer panic. Too late.

Something heavy pushed against her hand, weighing it down. *Dark. Air. Need air...* Struggling. Thrashing. Drumroll. *Drumroll?* Emu thought as she felt herself falling.

The darkness was giving way to light. Maybe the drumroll was her outro to whatever lay beyond. The white glow turned ash-gray. The afterlife looked like Puyallup, apparently, which Emu found a little disappointing. Then she felt pain. That didn't seem fair. You're not supposed to hurt when you're dead.

Oh. She wasn't.

The realization exploded into Emu's mind like a lead pipe to the back of her head—or maybe that was her hitting the concrete. Something wrenched her shoulder, crushed her arm, knocked the wind out of her.

She rolled on to her side, gasping for breath, trying to figure out what had just happened. When she looked up—well, "up" from the ground, behind where she'd been standing—she saw someone stumble and fall on their arse, clutching their leg. Someone holding a garrote.

The person who'd tried to kill her.

Adrenaline and Emu's cybernetic reaction enhancers finally started doing their jobs. Her arm wasn't moving properly, but she dragged her Crusader from its holster and made a game attempt to line up the sights, then pulled the trigger. Then she did it again, and again, and again, until all she heard was clicks and the gun stopped trying to buck out of her hands.

Emu didn't see her attacker moving anymore—and after a moment, neither could she. The Crusader clattered to the pavement, and her vision went black again.

Emu awoke with a start. It took her a second to realize she was propped up against a wall. She was in a dark room, and her head was killing her—and so was her shoulder, she quickly learned, when she raised her arm to clutch her head. A moment later, it registered that her hands weren't bound.

With some effort, she stood. Her legs were wobbly, but seemed to be functioning. Her entire body looked and felt encrusted in grime. When she looked around to get her bearings, she saw that she was in some kind of storage room. In the distance, she heard muffled screeching and banging, crunching noises, mechanical whines. There was a door in front of her. Emu twisted the knob, and to her surprise, it moved. She pulled the door open to reveal...Hardpoint, standing at the workbench and tinkering with his newfangled drone.

Oh. So that's what the storage room at Black's looked like.

Hardpoint looked up when he heard the door open. "Hey, take it easy. You should sit down, you got beat up pretty badly." He pointed at a nearby chair.

Emu was in no position to argue. She flopped down, wincing at the bright overhead lights. "The frag happened?"

"I was going to ask you the same thing," Hardpoint said. "I looked at the security feed when someone started shooting the windows out, and all I saw was you unconscious and some *bakayaro* trying to stand up to finish the job. Are you in trouble?"

It was a bit of a trick question, Emu knew; Hardpoint wasn't the type to ask something like that unless he already knew the answer. Making it a question just gave her the chance to save face by claiming it was no big deal, instead of forcing her to admit she couldn't handle it on her own.

"A Johnson backstabbed us," she said, figuring being honest was the least she could do when Hardpoint had just saved her life. "Renraku bloke. We did the job, and when we went to collect our pay, we found a Knight Errant HTR team instead. Someone knocked over one of our safehouses at the same time. We've been trying to track down the Johnson and get some dirt on him so he'll back off, but Rude disappeared the same night as the meeting, and Frostburn vanished the next day."

"*Chikusho,*" Hardpoint breathed. "Is the guy you were meeting earlier involved somehow?"

Emu started to shake her head, then changed her mind and began to nod, but gave up entirely when the all the head motions made the throbbing worse. "He's a dispatcher for Knight Errant. I asked him to find out who put in the 911 call the night of the ambush. The meeting just now was him giving me the paydata, but he was acting really strange, asking more questions than usual."

"Like he was wearing a wire."

"Yeah." Emu sighed. "I'd just gotten off the comm with Zipfile when the other slot snuck up on me. I honestly don't know how I survived."

"I'm sure Renraku's lax recruitment standards didn't help." Hardpoint raised a hand when he saw Emu's hurt expression. "That wasn't a criticism of you. Here, let me show you the cam footage."

The dwarf was silent for a moment as he accessed the shop's security system. The bright AR display hurt Emu's eyes a little, but she was able to take in most of the image. The camera had been at the wrong angle to capture her assailant's face—or, more likely, her assailant had gone out of their way to conceal it—but the view was otherwise decent. Emu saw the attacker sneaking up behind her while she chatted with Zipfile, then struggle, and then...

Emu's cheeks grew hot as she realized her savior had been the little Walther holdout pistol she kept up her sleeve. Her flailing had dropped the gun from its arm slide into her hand, so that when she'd reflexively pulled the trigger, the pistol's muzzle was already lined up with the would-be assassin's leg. Even a light round like the Walther fired left nasty wounds when six of them hit roughly the same spot.

"I see." Emu was too absorbed in her own thoughts to say anything else. Hardpoint had been kind enough to let her save face by pointing the blame at Renraku's poor hiring choice, but the reality was that Emu had only survived the attempt on her life because her assassin was too incompetent or overconfident to line up a headshot instead of walking across an empty parking lot. The idea that she was alive because someone else had made a mistake—instead of because she'd successfully defended herself—was too much to process immediately.

For a few moments, Hardpoint didn't say anything either, until enough time had passed that the topic seemed closed. "I've already contacted Yu and Zipfile about what happened, and programmed your car's autopilot to take an indirect route back to your safehouse to avoid any pursuit. I'll have one of my drones shadow you to make sure you get there safely."

"That's sweet of you, but I've driven in worse shape than this—"

The dwarf clucked his tongue in disapproval. "The medkit autodoc said you have a concussion. Black doesn't have a proper med-drone here, and I'm no doctor. If that blow to the head damaged your control rig, trying to jump in could fry something important. Manual or autopilot only until a cyberdoc clears you," he ordered in the tone of a disapproving parent.

"But..." Emu sighed. "Ugh, fine." She knew Hardpoint, as a fellow rigger, knew just how aggravating it was to be in a vehicle she didn't control. She also knew he was right about the risks of malfunctioning headware; Rude had told her once that his amnesia was caused by taking a blow to the skull that had made his augmentations burn out and cook part of his brain. Then again, the troll had a pretty morbid sense of humor, and so much of his feelings had been replaced with chrome that Emu could never quite tell when he was joking.

When she felt like her legs could carry her, Emu collected her gear from Hardpoint—including a few trinkets he'd taken from her assailant—and bade him farewell. True to his word, the dwarf sent one of his Roto-Drones to watch over her. As Emu trudged back to the Commodore, she noted that the would-be assassin's body had vanished from the parking lot. At least she wouldn't have to worry about it wrecking her rear bumper when she backed over it.

Inside the Commodore, Emu groaned when she saw the autopilot route Hardpoint had programmed—both because it was autopilot, and because it would take a solid two hours for her to get back to the safehouse. Resigned to her fate, the rigger sent Yu and Zipfile messages to inform them of her ETA, so they'd know to come looking for her if anything went wrong.

A two-hour road trip seemed like the perfect opportunity for Emu to take a nap, but once again, she was too tense to fall asleep. She was freezing, even with the heat turned all the way up. Every little noise made her jump. The sensation of having the life choked out of her played through her mind on an endless loop. When she reached for the steering wheel, trying to clear her head by focusing on the road, her hands shook. Emu swore in frustration. The danger was over, so why was she still so rattled? Sure, she'd almost died, but that was nothing new; her run-ins with the Knight Errant helicopter and the 405 Hellhounds could have killed her, too. How was almost getting strangled by an assassin any different?

Driven by the need to get the feeling of being strangled out of her head, Emu reviewed the events of the last few days. The fact that Yu and she had been ambushed at the warehouse didn't bother her; it wouldn't have been the first time a Mr. Johnson had decided he'd rather try to kill the team to tie up loose ends and pocket the second half of their fee than pay them for their work. Not that it wasn't annoying and dangerous when it happened, but it was purely a professional conflict, like the urban brawl matches Zipfile loved so much.

The attack on the team's safehouse, on the other hand, wasn't just a greedy, opportunistic employer trying to rake in a few extra nuyen under the guise of "tying up loose ends." No, this Mr. Johnson actually wanted the team dead—not just "the team who did this job," but "Emu, Frostburn, Rude, Yu, and Zipfile."

The weight of the realization broke a dam inside Emu, and the rigger slumped forward against the Commodore's steering wheel, sobbing. Logically, she had understood that she was in danger the moment she heard the safehouse had been attacked, but she hadn't really had time to process the situation before her run-in with the assassin. Now she had no choice but to face the reality of the situation, and the visceral fear that accompanied knowing her life was in danger crushed her chest until she could barely breathe—just like the assassin's garrote. The delayed panic was hitting her full force, making the Commodore's normally cozy cabin feel like a cage.

I could run, Emu thought. All she'd have to do is reprogram the Commodore's autopilot, give the Salish border patrol her real SIN so they wouldn't arrest her on the spot for having a fake, and she could leave Seattle behind forever. It wouldn't be the first time Emu had started a new life. She'd been on the move for as long as she could remember: between families as a young girl, from her hometown to university on a corporate scholarship, then off the path her parents had chosen for her and into the shadows, first in Australia and now in Seattle. She'd even gotten her runner handle from both her speed and her tendency to "migrate"—a side effect of never quite feeling at home.

You're letting your fear get the best of you.

The realization shocked Emu upright and out of her crying fit. She didn't like that thought, not at all, and tried to stuff it back into the recesses of her mind—only to have more unpleasant thoughts spill out, like her head was Pandora's bloody box. *You're right to be scared. They caught you when you were vulnerable, and they'll do it again. But being vulnerable isn't the same as being helpless. Are you going to give in to your panic and let them win, or are you going to pull yourself together and fight back?*

Emu sighed and slumped forward again. In her heart, she knew her inner lecturer was right: right now, she wasn't running the shadows so much as running scared. Renraku was one of the ten biggest corporations in the world. If they wanted her dead badly enough to hire assassins in the first place, skipping town wouldn't be enough to stop them from coming after her. The only way to do that was to fight back, and that would be a lot easier when she had allies on her side.

With that dilemma resolved—at least for the moment—Emu slipped into a dreamless sleep.

Emu and Zipfile decided to launch their raid in the early hours of the morning—too early for even Grounds for Appeal to be open, much to Emu's chagrin. The guards would have been up all night by then, they reasoned, and with a little luck, the two runners might be able to catch some of their opponents literally napping.

Neither woman would have any problem seeing in the dark, between Emu's cybereyes and Zipfile's dwarven thermographic vision, and it would give her Bulldog step-van a little more camouflage during the approach. Emu had opted to leave the quicker Commodore at home for this run, despite strongly preferring the smaller, nimbler sedan to the clunky cargo hauler, in favor of the Bulldog's tougher armor and larger storage capacity.

"I really ought to get one of those chameleon coatings," Emu mused aloud as the Bulldog rolled towards the Yakuza warehouse. She wasn't jumped in this time, partly to avoid risking any stress on her control rig—the street doc she'd browbeaten into seeing her on a moment's notice had pleaded with Emu to "take it easy," but admitted there was no reason to think anything would go wrong—and partly because it tended to creep passengers out when their driver was lying comatose in the front seat of the vehicle. "We could do this in broad daylight and they'd still never see us coming."

Zipfile glanced sideways at the rigger. "This is why you're in over your head with the Mafia. 'Oh, I should get a chameleon coating.' 'Oh, I should get a reflex recorder.' You should get a *money manager*, lady."

Emu smirked at her. "Is this when you give me the 'starving children in Africa' lecture?"

The dwarf grinned. "Hey, I would know, I was one of them."

"And look where you are now." Emu squinted at the Bulldog's nav system. "The target's in the next building over. Last chance to change our minds."

"We've got this. Jacking in now." Zipfile tapped her fingers against the cyberdeck sitting in her lap, and a moment later, her body went slack as she projected her mind into the Matrix.

"They've got their own decker," she continued, switching from speaking in person to "speaking" electronically without missing a beat. *"They haven't seen me, though. Seven other commlinks including yours, and a bunch of drones: Hornets, too many to all be friendly, plus a couple work drones."*

"Do they have a rigger?" Emu checked the sensor feed from her Optic-X2, which was dutifully circling dozens of meters above the Bulldog. She'd sent the drone ahead to scout the area before she and Zipfile arrived at the warehouse, but so far, there hadn't been much activity; the Yaks had mostly stayed holed up inside the warehouse, not really "patrolling" so much as sticking their heads out the windows every so often. Having a swarm of Hornets—surveillance drones descended from MCT's Fly-Spy, and too small for the Optic-X2 to spot—would explain why their security had looked so lax.

"Didn't see any RCC icons except yours." The rigger control console—or as many riggers called it, the "captain's chair"—was second only to the control rig itself when it came to the rigger's most vital gear. RCCs were designed to control large groups of drones, and the higher-end models provided extra-tough firewalls to keep hostile deckers from hijacking the rigger's automated army. If Zipfile hadn't spotted any of the Yaks using an RCC, their drones would be no match for hers.

"Found the package—drek," Zipfile said a moment later. *"The data on the RFID says the container's almost as big as I am."* The decker marked its location in AR for Emu. *"Checking out the warehouse's security now..."*

looks like there's one camera on the door closest to the package, one in the corridor leading to that part of the warehouse, and one covering the part of the warehouse where the package is. You said it was metal, right?"

Emu sighed and rubbed the bridge of her nose. "That's what my contact told me. Steel case with a blue stripe."

An image appeared in her AR field, showing the inside of the warehouse. There were shelves upon shelves of boxes, but the camera was focused on several messy stacks in the middle of the floor, all made of cardboard or dark plastic. *"If the GPS is right, it's in the middle of that pile."*

"Of course it fragging is." Emu's forehead hit the Bulldog's steering wheel with a *thunk*.

"At least we've got the layout of the place now," Zipfile said. A 3D map of the warehouse's interior appeared in Emu's AR field. *"I can make one of the hauler drones carry the package outside for us, and loop the cameras so the Yaks don't see it leave the warehouse. They'll still hear it moving, but that shouldn't matter as long as you've got your drones distracting them."*

Emu sent a series of mental commands to the Bulldog and her RCC. "How long will it take to get the package?" The van's rear doors popped open, revealing the small squadron of drones sitting on plain metal shelves inside; proper drone racks were yet another item on the list of Emu's things to get, though they were admittedly a few spots above the chameleon coating.

"How fast does an Ares Packmule move?" The question was accompanied by Zipfile's avatar shrugging.

"Tell me when it has the package. Mark the 'Mule's path for me?" The four Hornets immediately buzzed off toward the warehouse while the replacement Roto-Drones—now upgraded with FN HAR assault rifles and high-end targeting software—readied themselves for liftoff. The buzzing of various small rotors made the Bulldog's cabin sound like Emu was sitting inside an armed air conditioner until the gun drones also took off into the night.

A glowing line appeared on the warehouse map in response to Emu's request. *"'Mule's working, cameras are looped,"* Zipfile reported.

"Roger that." Emu settled back into the Bulldog's driver's seat and called up the Hornets' camera feeds alongside the one from the Optic-X2, marking the positions of each Yakuza member she could see on the map Zipfile had provided. The door the Packmule had to get through was directly below the warehouse's second-floor office, on the opposite end of the building from the larger loading doors. In the absence of enough team members to carry off a more complex diversion, Emu opted for the tried-and-true "shoot one side of the building while you sneak through the other" strategy. On the Optic-X2's camera feed, icons denoting the three Roto-Drones circled into position on the loading-door end of the building.

Then came the waiting. Emu wished she could light a cigarette, but neither she nor Zipfile had wanted to risk one of the Yakuza spotting the pinprick of light or its heat signature—not to mention that, the way this run had started, Emu was sure that fishing in her pockets for her smokes and lighter would take her attention away from the situation at exactly the wrong moment.

Instead, the rigger sat around twiddling her thumbs for an eternity that her commlink's clock claimed had only lasted five minutes until Zipfile spoke again. *"Packmule's got the package."* When Emu checked the camera feed Zipfile had hacked from the warehouse's security system, she was relieved to see that the work drone was indeed holding a steel case with a blue stripe.

"Distraction on the way." With a single command through the RCC, all three of Emu's Roto-Drones started pouring rifle fire into the warehouse's loading doors, and mayhem broke out. Emu grinned as the Yakuza soldiers flew into a panic, watching from the Optic-X2's sensors as four of them charged down to the main floor and out of the building to take up defensive positions, giving her Hornets a chance to dart inside before the doors closed. The four Yaks left inside the control room, busy trying to respond to the crisis, didn't notice the insectoid drones slip through an air vent until a Wasp had landed on each mobster's shoulder or neck—until all four collapsed, disabled by doses of Narcoject delivered through each Hornet's hypodermic "stinger."

With the most likely sources of interference busy or napping on the job, Emu signaled Zipfile. "Door's clear, get the Mule out!" The Bulldog's engine roared to life, and Emu guided the van to the warehouse exit.

"Got it. Shutting the cameras down so I can get the doors," Zipfile said. On the warehouse cameras, Emu saw the warehouse's interior maglocks flicker from red to green. A moment later, the dwarf started awake, shaking the virtual fog out of her head. Drones could do a lot of things, but they weren't any better at opening doors with their "hands" full than metahumans were, so it was up to the dwarf to play porter.

While Zipfile hopped out of the van to look after the Packmule, Emu checked her Roto-Drones' status readouts. The Yakuza weren't particularly good marksmen, Emu noted, but the muzzle flash of the drone's assault rifles gave them a pretty good idea of where to aim. All three drones had suffered enough damage that Emu wanted to pull them back, both to draw the Yakuza away from her exit route and to avoid having to replace the drones *again*.

Unfortunately, a retreat wasn't in the cards just yet. The Packmule was decidedly *not* living up to its nickname, the "Hauling Ass," but rather moving at the speed Emu would've expected from its namesake animal—maybe one with a case of chronic depression.

Even the normally-chill Zipfile was visibly agitated at how slowly the drone plodded through the warehouse—or maybe at the absurdity of having to hold a door for a drone in the middle of a firefight.

Eventually, though, the Packmule did saunter out and place the blue-striped steel case in the back of the Bulldog. When the package and Zipfile were both safely in the van, Emu recalled her Hornets—only to have all four of them explode into shrapnel and their video feeds cut to black. One of the Roto-Drones wasn't doing much better, and Emu directed it and its two counterparts to hustle up, up, and away before the Yakuza could finish any of them off. No sense trying to pick them up now when she could just meet them late—

"Mage!" Zipfile's warning came a split-second before a lightning bolt slammed into the Bulldog's side. Emu cursed a blue streak as the electrical surge caused the van's systems to flicker and reset themselves, scrambling to bring everything back online. A string of thunderclaps echoed through the van's cabin as Zipfile returned the spellcaster's fire with her Ruger wheelgun, and Emu matched the noise with a quieter, but no less emphatic *bang* as she pounded her fist on the Bulldog's dash out of sheer desperation. Thankfully, the impact was enough to get the van's controls functioning again, and the Bulldog's wheels kicked dirt and gravel everywhere as Emu stomped on the gas.

Any hopes the two runners had of making a clean getaway were dashed by submachine gun rounds pinging off the Bulldog's armored chassis; the Yakuza who'd engaged the Roto-Drones had realized they'd been bamboozled. Emu yanked the steering wheel to bring the van around a corner, then used the brief reprieve to order her Roto-Drones to turn around and strafe the Yaks from above.

"Zippo, make sure the cargo's tied down. Gonna try to lose these slots." Zipfile grunted an acknowledgment and shimmied into the cabin's cargo section.

Emu checked the Optic-X2's camera feed and cursed when she saw the Yakuza set off after her on their racing bikes, then activated her control rig. Compared to the Commodore, the Bulldog felt more like a bull than a dog—an *aging* bull, half-lame and arthritic after years of chasing rodeo clowns, and barely able to keep its footing when moving at any kind of speed, as Emu was rudely reminded when taking a corner nearly rolled the van on to its side. The internal cameras showed the steel case sliding across the floor with the momentum of the turn, then Zipfile bouncing after it a moment later, like the slapstick comedy beat of an action trid. It took the poor dwarf several more cycles of being tumble-dried before she was able to grab one of the case's handles and hook it to a cargo line.

Meanwhile, Emu kept the Bulldog zigging and zagging through the built-up area around the warehouse as the Yakuza bikers swarmed around her. One decided to get cute and pull up next to the driver's-side door with gun in hand, realizing too late that when an armored van swerves into a flimsy crotch rocket, the crotch rocket loses. The impact and the Mirage's own speed sent the bike careening wheels-first into a building, and left Emu with one less enemy to worry about.

"Their decker's trying to call for backup," Zipfile said, informing Emu that she was back in the passenger seat.

The other three bikers kept up their assault as though trying to take revenge for their fallen comrade. Every *spang* of a bullet against the Bulldog's sides, translated through Emu's control rig, stung like being hit with a rubber band.

Around the next corner, Emu spun the van into a hairpin turn—only half-intentionally, though she'd never admit that—and lined the nose up with a biker who was paying more attention to lining up his shot than to how the van he was shooting was headed straight for him. Emu had just enough time to see his Yak-in-the-headlights look through the Bulldog's external sensors before the two vehicles collided and the biker and his Mirage went bouncing down the street in the opposite direction.

With their numbers reduced by half, the Yakuza bikers fell back when Emu turned the Bulldog towards the freeway, only following close enough to keep the van in sight—and when Emu's Roto-Drones showed up and began raining bullets down, the Yaks gave up even that token pursuit. The rigger sighed with relief as she ordered the drones to follow the Bulldog, just in case the Yakuza sent any more trouble after them. Another minute or two, and they'd reach the freeway and make their esca—

Emu hadn't even finished inputting the Roto-Drones' commands into her RCC before one of them exploded into shrapnel. What the frag had caused that? Was there something wrong with the Bulldog's external sensors? Did the Yakuza decker get the better of Zipfile and hack into the van's systems?

The answer became clear when a fearsome-looking warrior riding a cloud threw a bolt of lightning at the Bulldog, forcing Emu to swerve to one side and confirming that the Yakuza magician had summoned a spirit to assist in the chase. Emu had seen Frostburn use spirits the same way, providing magical concealment that prevented the team from being spotted during runs, and soaking up bullets when Rude was off doing something else. As her Roto-Drones got back into firing range, Emu hoped the hostile spirit wasn't as sturdy as Frostburn's were.

The Roto-Drones swooped down on their targets, unleashing a storm of automatic fire, only for the bullets to flatten themselves against the spirit's supernaturally tough skin without so much as leaving a mark. The spirit returned the gesture with another brilliant elemental bolt that blew one of the Bulldog's rear doors off its hinges, leaving Emu groaning in simulated pain when her control rig translated the damage. The spirit was happy to drive the point home with another elemental bolt that blasted another Roto-Drone to pieces.

"*I just replaced those!*" That's what Emu would've shouted if she hadn't been jumped into the Bulldog. Instead, the outburst came through as an ear-splitting honk from the van's horn.

"We need to deal with that spirit," Zipfile said—rather unnecessarily, Emu thought—as she scrambled to draw her Ruger.

"Working on it." The assault rifles mounted on the Roto-Drones were the biggest guns Emu had, short of swinging the Bulldog around and ramming the spirit head-on, and she didn't particularly feel like giving it the chance to put a lightning bolt through the windshield. Short of conjuring a better-armed drone out of thin air, there was nothing she could—

Hmm.

Mind racing, Emu sent a series of commands to her commlink. Even that brief task almost prevented her from swerving the Bulldog away from the spirit's next attack, and the odd stray bullet that landed in the Bulldog's cabin made it feel like Emu had waited an eternity before the recipient of the call answered. "*Moshi moshi.*"

"Please tell me you got a gun mounted on that new drone."

Hardpoint's eyebrows rose. "*I did. In fact, I just finished calibrating it. Why do you ask?*"

"Because I'm mid-run up in Redmond with some kind of spirit chewing my arse, and my drones can't scratch it." Emu felt another impact through her control rig as she sent Hardpoint her GPS data.

The dwarf nodded gravely. "*I'm on a test flight in Snohomish. Head north, and I'll meet you as soon as I can.*"

"Got it." Emu killed the call and threw the Bulldog around a corner, giving the van as much gas as she could manage. Zipfile and the remaining drone were blasting away at the spirit, which utterly ignored their fire as it tossed lightning bolt after lightning bolt at the Bulldog like the van had called its girlfriend ugly. Emu's control rig made the Bulldog more nimble than a cargo van had any right to be, but she couldn't avoid every blast, and the rigger's worry grew as the Bulldog's status display turned increasingly red with each impact.

Over the next few minutes, and despite the dire circumstances, the game of cat-and-mouse between Emu and Zipfile and their pursuer became routine, even tedious. Emu would bring the Bulldog around a corner, the spirit would follow, and Zipfile and the remaining Roto-Drone would lay down as much cover fire as possible while Emu swerved to avoid yet another elemental bolt. Most of the time, the spirit's attack would miss. Then Emu would turn another corner to keep the spirit from getting a follow-up shot on the van, the spirit would give chase, and the process would begin over again. The problem was that every elemental attack that hit its target slowed the

Bulldog down a little bit, making the van a little more fragile and the controls a little less responsive. As the chase dragged on, the spirit got more accurate, or maybe luckier. Instead of every fourth lightning bolt striking its target, it became every third, and before long the Bulldog's cabin was filled with holes the size of Emu's fist.

Come on, Hardo, where are you? If Emu hadn't been so busy trying to keep herself, Zipfile, and the van in one piece, she might've called him a second time, even though she knew it wouldn't make his engines run any faster. Instead, she drifted the Bulldog around yet another corner—and promptly had a heart attack when she heard a deafening *bang* and felt the vehicle spin out of control, then pitch over onto its side. Pain shot through Emu's "feet" like she'd dropped something heavy on them, the control rig's way of telling her the Bulldog had blown two of its tires, and the sensation of gravel and asphalt scouring the van's side panels felt like someone had body-checked Emu into a belt grinder.

Emu barely got her control rig shut off before the pain from the Bulldog's "injuries" overwhelmed her, and even then, it still took several seconds for her brain to unscramble itself. Once the rigger had come to her senses, she slapped her seatbelt release and tried to climb between the front seats—the driver's-side door was pinned against the ground—only to see the hostile spirit floating outside the van.

Another brilliant bolt lanced forth from the spirit's hand, and out of sheer desperation, Emu flung herself back into her seat. A flash of light filled the Bulldog's cabin, accompanied by the stench of ozone and an electric tingle across her skin, followed closely by a drumroll of thunderclaps ringing through the air.

So this is how I'll die, Emu thought. There wasn't time for anything else before the spirit's attack hit home and the resulting blast pummeled her into darkness.

After an indeterminate amount of time, Emu's repose was cut short by an ear-splitting roar. When she opened her eyes, the dark sky was fringed with an orange glow, and the air was thick with stifling heat and an acrid chemical stench.

Panic flooded into the rigger's thoughts as she heard someone screaming nearby. *Frag off, Hell isn't real! It isn't, it can't be real...it...*

With her mind racing like an engine with the gas pedal floored, Emu jolted upright from where she'd been lying on the rough, sharp stone, looking for something, anything, that might prove her fears wrong.

The first thing she saw was the Bulldog's front grille. The vehicle's burning wreck was still tipped over on its side, and its windscreen was missing. Then Emu heard more screaming and another thunderous roar, and turned to see Zipfile nearby, jumping for joy like she'd just won something. "*Laduuuuuumaaaaaaaaa!*" The cheer was followed by the triumphant, bellowing *vrrr* of a vuvuzela being blown at volumes no metahuman lungs could match. It was the same audio clip that Zipfile played when her beloved Imikhonto scored a goal in an urban brawl game.

Emu gingerly pushed herself to her feet, her entire body aching. "What happened?"

"We got thrown out of the van when the spirit hit it after we crashed," Zipfile said. "But the spirit kept attacking the Bulldog instead of coming after us, until Hardpoint's drone showed up and wrecked it with that giant machine gun." The dwarf pointed off to the side, where Hardpoint's Shingetsu was sitting as patiently as the dwarf himself did.

"And the cargo?" The possibility that this whole debacle had been for nothing, that the goods Tommy D wanted so badly might've been destroyed in the crash, frightened Emu almost as much as thinking she'd literally died and gone to Hell.

Zipfile shrugged. "A little banged up, but I got it out of the Bulldog before anything caught fire. I'll need your help getting it into the car, though."

"Car?" Emu tilted her head to one side, confused.

"I had to steal a car to tow the case out of the Bulldog—it was too heavy for me to lift, remember? Besides, we needed a ride anyway." Zipfile grinned.

Emu couldn't help but laugh at the dwarf's logic, especially now that post-danger exhaustion was setting in. "Suits me fine, mate."

With that, and after a brief text-message exchange with Hardpoint—Emu tried not to think about how much it would cost to replace the explosive rounds Hardpoint had expended on the spirit—the two women loaded their cargo into their newly-acquired Americar and set off.

Rather than waste time going back to the safehouse, Emu pointed the Americar directly for the White Pine Casino. The place was open 24/7, and although Tommy D wasn't there—Emu doubted the mobster was even awake at this hour of the morning—his *soldati* were happy to take the cargo off the rigger's hands. Not feeling particularly trusting after the events of the last few days, Emu sent her own message to Tommy to make sure his goons didn't "forget" to tell him that Emu's job was done, then summoned her Commodore for a pickup. Meanwhile, Zipfile set the Americar's autopilot to return the vehicle to where she'd stolen it from. If Knight Errant bothered to investigate, all they would see was that some gambler had stolen a car to go joyriding to a casino.

Back at the safehouse, Emu found herself unable to fall asleep, despite her exhaustion. Instead, she passed the time by staring at the ceiling and wondering if the Mafia run had been worth it. It would give her a month's respite from Tommy D's legbreakers coming looking for her, but Emu's payments to the Ciarniellos were nothing compared to the cost of a new RCC—the device had been inside the Bulldog when it caught fire—let alone the Bulldog itself, or the drones she'd have to replace yet again.

It's just part of life in the shadows, Hardpoint had told her once, after the first time repair costs had turned a run from a profit into a loss. This one was by far the biggest lost Emu had suffered as a result of a run, but it wasn't the first, and she knew it wouldn't be the last.

With that "comforting" thought in mind, Emu finally drifted off to sleep.

When the rigger woke up that afternoon, she was assaulted by the smell of something spicy. Her growling stomach propelled her into the safehouse's kitchen area—and there, she saw Rude, sitting at the table with a pile of Taco Temple double-stuffed tacos in front of him. When the troll heard Emu enter the room, he looked up from his meal. "Yo."

"Where the frag have you *been*, mate?" Emu's surprise made her forget how hungry she was for a moment.

Rude shrugged. "Lookin' into somethin' I found at Elfy-Pants' little warehouse party. Got a little shot up, an' had to lay low for a while."

"And you didn't think to tell us?" Emu sauntered into the kitchen proper and retrieved a soybar from one of the cupboards. The tacos smelled damn good, but the rigger knew Rude and his troll-sized appetite weren't big on sharing food. Hell, they'd be lucky if he didn't start in on the soybars after the Aztláner food was gone.

"Nah, just bullets. Didn't want y'all to start naggin' me 'bout it. Already had seventeen messages tellin' me to come here." Rude grumbled toward the living room couch, where Zipfile was chilling as she surfed the Matrix in VR.

Emu snorted and plopped into the chair across from Rude. "Well, maybe they wouldn't back up like that if you answered your bloody commlink once in a while. So what's this thing you were looking into?"

Rude grunted around a mouthful of taco. "Tell you when FB and Elfy-Pants get here."

"You heard from Frostburn?" Emu's eyebrows shot up.

"Shorty did. Just said she was on her way. Elfy-Pants went to... fraggin'..." Rude paused for a moment, then growled and smacked himself in the forehead. "The food store."

"Stuffer Shack?" Whatever accident was behind Rude's amnesia caused other memory glitches sometimes, Emu knew.

Rude grunted an affirmative and went back to eating. Emu knew that was Rude-speak for "I have nothing more to say on this topic," so rather than try to engage the troll further, she started browsing through the messages that had come in while she was asleep.

Most of them were spam and went straight to the bin, although Emu did send the "Tír Tairngire prince" who wanted her help moving his nuyen out of the country a fake SIN that had already been burned, purely to see whether Knight Errant would go after the scammers for accessing a credit account created under a fake name.

With the spam messages out of the way, Emu finally got to something useful: a text-only message from Lyara. <*heard from Taco Shower, he wants 3k for info on your Johnson*>

<*tell him he can see plenty of Johnsons on the Matrix for free*>, Emu replied, snickering.

<*so proud of you*>, Lyara texted back a few minutes later. <*I meant the Renraku one tho*>

<*nvm then, 3k's too exy*>, Emu wrote back. Between the name she'd gotten from Draper and the commlink from the Renraku-hired assassin, she was confident Zipfile could dig up the same information as Lyara's contact, and with the bundle of expenses she'd incurred on her Mafia assignment, Emu wasn't thrilled with the idea of spending even more nuyen.

Several minutes passed before Lyara wrote back again. This time, her message led off with an angry-face icon. <*wow, after all I've done for you... not sending you tomtoms anymore*>

The rigger shook her head at Lyara's message. "Wow, rude."

"Mm?" Rude looked up from his rapidly-shrinking pile of tacos.

Emu waved him off. "Nothing. Not you."

"Huh?" Yu had naturally chosen that moment to return from Stuffer Shack, and as usual, Emu hadn't heard the elf enter the room.

"Never mind." The rigger sighed, but immediately perked up when she saw another figure enter behind Yu. "Frostburn!"

The ork magician waved. "Hey, gang. There a spare bed around? I haven't slept since...yeah." Emu could practically see fatigue gumming up the gears inside Frostburn's head.

"Coffins, yeah. Right-hand door," Emu said, pointing to the bedroom.

"Thanks. Oh, here. From Renraku." Frostburn fished a commlink out of her pocket and tossed it at Yu, apparently having forgotten that the elf's hands were full, then shuffled off to the room Emu had indicated. Luckily, Yu was able to catch the flying device with his foot before it hit the ground, kicking it up into the air like a hacky sack so it fell into one of the grocery bags.

Emu glanced at the others as she lit a cigarette. "You want to wait to talk until she wakes up?"

"Nah, fill her in later," Rude said, balling up his bag full of taco wrappers and tossing it into a nearby bin. Emu nodded and pinged Zipfile in the Matrix. The dwarf joined the others at the kitchen table a few minutes later, and Rude continued. "That thing I said I was lookin' into? The same guys who tried to geek Elfy-Pants at the warehouse also geeked a bunch of Renraku wageslaves."

Emu frowned. "From what my contact told me, it was a real HTR team at the warehouse."

"Or they hacked Knight Errant's dispatch system to cover their tracks," Yu suggested.

"Not likely." Zipfile shook her head. "Ares might not be a 'Matrix corp' like Renraku, but they still have wiz security on their most important systems. Hacking KE dispatch would be hard enough that a lot of deckers would only do it to say they could."

"Besides, you saw what they brought to the warehouse," Emu added. "Anyone with the nuyen to kit out three or four Roadmasters' worth of HTR troopers *and* the helicopter that came after us might as well just bribe someone at Knight Errant. If I can afford it, they sure as hell can."

Yu raised an eyebrow. "Your guy sold you out, remember?"

"That's not the point, and you know it."

"Fine, fine." Yu raised a hand to concede the argument. "The only thing I got out of Myth's guy was that he's no help. He just said he didn't know of any ops they were running against Telestrian."

Rude grunted. "Maybe he's lyin'."

"Maybe. I wish I could say I'd have known if he was, but I thought that about our Johnson, too," Yu admitted.

"Don't worry about it," Zipfile said. "Lying is what the corps do. That's how they keep people under their thumbs."

"You could ask him to run the name my contact gave me. Haruki Satou," Emu said.

Yu shook his head. "The guy I met referred to himself as 'Satou,' too. I think that's just the name Renraku Johnsons when they meet with runners."

"Don't worry, chummers. I already found the Johnson." Zipfile grinned, smug as a Tír-born elf. Emu and Yu both gaped at her, and Rude even raised an eyebrow at the dwarf.

"So we had three different commlinks for this guy, yeah?" she continued. "The one Yu called to arrange a meeting after the run at Telestrian, the one the Johnson used to call 911 at the warehouse, and the one he used with the assassin that went after Emu. So, I pinged some of Frostburn's old co-workers at NeoNET to see if they still had access to the routing data for Seattle's grid, pulled the GPSs of the burner commlinks during those calls, and got some friends to help me check the GridGuide logs." An image of an SK-Bentley luxury sedan—probably from a surveillance camera, Emu guessed, judging by the high angle—appeared above the table. "Is this your car?"

Emu whistled. "It will be if we steal it. We can do that, right?"

"Chummers, meet Simon Dennis, Renraku spy and former CEO of Rip Current Sea Lanes. He's—" The dwarf broke off suddenly, frowning. "Is everyone else getting that call?"

In the same moment Zipfile asked, an incoming-call notification popped up in Emu's AR field, claiming to come from a private commcode. The four runners nodded to each other, then picked up the call in unison.

The avatar that appeared was of an elven man in a business suit, wearing the kind of bemused smile that Emu used to get from her father's corporate superiors.

"Good afternoon, everyone," he said, words tinged with a mild but obvious Tír Tairngire lilt. "My name is Mr. Johnson, and I work for Telestrian Industries. It's come to my attention that you carried out an operation against this corporation several days ago, one which has inflicted significant financial burden on our company. I want to give you the opportunity to correct your mistake."

The team shared a series of "you've-got-to-be-kidding-me" looks before Yu answered. "That's generous of you, Mr. Johnson, but our team isn't in the habit of undoing our own work—unless you're offering us compensation for doing so."

Mr. Johnson smiled. "That depends. Would you consider an opportunity for revenge against the man who's been trying to kill you 'compensation'?"

If Yu had some kind of reaction to the elf's words, he didn't let it show. "I'm afraid I'm not sure what you're talking ab—"

"Let's not waste any time beating around the bush, shall we? A Renraku operative named Simon Dennis, whom you know as 'Mr. Miller,' hired you to infiltrate the Telestrian Industries headquarters on Denny Way and plant malicious code inside our corporate host. You did so, and when you went to collect your payment, he double-crossed you and sent Knight Errant to kill you instead. Much to his chagrin, you survived not only that attempt on your lives, but several further attempts against various members of your team. So, I ask you again: Would you consider the opportunity for revenge against 'Mr. Miller,' the man who's been trying to kill you, 'compensation'?" Mr. Johnson raised his eyebrows expectantly.

The team shared another round of glances. "We'd be open to the idea," Yu said.

"Splendid. Meet me at the Viridian Gardens at nine o'clock tonight, and we'll discuss the details. Don't bother dressing for the occasion, I'll send word to the front desk to allow you inside regardless." Before any of the runners could respond, the Telestrian Mr. Johnson ended the call.

Almost in unison, Rude and Zipfile spoke up: *"Fraggin' elves."*

"Yes, it's all our fault." Yu rolled his eyes.

"I'd love to know how this new Johnson knows so much about our situation," Emu said, frowning.

"Then I guess we're taking this meeting," Zipfile said.

Leave it to the daisy-eaters to build a place like this, Emu thought as she took her first steps into the Viridian Gardens. Calling it "a private club in Downtown Seattle's Elven District" didn't really do it justice; to Emu, it felt more like someone had taken a work of art and turned it into a building. If there was one thing elves did well, it was "pretty," and the Viridian Gardens' refined lines, rich colors, and all-elven staff—no serving drones here—all fit the bill nicely. Emu focused on the first two as the *maître d'* escorted the team through the club, since it let her ignore how the staff were giving the team the same questioning looks Emu had gotten at Powerline.

When the runners arrived at the meeting room, Mr. Johnson was already there, admiring something through a window on the far side of the room. He turned as the team filed in. "Ah, there you are. Please, sit." His aloofness was even more pronounced in person, the rigger noted, no doubt helped by the two bodyguards in severe black suits and serious shades at his side.

Emu couldn't help but smile when she saw Rude angle for the chair directly opposite the Johnson. The troll shot the suit an irritable, defiant glare as he plopped into his seat, hard enough that Emu thought she heard it crack under his weight. Frostburn and Zipfile settled in on Rude's flanks, as though they wanted to stay as far away from Mr. Johnson as possible.

Meanwhile, Yu offered the Telestrian representative a deferential nod as he slid into his chair. "Thank you for giving us the opportunity to meet with you, Mr. Johnson. We appreciate your restraint in deciding not to punish us for the losses you suffered as a result of our actions."

As she listened to Yu go through the ritual of paying social tribute to a potential employer, Emu felt a twinge of anxiety and resentment well up inside her. She'd spent enough of her life listening to corporate doublespeak to know that Yu was basically thanking Mr. Johnson for not sending people to kill them like Renraku had, and hearing it spelled out like that was an unwelcome reminder of how close Renraku's assassins had come to succeeding.

When Emu looked at the rest of the team, she saw Rude and Zipfile fixing sullen glares on both Yu and Mr. Johnson. Frostburn was likewise scowling around her tusks, although Emu couldn't tell whether the ork's expression came from being cranky about how Yu was kissing Mr. Johnson's ass on the team's behalf, or because they'd had to wake her up from her much-deserved rest to make this meeting.

Mr. Johnson didn't seem the slightest bit ruffled by the team's petulance, matching the glares with a smile infused with more smugness than a metahuman face should've been able to express. "I'm sure you've all heard the old saying about how the best way to judge a person is by the quality of their enemies. By that standard, being in the crosshairs of one of the ten largest megacorporations in the world is quite an endorsement."

"Doesn't feel like one," Frostburn grumbled under her breath.

"Imagine my surprise when, two days after one of Telestrian's most sensitive operations in Seattle was targeted, I received a dossier full of verified information on the team of freelance operatives behind the attack. What an incredible coincidence!" Mr. Johnson shook his head with a rueful chuckle. "The Renraku operative who hired you must be an idiot to think that we would fall for such a transparent ruse—but Mr. Dennis' loss is our gain. Which brings me to the reason for this meeting."

"Finally." Rude rolled his eyes.

Mr. Johnson gestured, and a trid projector in the middle of the table lit up, revealing a corporate logo Emu didn't recognize. "There's a company called AVR Optronics that produces...well, I won't get into the technical details. Suffice it to say, the components they produce are used in the manufacture of Renraku's newest model of cyberdeck, the Kitsune. AVR's primary assembly plant is here in the Seattle Metroplex, in the industrial area of Auburn. I want it destroyed, thoroughly enough that they'll know it was deliberate.

"Oh, and there are two other matters which you may find of interest. First, a man fitting Simon Dennis's description has just taken the position of chief operations officer at AVR. His office is located at the same facility, which would be extremely convenient for anyone who wanted to 'persuade' him to call off the attempts on their lives. Second, since you've already displayed your talents at infiltrating secure systems—" Mr. Johnson's mouth tightened at that, and Emu heard Zipfile snicker. "—I'm also prepared to pay you a bonus of five thousand nuyen each if you bring me the production schematics stored on their host."

"And what about the base pay?" Yu asked.

"Base pay?" The well-dressed elf scoffed. "It's been deducted. Consider it reparations for the losses you've inflicted as a result of your assignment for Renraku."

Rude snorted. "Sounds like a 'you' problem. I do a job, I get paid. I don't get paid, I don't do the job."

Mr. Johnson's gaze flickered toward Rude, but his reply was directed at Yu. "I would suggest you remind your teammates that it's *your* job to negotiate with prospective employers, not their—"

"*Hey!*" Emu nearly jumped out of her seat as Rude's shout shook the room. The troll leaped to his feet, far quicker than his bulk suggested he was capable of moving, and his fists slammed against the table with enough force to crack the hardwood surface. Emu couldn't tell whether Mr. Johnson's snub had genuinely set off Rude's temper, or if the troll was playing it up in an effort to intimidate the suit; most people, even corporate Mr. Johnsons who were used to dealing with shadowrunners, didn't have the nerve to face off against a three-meter-tall walking wall of enraged muscle and chrome.

Unfortunately for Rude, Mr. Johnson and his bodyguards were in the minority. A pair of HK submachine guns appeared in the guards' hands faster than even Emu's cybernetic eyes could follow, and the weapons came to bear on Rude before the troll's fists hit the conference table.

A split-second later, Emu's hand reached her Crusader, though she didn't draw it yet; she wanted to show Mr. Johnson and his bodyguards that Rude would have backup if a fight started, not to start a fight herself. A glance at the rest of the team revealed that Zipfile had reached for her revolver in the same way, and Frostburn was wearing the same deep frown of concentration she always got when she was preparing to cast a spell. By contrast, Yu had his hands up and open in an attempt to restore calm. He'd just opened his mouth to speak before Rude beat him to it.

"Ya got somethin' to say to me, ya say it to *me*, not him." The troll's gaze never wandered from Mr. Johnson's face, like he hadn't noticed or didn't care that two other people had guns aimed at him. His point made, Rude lowered himself back into his chair and folded his arms back across his chest.

"Very well. I'll even use small words to make sure you understand." The edges of Mr. Johnson's smile turned razor-sharp. "I couldn't care less whether you take this job or not. I only bothered to call you because your attack on the Denny Way offices proved that you know what you're doing. We can help each other, and frankly, you need the help a lot more than I do—but if the chance to get Renraku's assassins off your backs isn't worth taking a lower fee, so be it. So, are you taking the job or not?" The suit raised his eyebrows at Yu.

Yu's composure didn't waver as he tilted his head towards the rest of the team. "Would you mind if we took a minute to discuss this amongst ourselves?"

"By all means." Mr. Johnson rose from his seat and exited the room, bodyguards in tow.

The door had barely clicked shut before Zipfile spoke up. "*Eish,* he's as bad as the *wakyambi!* 'Ooo, I'm going to treat you like a

servant because you're short and you cost me money!' Drekhead."
The dwarf punctuated her tirade with a vulgar hand gesture.

"Renraku sent someone after my family," Frostburn growled.
"Frag the nuyen, I'll take this just for payback."

Emu's eyebrows shot up. "Bloody hell! Is that where you've been
the past couple days? Are they alright?"

Frostburn nodded, her shoulders sagging as some of the tension
flowed out with her words. "They're fine now, yeah. They want to
make an example of us, I say we do the same to them, even if it costs
us a little nuyen."

Rude grunted. "Frag that. Word starts gettin' around that we're
takin' jobs on the cheap, people'll start expectin' it. I ain't takin' a pay
cut just 'cause this keeb caught us at a bad time. We can deal with
Renraku on our own."

"You can, maybe," Emu said. "I wouldn't give myself the same
odds, and I sure as hell wouldn't expect Frostburn's family to be able
to fight back if Renraku comes after them again. No offense, Frosto."

"None taken."

Zipfile shrugged. "If these guys want to pay us to do something
we would've done anyway, I'm happy to take their money. If Yu can
convince Johnson to raise his rates, even better."

"I'm happy to try. Are we splitting it four ways or five?" Yu looked
at Rude, who made a noise that sounded halfway between a grunt
and a growl, but didn't exactly object.

Encouraged by the troll's non-rejection, Yu stuck his head into the
hallway to summon Mr. Johnson back into the room.

The two elves took their sweet time haggling, but Yu prevailed
in the end, and took Mr. Johnson's promise of seventy-five hundred
nuyen—with the customary fifty percent up front—along with what
little intel he could provide on their target. The meeting wrapped
up quickly after that, with the snooty *maître d'* returning to show
everyone out. To Emu, it seemed like the team was almost as happy
to be leaving as Mr. Johnson was to see them go.

As the five runners ambled down the front steps of the Viridian
Gardens, Emu looked at Frostburn and Rude. "So, what exactly
happened to you two, anyway?"

RUDE
BRYAN CP STEELE

Pinned down, low on ammo, and jammed by enemy IC across all channels—everything was fragged, and Rude knew it. The ammo counter in his field-of-vision HUD was in the low double digits, and the smartlink flashed warnings at every other firing solution.

What a total fragging mess.

He looked up to lock eyes on an old friend...no, his squadmate... standing out in the open. An easy target for even these ghetto rebels—

Incoming! Get down, Marcel!

Fiery plumes and shrapnel hailstorms erupting from a line of mini-missile impacts shoved the troll into a combat roll, diving away from the rapidly vanishing brickwork of the old Boston P.D. metroplex.

Boston? When the hell was I in Boston?

Rude blinked away brick dust and cordite ash, letting the polymer sheaths of his cybereye platforms auto-lube away the smaller particles into thin, greasy tears down his rawhide cheeks. His vision clear, he torqued his head back and forth. Where was Marcel? Where was the Southside battlefield? Hell, where was the metroplex? All that was around him now was the alloy-lined walls of...where? A prison cell?

Just gotta do my time. Serve my corp, keep the deal.

The pressurized *hiss* of the door sliding open spun Rude on his heels, the familiar cold of a handmade shiv in his hand. Beyond the open door, the complex corridor stretched outward an impossibly long distance. Running toward him, eyes wild with rage, the mob of other prisoners threatened to wash over Rude like a convict tsunami.

It ain't gonna matter how many of ya'll there are...I'll gut ya one at a time!

Rude stepped out into the corridor to meet the oncoming tide of jumpsuit-clad murderers, but between eye-blinks they vanished, replaced with the blinding fluorescent lights of an operating theater.

The floor shattered like glass under his next footfall, the troll spinning in the darkness of the resulting void. Grasping in vain at the emptiness, Rude lost himself in the vertigo. Frustrated rage poured adrenaline into his veins, and he pounded his fists angrily against the sides of his head, clenching his eyes so tight his head ached.

When will it end?

No. His head didn't ache. It throbbed. Throbbed with every beat of his bio-enhanced heart. Rude felt each pulse of pain as it radiated out from the base of his skull. Radiated out from...from...

Frag 'em all!

Everything was replaced by the roar of his modified Ingram in his hand, spitting death at a line of merc'd-out goons in a field of burned-out cars scattered throughout the parking structure. Rude's grin shone like a silver scythe in the blooming muzzle flashes of his gun. This. This is what he lived for. It made sense. It was what every cell and fiberline in his body screamed out for.

Everything moved at the speed of an action vid. Rude leaped over the car, letting the machine gun fall from his fingers to mag-clamp to the block on his belt before drawing the Dikote blade from inside his coat.

Let's get up close and personal! Yeah!

He moved like lightning from one merc to the next, cutting and slicing parts off each one in a grisly display of "aggressive incapacitation" that Rude had used so often in his U-Brawl days. For over two meters of bio-print, polymers, metal, and troll flesh, he had the grace of a ballroom dancer—if that dancer was a murder machine, and everyone else on the floor was his victim.

"Rude..." A familiar-yet-disembodied voice echoed across the scene, causing him to pause his slaughter for a moment.

Stupid AR echoes. Shut the hell up and let me work!

He returned to his bloody task, sending two more exec-tec armored suits spinning away from either side of him, their slashed faces spraying arcs of crimson that reached up and across his path. They collapsed, their blood splashing a staggered red 'X' on the ground before him.

"Hey, Rude..." That voice again, this time making the troll drive his sword into his target so deep that he lost his grip on the gore-slick hilt.

This is how it's done, chums!

Rude lunged forward at the last of the opposition; easily knocking the short pistol from the man's shaking fingers with the back of his bony-knuckled fist. He clutched the much smaller man by the shoulders, his own thick fingers pressing hard into the elf's back and chest.

"Rude, man... come on!" The now decidedly female voice was accompanied by a shooting pain at the base of his skull, just like before.

Shutupshutupshutupshutup...

He clenched his teeth and tried so hard to focus on the work, but between the throbbing in his head and the edges of his vision beginning to blur, it was hard.

Rude started to squeeze and twist the thin little elf in his grip, pushing enhanced musculature until his arms were filled with burning cords of sinew. He could hear bones crack and lungs wheeze. Through the sensory augments in his fingertips—fingertips that he knew should be metal and not meat—he could feel the uneven edges of new broken bones rubbing against one another, flooding the corporate wage slave with agonizing pain.

Wait. Corporate?

Rude looked down, shifting the broken elf's weight in his hands like a child's toy, using his thumbs to pull his jacket aside to reveal a bright and shiny clearance badge on his inner lapel. It was fuzzy at first, especially with the growing pain in his head, but the image began to sharpen. Who did they work for? What kind of mess had he gotten into now?

"Rude! Pick up, dammit!"

Oh...

The insignia came into focus. Saeder-Krupp. These guys worked for the same people Rude was...

...hells.

There was a series of blinding, sharp pains at the base of his skull. His hand went to dig at it, this increasing agony, but there was a blast. A flash from behind his eyes. Everything was washed away in an instant, leaving Rude alone and shaking in the darkness again. He knew something horrible had happened, but trying to remember what caused an even greater hurt deep within him.

"Rise and shine, you knobbly jackass!" this last time the voice was clear and obviously frustrated, but it was accompanied by the annoying claxon of Rude's AR wake-me-up program. The sound was somewhere between an Ares air raid siren and South Chicago goblin jazz. In other words, the perfect thing to ruin the best and most chemically-induced sleep sessions.

"Ow!" Rude shot up in his bed rack, slamming his forehead into the frame overhead, adding another small dent next to all the others. Lines of startup code blurred by his internal HUD, rolling through a dozen or more job offers automatically flagged for denial for one reason or another, landing squarely on the triplicate alert that Rude had an incoming call that he'd already missed a few times. The AR signature icon attached to them blinked like a hazard bulb.

"Dammit, Zip...never before ten on my damn day off..."

Legs heavy with both sleep and augments not fully powered up just yet swung out and planted onto the mock-hogony paneled floor of his tiny apartment. It was almost comical how small his place was compared to his bulky frame, but it served all the right purposes for a troll on the go.

Rude rubbed his eye sockets with the heels of his only remaining—mostly—"bio", hand, yawned like some kind of medieval beast, and slowly popped each of the knuckles on it individually, skipping the one poly-plast finger that he got in Reno a few months back. *Or was it DC?* he thought, rubbing the thick ridge of scar tissue at the base of his skull. "Frag it."

With a staccato series of *cracks* and a few matching groans, Rude rose out of his sleeper and stretched to his full height, the sudden drop in weight triggering the stowaway feature to slide the glorified cot into the wall. The tallest edges of his horns scraped lightly against the stucco of the ceiling, sprinkling chalky dust onto his lumpy head. There was a map of tiny, unintentional hash marks across the whole ceiling from similar scrapes and bumps, and he barely even noticed the contact anymore. Just another part of living a troll's life in human world. If it even was a human world anymore. Who could tell, really?

Rude reached over to the countertop, an easy feat considering he could flat-palm both parallel walls in his room, and grabbed the half-drank soycaf. He upended it into his mouth, winced, and struggled down an oddly-bitter swallow.

"Aw, drek." the floating filter end of a cigarillo stared up at him as it swam around in the brown gunk that was going to serve as breakfast.

The icon started blinking again; another incoming call.

"This better be important, Zip," Rude growled, his words translating into a text file within the AR connection with his "favorite" decker. "Ya don't even know the dream yer interruptin'."

<*Gross, Rude.*> Illuminated green letters scrolled across his AR view. <*I don't need to know that.*>

"Hazards of workin' with this pretty face," Rude flicked the soycaf cup toward his waste bin, hitting the lip and splashing foulness down the wall. Sure, he can put a Predator round through the eye of a ghoul at twenty paces, but he misses the shot that will keep his apartment from reeking. "Great. Now, what's so prime ya risked a smack down?" He sighed gustily. "What we lookin' at?"

<*You know you don't have to talk out loud, Rude,*> Zipfile's reply scrolled across his vision. <*I keep telling you that. Your Sony Emperor will totally translate to us as fast as–*>

"But I *like* ta talk!" Rude laughed. "Almost as much as I like ta sing—"

"Okay, okay!" Zipfile cleared her throat, hoarse from disuse, "We can back and forth like plebs if you want to. It's your call."

"Actually, this is *yer* call..." Rude plucked an old L.A. Tridents jersey off the top of his laundry pile, gave it a sniff, and ducked his head into it. Struggling to get it over his horns without ripping it, he spun in place awkwardly. In his twisting and bending to get dressed, he caught his back's reflection in the wall mirror and it gave him pause.

Puckered bullet wound scars formed a constellation of past combats across his corded, muscular trunk; matched by a roadmap of knitted slashes and surgical stitching. His arm was a quilt of medical wonderment where it went from warty muscle to hydraulically enhanced machine. Each one of these ugly marks came with a story about how Rude had survived something terrible before, but he struggled to remember them all. So much of his past should be easy to recall, especially with these physical reminders scattered all over his body, but things got so cloudy sometimes. It was so scrambled up there, he had to wonder if—

"Rude?" Zipfile's voice snapped him out of his fugue. "You okay, chummo? You kinda trailed off there."

"Yeah. 'Course I am!" He pulled down his shirt with a grunt and yanked up a pair of jeans that had seen better days quite a few worse days ago. "Just muted out for a second. Cut ta it. What's on the feed that has ya'll up in my ears this mornin', and so quick after our action yesterday?"

"Yu."

"Well, yeah." Rude snorted. "'Course it's about *me*, beetle-brain, why else would ya be callin'?"

"Ugh! Not '*you*,'" The exasperation in her voice was as thick as fog off the Sound. >*YU*.

The name popped onto Rude's HUD and he had to stifle a genuine laugh. "Honest mistake."

"Not if we were text—"

"Get ta the point, Zip. I gots a bunch to do today," Rude lied. "What about Elfy-Pants?"

"Frag." She sucked air through her teeth. "Yu was all over the wire this morning...*really* early this morning, something went awry with the rest of the pay for that Renraku run, so it looks like he wrangled Emu last night for a ride over across the stretch to, I don't know, meet up with their Johnson again? Apparently the guy wants to do everything analog, handing over encrypted sticks in person."

"An' ya'll call *me* old-fashioned."

"I know, right?" she continued. "It's why I'm actually calling you. I know he said he had it handled, and that he wanted to follow up on this thing alone, but that elven confidence has gotten him into trouble before, and I just can't shake the feeling that something isn't right. I mean, Renraku is a tech corp. Renraku *Computer Systems*. If there's anybody's Johnson that should be fully iced up for protected money transactions, it'd be a Renraku Johnson. Doesn't make sense and frankly, I don't like it."

Zipfile triggered a few subroutines and an address popped up into Rude's AR, internal positioning software already figuring out the best ways to get there.

"A Rip Current storage site? Ooh, nice. Blind alley on one side, and a speck of an office complex on the other. Not far from the waterfront to stem street-level obstructions. Tons of neighborin' buildings for lease or renno." He saved the information for later. "Great place fer an ambush. I could really mess some idiots up in that spot."

"My thoughts exactly. Even with Emu nearby to back him up, I don't like what Yu could be strolling in to find. He isn't exactly known for his self-restraint, and give Emu all night? She can talk anyone into a bad idea if it means an adrenaline rush." She was biting her lip, and Rude could hear what it was doing to her enunciation. "That's why I'm calling you. The meet isn't till later today, and it's all the way over in West Seattle. I know your place in Puyallup isn't exactly right next door, but it'd make me feel a whole lot better if I knew you were heading up to check it out. If you leave soon, you'll make it there long before he does to scope out the site."

"I dunno, Zippy." Rude groaned dramatically. "Can't see Elfy-Pants being terribly happy to see me hornin' in on his action. Not that I care what he thinks 'bout a babysittin' call, but he'll surely give *ya* hell over it."

"That's why I think it would be best if you just shadow it?" Zipfile added an innocent lilt to her voice, "Make sure it goes down like they think it will, just to be safe?"

"Aw, I dunno..." He fingered through weeks of empty entries in his personal planner. "I got a ton of heavy shit ta do today. This is a big ask on short notice."

"I know, I know." She sent a packet of pics to his viewer, "That's why I come bearing gifts."

The pics were digitally enhanced auction-tagged images taken from multiple angles of three specific objects. The first was a long, stormy-sky blue-black colored, NAN-styled duster with a row of internal sleeve and chest pockets perfect to hold all sorts of great toys for easy access; it was nice, and he *could* use a new coat. His was getting pretty worn out. The second was an automated software suite designed to speed up the friend-or-foe indication on a SmartGun link by putting an emoji-esque overlay of various programmable icons over the faces of pre-coded friendly SIN readouts; kind of a goofy thing, but it could make a firefight fun in the right circumstances. Lastly, a set of pics that left Rude's jaw open in awe—an autographed *physical* portrait of Geanna SINnamon, Rude's absolute favorite orxploitation action/adult-video star.

"Yes. Deal. I'm in." Rude accepted quicker than he'd wanted to, but damn...a *signed* SINnamon? Zipfile had her ways to get a hold of just about anything in the deep Matrix, so he wasn't about to question his good fortune.

"Just be careful not to let them know I sent you, okay? Yu has all those pointy-eared feelings, you know?"

"Elfy-Pants and Emo won't even know I'm there." He chuckled—the tiniest touch of malice in his voice. "'less they do somethin' too stupid, and go forcin' my hand."

"Perfect." Zipfile punctuated her statement with one last line of text. <*You be careful, too. I heard we got something big coming down the pipeline soon, and we'll need you.*>

>*ThANksoK@YY*, he comm'd back after a few seconds, knowing his purposeful delay and terrible textmanship would drive her nuts.

Rude shoved his finger against the activator for the UV panel that served as his place's window facsimile, a soft day-like glow cascading down on his far-too-brown-to-be-healthy thornapple cactus, and slid open the door to his cabinet/cooler. There was maybe three sips of H2-Faux in a plastic bottle, the recycled drinking water everyone in Puyallup used to avoid city plumbing charges. Giving the first two sips to his plant and taking the last for himself, Rude put the empty bottle back in the cooler and slid it shut.

"Hold down the fort, Sir Pricks-a-Lot." The door to his place clacked open halfway through the two steps it took for him to reach it, and he smiled at how odd his "leave the hab" ritual was. It was something his friends—no, his *squad?*—used to do back...back in...

"Frag it." He almost hated it more when the little things got foggy.

Rude's apartment door swung shut as he walked down the hall in his hab-slab, the automatic mag-locks engaging as soon as his AR signature got a meter away. Between that door, those locks, and hell—the walls; his place was not exactly a fortress. If someone really wanted in to his place, it wouldn't take much. Combine that with how Puyallup would *never* be called a "security rich environment" on the best blocks, and no one would question why Rude didn't keep anything of real value in his hab.

For that, there was Squid's Vaults.

Only a few blocks away from Rude's place, ol' Squid had made his claim on a quarter block of primo Puyallup real estate nearly a decade ago, buying up a row of rent-by-the-hour coffin sleepers and one dilapidated Stuffer Shack with a pile of nuyen. Over the next few weeks, he'd bulldozed the whole section and built up some seriously reinforced storage units—The Vaults.

A ton of rumors floated around about where Squid came up with the cash. The two leading theories were that he was named in a Russian dragon's will and—Rude's personal favorite—that he's a retired 'runner who brought down an entire Humanis Policlub cell. Wherever the funds came from, Squid wasn't telling.

The Vaults themselves were built like nothing else in Puyallup. Twin layers of ballistic fiber surrounding a living anti-astral algal web, maintained through internal nutrient threading, which is buried in twelve inches of polymer clay and rooted in place by aluminum posts every meter-and-a-half to form the walls. The scalloped design of the electronically, magnetically, and physically locked access gates were made to collapse inward like a closing flower on any impact with enough force to possibly bend the heavy alloy.

It took an active AR code, a biometric scan of the body part of the renter's choosing, and a physical keycard to open one of Squid's Vaults up—with a remote-triggered hardening foam deployable in each unit just in case. If someone managed to actually break in, in just a second or three they and everything in that Vault would be encased in breathable foam as dense and sticky as wet cement. This place was better protected than some of the corporate bomb shelters Rude had seen—and broken into—in the past.

Whatever Squid did in his former life, overdoing it on security was likely a plus.

"Hey, old man." Rude waved to the front gate camera, knowing the cranky dwarf was surely watching. "I need to come get a few things."

"Rent's due next Tuesday," a gruff voice barked through the speakers, *"try t'have it on time this month."*

The gate let out a grinding electronic *buzz* and slowly slid to one side.

"Thanks." He walked through, and not three paces later he heard the gate *clang* shut and its locks clamp tight. "Shouldn't be a problem," he answered, hoping it was the truth this time.

As Rude strolled through the rows of storage units, he wondered what kinds of treasures were hidden behind those sterilized, uniform-looking spaces. Guns, drugs, money, probably more guns...it was basically Schrödinger's Black Market. Even a powerhouse troll like him knew better than to try and open up any of these things except his own. Squid was always watching through the lens of his camera network, after all, and the locals swore that crazy old bastard had a fragging rail rifle in his office. Yeah, the last thing Rude wanted was an anti-tank round turning his insides into troll salsa, so he plays by the rules every time he stops by.

"Forty-one, forty-three, and..." he counted out loud, "here we go."

He stepped close to unit forty-five, a green icon appearing in his vision as soon as it recognized his AR signature, triggering a small security hatch to drop open to the side of the entrance gate. Behind the hatch was a simple circular slide with a straight slit down its middle next to a flat acrylic panel marked with a scanning grid. Rude fumbled in his pocket to produce a small, plastic keycard, which he carefully slid into the slot until it chimed softly, then turned it awkwardly counterclockwise until it chimed a second time.

Having set aside his discomfort about getting access to his Vault long ago, he stooped over and leaned in until his face was a few centimeters from the scanning plate—then opened his mouth, let his tongue drop comically out of his tusked lips, and smushed it against the cool, smooth acrylic. The plate lit up a neon green, illuminating his whole face and upper chest for a moment before going black once more.

"*Welcome, Mister Shaw.*" Hearing his most commonly used fake name in the soft electronic voice always worried him. Who else could be listening?

Prolly just Squid, he mused, pulling back from the security panel, flipping the hatch shut with a flick of his wrist, and turning to the entrance aperture. The metallic "petals" of the scalloped access hissed out a series of climate controlling gasps of pressure before shuddering to life, sliding into the unit's walls in three directions.

Rude stepped inside, the access mechanism closing behind him. *One set a' programs away from bein' in lock up*, he exhaled coolly. It always bothered him being in here too long. It wasn't like he was claustrophobic or anything; trolls get real used to being too big for human-centric construction early on, or they'll go crazy quick. This was something else. Something that reminded him of...*something bad.*

"Get it together." He shook off the feeling and waved on the blinking fluorescent bars set in the ceiling. Horrible, bleach-white light bathed the room. Rude smiled, the last flicker glistening off his titanium-tipped eyetooth.

The room was two meters wide, four deep, and just tall enough for him to walk around without banging his horns—but he did have to keep his hair down, or it would rub annoyingly against the ceiling.

Two long tables, stretched out on both sides of the unit to leave him a path in between, were strewn with scattered satchel bags, take out boxes, and shipping crates. In and around these containers was the epitome of organized chaos.

Bullets and casings of the same caliber were either piled together or stashed in plastic bags. Firearm parts and components sat nestled in black marker outlines drawn on the tables like chalked out bodies in old noir vids. A dozen and a half knives, spikes, and assorted killing tools jutted out of a battered medical training mannequin propped against the far wall. Rude's modified Desert Strike sniper rifle hung in a chain sling from the ceiling. Heavily marked and noted printouts of city area maps, building schematics, and his three favorite food delivery joints' menus were taped to the walls. It was a street sam's dream to have a prep room like this, and only Squid's renter regs kept him from simply living in the "Rudecave." Instead, it was the first stop on the way to any 'run.

Rude slowly walked the length of the unit, stopping briefly to consider each and every piece of equipment he passed. He may have had some seriously fragged up memories rattling around inside his thick skull, but the idea of "situational utility" was as hardwired in his instincts as the synaptic boosting chain was to his neural network. Each item was carefully optioned before he decided to bring it with him to West Seattle.

The Warhawk? His alloy fingertip traced the gigantic revolver, stopping to tap twice on the scorch mark where there was once a biometric safety. *Nope, haven't gotten the damn thing fixed yet.*

Could sling the Narco. Rude pulled the dart gun out of an old protein bar box and turned it over in his palm. His SmartGun feed synced up with its suite, throwing strings of useful data up onto the corner of his vision but a single, red blinking digit stood out. He blinked away the info and unceremoniously dropped the weapon back into the box. *Two tranqs. Really? When we get paid, I need to scrape up some more.*

Grenades? Rude laughed, not even picking up the container with his last three Aztechnology party favors—two frags and a flash-pak. *This is secret babysittin', not a full 'run.*

Yeah, yer comin' with me, Babydoll. He scooped up an Ares Predator anodized a dull cobalt blue and reached over to grab a chain-and-leather belt from a nearby box. Made for a gunslinger, the holster had networked magnetics to either hold its weapon in place or help shunt it out for an even quicker draw. Rude checked two magazines for live rounds, slapped one into the pistol before holstering it, and slid the other into his pocket. *Even if I prolly won't need ya.*

Stepping to the end of the unit, he came eye-to-chamber with the hanging sniper rifle. *Wish I could take ya out,* he ducked beneath it and headed to the half-destroyed mannequin, *but your kinda attention's the last thing I need.* Legal enforcement of self-defense weaponry was a lot stricter in West Seattle, not to mention the ride across town.

Rude plucked two long knives out of the mannequin's shoulders, ballistic gel inside sealing up as they *shlucked* upward, and tucked one into the side of each boot. He shrugged on the wide, over-the-shoulder sword-sheath and its deadly contents, adjusting it almost absent-mindedly into its place between bony growths jutting up from his shoulder. *Never leave home without ya'll.*

He traced a few possible routes on his combination subway/monorail map, figuring out the best ways to get across town in the next few hours. It wouldn't be a fun ride, that's for sure, but considering that he couldn't exactly call Emu for a lift, it was an option. This part of planning a mission made Rude really miss having a dependable rigger to call in a pinch.

Waypointing all the stops he'd have to transfer at to make the trip, the troll turned back to the door. Displayed above the access mechanism was his most treasured possession—and the only thing he could clearly remember from before waking up in Chicago—an old wooden sword wrapped in a black ribbon.

"*Animam gladius*," Rude remembered out loud what the old, tattooed man said when he gave it to him, "*Meus rudiarius.*" Taking a deep breath, he took two steps toward the outside and then froze once more. His chin dropped to his chest heavily.

Well—his cyberarm shot out and plunged into the box to his right and popped back with a small, matte black spheroid in his fingers—*just the Flash-pak wouldn't hurt*. With a happy whistle, Rude waved open the door and headed back outside into the unit walkway.

"*Looks like somebody's in for a rough night, eh?*" Squid chuffed, the voice eerily coming from no specific direction and changing from speaker to speaker as he walked through the facility. "*Go git 'em, lad.*"

"Drek, man. I wish it was like that." The exit gate pulled open to let him out, and Rude paused for a moment to address the disembodied old dwarf, "Ain't gonna be much more than dryin' paint."

"*Go ahead, 'runner,*" Squid laughed himself into a lifetime smoker's cough, "*keep yer secrets.*"

"Thanks, old man."

Rude was used to getting drek looks on the streets of Seattle; most trolls were. It got better in Redmond and the Underground, but even in the gangland ghettos and industrial sprawls of Puyallup he seemed to bring out the worst in passersby. If they didn't just avert their eyes completely or stay lost in the AR Matrix miasma, it was a flip of a coin whether the look in their face was going to be the pupil dilation of abject fear or the skin flush of a possible threat. It was a rare treat when he didn't see someone's pulse quicken or their muscles tense as they crossed paths on the sidewalk. That is, if they don't just cross the street to avoid him altogether.

That's what made Rude so hyper-aware of the people around him—when they didn't fall into the common classifications his combat instincts put them into. Almost halfway to the subway station, there were two otherwise normal Seattleites that were raising his hackles pretty bad.

He knew what he had to do.

Rude slowed his stride by a quarter-step every ten paces; slow enough to be discreet, but an adjustment that would put him in striking range right at the open alley at the end of Meridian.

Five.

Rude's AR overlay monitored the distance between he and the alley—ten meters. He and his followers—five meters. The distance between his hand and the hilt of his blade—ninety-eight centimeters.

Four.

Eight meters. Four meters. Eighty centimeters.

Three.

Five. Two-and-a-half. Sixty-three.

Two.

Three. One. Forty... *careful now, don't give it away...*

"Alright ya'll—" Rude suddenly took a sharp step *backward* between the two men, his strength and size plowing through them like an ax splitting a log. One hand already clasped tightly around the hilt of his sword and the other anxiously hovering over his sidearm, ready to draw. "Who's payin' ya to creep on me?"

"What the frag, man?!" Knocked aside by Rude's maneuver, the man barely kept his footing. His eyes wide with shock behind green-tinted shades. Immediately throwing his hands up, he stammered, "H-hey hey now..."

"Damn it!" The other man, a shorter sod with a glossy, black plastic fade, didn't fare as well—and was knocked completely off his feet. There was raw anger in his face; the kind of anger that the threat of great bodily harm doesn't even dull. "Watch it, trog!"

"What the frag'd you say?" Rude was an incurable asshole with a kill count he *literally* couldn't remember, but some things still caught him flat-footed—like fearless racism out of a worm like this.

"Hank!" The first man scolded the second. "You can't say stuff like that!" He took a step backward, and shook his head at Rude in disbelief, "I'm so sorry, man. I ain't like that. I don't want no trouble."

"*He* does," Hank spat venom in his words at the towering troll, picking himself up off the ground. "They always do. But I'm not giving you anything. Not one nuyen!"

"Bless yer heart, ya stupid runt." Rude's laugh was terrifying. "Ya think I'm *muggin'* ya'll?"

"Aren't you?"

"Ya'll ain't after me, are ya?" Rude folded his huge arms and took a step sideways, "Yer just fraggin' idiots. Go on. Take off."

They didn't waste any time putting to heels and jogging away, the black-haired bigot sparing one hateful glance back at Rude before turning the corner. They were probably already calling the Knights about it and this whole block would be crawling in no time. Well, it *was* Puyallup...so, maybe not.

"Get a hold of yerself," he said, shaking his head in disbelief and coming around to the present again. All too aware of the sixteen pairs of eyes—at least two sets augmented and possibly recording—watching him now, Rude ducked into the alley and thumbed his commlink to start searching for local reports. Keywords *troll, assault,* and *dumbass-rookie-mistake.*

Maybe the subway-to-monorail-to-subway route wasn't going to be the best option today after all. He could call a Kombat Kab, which would have to be an XT model because...troll, but their rates were pretty ugly for a drive that far. Rude cycled through his commlink protocols and sent his current account totals to his HUD.

"Seventy-eight nuyen?" An alloy-knuckled punch of frustration buckled the steel of the dumpster with an echoing *bong.* "Are ya kiddin' me?" The money from yesterday's little jaunt hadn't come over yet, which left him with very few legitimate options. *Mass transit it is.*

Taking it slow and additionally careful, it took Rude almost an hour to reach the subway station. He was sure to use blind walkways, covered passes, clouds from broken steam vents, and one sewer junction supposedly "closed for safety reasons." Nothing had rolled in on the feed about him this entire time, but he still wanted to be careful. Zipfile asked this to stay as anonymous and down low as possible, and Yu would surely have his ear to the pavement, too. Shadowrunners are the perfect mix of skill and paranoia, and Yu wore his like a badge of honor sometimes.

Subway stations and the trains heading in and out were a great way to travel incognito, even if they weren't the cleanest, safest, or most timely method. In greater Seattle, two-thirds of the subway trains had been vandalized, damaged, and muddied up in the Matrix enough that surveillance is limited to "eyes only" most of the time. Quite a few were actually run by the Ork Underground these days, and Rude had spent enough time on them to generally recognize the Or'zet graffiti on the doors to know the best ones to use when you're a troll on the lam.

It took him all of nine minutes to know he needed to be on the Green Line.

Two hours on the Green, a quick hop on the monorail to cross Downtown, then dealing with all the stops on the Violet to get to the Waterfront.

This ain't worth a damn coat and some goofy software, Rude sucked through his lustful grin loudly as the subway car doors hissed shut, *but SINnamon is.*

"Ugh." A troll's sense of smell wasn't as refined as some of the other metahumans out there, but it was heightened enough for Rude.

Stepping up those last few stairs into the evening air, he forgot what a displeasure it was; a foul combination of salty sea, urban pollution, homeless dinge, and that weird ozone smell that only seemed to blow in from the south sometimes.

He fished around his pockets for a slightly crumpled pack of cigarillos, plucking the last one out and tucking it into his lips. He wouldn't be able to keep it lit for the actual stakeout—Yu would see the cherry from a block away—but if he dragged deep enough off it until he got close, it would keep the Sound's stink out of his nostrils.

The directions to the Rip Current storage warehouse were pretty straightforward, and Rude wasn't even going directly there anyway. It would be a short trip to the building across the way, and the best vantage point to get a good look at the site.

<Rude. Hold up a sec.> Zipfile's text blinked across the troll's field of vision. <You might want to get a leg up to the meet site.>

"What's the rush?" Rude checked the timestamp and raised an eyebrow, "It's like seven blocks."

<Eight.>

"Alright, eight. Whatever. Wait just one fraggin' minute, how do you—"

"Emu and Yu rode into West Seattle together," her voice interjected, briefly switching away from text in order to interrupt the troll's impending line of questioning. "But Emu's nowhere nearby, and Yu's headed in alone." <She just dropped him off like three blocks away and is sitting pretty.>

"Ooh." Rude gestured with fake shock despite no one else in the conversation being able to see. "That's terrifyin'. Three blocks and a half-klick walk all alone on dainty elfy toes?"

<Come on, be real. I'm talking straight, Rude. With Emu leaving him, that means Yu's walking in to this blind AND alone. I really don't like it, I'm watching his tag get closer and closer and I have a terrible feeling about this. I'll see if I can get Emu back over there, but I'd feel a thousand percent better if I knew you were chugging over there instead of moseying around in a blind damn subway.> Her words were in a simple font cast in flat green, but her tone was quite clear.

"Alright, Zip. If it'll make ya feel better." Rude began to pick up the pace, "but while ya'll are chit chattin' about her choice of parkin' spots, figure out what happened to our shares of the Telestrian gig. I've smelled enough subway train vomit and ork piss today, and I need cab fare."

<Will do.> Her font grew in size by five points and turned a glowing, warm fuchsia. <Thanks, big guy.>

"Don't mention it," he growled into the comm, "I mean it."

Putting more pavement between his strides, Rude began making short work of those eight blocks. Unlike the streets of Puyallup in the middle of the day, West Seattle was far more sparsely populated in the evening—especially this close to the waterfront. Sure there were scores of homeless and wage slave laborers, but seeing a troll taking two-meter paces down a dark street wouldn't leave quite as lasting mark as one might think. If they even unplugged from their BTL feed or put down the chem-burner long enough to even notice him at all, that is.

It was odd. Rude didn't really *care* about anyone, not especially, but he had come to at least respect the roles Frostburn, Zip, and the others filled for him. They scratched an itch that he couldn't quite understand. Yes, even Elfy-Pants. Knowing they *needed* him somehow invigorated him on a core level; like a hero complex he didn't actually know he had. Running toward this secret stakeout of his foolish teammate's wasn't how Rude expected to be spending his evening, and should have pissed him off hours ago.

Yet, it didn't.

Quite the opposite, in fact. He found his running gait opening up even further, each step a leap longer than a Tír-born elf was tall. The reinforced soles of his combat boots clomped on the concrete, and the tattered tails of his coat trailed behind him like the cape of the world's dirtiest superhero. Rude would never say it out loud, or even admit it to himself, but he *liked* being a part of the team. There was so much that he couldn't remember from before Chicago that he didn't spare much thought to some of those hardwired feelings that occasionally popped up—but he always knew they were there.

Like that moment. Running full tilt like a two-and-a-half-meter tall lion bounding across the Serengeti, he could feel a memory scratching at the inside of his skull. His cybereyes outlined parked cars and urban debris as obstacles seconds before he would zigzag around or vault over them, but Rude's mind's eye wanted to see them as something else—*riot barriers?* It was a real mess in his head, like a knotted-up ball of wires, both figuratively and literally. It was always worse when he slept, especially when it was without proper pharmaceutical aids.

<You're almost there.> Zipfile sent. <*Yu's almost a block farther, too. Damn, chum, got some legs on you! #TrollOlympics #GoldMedalRude #Thanks!!*>

Rude didn't respond. He hated conversational hashtags, and *really* wanted to grind some ear-numbing profanity into Zipfile's comms, but he was moving along too fast to grab or talk to his Sony. The idea that she knew exactly where he and Yu were—probably by the ping of their various gears' AR signatures—was a little troubling. Yeah, Zipfile was their team's go to Matrix expert, and the best ass to have in the C&C hot seat when on a mission, but real time tracking on a little personal side job like this? That kind of "Big Sister" shit made him nervous. What else was she watching and keeping tabs on? What else has she seen? He couldn't exactly turn off the networking to most of his internals; he'd be a one-armed, blind sloth with a heart arrhythmia! *We might need ta talk about some privacy settings,* he thought as his waypointing suite signaled his arrival, *but that'll have ta wait.*

The "West Campus Rip Current Shipping Lanes Office and Alpha Supply Depot," a mouthful of self-aggrandizing corporate label if there ever was one, was two stories shorter than the Argyle Fields Park-n-Go. This meant that Rude couldn't see Yu's meeting site from where he was currently standing, but it also meant that anyone over there couldn't see him, either.

Higher, he looked up the side of the parking garage, *Up there.*

The pedestrian entrance was on the side facing Rip Current. Rude wasn't about to stroll around to where everyone could see him in order to get inside, but he was not equipped for scaling a five-story building, either. For security reasons, there were no access openings aside from the main entrance on the first floor, but the second floor windows were probably big enough for him to squeeze into if he could reach them.

A single sweep of the immediate area gave Rude a few different ideas. Because the refuse drum looked too flimsy and the lid was missing from the recyclables dumpster, that left the burned out hardtop a little too far away to be an easy step. He backed up a few paces, judged his distance, and sucked in a deep breath.

Surging forward, he leaped onto the hood of the old car and pushed off with every ounce of strength in his legs—which is to say a lot. Over three hundred kilos of troll flesh, cyberware, and equipment launched up into the air toward the building.

"Oh—" Rude arced through the distance with the right amount of force and speed, but geometry was not his strong suit. The angle was off, and he was headed for a face full of siding. "—frag."

Fortunately, trolls have long arms, and *this* troll also had a military-grade prosthetic fist. The shining metal fingers of Rude's left hand slammed against plastic-coated concrete, biting like five mountain climbing pitons into the wall. Metal-capped boots scraped and scrambled against the wall beneath him and his right arm stretched up to grab the window ledge. "Fragfragfragfrag." It wasn't a pretty landing, and he was glad no one could see it, but it worked.

Straining his muscles, Rude lifted himself into the window ledge, smashed the double-thick panes with a trio of quick head butts, and rolled inside. Glass fragments clinked and tinkled onto the pavement as he stood up to take in his surroundings. There weren't too many cars logged in their spots on this floor, which likely meant there were even fewer on the levels above. All of the apparent security cams in the main parking rows that Rude could see were shattered or spray painted over, but the lift between levels was sure to be fully gridded out. *Stairs it is.*

The rooftop access door wasn't even locked. It looked like it might have had a deadbolt at one time or another, but that had been wrenched out of its frame at some point. The door basically was being held shut by the seal around its own weight, and didn't look like the kind that would latch behind him when it closed or anything. There was a chunk of broken cinderblock sitting right next to it on the outside though.

Prolly to keep it from blowin' closed when it comes in hard off the Sound. Rude sat the manmade stone trapezoid in the obvious path and started to let the door swing shut—but caught it with his ankle at the last moment. *Don't get sloppy. Yer better than that,* he chastised himself as he slowly let the door close to 90% with a barely audible *klok.*

The rooftop parking sleeves were reserved only for utility employees, garage staff, and special permits, explaining why there were only four vehicles scattered around up here; two security sedans, an Ingersoll delivery truck, and an enormous Monohan charger-construction Roadmaster taking up two rows of spaces on its own. There were scattered illumination pylons around, and a few climate control nodes, but it was otherwise pretty wide open.

Surrounding the roof, for safety reasons, was a meter-tall border wall topped with ten centimeters of anti-gull wire mesh. It would be great cover for a normal sized person skulking around the roof, but Rude had to crouch-walk like some kind of beast to take advantage. It was uncomfortable, undignified, and smeared the hem of his coat with road oil, but there was no way anyone in Rip Current could see him.

He awkwardly scuttled up to the edge, being sure to keep the wall between him and the street and the parked vehicles to block out the blind angles in case someone came up the stairs. A quick tug on his pistol to break the magnetic seal and he lifted his Predator carefully over the lip of the wall so the barrel could "see" toward the building beyond. The fibrous pad in his palm made the connection to the pistol's integral SmartGun link and Rude synced his eyes into full view so he could see what was going on, making his gun into a "bullet's eye periscope" so he could keep his horny head down.

The streetscape filled his eyes. It was a green grid of topographic lines and data signatures, outlines of objects and highlighted potential threats, and a few flashing silhouettes of targeting solutions. A few neutral non-classified guards patrolling near the main gate, a pair of blue-level armed drones whirred around the window line of the smaller building, but nothing highlighted with "imminent danger red."

One flashing signature blinked the bright green of "friend" nearly a half-block away near the line at a brick of angles that had to be a soycaf stand—Yu.

See? He's fine. Rude clipped the image and sent it to Zipfile's link.

Or tried to, anyway. *<kjaf@$ila(&iugvb^^vbljkbaqlu...404.>*

What the frag? He wasn't a complete rube when it came to computers, but Rude didn't think he'd done anything wrong. *Stupid Sony. Knew I shoulda nabbed the Hermes.*

Yu's flashing indicator was moving again. It paced a few times in front of the building, but vanished along the wall of gridlines next door to it after just a minute or three. Seconds later, the green icon appeared on top of the small office complex across the alley. Whatever Yu was up to, he was at least trying to be careful and clever about it. Rude rolled back the last few seconds and tried to pop it to Zipfile again.

<hhneFHISEFOH&$ii))@hjklh123...404.>

Again, the data packet didn't send. Once was a technical hiccup, but twice in a row—something wasn't adding up. The noise here shouldn't be high enough to muck with Rude's gear, but an internally encrypted simple message with the same routing hub? No way. This wasn't normal. He made a note of the timestamp—20:58. That could be important information later on if they need to track the problems and see what happened.

Maybe Zippy was right to be worried...

Rude took another quick scan of the street level using the Predator, saw that nothing really had changed across the way. Yu was still watching from across the alley from a high vantage point—although not as high as Rude's. With this whole Matrix glitch thing that was happening however, it couldn't hurt to be a little extra thorough.

Pulling himself out of SmartGun mode, the gray and murk of the real world snapped back into view. He readjusted his stance so he was facing the wall and rose slightly from sitting to kneeling so he could look at things in better, sharper detail. Rude scanned the rooftops—both Rip Current's and the parking tower's—as slowly as his patience would allow. Nothing seemed out of place, not really, not even—

Wait a sec. Rude focused on a shining sparkle on the wall's ledge just beyond the AC block. It was a piece of mechanical something. *What the hell is it, though?* He zoomed in tight on the weird chunk of metal, and even then it took a moment to recognize...the mangled deadbolt from the door! Switching from the common wavelengths of his cybereyes to their high-powered recreation of his natural thermographic vision, he squinted at the scene like a jeweler peered through their loop at an unknown piece.

There it was, just beyond the broken AC unit, the faint outline of a person sitting cross-legged.

Frag. Rude took a steadying breath. *I ain't alone up here.*

There wasn't much in the way of heat being given off, but enough that Rude was sure that it wasn't a trick of code or even some homeless guy who managed to get stuck up here and die in a weird position.

It was the kind of heat signature that looked like it was purposefully obscured, *because that shit don't happen by accident.*

The mere potential that this babysitting gig might turn into something exciting quickened Rude's heart rate, a trickle of his triple-strength adrenaline being released into his veins. That familiar tingle rose up to meet it, his muscles starting to buzz, and he was yanked back to that Meridian Street sidewalk earlier that day. *Might be nothin'*, the terrified eyes of that racist's hopefully now *ex*-friend like a billboard in his thoughts, *don't lose it.*

Careful not to reveal himself just in case it was just some guy in the wrong place at the right time, Rude crawled in a wide arc so as to get a better vantage point on this stranger. He needed to *see* this person before making some kind of judgment call. Having to end some meditating utility worker's life wouldn't cost him any sleep or anything—but he wasn't getting *paid* for that kind of heat. It's a lot of work to make somebody disappear in the '80s, and not something he does for free.

Guy chose a good spot, Rude growled internally, *better than mine, for damn sure.* He had to keep adjusting his angle of approach, because the few random objects on this rooftop overlapped the lanes of vision to this mystery person perfectly. Rude was nearly back at the access door by the time he could lay eyes—shifted back to the visible spectrum for full effect, of course—on his little rooftop friend.

I knew it was too goddam perfect!

This elf, by the pointed ears jutting out from the sides of her combat helmet, was hunkered down behind a curtain of high-tech plastic interwoven with circuitry. Rude wasn't familiar, but he could tell the strange patterns were technomantic. That cloak must have been hiding her from more than just thermals, because he didn't pick up any static or scan blips when he swept the rooftop. Hell, maybe it even clouded her from his mind in some way. *Magic's like fraggin' cheatin'.* His teeth ground against each other. *But techno-magic? That's like double cheatin'.*

Whatever this elf was up to, Rude knew it wasn't good. He leveled his sidearm at the back of her head, about to send her face splattering out into the street, but then paused. *Too loud. Need something else, something quieter.* He drew one of his boot knives. *Perfect.*

Feeling the weight in his hand and judging the wind, in one swift motion Rude cocked back his arm and launched it back forward. The blade spun forward with the force of a bullet. His skills said that it was going to hit point-first, but when thrown by a cybered-up troll—even the blunt hilt would probably break bone.

If the knife would have hit at all, that is. Striking some unseen barrier—maybe whatever was shielding her thermographics—it ricocheted away and clattered across the top of the AC unit.

His target leaped to her feet and spun around in the same fluid motion. The plastic sheet loosely tied around her neck crinkled and flipped behind her like a cape, motes of glittering energy dancing across its surface.

Under that weird cloak her thin, elven frame was partially hidden by a suit of ballistic armor emblazoned on the chest with the silver badge icon of a Knight Errant street agent. The uniform wasn't standard though, as she didn't wear the normal reinforced gloves and boots. Actually, she didn't have shoes on at all.

"Guys," she hissed into her chinstrap microphone. Lightly glowing sapphire eyes peered out from behind her helmet's clear visor, surely seeing things that even Rude's augmented eyes couldn't even imagine, and she was already moving her fingers like disjointed worms at the ends of her hands. "Move in. Go time."

A streak of white-blue fire leapt from her fingertips with a *fwoosh*, forcing Rude into a sideways roll just to avoid it. He could feel the spell's energy through his clothes and thick skin, like the meat under his dermal layering was trying to cook from within. Where the bolt hit the access doorframe behind him, a blackened flower of a scorch mark bloomed.

"Frag it." Rude's voice was full of venom, letting his instincts take over. Using one knee as a pivot point like a Renton street dancer, he turned in place, snatched up the closest thing to his open hand—the broken cinderblock doorstop. He hurled the glorified brick with all day's pent up frustration at her.

There was nothing to say that the cinderblock would fare any better than the knife against her invisible shielding, if it was even still there, but Rude wasn't just some dumb troll from the Barrens. He was full of skills he couldn't remember learning, instincts that made no sense for a professional thug to have, and experiences that came back to him at the strangest of moments.

The elf put up her hands to block it, but the tumbling, soaring, manmade meteor struck its target dead on—which wasn't her at all.

Nearly a meter to her left, it tore through the pressurized coolant tank attached to the AC block unit. While she was preparing to deflect a physical attack from her front, the actual assault sprayed at her from the side and coated her with toxic, semi-acidic foam. It crept in like rain through the gaps in her jumpsuit, across her exposed chin, and thoroughly onto her bare hands and feet. Not only was it excruciatingly cold, but it was also slick like motor oil. As soon as it touched her bare skin, it started to immediately draw out the water in her flesh. She slipped to the ground to flop about in the steaming pool; the arc of slowly drooping liquid from the de-pressurizing tank coating her with even more.

"Unh... g-ge... hnurhk!" she tried in vain to speak, to call for help, but Rude wasn't about to lose the upper hand. "Ah'm... attack..."

He crossed the distance between them in two great leaps, the second of which allowed him to land within arm's reach of her kicking, bare, and blistering feet. He clamped his cybernetic hand around her ankle like a vice. It was surely painful to be in his bone-splintering grip, but her exposed skin was already black with chemical freezing, so she felt nothing when the troll yanked her up and out of the coolant spill. When he swung her at waist level into the nearest light pole however, she definitely felt it.

Her upper body bent around the anchored pole roughly halfway up her ribcage, shattering her midsection into a grisly obtuse angle. The Knight Errant armor couldn't protect her from this impact, yet it was likely the only thing keeping her from tearing in two. When her head snapped around to face her pelvis, the helmet that was protecting it popped off and spun away like a top. She was a fish pulled from the river, her mouth opening and closing soundlessly in vain. No words came out; only a bloody froth.

"Goddam mages," Rude watched as the glittering sparkle in her eyes faded away along with her life. "Wait. What the hell is that?" He stooped down and turned her head to the side with his mechanical index finger. There on her neck, disappearing down into the collar of her armor was an elaborate tattoo of a white-feathered flying serpent. "Ya'll ain't KE standard, are ya?"

"*–on approach–*"

Tinny little words trickled into Rude's ears from somewhere nearby. He tilted his commlink's screen up to see if he was accidentally channel surfing or something, but no, he was still dealing with too much noise to be receiving anything.

"*—contact…ten–*"

There it was again, but this time he knew to listen for it and homed in. *Her fraggin' helmet!* The modified Knight Errant riot helmet, altered so she could have her open ears and half-visor for some weird magic-using reason, was tiny in his palm. Like trying to hear the ocean in a conch shell, Rude lifted it up to his ear.

"*—Spotlyte isn't answering for sitrep,*" a deep but feminine voice, possibly an ork's, crackled across the helmet's internal speakers, "*but the target is supposed to be here. We're going in chummers, hard and hot. Get ready!*"

Over the ledge, from down in the street, it was suddenly a war zone. Rude heard the staccato reports of submachine gun fire answered by higher caliber assault rifles. Multiple sets of tires screeched on the pavement, but the echoing *spwang* of assault vehicles tearing through the fencing put a little more pep in his step.

Rude kept the helmet in hand as he ran to the street side ledge, looking over it at the Rip Current building and just how much the scene had changed in just a few minutes. A trio of Knight Errant armored cars were on the scene, the last of which Rude saw drive straight through the gatehouse and the unfortunate guard standing beside it. Heavy gear response agents from KE spilled out three at a time from these vehicles as they slid into position. This kind of mobile attack unit was paramilitary in nature, and not something that could be planned quickly or as a reaction—these corporate soldiers were here at this time because they had been *told* to be here at this time.

Guards and other strangely well-equipped employees from within Rip Current began exchanging fire, bursts of bullets turning the side of the warehouse into a modern art piece and denting the plating of the armored cars like weird, violent constellations on their black paint. A handful of Knights began moving around to flank, but they missed the tell-tale *whump* of a 40mm grenade round being fired at them. The resulting explosion sent the agents spiraling in several directions and forced them to hunker down and take note of the situation. All the while, Yu clung to the rooftop of the office building and did his best to stay out from between these two forces.

"Serpent Squad," a voice with some authority came from the helmet, *"fan out! Search everywhere! Find the target, shoot to kill."*

Rude watched as the Knight Errant agents did as instructed. Teams of two or three vanished into all the neighboring buildings. They were all wearing Knight Errant armor and possessed sidearms that matched, but that was where the similarities end. They were mostly metas with a few humans, but even the humans looked like they didn't belong in everyday society.

Another grenade nearly tipped over an unmarked deployment van, leaving one of the Knights Errant dead in the street and two others reeling. *What has Yu gotten us into now?* he was genuinely curious, because this was one serious escalation from a few guards and drones.

The sound of a familiar weapon's—Yu's machine pistol—signature gunfire caught Rude's focus. Elfy-Pants had lost his cover and was now showering some KE troll with small caliber rounds, barely forcing him to shield his eyes. It was a good enough distraction to let Yu duck past and into the stairwell access.

"We got him trapped! Move in!" The helmet speaker's message matched the fact that three of the Knight Errant soldiers had just blown the street-level emergency doors on the first floor and were disappearing into the smoke. The troll from above and the soldiers from below; they were going to catch Yu in the middle, and he had no idea. Rude could see flashes of gunfire in the windows of multiple floors in that building, and he hoped Yu wasn't already getting chewed up by that crossfire.

"Babysittin' my ass." He cynically laughed. "Time ta save the fuckin' day."

The situation called for quick action, and Rude was built for it—literally.

Somebody—who, Rude had no idea—had paid a *lot* of money for the gear all wound up in his body. Hardwired reflex boosters, a synaptic crash suite, state-of-the-art cybereyes, and his augmented forearm would be enough to bankrupt a small business or starting runner. That didn't even take into consideration his non-combat enhancements like the tracheal filter, commlink bridge, or his secondary—and *tertiary*—redundancy livers. Rude was one hard ass, troll-shape meat sack worth *millions* of nuyen.

Time to put all that money to work.

Most people will tell you how fast things move in a violent conflict; that it's over so fast they barely know what's happened. For Rude, it was the exact opposite. His mind was always a jumble of broken memories, disturbing dreams, and somewhat wrangled chaos—except when he went into full combat mode.

Nano-catalytic converters interwoven to his glands triggered, sending a full adreno-endorphine cocktail flooding through him. A cold numbness spread out from his core, the familiar tingle of his neuro-muscular network beginning to heat up inside his limbs like the glowing element inside a twentieth century lightbulb. After the initial throb of his body adjusting to the nearly euphoric shift in chemical saturation, the stillness that followed was the closest thing to a meditative state Rude had or would ever know.

The world slowed down around him. The cycling rates of machine gun fire ticked back slightly. Shouts both fearful and aggressive became longer and more exaggerated. More than anything though, Rude's thoughts became so precise and focused that he measured every decision and action three times before enacting them. Only someone with similarly augmented synaptic functions knew the momentary Nirvana of using them at full tilt.

Have ta get down ta the street. Less than two seconds and Rude weighed the options:

Jump across? It was more than six meters to cross the street. Leaping off the parking tower, even with the angle of descent to the shorter building, was unlikely to be successful.

Jump down? Rude was a badass, but five stories straight down? Even with his upgrades, a broken pair of ankles was the best case. Worst case? A shattered everything.

Lightpole? He could probably bend it at the middle and try to use it like a vault to get across, but the wiring was live—it was currently lit—and even *he* might not be able to crack that alloy casing.

Door? He could easily rip it off the hinges and concrete-surf down the slope of the garage, but probably only in a straight line, and re-adjusting descent angles would actually take more time than just running.

Run. Using the ledge as an anchor for his starting foot, he shot forward, easily stepping over the crumpled elf corpse on his way to the descending ramp leading to level four. Rude swung his arm in a wide arc, smashing her helmet against the lightpole as he passed by. Impact-resistant plastic shattered like an eggshell, leaving not only a black scuff and small dent on the pole, but also the formerly internal wire harness that connected the microphone, Matrix power receiver, and speaker suite—and still did! Rude shook off a few fragments of plastic and shoved the tangle of strangely functional electronics under his collar, *Might need that later.*

He pumped his legs harder, picking up speed as he rounded level four to level three. There were more parked vehicles on this floor, increasing the chance for additional security issues, but Rude wasn't terribly worried. If his Zipfile-doctored Sony was still getting scrambled by the noise—it was—there was almost no way a commercial vehicle suite or garage rig was getting through to transmit. With the firefight outside, the chance of anyone seeing and remembering him were pretty low, even with the streetlamp light coming in through the garage windows.

Windows!

Rude did some mental navigation as he got to the wall on level three that faced the cross-street alleyway and picked up speed. Right before the turn, he leaped into the air and straightened his body into a feet-first spear to crash through one of the windows into the open space above the alley. As soon as the dense brick wall of the neighboring vacant renovation met the flat of his boots, Rude let his joints become crumple points and he sat up into a sort of vertical crouch. Gravity caught up quickly, and he started to slide down to the ground below. He used his cybernetic fingers as a dragging anchor to slow his descent in a shower of red dust and stony shrapnel, but as soon as he could he stepped back and leaped the rest of the way down.

He hit the ground running, knowing that every second counted in the firefight Yu was in. The two grenades that went off in the street did an admirable job putting a haze in the air and had set one of the Knight Errant vehicles ablaze with a wonderfully smoky fire. Rude didn't even have to pause for a better opportunity to cross the street, ducking slightly to make sure he stayed in the thickest of the shroud.

His luck continued. When the Knights had breached the building, they'd blasted the ground floor doors nearly off their hinges, leaving the entrance open enough that he barely had to slow down as he crossed into the downstairs lobby. Once inside, luck was no longer a factor—it was time for skill to shine.

The lobby was sectioned into roughly three parts: the stair landing, the front desk/waiting room, and the back hallway that likely led to the rest of the first floor. Burned cordite filled the air with its tangy odor, and the strobing muzzle flares from weapons fire flashed all around the landing.

Two of the three agents Rude saw enter the building were at the foot of the stairs, firing short bursts from their shortened assault rifles up into the corridor above. They took alternating turns spraying bullets into the empty space, checking their own ammo supplies to reload accordingly, and taking cover from return fire. It was an excellent coordinated effort. The third Knight, the ork, was nowhere to be seen, and Rude assumed he must've gone up to make it a close quarters fight.

Military training. Maybe Ops. Rude was actually a little envious of a well-oiled team like this, really something you rarely saw in corporate security. *They're just doin' their jobs,* he mentally sighed, *leave enough of 'em for the Doc Wagon to patch back up.*

"Ya'll should've taken the day off," he drew both his sword and the Predator, the first blast from the latter catching one of the human Knights in the shoulder. Their thick armor padding stopped the round from penetrating, but the impact nearly spun him one hundred and eighty degrees.

"Secondary target! Floor one!" the other agent shouted into her helmet microphone loud enough that Rude heard it in stereo—once from her lips and once coming up from the knot of wiring under his coat collar. She swiveled her weapon and spat a burst toward the troll barreling down on her. Sadly, it wasn't the first time Rude had taken a few Knight Errant rounds.

"*Frag!*" he shouted when the first AP round speared right through his armor—both worn and natural. A squirt of hot red blood spurted out of his bicep, the pain cutting through chemical compensation. It was everything for him to maintain his grip on his pistol. *That was not standard KE munitions,* the burning in his arm kept throbbing angrily, but Rude wasn't about to let it slow him down. He just needed to change his plan of attack to compensate.

He slid to a stop, grinding broken glass and bullet casings into the glossy tile floor under his boots. Using some of that momentum, he swung his leg forward into a lobby chair *formerly* bolted to the floor. Like the kicker for the Seahawks he sent the furniture careening across the room toward her. Rude could see the shock in her human face disappear into the growing reflection of the chair in her visor right before it collided with her upper body and exploded into chunks of metal, plastic, and faux-wood. The impact knocked her on her back, flat on the landing with a lung-emptying "*Oof!*"

Having only the Knight Errant he had first shot as a momentarily active threat, Rude tried to put a few more bullets into his more armored sections. They weren't likely to kill him outright, but they'd put him down for sure. Rude's arm was more wounded than he'd first thought, putting a terrible tremor in his aim, and the shots bucked wild. Not wild enough to *miss* the Knight altogether, but enough to miss what Rude was trying to hit. Instead of simply doubling him over with easily patched up tissue damage, the bullets slammed into the fist clutching his rifle. In a cloud of red mist and flying bits of black glove, his hand disappeared and was replaced with a ragged, gushing stump. He fell to his knees and mumbled incoherently in shock, his other hand trying in vain to pull the ribbons of meat together again.

"Aw hell." Rude was upset. His aim was off from the injury, and he *actually* didn't want to kill these guys—but seeing a soldier fall apart like that was too much for him to handle.

He'd want it this way. He crossed the distance in a few strides, holstering his currently unreliable sidearm. His sword flashed forward, nearly taking the Knight's head clean off. Rude looked down his extended sword arm, his eyes lingering for a moment on the fresh blood spatter dotting his cyberlimb, and he wondered for a moment if something similar happened to *his* hand, when it was still flesh and bone.

"Claymore, no!" The woman agent had apparently caught her breath. She rolled over to her knees and screamed dramatically at her dead teammate. *So much for military discipline*, Rude judged her emotional outcry, but it added to her resolve. Her rifle had fallen from her fingers when the chair hit her, but she wasn't out of the fight.

"*Altered vehicle approaching–*" the radio eavesdropped into Rude's ear, "*unexpected tertiary target. Bug out, now!*"

"No way," the Knight Errant stood up, plucked off her helmet and tossed it aside. Her face was a scowl of hatred, and she wasn't about to obey those commands. "You killed Claymore, you trog bastard! I'm gonna enjoy this," she hissed. Two sets of shining cyberspur blades ripped out of her gloves, clenched fists shaking with rage.

When she pounced like a predatory cat, Rude almost felt bad for her. She had lost someone obviously important to her, and now this. He was going to let her live, maybe just break a few important bones so he could get back to making sure Yu was okay, but now that she'd made it about his race? He just couldn't be bothered to hold back.

Her anger made her sloppy, and she overextended her attack. Her arms thrust forward, blades trying to find him, but he sidestepped her completely and brought the heel of his metal hand down hard on her lower back. The resounding *crunch* was replaced immediately by the *squelch* of her body getting trapped between the crushing force of his pressed attack and the unforgiving marble stair landing. Looking down at his grisly handiwork, Rude assumed she might live for a few more minutes, but he didn't have time to spare her a second stroke.

"Another one?" He did notice the white-feathered serpent tattoo on the back of her exposed neck again. Something was definitely strange about these guys, and it made Rude seriously wonder if they were KE street agents at all. *What have ya'll got me into?*

The *ding* of the elevator in the back of the lobby grabbed Rude's attention. The doors slid open, revealing that third Knight Errant he was missing—the ork he believed was probably calling the shots. Under one arm he had tucked a bulky satchel, while the other lifted a beat-up machine pistol tipped with a savage-looking bayonet.

"*Druik pokk nongh!*" Or'zet profanity always made Rude smile whenever he heard it because it was *so* grossly literal about what you should do to combine parts of your own body. This ork's words were no different, spawning a chuckle from the troll as he turned to flee out the back. Over his shoulder he let the machine pistol belch lead wildly into the lobby, generally at Rude, who plunged his sword down into the now very dead woman at his feet and lifted her up in the path of any shots that might have randomly found him. The ork shouldered his way through the emergency exit, the noise of the klaxon alarms replacing the popping machine pistol fire.

The whine of rotors outside came in through the open door, joined by the hum of a fast engine and the rattle of automatic gunfire. Rude took a moment to look over his shoulder and saw Emu's ride drift sideways onto the scene, her two support drones opening up down the street. *Backup's here*, he thought as he looked back at the slowly closing back door. Rude swung his meat-shield off his sword, slid his blade into the scabbard on his back, and followed the fleeing ork out into the rear lot. *Time to tie up loose ends.*

As soon as he emerged into the night air, warning klaxons inside the building blending noisily in with the emergency sirens outside. There was so much gunfire echoing from the street in front of the building, Rude didn't hear the lower caliber *pops* of the ork's machine pistol. Plastic splinters showered the side of his face as the rounds stitched up the doorframe next to him, one barely grazing the edge of his horn.

Rude turned to face his attacker, currently using a parked Econocar as cover, and narrowed his cybereyes with a look that said, *"Oh no you didn't..."*

"Oh *drek*," the Knight knew he had one good chance to get the jump on a monster like Rude, and he had just fragged it *bad*. Once more the agent scrambled on his heels and moved to flee.

"Not this time," Rude growled, reaching into his coat's pocket. *Damn, that really hurts*, he thought as his wound flexed to grab the small oval within. Ignoring the growing ache, he thumbed the activator to "impact" and hurled the Flash-pak across the lot.

Most people are trained to toss grenades of any kind in a wide, parabolic arc in order to avoid obstacles and potential scatter-causing impacts while maximizing area of effect. Rude was *not* like most people. He whipped that grenade side-arm like a college ball player looking to make the major leagues.

The Flash-pak punched through the Econocar's passenger side window like a bullet. Even though it was set to detonate on impact, there was still a fraction of a second's worth of delay. A muffled *whump* followed by the crash of broken glass blasted out of the car as the grenade went off. Used for nonlethal incapacitations, Flash-paks generate a tremendous amount of light and sound in a large radius carried on a short lived, powerful concussive wave. Within a confined space—the driving compartment of a compact car, for example—the pressure is multiplied dramatically.

Shards of glass sliced outward in all directions, cutting a thousand tiny slices into the ork's uniform and exposed skin. Little wounds like that were annoying to a toughed up meta like him, but the shockwave of force that followed was another story. The Econocar's plastic shell and alloy frame could not hope to contain the doubled-and-re-doubled blast. The hinge buckled, opening the driver's side door into the Knight's center mass with nearly as much force as what Rude himself could managed with a kick.

He flew backward onto the asphalt, ribs broken and lungs burning for fresh air. The machine pistol flew from his grip and, more interestingly to Rude, his underarm satchel took the brunt of his fall. Its flap rolled open and an assortment of broken tech components, sparks, and other smoking bits of metal or wire spilled out to join the shards of window glass. Like looking at the fragments of a shattered vase, Rude could tell the parts were once whole, but he had no idea what that could've been.

<*Frostburn? Rude? Are you there?*> His commlink suddenly crackled to life with Yu's chatter. The Knight Errant team had a damn jammer; some kind of Matrix noise generator.

<*Easy, elfy-pants, I'm here.*> Yeah, Zipfile wanted this to be a quiet thing, but enough stuff was adding up to a nasty double-cross that Rude risked her wrath anyway by responding. He stayed text only as he stepped across the lot toward the ork. <*Just hadda finish a little business of my own. Made sure everything's nice and tidy after yer little sneak-and-peek.*>

"Targ...et," the ork on the ground started to groan, and Rude heard it from his collar. He picked up the pace for a few strides to plant his boot onto the Knight's chest. He didn't even have to put on any pressure; between the broken rib and half-a-troll's weight, his lungs squeezed to a third capacity.

<*Ya don't think I'd be lettin' ya fall to a couple of KE goons, do ya?*>

The ork wriggled under his boot, and Rude saw yet another of those white-feathered serpent tattoos on the back side of his lumpy head.

Yu's signature blinked in his HUD. <*Thanks, Rude. I owe you.*>

<*More like ten or twelve by now. I stopped countin'.*> He replied, half-aware of the other conversations going on the channel, focused more on why this Knight Errant squad just felt somehow wrong. The whole thing just felt somehow *off*.

Rude knelt down, careful not to give the ork too much freedom. He straddled him, planting one knee onto each arm and pressing the rest of his weight on his midsection. Anti-ballistic plating aside, having a troll sitting on you is not only undignified—it is a remarkable handicap.

Rude's reached back and slowly produced the shining combat knife from his boot, thankful he didn't have to move his arm that much. Each twist or pull sent fire throughout his right side. *What the hell did she hit me with?*

"You...you know how it is, chum," the ork coughed out the words and twisted his face into a forced smile that did nothing to hide his panic, "'runners gotta...run. Just a job..."

Just a job. He'd heard that before. Hell, he'd *said* that before. It was definitely not something some corporate agent would say. This ork, no matter how he was dressed, was not a Knight Errant. None of them were. This was a mission team, and like it or not, Yu's warehouse meet up was the target.

<*–where no one will think to look for us. Either that, or we scatter to the winds to wait for this to blow over and take our chances.*> Yu's text continued to scroll through Rude's vision, but he only really paid attention to those last few words.

"Fuck that," Rude's talk-to-text suite on the Sony translated it for him. He wanted the ork to hear what he was about to say. "They wanna hit us, I say we hit 'em harder." He grabbed the fake agent's chin—more like the lower half of his head, really—in the fingers of his cyberhand to hold him still. The ork's pleading smile contorted around his tusks and he let out an indecipherable slur. Rude lowered the knife slowly as he spoke, the tip lightly touching the chromed lens of his captive's augmented eye with a barely audible *click.* "Just tell me where to start shootin'. I think I know just where to start lookin' too."

A sound that could be mistaken for words drooled out of the ork's restricted mouth, his eyes blinking deep and deliberate, and his hands tapping out his submittal on the pavement.

<*Hold up, Rude.*> Emu added. <*Let's take a quick breather and check back in tomorrow. Then we can set back to it fresh and out of the line of fire, okay?*>

"Yeah," Rude pulled the knife away and held it up like a finger against his lips in a *shhh* gesture, "ya'll hit me up tomorrow." His mechanical strength effortlessly turned the ork's head to one side, exposing that tattoo more clearly. "I've got a lead."

"I knew it..." the ork grunted angrily, "I told Spotlyte the Renraku hit...was gonna be a fraggin' bloodbath...!"

>*Rude? Who was that? What are you doi–*>

Rude flipped off his comms. "Keep talkin'." He relaxed his grip so the ork could continue, "and I might let ya'll live. Who're ya with? Who hired ya'll to kill my shelf's elf?"

"Serpent Squad," he admitted, "Runners out of Renton. That's all I can give you. You know how it goes."

"Yeah, I hear ya." Rude sighed, pressing the knife's edge just above where that tattoo started, "but we both know ya got more to give..."

"Hez ain't been 'round yet," the bartender, a smarmy-looking goblin with a face like a lost dog fight and a prosthetic ear two sizes too big, stretched his neck up to look Rude in the eyes. "Buys y'rself a drink, a dance, or a private. I don' care, just get t'steppin' on somethin', hightower. Ye'r spookin' the ladies!"

Horneez Gentlemeta's Club was a favorite hangout in Renton for those metahumans that really stretched the limits to the "human" part of that nomenclature. It was one of the only places where, if you had the nuyen, you could have a drink with a half-shaven sasquatch, get a lap dance from a centaur, or—as Rude was hoping—get the dirt on a nasty piece of work that had nearly gotten one of his teammates killed.

"One of those," Rude pointed his finger at the dark brown lager disappearing down another patron's gullet. He checked off the AR swipe, his eyes going wide for a moment when he saw nineteen nuyen vanish from his account, and jerked the glass out of the goblin's hand. The bartender stood there for a moment, the green "*add tip*" flashcode blinking in the air between them. Rude smiled his favorite "screw you" smile, and turned away toward the main body of the club.

Horneez was pretty busy tonight. People from all walks of street-level life danced, caroused, drank, and seemed to be committing a *variety* of other activities in the flashing lights and sickly-sweet vanilla scented fog machine exhaust. Three different stages lifted a beautiful elven woman, a perfectly sculpted ork male, and a heavily animalized modified human that seemed to be more feline than either male or female above the crowd. They danced with great skill to use their bodies seductively and suggestively to the intensely loud music flooding the entire building. Glowing payment receivers blinking in the AR around their stage platforms allowed patrons to tip the entertainers of their choice, possibly opening up alternate "option tabs" for additional services closer to the end of each dancer's set.

Maybe if I had the extra nuyen, watching the gyration sync up with the beat of the music, he lifted his pint in three fingers and took a sip, thankful for the numbing chems in the slap patch on his arm. Even so, Rude rubbed the cold throb in his bicep, pulling his hand away and looking at the thin crimson film on his thumbprint.

"Hoy oy, chum." A familiar voice broke through the bassline, half a laugh in his tone. "Might wanna get that checked out, mate."

Hez was small for an ork, but nearly every inch of his exposed skin—and even more that wasn't—was covered with tattoo work. He was a living gallery of arts varying from jailhouse tats done with ink and a razor, watercolor-styled paintings that look like they stepped out of the Nu Louvre, and bio-luminescent patterns engineered from some deep-sea beast. "Inna spot o' trouble, are ye, Rude boy? What cannae help ye wit', and what does't pay?"

Hez was a ranking member of the Skraacha, a group of metas from the Ork Underground that took it upon themselves to play night watchmen, and one of the only magically-inclined people Rude trusted—mostly.

"Can we go somewhere private?"

"Why?" Hez's laugh was sinister. "Ye gittin' plans on me, mate?"

"Naw." Rude's smile was totally genuine. Hez had a way of making everyone around him just a shade happier, even troll killing machines. "I need to show you somethin'."

"Exactly." He winked, the sworl tattoo around that eye shifting colors from blue to pink to that strange yellow of a soynana peel.

"Ha!" Rude laughed out loud halfway through a pull from his drink and sprayed foam into the air. "Yer killin' me."

"Looks like somebody already tried tonight, mate." Hez leaned in and a shine crossed his eyes that didn't match up with the lights of the room. His demeanor suddenly changed to much more serious. "Yeah, let's take this elsewheres."

Hez held up an awkward hand gesture—something between a gang sign and an arthritic palsy—to the bartender, who returned it with a curt nod and the press of a button under the bar. Without a further word, the ork grabbed Rude by the mechanical hand and led him toward the far wall.

"Hey gorgeous." A thick-horned troll wearing little more than a red leather bandolier tried to interject in their path, but Hez shot her a look and she stepped aside knowingly. "You go get yours, sugar," she added loudly, spinning back to the crowd.

Rude was led to the bright glow of the back kitchen hallway, but he and Hez took an abrupt turn through a deceptively difficult to notice panel into a small room with a private table.

The troll shrugged off his sword scabbard and strap, sliding it onto the table with a dull *thud* before swinging off his coat, draped across the back of one of the chairs and plopped down into another.

Hez took the chair across from him, pulled a small gold-plated box out of his mock-snakeskin jacket and thumbed it open. He plucked a small, thin cigarette from within, clasped the box shut, and started to tap the filtered side against the top. Popping it into his mouth, he lifted a single finger to the tip. Smoke immediately started to curl up from the bright red ember flaring to life beneath his touch. "Awl'raight, show me whatcha got."

"What do ya'll know about these guys?" Rude drew a plastic baggie out of his pocket, pinched open the sides, and let what looked like a lump of bloody, grey-blue lunchmeat flop onto the table. Poking at the folds with his finger, the lump flattened out to reveal an oblong patch of leathery skin tattooed with a somewhat stained version of a white-feathered serpent. "Snake Squad, or somethin' like that."

"Wow, mate." Hez recoiled a bit, less in horror and more out of surprise. "Now I see why ye dinna wan' to yank that out in public. 'Tis quite a shock." He carefully turned the flap around to face him. "Oy, Serpent Squad. Nasty pieces o' work that hire out from al'ovah. What'cha need from them?"

"They went and tried to kill one of mine." Rude smirked. "But I took 'em down a few pegs. One of 'em said somethin' about bein' hired to a job on a corp that just so happen to have just double-crossed my team. I might not be the smartest troll around, but that seemed too much like a coincidence."

"Stranger things been known t'appen, mate."

Rude pulled a second baggie out of his other pocket and pushed it across the table; it was full of assorted broken bits of electronics sprinkled with tiny motes of broken glass. "These Serpents were jammin' our comms. *Our* comms. Like they knew the link codes t'our private network. Not just that, but they knew where my guy was supposed ta be meetin' a Johnson. They came in like the Law, and hit hard. If I wadn't already there scopin' the joint, one of my guys'd be an elfy-shaped stain on the street."

"Oi," Hez took a deep drag off his cigarette and blew out a plume of blue-gray smoke, "sounds a roughin'."

"I've had worse." Rude snorted. *Prolly.*

"Ah'm sure ye 'ave." The ork sat back in his chair, blew more smoke toward the ceiling like some kind of orcish dragon, then looked Rude in the eyes. "But this'n still sounds a sight awful, mate. I don' know much about the Serpents, but I 'ear things."

"What kind of things?"

"Nae much, really." Hez drummed his fingers on the edge of the table, "but ah do know where ya maight dig up sumfin'."

"How much is this gonna cost me?" Rude took a drink, leaving just enough to swirl around at the bottom of his glass as he spoke, "'Cause my nuyen's all tied up at the moment."

"Nuffin', mate." He shook his head and fidgeted with the ring on his pinky. "Call us even. Ah still owed ye fer that Tacoma job."

Hez searched the ins and outs of his jacket and found a folded napkin with a purplish-brown wine stain on the corner. Flattening it out on the table, he smoothed it down a few times with his hands before tracing across it with his finger, with the paper smoldering into the dark letters and numbers of an address.

"Show off." Rude finished his drink and slid the napkin away from the ork. "Ya could've asked if I had a pen, you know?"

"Just be careful, mate," Hez warned him. "That 'ole block be crawlin' wi' problems. Call if ye get in some trouble."

"Trouble?" His grin was wide as he stood, and he dramatically clutched invisible pearls. "Little ol' me?"

"Ah mean it." All of Hez's illuminated tattoos shifted color to various shades of violet, casting the ork awash in new darkness. "Sumfin' big is brewin' out there, an' even ah dunno what it be just yet."

"I will." Rude shrugged on his coat again, slung the bandolier back over his shoulder, and adjusted the sword to sit between the worn calluses in the leather. "And thanks."

"Don' mention it, mate." He chuckled. "No, seriously, if ye get busted—ah don' know ye."

Rude nodded and headed back out into the club. He returned his empty pint to the goblin at the bar, made sure to throw him a good *"Next time don't question me"* look, and crossed through the crowd to the weapon check at the front doors.

"Have a good night?" the dwarf minding the vault scanned his AR signature and handed over the mirrored plastic storage pouch that held the troll's sidearm.

"Just gettin' started." Rude tore open the bag with his teeth like a snack-n-seal. "Ask me in the mornin'."

"That's the spirit!" The dwarf stroked his beard suggestively. "Have a good one then, chummer. Come see us at Horneez again real soon."

Rude stepped out in the wet night air, the thrum of the electronic dance music of the club dulling to a muffle as soon as the doors hiss shut behind him. He flexed his injured arm a few times, still thankful for the patch pouring anesthetic into him, and opened the napkin-note from Hez. Aside from the address and Hez's personal link info, there were four words scrawled across the top like a newsblog headline...

Here There Be Monsters.

Rude held the note up and matched it to the giant plastic lettering nailed to the marquee of an ancient, dilapidated concert venue. The sign letters didn't match each other; some were likely originals from when they put names of bands or artists up, a few were taken from other signs on other businesses, and the two "S's" were just spray painted on. Whatever this place was, its advertising either was greatly wanting—or it spoke volumes of the establishment inside.

This part of Renton felt like a baited trap during the day, but at night Rude could feel all the eyes cloaked in cover and shadow watching him, many of them probably through a set of crosshairs. Everyone knew the gangs really ran this part of Seattle. The Underground maintained a powerful presence here, too. It was Rude's longstanding rep with a few of their "middle management" members that he hoped would carry him safely through this.

I hope the intel's good, he took a deep breath and stepped through the curtain of hanging chains that made up the front doors to Here There Be Monsters. Like the two seals of a hermetic airlock, there was a second curtain a dozen steps or so inside the first; this one constructed from hundreds of straps of leather. He could hear a variety of different sounds and noises from inside that heavy curtain, many of which honestly piqued his curiosity more than anything.

Before passing through to whatever was...*hissing?*...on the other side, Rude took a moment to turn up the read on his Sony, thumbing through his contacts for any familiar signatures to turn up. *Nobody around. Great.*

Rude swept a section of the curtain aside with the sweep of his arm, his senses immediately bombarded with new-yet-familiar foreign stimuli. There was the mustiness of an apartment that had too many cats in it, or that pungent tang of rat piss mixed with just enough sick-sweet of rotten food. It was a *hairy* smell that you could somehow taste.

What used to be the venue's stage center had been gutted and torn down to the basement level, creating a pit of sorts. A rough cement floor stained with blood and *other* fluids stood there gaping in the floor like a stone grey eye staring at the ceiling.

Rude knew what he was looking at—a paracritter-fighting arena. He was no stranger to these types of barbaric entertainment centers, and they'd never even left a mark on his conscience; he'd given more than his share of nuyen to the bookies over at The Coliseum. Even so, the way this place was put together, the way it *smelled*...Rude felt greasy as soon as he took three steps inside.

There were pens and cages of various sizes and shapes standing, lying, hanging and leaning throughout the huge chamber that made up the floor plan. More than half of these pens contained a myriad of beasts. Augmented fighting dogs, a hooded firedrake, a thornquill bear, and other creatures all made their strange sounds from around the room. By the ropes of its glowing saliva falling from obscured jowls, even a barghest hung in his cage, ready for his turn in the pit.

"Fights're cancelled this week," a heavily cybered human shouted down from her perch on the far balcony, the shine of a chromed-out pistol in her equally chromed-out hand. "Whaddaya want?"

"Info, I hope," Rude replied, holding his arms out wider to show he wasn't looking for a fight. "I was told ya'll might know something about a job gone bad by a local crew."

"Depends." A second voice surprised him from behind, a dwarf holding a shotgun emerged from a side office. A ring of maglock key fobs dangled from a stretchy bracelet around his wrist, meaning he was likely the boss here.

"On?"

"What crew, what job." The dwarf spit a foul glob of phlegm on the floor, "And what's it worth." He lifted the barrel of the shotgun so that it pointed at the small of Rude's back.

"Whoa, whoa," Rude gestured with his open hands again, trying to reinforce the fact that he wasn't here to start something, "I'm not here to ruffle ya'll. I was told you might have the dirt on the Serpent Squad hit that went south…"

There was a look shot between the dwarf and the woman as soon as the words left Rude's mouth. It was subtle, and it was the kind of look that spoke volumes. A tiny surge of adrenaline shot through his system in anxious arrival of what part of him knew was going to be the ugly moment about to start.

The dwarf scowled. "Earn your wage somewhere else, bount."

"No, wait." Rude tried to diffuse the situation, but part of being a troll meant most people always thought you were about to start a fight. Most of the time he would lean into it, use this natural intimidation to his advantage, but Rude had already been through one ugly scrap today, and didn't have anything against these guys. *I don't wanna kill anybody else tonight.* "You've got this all wrong. Just hold on a sec—"

The *clack* of her pistol behind him was the proverbial pin dropping in a quiet room. Despite the sounds of the beasts around him, the jingle of the chains at the front of the building, someone shouting at their significant other in the alley, and one wild siren down the block— the hammer of that chrome pistol clicking into place was louder than anything else in Rude's ear. More than that, it was something that rang in Rude's *head*.

"*I hate Boston*," he muttered as the world fell away into the haze of a broken memory. Here There Be Monsters vanished and it was replaced by a smoke-filled, brick-walled office hallway. The swarthy dwarf in work overalls shifted into a broken and bleeding elf in an Armani three-piece. The arming of a pistol twenty meters away on a balcony became a revolver's cylinder wheeling into place right behind him. "*Ya'll can't fool me twice…*"

Rude moved so fast the dwarf was completely caught off guard. The metal fingers of his left hand swung forward and clamped around the barrel of the shotgun and shoved it sideways a full second before the trigger was pulled; making sure the buckshot that exploded from the end missed him entirely. A cloud of metal pellets passed by, ripping into a row of nearby cages. Sparks showered from where they struck metal, and a mix of howls and growls from where they met the flesh of the animals inside.

"Knife-eared double-crosser!" With a shout Rude pushed the hallucinatory-elf's outstretched arm forward, popping it fully out of the socket and collapsing the elbow. In reality however, he had just shoved the stock of the shotgun into the dwarf's face—but the *ke-runch* of bone from the impact and the accompanying scream sounded exactly the same.

"Chiphead! What the hell're you talkin' about?" The dwarf's hands flew up to his shattered and gore-spattered face, shouting and spitting pieces of teeth. "Bag and tag this crazy prick, Dollie!"

The troll spun around, trying to bend his thick trunk in a way to avoid the double-crossing wage traitor in his mind putting two Ruger slugs into his spine. However, as that the gunman wasn't actually standing right behind him, and instead was up on a balcony, all Rude did was toss the dwarf's firearm away and do a strange little dance move.

Rude didn't go into these memory-fugues often, and they never lasted long at all; even less when something in the real world couldn't match up with the memory landscape—for instance, when a bullet hits him. Or four.

Dollie's first slug embedded itself in his armored jacket just above the ribs as he spun; he barely felt the impact. Her second, third, and fourth however, were a different story. Pain rocked through him, starting at his armpit and traced around to his navel. Her pistol wasn't a hand cannon or anything, but she was fast on that trigger and had a good eye for where to put her shots.

"GodDAMN IT!" Rude roared, half in pain and half in frustration with how this situation had turned bad so quick, diving for cover behind a big cage covered in a black tarpaulin. "Stop! Stop! I'll go! Frag!"

"You broke my face," the dwarf shouted, scrambling to get at his gun in the chaos. "Now you gotta pay!"

With that, Rude knew that things had gone fully sideways. After smashing up the dwarf's face, if he was going to get out of here, it was going to be over their dead bodie—

"FRAG!" Fire flooded his hip, and Rude recoiled from it, stumbling backward into a row of benches. He looked down, expecting to see another bullet hole—maybe from some ricochet or lucky shot—but instead there was just a small ring of slowly spreading red flowers. He wasn't shot, well not beyond the ones he already knew about. If he didn't know better, he'd say it looked like...

A bite mark?

Rude looked up from the wound at the cage he was hiding behind, saw a flicker of scaly movement at the edge of the tarp, and honest fear froze the blood in his veins—or maybe that was the venom surely seeping through his most recent wound.

Can this day get worse?

A shotgun blast turned the old church pew next to where he ducked to splinters.

Yes. Yes it can.

He wanted to do nothing more than take out every ounce of his anger and regret he had accumulated over the course of these last few days on these two. Maybe shove that gila demon into the dwarf, and the dwarf into the breeder before feeding them all to the barghest like some kind of vengeance turducken—but there really was no time for that now. Between the patch on his arm losing potency, the growing pain in his hip, and the fresh bullets worming around in his torso, Rude was growing a little shaky around the edges.

Calm, Rudiarius. Find your calm. He heard the old man's voice in his head, and knew it spoke the truth. The venom was going to circulate, but if he kept his heart beat slower—slower than what it would take to murder these two—he could get help. Rude took a better scan of the room. Focusing on ways out of the room rather than how to conquer it.

There it is. He drew his boot knife—ironically, the one that he used to carve up the ork runner that brought him here in the first place—and took a slow breath to calm his shaking arm. He hurled the knife up at one of the hanging cages, sinking it into the reddish-brown flank of the beast inside of it.

"Sorry, Fido."

The fire drake inside the tempered steel bars let out an angry screech—followed by a plume of flame that streaked across the ceiling like a sheet of blazing light. Rude's eyes were fitted with integral flash compensation, so it was nothing more than a color shift in his vision for him, but the human and the dwarf—two low renters that had to host paracritter fights just to get by—were not remotely as fortunate. They both shouted and cried out, shielding their faces from the dazzling flame.

Rude used the few seconds it bought him to scramble up to his feet and back out the front. The leather and chain curtains slapped at him annoyingly as he passed out onto the sidewalk, but the spreading wetness from his wounds and the venom's somehow icy heat were causing a variety of internal alarms to blink to life in his HUD. He had no idea how long he was going to be able to stay on his feet, but he knew he couldn't stop to rest too close to Monsters. They'd find him for sure and, misunderstanding or no, who knows what they'd do to him now.

He found a burned-out collection van on a side street and used his metal fingers to unzip the pollution-corroded siding, half sitting and half collapsing on the devil rat-infested bench within.

"Come on, Hez," he whispered, a strange taste of copper mixed with bitter salts suddenly on his tongue as he fumbled with his Sony to send the message.

<Monsters was a bust. Need help. DRT wreck on Calliope and Station. Need khlbn nnnnnnnnnnnnnn...>

With a heavy *thump*, Rude landed on a long metal table. The last half hour or so was a blur, but he vaguely remembered somebody scooping him up out of the van and putting him in a beat-up old Docwagon rapid-response vehicle—a luxury he definitely couldn't afford.

Everything was a haze; the venom tearing through him unabated and strengthened by the blood loss.

"I can start work on him," one gruff voice said, "but this is a fraggin' mess, Hez! You already owe us for that ghoul nest. This is already a blood—"

"Bloodbath," Rude muttered, remembering why he was in this mess, "Renraku..."

"What'd you say?" another voice chimed in, "You know about that?"

"Serpent...Squad."

"Go ahead and start stitching, Doc. Sounds like we've got a lot to talk about—if he lives."

Take more'n this to kill me, Rude hoped inwardly as he lost consciousness.

Get down, Marcel! Incoming!

That same dream again. A firefight. Dead friends.

Man, Boston really is a shithole.

This wasn't a dream, but it wasn't a nightmare, either.

When did I ever work for a corp direct?

Whatever it was, they had a loyal soldier in Rude. In the dream he saw himself in a picture frame. His head was shaved, and he wore an earpiece like he has seen in CorpSec agents.

Time to kill some prisoners, I guess. Musta been framed or somethin'?

Rude looked down at the elf in his grip. The elf that, in the last few days, he had crushed, beaten, shot, and eviscerated in his mind a dozen times or more.

Time to die, Agent Garton...

That was a new voice. The guy from behind him. The guy with the hand cannon at his head.

Wait...not behind...

The voice warning him, high-pitched and feminine, wasn't coming from a gunner.

It was in my earpiece!

This was it! Rude was on the edge on knowing what this was all about. He needed just a few more sentences; needed to hear it a little more...

"You still with us, Rude?" A deep, baritone boom in the ether of his mind.

That's the wrong voice! No, wait!

"Dialed up to eight-forty. Clear!"

A blast of raw energy surged through Rude's body. Lightning flooded his nerves, his wires, and bounced around inside his body like frag shrapnel in a bunker.

His eyes flew open, a field of static and reboot code flipping across his HUD, but he could see the ceiling. Surgical tools hung on dangling racks between yellowed fluorescent light bars, some of which shined with fresh blood. At the edge of his vision he could see the shape of a wide-shouldered ork shuffling about, the plastic visor-mask of an ops surgeon currently lifted in the "up" position. It was some kind of street clinic—a nasty, low tech one, too.

Frag! I'm gettin' cyberjacked!

Rude had to move. He had to get out of there! He tried, but his body felt too heavy and numb. He lay there, trying to will everything into motion. All he could do was lie there and listen to the out-of-tune operatic music coming from somewhere nearby.

Then the ready lights to his arm blinked live in his feed, *Just in time.*

"It worked! Almost shorted out the genny, but—" The ork leaned over into Rude's view, a pleasant smile on his leathery face—that was immediately pressed into a grimace as Rude's cyberhand shot up and caught him by the chin. It was a familiar grip, even if last time it was the troll that was on top.

"None of that now," a cool, calm voice purred into Rude's ear at the same time the cold barrel of a pistol pressed up into his nostril, "Doc just saved your life. Don't go making me waste all of his effort and expensive chems by making brain pudding, puddin'."

"Heshz," the ork slurred, "Heshz shent ush." Rude relaxed his grip, and he laughed out his words again, a slight nervous tremble in his voice, "Hez sent us. I'm Doc—the guy who just patched you up. That BA chica who's trying to pick your nose with a forty-four-caliber dep round? That's Crow. The angelic tenor finishing his shower next door is Toro. Syd and Fritz are outside. We do a lot of work for the Underground."

"Why can't I move?"

"The big ones really are thick sometimes, aren't they?" Crow holstered her pistol and hopped up onto the back of a chair, perching her elven litheness on it like a bird of prey. "Doc pumped you full of happy-sleep-o-meen or zonk-a-trol or something like that. Dug four damn bullets out of you, and filtered out all that nasty lizard spit. You'll be fine."

"Not if he keeps digging up garbage on that job with the Telestrian fakes, he won't." In clomped a massive wall of a minotaur. Toro's deep chocolate flesh was a road map of dazzling white tribal tattoos and bioware scarring, all much too visible due to the comically small pink bath towel around his waist fighting against his every movement. He wrung water out of a clump of dreadlocks that sprouted from around his curved, silver-capped horns, and the occasional droplet fell from the brass loop piercing jammed through his nostrils.

"Let me help you up, tough guy." Without so much as a strained sigh, Toro carefully pulled Rude up by his armpits and leaned him against the wall so he was sitting up and could look around. "You'll be okay, cuz. Doc does real good work. Used to work on a 'wagon and everything."

"Go get dressed," Crow said, snickering. "Poor guy doesn't want your moo meat draggin' all over him while he's on the mend."

"You're just jealous." Toro laughed and gyrated at her suggestively, but then disappeared into the far room again.

"What..." Rude coughed, realizing suddenly that whatever the ork gave him must have been pretty strong, because even his tongue was numb, "did he mean by *fakes*? What does Telestrian have to do with Serpent Squad? Why'd they try to kill my, uhm, elf?"

"Why wouldn't they? After the nasty mess they left when they butchered that Miller guy and all those Renraku wageslaves," Doc shook his head, pouring a vial of neon green *something* on a delivery patch and turning it slowly in his fingers to evenly spread the fluid on the microscopic delivery fibers. "It was savage. Some of them weren't even armed. Half of Serpent Squad, claiming to be Telestrian corporate, came in and did the gig. It was *so* dirty." He flipped the patch down onto the troll's thigh with a *slap*. "There. You should start to feel like yourself soon."

"Woo." He was right, Rude's body came to life in a few seconds— but so did the pain from all the surgeries and chemical treatments over the last two days. He grit his teeth and exhaled slowly, trying to expel as much as he could before he passed out. "How do you know all this?"

"Well..." Doc smirked. "About that."

"We found 'em," Toro added, coming back into the room. At least now he was wearing pants and a tight vest made of interwoven shipping cord and carabiner clips. "Our team got hired to—"

"Whoa!" A skinny man with the world's tallest flashing blue Mohawk burst into the room carrying two big sacks of greasy "burgers" from Chewy's. "Can we trust this tall drink of chowder?"

"C'mon, Syd. He's been through the drek." A shorter blond guy with visible hardwires running up through his arms and an expensive-looking rigging node on his temple followed him in, half a dozen to-go cups balancing in a cardboard carrier. "Hez vouched for him, that's good enough for me."

"Hez owes us for another job, Fritz." The scrawny one who must have been Syd plopped the bags of food on the countertop, far too close to a jar of unrecognizable organ parts drifting in oil. "I don't trust 'im as far as I could throw 'im."

"Not far, then, by the looks a'ya." Rude chuckled, and everyone in the room—except Syd—joined in the laughter.

"As T was saying." Doc rummaged in the greasy sack and pulled out an equally greasy sandwich. "We were on a job, taking out what we were told was a new designer drug den that was cutting up the streets real bad. We didn't do enough research—"

"That's on me," Syd admitted, shoving a handful of tofu fries into his noisily chewing mouth.

"We walked right into a setup," Toro added.

"There was a whole room full of Renraku wage slaves getting cut to ribbons." Crow continued the story between pulls of cola. "This team of Telestrian wet ops was in the middle of the hit when we rolled up."

"We bounced a few shots back an' forth." The minotaur snorted. "But they bugged out as soon as we brought down one of 'em."

"Lil' dwarfy fella." Syd whistled and traced his finger in the air, causing the white-feathered serpent to appear as a glowing image in the AR fields of the Matrix. "Fuckin' Serpent Squad went an' gone corporate."

"When they were comin' after *my* guy," Rude added, "they were all dolled up to be KE riot response, not Telestrian."

"That's so weird," Syd mused.

"I know, right?" Fritz shook his head. "Why change gears between gigs unless they've been told to by an employer?"

"Nope. Not what I'm talkin' about," Syd swallowed the mass of half-chewed horribleness in his maw. "It's weird that the Sony Emperor over there, the one in the pile of Rude's gear, won't shut up."

"*Syd!*" half the room scolded him with well-practiced cadence. Syd shrugged in response and wandered off, muttering to himself about "the predilection of the governmental promises of the Man in the UCAS."

"Frag—Zip's prolly losin' her mind, since my link's still dark." Rude swung his legs off the table and carefully put his weight on them. He started fishing through his things, strapping them on until he got to the small glowing screen of his Sony.

Nineteen messages. He stifled a smile before realizing that it actually could be important with all the crazy stuff going on. Something was really not right about all these things, and Rude wasn't sure if he could actually trust the team standing around him just yet. "I'll hit her back in a few."

"You gonna be okay, cuz?" Toro spun a pair of billiard balls in his hand like meditation orbs.

"Yeah. Ya'll were right. Doc does good work." Rude knew he'd be hurting for a little while, mentally already asking Frostburn for some of her magical healing later on, "I'm glad Hez hired ya'll to come get me outta that mess he sent me to."

"Yeah, Hez ain't payin' for you. The Underground hasn't even paid their debts from our last mission on their creds," Crow steepled her fingers, putting her index tips onto her chin, "so all of this...it's on you. Will that be stick or AR swipe?"

"Good luck with that." Rude clicked his tongue cynically. "Until we get this whole Renraku-Telestrian thing squared away, I'm pretty much broke." He was surrounded, and not going to be able to fight his way out of here. "So where does that leave us, then?"

"Oh," Doc waggled a finger in the air, "with all that's going down around you right now, we're fine with doing this on the borrow. If whoever hired the Serpent Squad to get in our run is also mixing it up in your biz, I'm sure there'll be the chance for your guys to pay us back soon enough."

"Speakin' of—" Rude held up his Emperor."—I should prolly find out what's happenin'. Zippy worries." He looked down at the screen.

<Where the hell are you, Rude? Call us back ASAP.>

"I know the feeling." Crow smiled.

"I'll walk you out, Rude," Doc said, swiping open the door.

"Nah." He waved him off. "I can take it from here. Hit me up if ya'll need. You need my inf—"

"Already got it!" Syd shouted from the other room. "Thanks! Drive safe! Don't die!"

Rude steps out into the clinic's parking lot, putting several paces between its door and the edge of the street before pulling up his Sony's feed live on the Matrix again.

<Hey Zip,> he sent the message, then counted, *Three... two... and...*

<What the frag, Rude? Why are you in Renton? We said ONE day! ONE! Where the hell have you been?>

"Long story. Tell you later." Rude glanced over his shoulder and saw Doc and Toro standing at the window, watching him.

<We're in big trouble. I KNEW this was going to happen! Just get to the House. There's a lot you need to know.>

"Frag," Rude growled, "I've got stuff for ya'll, too."

<See you soon. Don't go dark again   like EVER. #TeamPlayer #WorldOnFireWithoutYou #WindBeneathOurWings>

"Zipfile?" Rude wrenched open the ignition panel of a beat-up old Nightmare—the only thing big enough to carry him within jogging distance that he knew how to hotwire, "can you scrub this bike's sig for me? It'll be faster than tryin' to get a Kab to ya'll."

Back in the window of the clinic, Doc and Toro watched his patient steal one of their neighbors' ride. The minotaur sighed, and Doc mimicked the sound. He folded his arms across his chest and slowly shook his head.

"What's up?" Toro furrowed his brow.

"You think he knows?"

"About what? Why the inside of that lumpy skull of his is a scrambled memory omelet, or why a bunch of his older 'ware is experimental paramilitary stuff?"

"I bet he'd be interested to know all that, yeah, but not as much as the fact that those Telestrian hit-drones are following him." Doc sucked air through his tusks.

"Oh...frag."

FROSTBURN
CZ WRIGHT

Spirits do not require eyes to see, but sometimes they work them into the form they assume when summoned to the material plane. This night, a spirit of beasts wearing bright, blue eyes spotted a metahuman creeping around where it did not belong. The metahuman was an ork, a woman, neither young nor old, who—the spirit tasted the unfamiliar emotion, trying to define it—felt disconcerted.

The spirit crept closer.

The ork crept up to a structure that was no more than a dark silhouette against the navy, starless sky. She pressed her hands against the smooth walls, and leaned her head closer to a half-broken window. The trespasser's attention focused upon the spirit's master. The spirit's master would not be able to see her sneaking about, but the spirit could see her without difficulty.

Now was the time to act. Materializing directly behind the ork, the spirit let out a deep, guttural growl. The ork whirled to face the spirit, and although she tried to keep a stony expression on her face, the spirit sensed the fear she struggled to keep locked behind it. The spirit rejoiced at the impending battle as it leaped for her throat.

Traffic murmured around Frostburn as she merged onto the freeway. Technically, it wasn't her doing the merging; it was just the car, piloted by a program and directed via GridGuide. Using GridGuide meant never having to check a map, which was a good thing, because Frostburn was intensely distracted.

"Record, love?" She had installed a voice mod into her commlink that gave it the voice of trid star Tommy Murphy. Normally, his

gorgeous, deep brogue requesting that she unload all her thoughts and troubles soothed her, but today wasn't a normal day.

"Record," the ork agreed, and waited for the recording light to turn red. "Someone burned down our safehouse," she said. The memory of earlier today—a tower of flames lighting the shocked faces of her crew—flooded into her brain. She cleared her throat and pushed away the worry and fear it ignited. "Luckily, no one was inside at the time, so no one got hurt. One of us got roughed up—" That was Yu, her team's face and stealth specialist, but she didn't like to use names on these recordings. "—but that was during the job he ran earlier, which turned out to be a setup. Then they hit our safe-house." Frostburn trailed off and growled under her breath, thinking. "I don't know what we were thinking, agreeing to him going in alone like that. Maybe we're getting sloppy."

Frostburn found herself chewing on her thumbnail and stopped the tangled mess that was her thoughts before it could unravel any further down a dark, worrisome path. It always happened when she didn't take proper care of herself, at least according to her records. She never seemed to notice while in the middle of it.

She stared at the lights of sunset reflecting off Lake Union as she and hundreds more crossed Ship Canal Bridge. Seattle rose like a wall: a silhouette of skyline to the west curved around the edges and reflected off the surface of the water, which was only visible for the height and relative empty space around the old bridge.

"Regardless," she said, "We're going to find out who's got it out for us, and we've each got a job to do. But first, I need to make sure my family's okay, and I'm happy the team was all right with my taking the time to check on them." She could just call, sure, but she wouldn't feel satisfied unless she'd taken a look around there, too. And since she didn't know who had it out for them, she couldn't know whether they'd trace her call home. "After that, I need to get some astral scouting done. That's the plan, at least."

She paused, unable or unsure of what to say more. "Stop recording," she told Tommy Murphy.

A foul odor assailed her nose, and when she wrinkled it in disgust, her tusks brushed either side of her nose with the expression. The awful smell of industrial fire smoke came from—she sniffed to double-check—herself.

She pawed through a duffel bag she called her not-an-emergency-bugout-bag. She kept the emergency bugout bag stashed in the smuggling compartment she'd paid her brother Jules to install, making it much harder to find. Pulling a packet of shower wipes and a grey and faded University of Washington hooded sweatshirt from the duffel, she cleaned off the physical remains of the day and changed into clean clothes, heedless of onlookers, thanks to the one-way glass that had become the norm among auto manufacturers, because no one wants to become the target of a spell in your car during rush hour. Stuffing her smoky armored jacket back into the duffel, she zippered away the stench of smoke and sweat.

Holding a hairband between her teeth, she smoothed her dreadlocks into a bunch at the crown of her head, then wrapped them in place with a little tug to keep them secure. She took a deep, long breath and shook herself out. She needed to get rid of this worry before she got home, or her family would pick up on it. They always picked up when she was worried. Except this time, they would start asking questions she didn't want to answer, and Frostburn didn't like lying to her family.

Well, she wasn't lying, per se. She just didn't correct them when they assumed she still worked as a corporate magical security officer.

When NeoNET, the corporation that had employed her until recently, had crashed, Frostburn had panicked. Working for the corporation had become a literal lifeline for her and her family. All of a sudden, she could buy her mom a house of her own, in a safe neighborhood away from—or at least just across the border from—the Redmond Barrens. They were able to afford medicine that kept her mom alive a little longer than she otherwise would have been able. The doctors said they would have a good couple of years more with her, just make sure she kept taking that medicine. Facing the prospect of losing that security was more than Frostburn was willing to deal with.

She had made a call to the headhunter who had approached her months earlier. At least, "headhunter" was what Frostburn assumed was the pretty troll's title. She had handed over a business card and said to give her a call if Frostburn ever needed or wanted a change of pace. Frostburn thought maybe the troll could at least help her find a way out of her non-competitive agreement—did it even matter anymore when the corp that made her sign the agreement had dissolved? Better yet, maybe she could help her get her a replacement corp job that paid similarly.

Instead, the troll—who called herself Ms. Myth—had introduced Frostburn to the lucrative and dangerous world of shadowrunning. Frostburn began to earn more than she'd thought possible, but at no small cost to her sense of staying honest with people close to her. Her whole family had naturally assumed she'd gotten work with another corp, particularly when she earned enough to move her aunt and cousins into the house in Snohomish after Frostburn's mother passed. Though she had initially considered finding another corp job, ultimately she decided against it. At least working in the shadows made her something of her own boss, but to be honest, she was satisfied to have finally found work that both paid the bills and gave her a thrill.

Ms. Myth had introduced the employment opportunity to the newly-unemployed Frostburn as "not exactly legal." The phrase had given her pause at first, because back when Frostburn went through her magical Awakening, she'd become the Girl Who Couldn't Lose: Corporations wanted her. Colleges wanted her. And once she graduated from college, she became the Girl With a Steady Paycheck. She could buy her mom a house—a whole house!—in a neighborhood that wasn't the Barrens. Through it all, though, Frostburn had always been the Stand-up Kid Who Did the Right Thing. Did she really want to become the Girl Who Has to Hide What She Does?

As Frostburn's car glided off one freeway and onto another, the route wound her between the largely working-class neighborhoods of Snohomish to her left and the hellscape that was Redmond to her right. The shades of golds and reds in the sunset shifted and glinted with the change in direction. The colors shifted her thoughts back to the memory of the flames—flames that, in all likelihood, served as retribution for their actions. The tentative connections forming between the Girl Who Has to Hide and the Girl With the Steady Paycheck gave her pause again, and she shoved the troublesome thoughts away.

I've got to get back to the team, she told herself. *We've got drek to do. Just a short visit, make sure the fam's okay, and back to work. Tonight if possible; otherwise, first thing tomorrow morning.*

Forty minutes later, the sun had disappeared behind the horizon and the headlights came on automatically, illuminating the road as she turned into her family's driveway. The car chimed arriving at her destination as it rolled to a stop, , and Frostburn's heart hiccuped. Draped across the garage above the opened doors was a hastily hand-painted banner that read "*WELCOME HOME.*" Crowds of people were packed around tables inside the garage; some she recognized as her relatives, others she didn't know at all. They all cheered her arrival.

Frag.

Frostburn crouched before a tiny girl she thought might be her second-cousin Ida. In her outstretched hand was a small, blue, plastic wolf figurine. Too much time in the heat of her car's glove box had warped the animal's limbs, so it stood on splayed legs that curved out and back to meet the base, like a cartoon caricature of bowlegs. Ida didn't seem to mind. She stared at the trinket, enraptured, with wide, brown eyes.

"You, my dear," Frostburn said, "are the proud recipient of the Wolf of Courage."She looked over the plastic, cereal-box toy, the last thing she was able to scrounge up to serve as a gift for the horde of kids that swarmed her car upon her arrival. One of the crowd got the remaining package of her shower wipes, and another group of them ran off happily and excitedly fussing over a still-wrapped carton of NERPs, arguing over who got what. Once the tide of children had receded, there stood little Ida, shy and gift-less. Frostburn's heart melted a little and, although it had taken her a good five minutes to find another present, she was grateful to have scrounged up this figurine.

Frostburn presented the Wolf of Courage to Ida, reverently holding it out to the little girl with her head bowed. But then, an impulse took hold of Frostburn. She clasped her hands around the toy and snatched it back close to herself. She pierced Ida with a fierce expression and said, with far too much urgency for the occasion, "Seize the power of the Wolf, oh Courageous One!" and thrust the toy back at the little girl.

Ida recoiled from her exaggerated performance, and her lower lip began to tremble.

Regret and embarrassment flushed through Frostburn, and she melted down onto her knees, cooing, "No, baby, please don't cry. I'm sorry, I was just trying to be silly, and I failed miserably. I didn't mean to scare you. Please don't cry."

With a wary glance up at Frostburn, Ida sniffled a little and wiped her nose on her sleeve. Then she reached up slowly, snatched the toy, and ran off as fast as she could around the side of the garage. A few seconds later, Ida peeked out and studied Frostburn from behind her cover, a look of utmost distrust on her small face.

Frostburn hung her head and sighed.

"Scaring babies for fun now, are we?"

Frostburn looked up, then jumped to her feet. "Holy drek, Emilia? It's been forever! It's good to see you!" she said as she stretched her arms wide for a hug.

The younger ork woman shook her ash blond curls with a mirthless chuckle and took a step back, her palms held out. "Yeah, I'm not much of a hugger."

"Oh," Frostburn said and started back, embarrassed. "Sorry. I'm just happy to see you is all. Man, it's been forever! I haven't seen you in...what—"

"Yup, it's been a while," Emilia said in a bored tone. She crossed her arms over her chest and took a drag off her cigarette as she scanned the street.

Frostburn nodded and shoved away a pang of hurt. She and Emilia, her cousin and junior by about three years, had been inseparable when they were kids. Their mothers, who were sisters, rented apartments in the same nasty, should-have-been condemned building in Redmond. Redmond being Redmond, though, living in a should-be-condemned building was par for the course.

When Frostburn developed magical powers just after puberty, everything had changed. Upon her Awakening and the subsequent drama of being courted by corporations eager to hire yet another mage, Emilia and she grew apart. When NeoNET fell over itself to hire her and gave her a full ride to the University of Washington, Emilia stopped calling. By the time Frostburn settled her mom in Snohomish, she and Emilia had fallen completely out of touch.It made perfect sense to Frostburn that they'd grown apart. Not only was this the start of those formative teen-age and early adult years, but life at the corp took up all of her time and attention. If she were being completely honest with herself, she'd forgotten about Emilia in the rush of attention, but she figured her cousin would have done the same thing. Everything was exciting at that age, and the sort of attention Frostburn got didn't get paid to orks and trolls very often. Still, seeing Emilia's apparent brusque acceptance of their distance still hurt.

"So," Frostburn said and tried to affect a casual stance, "what have you been up to?"

"Not much, just stuff," Emilia said.

Frostburn nodded and pursed her lips. *So it's gonna be this way, huh?* "Okay then," she said and sighed. "Well, I gotta get going soon anyway. It was nice to see you," she added uncertainly.

Emilia flashed her a quick, tight smile. The smile might have appeared genuine, had it not slid off her face immediately afterward.

As Frostburn cut through tables and crowds, needing to find somewhere—*any*where else to be—she headed across the garage toward her aunt. *Insult to injury,* she thought and shook her head. She didn't have time to worry about her younger cousin or the chip on her shoulder. She was here for a quick visit, nothing more. Make sure everyone's okay—basically, to put in an appearance. This would have been much simpler if her Aunt Gloria—Emilia's mother—were not the most social of butterflies. When given the slightest heads-up that Frostburn was coming to visit, the woman threw a party. And truth be told, there was a large part of Frostburn's secret heart that hurt to think she could have visited her mother more often while she was still alive. She did not want to make the same mistake with the rest of her family. Moving them in to her mother's old house was just a first step. Now that they were safely out of Redmond, she could certainly visit more often. Just so long as work didn't follow her home. That thought stopped her cold and she shoved the thought away. Aunt Gloria missed very little, and the last thing Frostburn needed was any questions about what was bothering her. No, she was just here to make an appearance and cut out gracefully.

She moved through the crowd, handing out hugs here and there, and got close enough for her elderly aunt to hear and see her. She was wrapped in a fuzzy purple blanket that resembled a royal robe, and sat on a floral-print, stuffed armchair that was her constant throne.

Someone had carried it out into the garage for her. The side table and lamp that usually sat next to her chair in the house had been brought out, too. Even her faded, rainbow-colored bread bag rug sat beneath her slippered feet.

"Hi, Auntie," Frostburn said. When her aunt beamed a crinkly, bright smile up at her, Frostburn felt any resolve she still possessed to dash out the door crumble away. Once an active, jolly figure, her aunt had grown ill and feeble over the past few years. Frostburn wondered how much time they had left.

Aunt Gloria pulled her hands from beneath the quilt and lifted them to Frostburn, who clasped them warmly as she sat down on a folding chair across from her.

Her aunt looked her over with that same penetrating stare that always made Frostburn feel like she was seven years old again. "You're too thin," she said in a strong, gravelly voice that belied her frail frame.

"I know. I've been busy, and haven't been able to start cooking at home like you told me—"

"Your hair is green," Gloria said, peering at her dreadlocks. Frostburn nodded. "The last time I saw you, it was red like a fire engine."

Frostburn grinned down at her boots. "Yeah, I suppose it was."

"I prefer green. But!" Gloria slapped her on the forearm. "I should see you at least *twice* with the same hair color; otherwise, you're not visiting often enough."

"You do know they make hair colors you can change in less than a minute or two, right, Auntie?"

"You know..." Gloria put her index finger beneath the point of Frostburn's chin, as though she were going to divulge a great secret.

"What do I know?" Frostburn said.

"Taking time off work to visit home once in a while won't kill you," she said with a conspiratorial wink.

Frostburn smiled with a wince and nodded. "I know. I know! You're absolutely right. I'm sorry," she said and sighed. "It's just that work has been so busy—"

Her aunt's wrinkles deepened as she smiled and patted Frostburn on the cheek. "I'm sure it is. But you still don't visit often enough."

Time melted away in warmth and camaraderie. Frostburn slowly made the rounds of her party, reconnecting with relatives she hadn't seen in ages, and tried to take her mind off the team's troubles, even if only for a bit. Even if the dark thoughts spilled back into her conscious thoughts every few minutes.

No one questioned her vague answers when she answered their "So, what are you doing these days?" questions. No one demanded anything more specific, which, if she were being completely honest, is one of the big reasons she'd stayed away from these kinds of gatherings in the past. She was sure her family would get everything out of her. Someone was going to throw a fit and get dramatic⊠—but none of that happened. It was a damn miracle.

Rounds completed, she retired inside. Maybe with everyone chatting, eating, and drinking out there, she could slip away to get a little work done. She poked around, snooping in the rooms of her aunt's house, feeling a little like a trespasser, even though she went through the better part of adolescence living under this roof.

Emilia had gotten Frostburn's old room when they moved in. The room could have still been hers, for how similar their tastes were. Punk rockers head banged from their AR posters draped askew over every wall surface. She sat on the bed and stared dryly at the moving posters, briefly flipping off Johnny Banger, who riffed in a never-ending loop. It was more of a salute to the legend than an insult, and she thought he would have appreciated the gesture.

But she couldn't work here, not with the *ick* of her interaction with Emilia earlier still lingering in her mind. She went into the master bathroom instead, locked the door, and lay down in the bathtub.

She closed her eyes and tried to settle her thoughts. Inhaling deeply, she visualized sloughing away the house, the family, and the physical plane altogether in an attempt to head into astral projection. She needed to find out more about the person who had hired Yu, and she had a decent idea of where to start—

A three-round burst erupted outside.

Frostburn leaped out of the tub and nearly tore the door off its hinges in her rush to get out of the room. Once outside, she spotted the source of the gunfire. Emilia stood in the middle of the front yard, pointing a pistol in the air, her eyes bright and a wild grin on her face at the crowd of children gathered around her.

Blood boiling, Frostburn ran to and disarmed her cousin within seconds, sped along by old muscle memory. She grabbed Emilia by the shoulders. "What the hell is wrong with you?" A wall of fumes hit her square in the face, and she recoiled. Her jaw dropped open and she worked her mouth without words for a moment before she spat out, "Are you drunk?"

Emilia scowled and swung a fist at the empty air between them, far too late to catch Frostburn in the face. "Gimme my damn gun back, slitch. No one fraggin' cares if I'm drunk."

"I fraggin' do!" Frostburn shouted. She glanced around at the neighbors' houses and lowered her voice to a hiss. "Especially if you're going to fire your sidearm in the fraggin' yard!"

"Don't yell at her. It's okay!" one of the little ones said. "That was siiick!"

"No, it's not okay!" Frostburn snarled and shoved Emilia away from her admirers.

Emilia pouted theatrically and generally fell in the direction Frostburn shoved her, barely getting her feet underneath her along the way. Brought to a stop, she swayed on her feet with a grin and a little giggling, but a fire burned somewhere below the drunkenness in her eyes.

"I'm taking you home to sleep this off," Frostburn said through a clenched jaw.

"No you're not, 'cause I'm not going home," Emilia said with a scoff. "I got work to do." She stabbed a finger into Frostburn's chest at the word "work."

"You're in no state to work. You're going home." Frostburn unlocked her car. "Get in."

Emilia swayed, cocksure yet guarded, and began to laugh. She shook her head as though Frostburn had just said the funniest thing. Then she sighed and wiped her eyes, turned, and walked unsteadily away down the sidewalk without another word.

"Oh, for frag's sake!" Frostburn muttered through clenched teeth. She turned to see the crowd of kids standing behind her, having obviously seen the whole thing. "Git!" she roared and lunged toward them. They scattered.

She pulled the car over and drove slowly alongside Emilia. "Get in the car."

"Fuck off," Emilia sang in an off-key fanfare.

"Oh my God, you have no idea how much I do *not* have time for your drek right now," Frostburn said. "Get. In. The. Car."

Emilia stopped and turned to stare at Frostburn with wide eyes. Frostburn sighed and stuck the car in Park. Emilia walked around and over to the driver's window, staring at her all the while. She squatted slightly, putting her head level with Frostburn's and said, "You 'don't have time'?" She paused for effect and wobbled slightly. Frostburn glared straight ahead out the windshield. "Well frag me, when did you ever?" Emilia popped back up to her full height and continued on her way.

Frostburn pinched the bridge of her nose. "You know what?" She slammed her palm down on the steering wheel and threw the car into reverse. "I don't have time for this. You want to act like an asshole? Go ahead. Just do it far away from here." She gunned the car backward to its parking spot outside the house.

Frag her! she thought. *She's a grown adult. If she wants to act like an ass, let her.* She slammed the car door shut, took one last look at Emilia, who continued away unsteadily down the sidewalk, and went inside with a shake of her head.

Back inside, Frostburn tried her best to be a good party guest, but she was fuming. She hadn't gotten a chance to get her work done, she was already late getting back home, her cousin was acting like a crazy asshole... Her welcome-home party had finally begun to wane; more than half the crowd had gone home already. The childless adults lingered, though. Probably wondering who they could get to take them home afterward. Gross. Better hope beer goggles didn't keep you from recognizing your relative before you let things get out of control.

Frostburn was all socialized out and bone-weary. She didn't perform well on the social front when in the best of spirits—that catastrophe with little Ida attested to that—but on not enough sleep, with a torched safe-house, fear for her friends's and family's lives, and after a fight with her childhood best friend? All things considered, Frostburn thought she was doing pretty well on the social front. She hadn't even hit anyone yet.

She leaned against the kitchen counter, distracted by her thoughts, and noticed she had taken her commlink out without thinking about it. She also found she had dialed all but the last two digits of Emilia's commcode. She paused and scowled, unsure of what she was going to say if she answered.

After a beat, Frostburn decided to plow ahead and finished the code. She waited, listening for Emilia to pick up, but the call went to voicemail. Emilia was probably still ticked off. Or maybe she'd passed out. Frostburn wondered whether Emilia was with friends and whether they were on the up-and-up. Once upon a time, she may have allowed herself a cozy daydream of Emilia's friends exchanging amused glances over their sleeping friend, and of one of them lovingly tucking an afghan over her. But experience and adrenaline shouted that down as nothing but naïve, and etched an altogether different and far less sweet pathway of thought.

She hit redial. No answer.

She yanked open the fridge door. Glass receptacles in the door clanged together noisily.

She dialed again.

Voicemail.

Clusters of her relatives approached to say goodbye. Frostburn suppressed an enormous sigh, smiled dutifully, and passed out hugs, but soon found herself pacing and gnawing on her thumbnail. She had to get back to work, regardless of whether she could work things out with her cousin. Smoothing things over would just have to wait.

She went back to the refrigerator for the bottle she'd been after before the last batch of goodbyes. She set the cold soda onto the chipped, laminate countertop and yanked open the silverware drawer. Rummaging through four types of tongs, five types of spatula, and six types of spoon, she retrieved the bottle opener. With a grunt, she picked up the bottle and ripped the cap off.

She set the bottle opener down and, with her thumb, she redialed Emilia one last time.

Voicemail.

Frostburn slammed the opened bottle to the counter, sending up a shower of foam.

She cursed under her breath and went to the bathroom to grab a dry towel big enough to handle the mess. The window of the bathroom looked right out onto the driveway, where she now noticed that her car was no longer parked in the driveway. She did a double-take and peered in every direction she could see from the window. Her car was nowhere to be seen.

She marched out of the bathroom.

One of her uncles was in the living-room in mid-stoop, placing Aunt Gloria's bread bag rug back on the carpet.

"Where the hell is my car?" she asked.

"Emilia borrowed it," he said. When he rose to his feet again and saw the look on her face, he hastily added, "She told me you said it was okay."

Frostburn made a guttural growl of frustration and whirled back into the kitchen.

Dial. Voicemail. Dial. Voicemail. Frostburn's blood ran hot when she was frustrated, and she couldn't help but leave a message. "You get drunk, shoot off a gun in front of the kids, and now you steal my car? What the hell, girl?! You'd better have that car back to me in one piece—and soon, or I'm gonna—"

The recording time ended with a *click*.

"Why the hell can't I leave an hour-long freaking message, huh?" she yelled at her commlink. "It's not like we use tape anymore! For crying out loud!"

Her uncle looked in from the living room, with a chagrined expression. Frostburn felt herself flush a little. "I'm sorry, it's not your fault. I'm just..." she hunted for words.

"I'd be ticked if someone took my car, too," he said with a smile.

Frostburn nodded, flushed even harder, and offered her own wan smile in return. "Sorry," she muttered, and then retreated to the bathroom again. She paced, clawed at her hair, and gnashed her teeth in silent fury. Then with a sharp sigh, she threw her hands down and centered herself, calming her brain.

She took a few deep breaths, closed her eyes, and began the process of summoning a spirit. In her mind's eye, she plunged her hands across the border between the physical and the meta planes. She conjured and pulled forth an assemblage, the threads of raw energy from the plane of kin and brought them into the physical plane beside her. There, she willed and shaped the energies into a magical construct—a spirit—that would obey her orders. Once its services to her were up, the energies would return to their native plane of existence. It wasn't really how it worked—rather, no one really knew exactly how it worked—magical scholars said it worked in any number of ways, and each way was often slightly different for each summoner. But at least she was confident in the structure of the thing. Other traditions insisted the things had minds of their own, which Frostburn felt was patently ridiculous.

The spirit of kin construct took shape in astral space. So closely related to the metahumanity on the physical plane were they that spirits of kin showed up resembling metahumans. This spirit had taken the appearance of a farmer. Farming had been big in Snohomish for a long time, but this looked like none she'd seen before. Modern farmers wore corporate uniforms and weren't typically more than drone operators, but this one wore bib overalls and appeared—but thankfully didn't smell—like he'd been rolling in muck. Spirit constructs could be strange.

"Find Emilia, and let me know when you have found her. When you do, I will have you guide me to her."

The spirit telepathically assented to its assigned tasks and disappeared. The task could take hours, if the spirit could find her at all, and Frostburn let out a heavy sigh. Maybe she could get some sleep and call a cab in the morning if she couldn't get her car back before then. But she'd be sending that bill to her cousin, damn it!

In the wee hours of the morning, Frostburn slumped in her aunt's chair in front of the trid. Her head drooped and woke her up with a start for the fifth time in a row. If anything, she wanted to be awake if Emilia returned to the house so she could rip her a new one. She considered getting up and pacing to stay awake, but it seemed like far too much work.

An impression arrived to her consciousness and snapped her fully into wakefulness. Her spirit of kin had returned. Its telepathic missive to Frostburn was simply that it had located a sign of Emilia. Frostburn hoisted herself out of the recliner, arched her back in a stretch, and groaned. The on-again-off-again napping had worn her out more than if she'd stayed fully awake, but the fight she had with Emilia bubbled back up to the surface. Adrenaline worked better than caffeine.

Hell, she could have just *asked* to use the car. As long as her cousin had said where she was going and when she'd be back, Frostburn probably would have agreed. But instead, Emilia had stolen the car, and now Frostburn was pissed. She couldn't imagine what had prompted Emilia to do it. She probably wanted to drive her friends around town and deface property or something. The most dangerous part of getting her car back was going to be losing her voice from yelling at Emilia so much once she found her.

Frostburn snuck out of the house, easing the door closed until the latch engaged with a soft *click*. She took one last glance around the quiet cul-de-sac to insure no one was looking her way, then headed into the empty garage. Although she wasn't doing anything illegal, the less often she had to test the resiliency of her fake magical practitioner's license, the better. Sure, she had a real license to practice magic, but things would become much harder for her if the cops pinged the real license; at least a fake one could be replaced if burned. And there were still some people around who, if they spotted someone summoning spirits, might decide to call the cops. Magic was widely known, but more than a few folks still got jumpy about it. Or maybe it was just that they got jumpy watching an ork practice magic. Either way, she preferred to remain unseen.

Mostly hidden in the garage, she summoned a spirit of air. It gave off the odor of burned wood as it materialized, and resembled nothing more substantial than a plume of smoke, but this was a stronger-than-average spirit she had summoned. It had a particular job to do. She gave the air spirit orders to transport her via air and to conceal both her and itself while they traveled. Using her spirit of kin's guidance, she would direct the spirit of air where to go. The air spirit should be able to carry her, and indeed, upon receiving its orders, the spirit took on a shape resembling a large bird of prey, hooked its talons painfully around her upper arms, and hoisted her up into the air. The spirit appeared to struggle to lift her, and she tried to help by kicking off the ground. Eventually, they were airborne, but the spirit kept dipping down every so often, forcing Frostburn to pull her feet up several times to avoid catching them in treetops or on rooftops.

In a strange sort of telepathic game of Hot and Cold, the spirit of kin led Frostburn and the flying air spirit to the location where it had found Emilia. The path took them over the residential neighborhoods near her aunt's house, making the houses, yards, and garages look more like a city-building simulation game as they grew ever smaller; over the big agriculture operations that took up much of the district's east side⊠—a patchwork of genetically-engineered crops; and then they approached a small patch of crumbling commercial development attached like a tick to the side of a block of low-income housing. The typical sorts of businesses⊠—a payday loan office, two liquor stores, and a pharmacy—all eager to feast on the low-income residents.

The spirit of air descended swiftly and unceremoniously dumped Frostburn about a meter up from the pavement. She yelped and barely caught herself from smashing her face on the asphalt, skinning her palms instead. With a glare at the air spirit, she stood, brushed herself off, and ordered it to await further instructions. If she didn't know better, she would have said the magical construction was pissed at her. Her midsection ached from all the abdominal work on the ride over, pulling her feet up over and over again.

A gate—no more than a rusting bar with chipped paint—crossed one open end of the driveway that arced in, past, and back out away from the strip mall. The other side of the driveway sat wide open, The gate on that side lay on the pavement, rusting, bent out of shape, and forgotten.

"All right," she said to her spirit of kin, though it was unnecessary for her to speak aloud to communicate with it. "Show me what you found."

She followed the spirit's guidance—hot, cold—past the stores, past patches of grass gone to seed that grew through the broken pavement out in front. She shifted to astral perception.

The world shifted and filled with color. Magic and life were the wheat of the astral realm and technology was the chaff. Anything that lacked that spark of life—things like buildings, parking lots, cars, commlinks—were a dull grey in astral space. Magic and life, however, glowed with brilliant color. Skilled magicians could learn to read the auras and colors to determine all sorts of things: health, age, mood, magical ability, the presence of cyber- or bioware, which, like the buildings, cars, and 'links, appeared as dull, gaping holes in the otherwise colorful aura of life. She didn't like to examine those with 'ware if she could prevent it; she found their lack disturbing. But she had the skill to look deeper, even if it was not one of her strongest skills.

A faint glimmer of something out of place caught Frostburn's eye, and she noticed a magical signature hovering in astral space near the corner of the liquor store. Magical signatures were created when someone used magic, and they bore qualities that made them resemble the aura of the person doing the casting. But signatures and auras were two completely different things. Frostburn did a double-take: this magical signature bore all the traces of Emilia's aura.

Frostburn shook her head, astounded. Her little cousin was Awakened. As far as she knew, no one else in the family was Awakened. Frostburn's heart ached for her cousin. To have to go through Awakening alone?

She studied the signature with curiosity. Her experience working with the astral, plus her time earning a degree, granted her quite a bit of knowledge. She could tell that Emilia had been feeling happy and not a little bit cocky when she cast what left this signature. The signature was created when she used a Health spell, though she couldn't pin down which one it was. Frostburn could tell that Emilia was as strong magically as she was, and shook her head in amazement again. *How the hell did I miss that?*

A couple more steps put her around the corner where she found her car parked. She approached cautiously and laid her palm on the hood; the engine was still warm.

Birds had begun to call. A little thrill in her gut at the sound of their songs told her it was probably nearing dawn. Checking her commlink verified that it was close to four in the morning. A weak wind gusted her way, carrying the sound of not-too-far-away voices to her ear.

Frostburn stealthily headed toward the direction the voices came from. She maintained a habit while on the job of shifting back and forth between astral and physical perception. There were just some things you could see better using one or the other, even if your ability to notice...well, *everything* other than what you can see better takes a big hit. When you're looking at the world in astral space, you can't see things in the physical realm as well. Just as when you're looking at the world in physical space, you can't see the astral. She had tried to explain it to Emilia once. She used words like "glow" and "sparkle," and soon lost the girl's interest as quickly as she disgusted herself.

Frostburn found it all difficult to explain. She just groked it; knew how to harness the winds, so to speak, and sail her ship in the direction she needed. And when she looked over the world using astral perception, and when she sifted that information through her studies and mother-fragging degree from UW, she could tell quite a lot, actually.

She stepped off the parking lot and into the weeds, searching using her physical perception, and was quickly rewarded when she spotted a recent shoe print. Switching to astral perception, she spotted another of Emilia's magical signatures a short distance from the print. Then she heard another snippet of talking: it sounded like one of those talking heads on the trid. At least she knew she was going in the right direction.

Butting up against the property in the back was the backside of an old gas station. Maybe they were trying to diversify as a junk yard, too, because numerous cars and trucks littered the area. Most appeared inoperable in some way, and one or two were verifiable hunks of junk.

She used the cars as cover as she closed the distance. The voices grew louder, and she knew they must be coming from inside. Sure enough, once she got close enough to get a better look, she noticed the back door hung ajar. She flattened against the wall a short distance from the open door, scooched forward, and listened.

The voice she had thought sounded like someone on the trid definitely sounded from here as though the speaker were just inside and not on the trid. "—And that's because they underestimate you. You're strong, and they're afraid of you. They'll do anything, everything to get a leg up, even if that means killing everyone who doesn't look like or behave like they do."

Murmurs of agreement rose to meet Frostburn's ears. There didn't sound like there were all that many people inside.

"It's up to us to put the balance right again," the speaker continued. "We need to be the ones to stand up and say, 'No More!'"

"Yeah!" A different voice. A young woman's voice, but not Emilia's.

Frostburn moved toward the opposite side of the station, hoping to find another way inside. She didn't want to astrally project out here alone, with nowhere to stash herself and no one to watch over her body. She spotted a broken window next to the front entrance and approached with caution, listening intently. The man inside continued his speech. She caught a word or two: he talked about justice and injustice. From the vocal agreement during his pauses, he seemed to be riling up his audience.

Frostburn reached the window and leaned in to get a better look inside. A blue glow shone on either side of the window frame. Frostburn frowned for a moment before it dawned on her that the glow was a reflection and it originated behind her. She readied herself to counter spellcasting, and turned to face an enormous, blue, glowing manifestation of a wolf. A spirit of beasts of strong-to-moderate force, its muzzle wrinkled and teeth bared, issued a deep, low growl from the back of its throat.

Stay with Emilia. She sent the silent order to her spirit of kin just as the wolf lunged at her.

Frostburn dodged its leap and instinctively brought her hands up to throw an Ice Spear spell at the spirit, even if she knew she didn't need her hands to cast. However, she second-guessed herself at the last moment and released of the threads of magic she had gathered: she didn't want to alert the group inside to her presence, and magic could be quite noisy. Instead, she switched to astral perception, and barely dodged as the spirit jumped toward her again. Her astral-self grabbed the beast spirit's astral form, and the two grappled in close combat, silent to everything in the physical.

The beast struck at her with its teeth—or the astral impression of teeth, anyway. It got a snap in on her forearm, which wouldn't result in a bleeding wound, but instead battered her will. Physical damage could be seen; stun damage couldn't always be seen, and that's the kind of damage dealt to the astral form. But stun would knock you down just as quickly as physical damage. Sometimes it could do you in faster, particularly if no one could see what's wrong with you and couldn't know to put forth any effort to help. A silent fight resulting in silent, invisible wounds.

Frostburn swung and landed a punch on the spirit in astral space. The blow seemed to knock some of the spirit's essence away, like a plume of cloud blown away by a strong breeze. The wolf pounced and leaped on top of Frostburn's astral form. They fell together, grappling, each trying to gain an edge over the other. Frostburn pawed at the beast spirit's muzzle, trying to get a hold, and the beast spirit snapped at her astral fingertips. Again, the beast tore into her arm as she blocked it from her face.

With a surge of will, Frostburn shoved her arm into the wolf's muzzle, wrapped her free arm around it, and lay atop the thing. It bucked and threw her off its back. Frostburn landed, rolled over, and cast a Mana Bolt at the spirit. Because the spell was wholly present on the astral plane, it made no disturbances in the physical plane. The Mana Bolt ripped through what little energy the beast spirit had left and tore the thing to shreds. The spirit dissipated to whatever plane from which it had originated, and Frostburn returned her attention to the physical with instant regret as the drain of the last spell washed over her

She lay her back against the wall and let gravity draw her to the ground. A double-shot of spell drain and injuries caused her head to scream in pain, and weariness and nausea blotted out everything else for a few heartbeats while she tried to fill herself with clean, cool breaths.

Spirits didn't usually bother with the physical plane unless they had orders to do so. Where was its summoner? She put her face up to the window again, but could hear no voices. Warily approaching the still-open back door, she listened again but heard nothing. She snuck inside.

She had barely taken two steps when a Stun Bolt hit her in the back, clobbering what was left of her will to the ground. With it, Frostburn fell, unconscious.

When Frostburn came to, her wrists and ankles were bound with zip ties that dug into her skin. She was tied tightly around her middle, attached to a chair, and wore a blindfold and a gag. Panic welled up inside her, and she quashed it back down: if whoever did this had wanted to kill her, she probably never would have woken up. The fact that she had told her that her captor likely wanted something more from her, and that would give her a chance to come up with something. She was careful to avoid any movements or noises that might alert whomever had captured her.

The odors of oil and gasoline told her she was probably still in the gas station. She could also hear very soft footfalls. A louder scrape of chair legs on cement startled and froze her in place.

"I see you've rejoined the land of the living. How lovely for you." She recognized the voice of the person who had been speaking earlier.

The voice, cheerful and matter-of-fact, grew closer. "You can call me Sir. Well..." He chuckled. "You can't call me anything at the moment, can you?" he said, and a gloved hand patted her face roughly where her gag dug into her cheek, "But you know what I mean."

"First, we're going to have a conversation," he said and moved away slightly. "You're going to tell me everything you and your team know about a job you just pulled against Telestrian Industries. After that," he said in a breezy, how-about-this-weather sort of way, "I'll kill you. Loose ends sink ships, you know. Or something like that, anyway."

Frostburn remained very still. She couldn't telegraph anything using her eyes or mouth, so it was best not to show him in her posture that she intended to fight back.

"I have to say, this *has* really been fun," he said in a conversational tone that suggested she hadn't awakened his suspicions yet, though she wasn't always the greatest judge of character. "Getting the chance to play fixer to a bundle of little baby runners. They're so cute. And dedicated, my goodness. Did you know that it took only the tiniest push to work them up to practically foaming at the mouths to go right all of society's wrongs? They're simply full of the fires of injustice." He chuckled and sighed. "So full of piss they are. So full, in fact, that I was able to get them out the door on a mission just as soon as I knew we had company."

He continued talking as he approached and moved around to behind her right shoulder. "You showed up earlier than I'd expected, I'll admit. I had a terrific plan all laid out, too. You would come looking for young Emilia—or so my research said—and *poof*, here we'd be: me with you under my boot, and you all alone. But you came early. I had to get them to work so quickly that I might have forgotten to tell them some important information." His tone lightened with amusement. "The corporate stooge they're off to egg may have gotten an anonymous death threat within the past, oh, six hours or so? And so the stooge's guards will certainly be on their toes. Hell, they'll probably shoot anything that moves. Ah well, that's what you get for trying to change the world. And what budding revolutionary wouldn't love to become a martyr for their cause? Down with the Industrialized Food Chain!" he shouted. "Or was it a more general 'down with industry?' I can't keep these pet causes straight." He sighed. "No matter. Let's begin."

A cold band of metal lay across her cheek where he'd patted her earlier. The gag around her mouth tightened for a moment and she heard a soft tearing sound. The fabric loosened and fell into her lap. The metal blade moved smoothly along her skin to rest on the side of her neck, where he pressed in. She noted he seemed careful not to touch her.

"Now," he said, "start talking about your job." His tone of voice turned into one of mock-intrigue. "Tell me everything."

Frostburn worked her mouth carefully, grateful to get the function of her mouth back to her, though mindful of the blade on her throat. She was never a good talker, even at the best of times, but she started in, talking empty information while her brain sorted for a good plan.

"Well, I wasn't there for the job itself, so I don't know much about it⊠—"

The blade pressed into her neck, and she grunted in pain. Warmth seeped down her neck. "Don't tell me what you don't know," He said quietly into her ear. "Tell me what you do know. Things will go much easier on you that way."

"Okay, okay." Frostburn swallowed. "We got approached by a guy who wanted us to hit a warehouse," she said haltingly, acting as though she were flustered and scared. Trying to take her time. The guy seemed to buy it. At least, he hadn't called her on it yet.

Her brain stumbled over the fatigue and the worry and the pain, sifting through coherent thoughts and blind, lizard-brain reactions to formulate a plan, all while trying to speak in complete, understandable, not entirely true sentences. She made up facts off the top of her head, mostly pulling from vague memories of the last action trid she watched. Careful to insert plausible details in among the bullshit.

A plan began to coalesce in her mind, and Frostburn knew she had just the one chance to try to get it to work. He had neglected to lash her legs to the chair, though her ankles were tied together, and she knew from the direction of his voice and the blade that he was behind her right shoulder. In mid-sentence, Frostburn pretended to be caught by a fit of coughing. Her captor, who was apparently eager to hear all she had to say, lessened the pressure on her neck ever so slightly. At the easing of the pressure, Frostburn shoved her boots hard into the floor and threw herself backward and to her left.

He squawked in surprise and managed to dodge out of the way of her fall.

When Frostburn hit the floor, she pulled up her feet and kicked out, viciously, with all of her strength. He snarled and cursed in a lilting language she didn't understand as she thought she heard him land in a heap.

She shot a silent order to her spirit of air to free her from her restraints. She could hear the man hacking and coughing and his boots scraping the cement floor as he scrambled to get back on his feet.

The air spirit assented silently. Frostburn heard a rush of wind as the spirit materialized at her side and removed her blindfold. She locked eyes with her captor—a young, well-suited elf—as the spirit pushed electricity through the plastic around her wrists. Frostburn yelped as the jolt burned her skin. The spirit zapped the plastic around her ankles, and she got to her feet, and kicked the chair away.

The elf glowered at her from the other side of the room while he summoned a spirit of his own. A humanoid shape comprised of fire materialized beside him.

"You've only bought yourself a few seconds, my dear," the elf said. "You and I both know you're barely on your feet. Tell me what you know, and I won't even cut you. I promise!"

The air spirit dove for the elf, expanding as though inhaling a massive breath. It spread out and tried to engulf the elf within its form, but the fire spirit counterattacked, breaking up the attempt.

Frostburn dashed out the open door at the back of the station. The sky had lightened considerably since she first arrived: the rosy hues on the horizon had paled and almost disappeared in the lightness of daytime.

The elf was right. Even now, she was barely upright after the barrage of drain and spell damage nearly put her on her ass, and the drain from summoning that latest spirit felt an awful lot like shoving a knife through her third eye. She ducked behind an old, electric-blue Nissan Jackrabbit that looked like it had been driven into every light pole in Seattle. Distant sizzling and whooshing came from the interior of the station as the two spirits battled one another. The elf would be out here and on her in a second. She had to get away.

With every instinct in her screaming to just run, don't fight, she summoned a third spirit—the last one she could keep under her control—and nearly fell over from the effort. Her eyes watered from the pain in her head as a column of white and blue fire materialized next to her.

She peered over the roof of the car and spotted the elf, who had indeed followed her out. He was hunkered behind a junked Toyota Gopher a row over and peered back at her. Like two opposing kickers in a sports match, Frostburn and the elf eyeballed one another and readied their attacks. Frostburn stood and let loose a Flame Strike down on her opponent, suppressing a gasp from the effort. But the elf was ready for the spell and dissipated the magical energies before they could do him any damage with nearly effortless counterspelling.

"Attack!" She ordered her own fire spirit into action, and it closed in on the elf. With his spirit of fire busy with her air spirit, she took a chance and sprinted for her car.

A *whoomf* from behind her was her only warning, but she knew that sound and threw herself to the ground. A ball of flame flew over her—right where she'd been standing a moment ago. The heat seared her back, eliciting a cry of pain and an acrid stench from the scorched synthetic fibers of her sweatshirt. She scrambled back up to her feet and continued sprinting. The row of bedraggled trees at the back of the lot took the brunt of the spell. Leaves sizzled and smoldered as the fire burned off the morning dew.

Frostburn slapped her palm on her car door. The biometric reader recognized her print and unlocked the door. She leaped inside, hearing the sound of small arms fire battering the lightly-armored back of her car as she sped away.

Frostburn reached out to her spirit of kin as she drove. The spirit assured her it was near Emilia, and offered directions to reach their location. Frostburn navigated the district and tried to follow the spirit's instructions, an enormously difficult task given that spirits don't consider streets and city layouts when guiding their summoners around. So, while the spirit would indicate *that way*, Frostburn had to deal with city blocks, traffic lights, and one-way streets.

She'd done her best to keep an eye out for anyone trying to follow her. She kept an eye out in astral space, looked behind her in physical space, and saw no one matching her route. So she was in the clear for now, but would have company soon enough.

The destination the kin spirit directed her to was the Ingersoll Aquaculture. Perched on the south bank of the Snohomish River, the facility was one of many owned by food giants Ingersoll and Berkeley. Eat anything produced in 2080? Chances were extremely good that whatever you ate was made from one of their products. The facility wasn't a very large one, but like every other piece of corporate property, Ingersoll and Berkeley was a subsidiary of Universal Omnitech, which meant that Knight Errant didn't even go in there. If you stood within the corporate limits, you played by the corporation's rules—rules that generally permitted them to shoot first and ask questions later, if at all. And considering the elf had said he'd called in an anonymous death threat, "shoot first" was certain to be the course of action security would take.

A stone wall encircled the perimeter, with a sign that read *"Ingersoll Aquaculture"* in enormous green letters standing upon it. Greenery of many types, none of which Frostburn could name, grew along the front and the top of the wall, lending the place a refined appearance.

Dawn sunlight glinted off the one-way glass covering the four-story building at the center of the property. It wouldn't be long before the morning rush of employees began streaming inside. Of course the place would be filled with guards, as any self-respecting corporate facility should be. Honestly, a part of Frostburn—the part that bought and consumed groceries from the greater Seattle area—kind of hoped the place had decent security, if only for the sake of public health.

She stashed her car on a corner up the street from the plant, . It wasn't illegal to park outside the place, even right next door, but she preferred to keep it as out of sight as she could—no sense in having her vehicle appear on a sec drone's camera.

Her head hurt terribly. Now that she had her car back, she had access to her supplies. She popped a pain pill and considered applying a stim patch—the only way short of a nap to rejuvenate herself—except if she couldn't finish her job within the half to full hour the drug remained active, it would wear off and she'd probably crash hard. She couldn't afford that. Nevertheless, she pocketed a few, just in case. She also grabbed the Ceska Black Scorpion machine pistol she kept hidden in the car for True Emergencies. And finally, she shoved herself and her bulky sweatshirt into the smelly armored jacket she'd removed on her way home. It might stink, but smelling bad beat getting dead any day of the week.

More properly equipped, she considered her options. The spirit said Emilia was inside this facility somewhere. From what the elf had said, there was a group of them here, waiting to egg some suit. She only knew Emilia, not the others, and she honestly didn't know what to expect from any of them. She was going in blind. Hell, maybe the elf was lying, and he hadn't sent them here at all. Maybe this was just one more convoluted way to try to get her killed. She'd take a look around, avoid trouble, and come out for backup if necessary. With luck, it wouldn't be necessary, but she crossed herself for good measure. She would have tried to call Emilia again, but the elf must have taken her commlink. It made her extremely grateful she kept her notes generic.

The telepathic connection between spirits and their summoners made it possible to know whether a spirit had been dissipated or whether it remained available on the physical plane. The spirit of kin was still around, but the spirits of air and fire had been sent back to their home planes. The air spirit had "popped" during the first few minutes of her drive; the fire spirit soon thereafter. That meant she had the freedom to summon up to two more spirits. A good thing to know, just in case. Of course, it also meant that the elf and his spirit had won the battle back at the gas station.

Frostburn closed her car up and walked deeper into the block, away from the road. She backed up against the side wall of the property where she was hidden by the masses of greenery and the shadows produced by the morning light. There, she cast an Improved Invisibility spell on herself. A wave of nausea passed through from her stomach, up her core, and into her head. Sometimes magic was like that, though. Some days you could cast spells all day, it seemed, with little to no trouble. Other days—particularly, she had noticed over years of experience, on those days she succumbed to worry or fatigue—even a simple spell could knock you down for the count.

Considering the stressors in my life at this very moment, she thought wryly, she could understand taking some drain.

Her physical form vanished from view. She could still be heard— or smelled, she supposed, and briefly wondered whether the smelly armor jacket was such a good idea—but she'd just have to be careful. She tied off the threads of magic to sustain the invisibility and then cast Levitate on herself. The drain on her system after the second spell could have been harder to resist alongside having to sustain the first spell, but she managed without a twinge of nausea.

Enveloped in invisibility and with the ability to fly, more or less, she lifted herself into the air in order to better survey the grounds of the aquaculture. At first, she lifted herself only so far as to see over the wall. There, she waited and watched astral space, looking for magical security. If anyone would be able to easily notice her, it was magical security. That invisibility spell made her invisible in physical space, but the spells lit her up like a spotlight in astral space. Once satisfied she could move around without attracting attention, she rose further into the air and floated within the bounds of the property. She perched, but did not relax, over the roof.

Ingersoll Aquaculture was predominantly focused on the growing and farming operations on the river. A large grid of pens and their accompanying harvesting drone tracks covered the shoreline. The surface of several of the pens glinted and bubbled with jumping fish. Outside the perimeter of the grid, a line of buoys marked the boundaries of the operation, and Frostburn figured the corp probably had some other painful goodies waiting for anyone trying to gain entrance from that side. She'd heard rumors of modified guards (either with 'ware or genetic modifications) who spent their entire shifts underwater. Though she wasn't sure they were that intense for guarding something like this place, she certainly didn't want to test that theory, either.

South of the river and the pens lay tens of meters of dock on which cranes and larger shipping drones labored, hauling stock back and forth between the farm and the facility. The north side of the main building had several enormous dock doors, behind which was probably the packaging operation. Inside the building, who knew? Offices, surely. But with any luck, she wouldn't have to go inside to find out. There was, of course, the chance the kids had already been caught or worse—she swallowed down the lump of that thought and pushed it away. But she'd best do a thorough search here before moving on to investigate that possibility. If the patrolling guards weren't up in arms, then the kids were probably still hidden around here somewhere.

She spent a few minutes hovering far above the aquaculture, noting the routines of the drones and guards who manned the place.

She spotted the locations of the guard shacks, spaced evenly and sparingly around the grounds.

Movement that didn't belong to either drones or guards caught her eye. Down below, near the corner of the facility just past the docks, a line of four people moved in a line from under the flatbed of one large truck to another, moving as though they definitely were not supposed to be there. *Bingo.*

Frostburn slowly floated down to the ground near the cabs of the trucks. Her boots scraped a little gravel underfoot when she landed, and she heard a small choking sound emanate from under the truck, followed by silence.

She took a quick peek in astral space and leaned over to get a better look. Huddled together were four glowing forms of metahumans. Being a skilled magician, she was able to read some information from their auras: they were young; they were two orks, a human, and a dwarf; and they were scared drekless. None of them was Emilia.

"Hey," Frostburn said in a whisper, and someone let loose a tiny cry that was quickly shushed. They heard her, at least, and they weren't jumpy enough to shoot at her. *So far, so good.* She returned her perception to the physical plane.

"I'm Emilia's aunt," she said, "and I'm here to get you out."

Silence greeted her and she waited. After a few seconds, a voice whispered back. "How do we know you're telling the truth?"

Frostburn snorted. "Well, I haven't started shooting you, have I?" It came out without much prompting. She was more than ready to be done with today.

After a few heartbeats, a low voice murmured, "Good point."

Soft scraping sounds preceded the appearance of four young faces under the truck. Two of them had tear tracks running down their faces. All of them looked shell-shocked.

She scanned the vicinity, found it was clear, and motioned for the kids to come out. Then she shook her head at her own stupidity. "I'm invisible, so you can't see me," she said. "But you can come out from under there. Do it quietly. The coast is clear for now."

One by one, they scooted and crawled out from under the flatbed. They were just a bunch of kids. Hell, Emilia was probably the oldest one of the bunch.

"Where's Emilia?" she said. "What happened?"

The kids exchanged worried glances, and none of them seemed to want to speak up.

The black-haired human boy said tentatively. "We were gonna do the thing, but..."

"But we lost our nerve," a small, red-haired ork girl offered, her eyes scanning the area for the source of Frostburn's voice.

"And then we couldn't get back out," said the sandy-haired ork boy.

"So Emilia went to look a way for us to get out of here," said the ork girl.

"But she's been gone for a while," added a blond dwarf boy.

Frostburn scowled and pursed her lips in thought. "Have you noticed any activity from security?"

The kids shook their heads.

"Any alarms go off since you showed up?"

They shook their heads again.

Frostburn nodded and sighed. They weren't far from the wall. She was confident she could get them out that way, so long as they avoided being spotted.

"All right. I can't make you all invisible, but you were able to get this far without getting spotted. If I can get you to the wall, I trust you can get over without being seen?"

The kids nodded with varying degrees of confidence.

"Good—" Frostburn heard the hiss of a voice over a transceiver from not too far away on the other side of the trucks. She cursed under her breath. "Someone's coming," she whispered. "Get back under there and be silent!" she said. The blond dwarf suppressed a sob as they all scrambled back under cover.

Frostburn readied herself for...she didn't know yet, but she was ready. A pair of guards walked in tandem a couple meters past the ends of the parked vehicles. Frostburn stayed perfectly still, watching them proceed, and examined them in astral space.

Neither was Awakened, and they had a little bit of some kind of 'ware, but not so much that they resembled the cheese with the holes in it. They moved along at a good clip, apparently oblivious to her—and the kids'—presence.

She waited to the count of ten after she lost them around the corner, then returned to the kids and to physical perception. "They're gone. You can come out again."

The kids crawled out quietly and quickly.

"I wouldn't normally do this," Frostburn said, "but I need to keep this invisibility spell up and I don't want to have to recast it. So all of you, hold hands now."

They glanced nervously between themselves, but obeyed. Once they all were holding one anothers' hands, Frostburn took the hand of the ork boy at the front of the line. He jumped in surprise, then flushed with embarrassment.

"Here's the plan: I'm going to get you over the wall. You're going to follow the wall to your left and find a car on the road. You're going to get into the car. You will stay put. You will stay quiet. Any questions?"

The kids shook their heads.

"Good. Come on." A last glance around, and Frostburn led them straight to the wall. One by one, she helped to hoist each kid over the wall. The last one in line was the dwarf boy. Frostburn wasn't the strongest ork in the world, but she could hold her own. Still, the kid was stocky and heavier than he looked. It was a challenge just to help him reach the top of the wall. She tried to get him to put his foot in her clasped hands, but it was impossible. With heavy regret and a sigh, Frostburn dropped her invisibility spell. Now that he could see her, she was able to help him up to the top of the wall.

The boy struggled, looking like he was doing an army crawl on his belly on the top of the wall. As he teetered at the top, barely out of Frostburn's reach, she heard a voice shout, "Stop!"

Frostburn cursed, jumped as high as she could, and literally shoved the boy's ass over the wall. She heard him land with a loud *thud*. She hoped he wasn't hurt, but even if he were, it was better than getting shot.

The two guards who had passed just a little while ago were running back toward her from the left.

She dashed back between the trucks and slithered over a couple of spots, between the wall and the cab of the truck the kids had been hiding under. Just as the guards came into view, Frostburn let loose a spell on them.

Her street name, Frostburn, was not her choice of names. That's just the way street names work; it's generally a nickname someone else gives you. However, it was an appropriate name for the ork for a couple of reasons. The first reason—and something she'd only noticed about herself recently—was that she tended to run hot when frustrated, but frosty under real pressure. The second reason—and the real reason behind her street name—was her trademark spells of Flame Strike, Fireball, and Ice Spear. Combat spells were showy, sure, and tended to get people's attention, but her preference actually lay with quieter effects, such as the Mass Confusion she imposed on these two guards.

Both men stopped in their tracks. The taller of the two yanked off his helmet and dropped his mouth open in awe. The shorter opened his visor and raised his eyebrows so high, they disappeared beneath it. Taller started to spin slowly in a circle, gaping at the world around him. Shorter scowled in consternation and shook his head vigorously.

She didn't know what they were reacting to, but that was part of the fun of this spell. As she watched them warily, she drew her Ceska and attached the silencer. Although the spell was meant to get them off her back, it was sometimes just as likely that they'd get confused enough to view her as some mutant monstrosity that they needed to kill, like, right the hell now.

Shorter said, "Wait...what were we doing? Focus!" He rapped his knuckles on his forehead. "There's an intruder. No, there's an escapee? One of the animals got out of its enclosure!"

Taller gazed at Shorter lovingly. "I never noticed it before, but your voice has a lovely aroma of blue."

Frostburn shook her head in amusement, double-checked she'd loaded stick-and-shock ammunition, then fired a burst into each guard. They grimaced, grunted, and shook as the electricity coursed through their systems, and then both fell to the ground.

Frostburn slunk forward, grabbed each of them in turn, and dragged their prone forms underneath the trucks. That should buy her a little time.

She reached out and tried to contact her spirit of kin. It responded that it was near. The spirit transmitted a telepathic impression of Emilia: her form in astral space glowed, and she huddled in the midst of grey tech. That didn't help much.

Frostburn sneaked deeper into the facility grounds. It wasn't well-guarded, as she'd surmised. She made a mental note to avoid consuming Ingersoll products in the future, though. There had been no sign at all of any uproar from security. Either they hadn't found Emilia yet, or they already had her in custody. The kids said they hadn't heard any alarms, but that didn't mean Emilia couldn't have been grabbed and either brought inside or sent away with the cops already.

She had just about finished a lap around the place by now. To her right was a tall, pale gray set of stairs leading to a landing and a metal door set a story or two up. One set of stairs stretched up before her; the other went down in the direction she was headed.

The door slammed open. Frostburn leaped forward out of sight and tried to become one with the wall underneath the metal landing.

Boots stomped overhead.

Can I risk another spell?

The sound passed over, then ahead and behind. She could see their black-clad elbows coming down the railing ahead.

They're coming down both ways–where can I go?

Frostburn whipped her head back and forth. The ones behind her were closer. She spun to face them and stared as they descended the last few steps and hurried around the corner at the bottom.

She turned. The other group headed away from her, too. Straight away. Not one of them turned to check their six. She gawked, unbelieving, then darted after them.

Looking the guards over in the astral, she noted how all of them weren't more than kids. Fresh-faced, the lot of them. And not a little bit scared. No cyberware or bioware. And, most importantly to her, none of them appeared magically active. Appeared being the operative word here, because there were ways to mask the aura, or just plain project false information: make yourself look like a badass when you're just a little newbie, or vice versa. Extrapolating from the rest of what she gleaned off this bunch, though, she doubted any of them were Awakened, let alone advanced enough to know masking.

Frostburn returned her perception to matters of the physical plane, and followed in the guards' wake. She yearned to move past them, to see what had kicked the hornet's nest, but she didn't trust herself to move unnoticed ahead of their line.

Instead, she waited until they turned a corner, then leaped and caught hold of the top of the shipping container and pulled herself up on top. Here she crouched, so as not to be spotted from the ground. The guards appeared not to notice, and hurried away toward the docks. There, near the furthest pens, a ghostly dog growled, ran a few meters away from, stopped and growled again at the approaching guards.

Frostburn scowled—this seemed too familiar—and scanned the rest of the piers. Far on the opposite end of the docks from the guards, enormous tanks cast deep shadows that the mid-morning sun had not yet scrubbed out. From the shadows, a glint of light. Movement where it should not be. Frostburn glanced around and behind her, but all the guards had run off toward the dog on the docks. She scrambled down and crossed the distance to investigate the movement in the shadows.

As she approached, a shift to astral perception revealed a figure crouched in the shadows, metahumanoid in shape, magically Awakened, and directly beside the figure, Frostburn's spirit of kin floated.

"Emilia!" she said as loudly as she dared.

The figure's head whipped around at her approach.

When Frostburn reached the sharp edge of the shadows, she practically dove head-first to get her eyes adjusted to the dark and verified her aura reading.

"Was that your distraction?" she said and hitched a thumb in the direction of the ghost dog

But before Emilia could reply, a voice shouted from nearby, "Stop right there!"

"Come on!" Frostburn shouted and reached a hand toward Emilia, who clasped her hand. Together they ran, out of the shadows and back toward the facility where they would be less in the open. The guard who had shouted started shooting, which alerted the guards on the opposite end of the docks, which brought bullets whizzing past them on either side. Frostburn and Emilia rounded a corner to break line of sight from the guards, and dashed up the ramps that led them back above water level and behind some semblance of cover.

They closed the distance toward the portion of wall over which Frostburn had dropped the others, and the door from which the guards had poured earlier crashed open again. Several more black-clad Ingersoll guards sped down the stairs.

Frostburn grabbed Emilia by the back of her jacket. Her cousin squawked and nearly fell, but regained her balance in short order. Frostburn heaved Emilia back the way they'd come, but instead of turning one way, she turned the other direction and stuffed herself and Emilia behind a large electrical box. She didn't know whether the guards had seen them, but she'd find out soon enough. She stabbed her elbow into Emilia's side, put her finger to her lips, and pointed in the direction they'd come.

"Commlink," Emilia whispered and made some kind of motion with her hand that Frostburn did not recognize.

Frostburn shook her head, confused. "I don't know what that is," she said mimicking the gesture, "but I don't have one; the elf—*your fixer*—took it. Where's yours?"

Emilia frowned. "I, uh, think I left it in your car."

Frostburn sighed. She was about to dive in to her planned tirade against her cousin when she caught a glimpse of movement over Emilia's shoulder. She pulled her cousin back toward her while she tried to make herself smaller and shuffle back a little herself.

The movement Frostburn had noticed was another patrol. They crept forward, but neither their eyes nor their barrels pointed their direction, though the helmets they wore made it tough to know what they were really looking at. Considering advances in audio engineering, she could bet on them hearing anything she or Emilia said. Maybe they didn't have 'ware, but chances were good their uniform helmets were outfitted with all sorts of fun toys.

They waited and watched: Emilia growing ever more bored; Frostburn growing ever more anxious. The patrol made its way around the corner they were approaching. Seeing no threat and having not been suddenly killed, the guards' postures relaxed a little and they continued on their path, which lead directly away from the two orks.

Frostburn let out a long, slow breath.

Emilia whispered, "It's a commlink. I'm answering a call?"

"What?"

"This?" Emilia made the odd gesture from earlier.

"Are we seriously discussing the latest trends in hand gestures now?" Frostburn said and craned her neck to get a good look around before she stood up from their hiding spot.

"You're just an old fart. What are you going to do when they do away with keyboards altogether?" Emilia said.

Frostburn shrugged and straightened her jacket. "Complain about it, probably. I'm sure as hell not getting a datajack installed." She rapped her knuckles on her temple. "No entry."

"You ever hear of 'trodes?" Emilia said. "I hear they're the latest new thing."

Frostburn screwed her face up and mocked Emilia's tone in a singsong voice. "Naw neh naw neh naw nee naw."

"How old are you?" Emilia said with a scowl.

"Old enough to know better not to run off on your own like that, at least!" Frostburn said.

"Oh *really*?" Emilia said and tipped her head to one side, deeply doubtful.

Four guards rounded the corner ahead, rifles at the ready. Both women jumped in surprise, and Frostburn launched a fireball.

The massive ball of rolling fire careened toward the guards, who valiantly attempted to leap out of its path, but the spell caught most of them, if only on their pant legs. They screamed and rolled on the ground, trying to put out the flames.

Only one of the guards avoided the blast. She lifted her rifle after having leaped clear. Emilia pointed at the guard, and a Power Bolt seized the woman. She cried out, her body seized up, and she fell in a heap.

Emilia grabbed a wobbly Frostburn by the elbow and led her away as fast as they could run. They darted around corners, momentarily moving into doorways and behind cover, and successfully eluded the guards long enough to briefly catch their breath.

"What the frag are you doing out here, anyway?" Emilia said in mid-evasion.

"I'm saving your ass. What did you think I was doing here?" Frostburn shot back.

"Although I appreciate your stupidity, I certainly don't need you coming in here like some great, holy savior. I can take care of myself."

"Oh, yeah. That much is *obvious*," Frostburn said. "Tell me, what was the next step in your plan when they caught you all alone out there?"

Emilia made a *pfft* sound and scowled. "Plans are overrated."

"You don't seem to know the first thing about plans!" Frostburn said.

"I know you think plans are downright plan-tastic, but look," Emilia said, scowling, "I know what I'm doing. You need to be able to be spontaneous. Keep your enemy guessing. Do what they don't expect." She rolled her eyes and shook her head. "You don't know *half* of what I do out here, so stop pretending you know everything."

Frostburn barked a laugh. "Listen to you." Then a dawning realization crept into her thoughts. "Wait a minute. You really don't know what I do every day, do you?" Gunfire erupted nearby, and bullet impacts pinged all around them.

"Frag it!" Frostburn and Emilia said in unison, and they ran.

"We gotta get out of here!" Emilia shouted.

"No drek!" Frostburn said. They ran, gasping, toward the back of the facility and the docks again, Frostburn leading the way. If they could just lose their tail long enough to get off the property, maybe they could get away. She considered the river, but did not want to contend with aquatic security, especially when swimming was not her strong suit. They'd have to hide somewhere, wait it out.

Before they reached the docks, Frostburn doubled back toward the heaps of shipping containers. "In here!" She motioned for Emilia to dive into one near the back and on the second row up. They helped each other crawl up and inside. With a quick glance behind them, Frostburn didn't see anyone obvious right away, and pulled the door closed before crouching behind the heaps of tarps mounded near the back.

The only sound inside the container was Emilia's and Frostburn's breathing, which gradually slowed as they regained their breath. They both froze when the sound of the guards approaching reached their ears. Boots ran around on the pavement outside, and they could hear the sound of radio chatter, but couldn't understand it. Frostburn could tell from the clarity of a voice when he called back to his team that he had just cleared the container underneath them.

A full minute after the guard sounds moved away, Frostburn said in a hiss of a whisper, "So what's the big deal stealing my fraggin' car after you got trashed? You're lucky you didn't crash it, because then I would have killed your drunk ass."

"I don't know if you noticed," Emilia said condescendingly, "but I have the ability to cast magic!" She waggled her fingers in front of her. "Ever hear of a little spell called 'Detox'?"

"Oh, for crying out loud, you're one of *those*," Frostburn said with a shake of her head.

"One of who?"

"One of those people who uses magic as a shortcut. Let me tell you, you can try to take shortcuts, but magic isn't going to save you from wear and tear. You'll succumb to it eventually."

"Whatever." Emilia shook her head. "Oh, and to answer your question from earlier, I *don't* know what you do, but frankly, I can probably imagine."

"You can, can you?"

Emilia snorted softly. "Yeah. Let me see, you sit on your ass all day, monitor screens, drink coffee... Let's see... Oh yeah, eat all the doughnuts—"

"That's cops," Frostburn said flatly, but Emilia continued as if she hadn't spoken.

"—And once in a great while, you get to play dress up! You and your little security team buddies suit up and go play shoot-'em-up! You shoot the drek out of some SINless losers... basically whoever your handlers tell you to shoot, you shoot them. Does that about cover it?"

Frostburn shook her head. "Actually, no. That doesn't even cover the job I did when I *was* a corporate security mage. Not that I expect you to care, but I haven't been employed by a corporation for a while now."

"Sure," Emilia said. "To be perfectly honest, you're right: I *don't* care. I know all I need to know."

"Excuse me?" Frostburn said, a little more loudly than she'd meant to.

"There's no excuse *for* you!" Emilia said. "It's people you who've—" Emilia clawed at the air with both hands, trying to find the right words as the anger erupted out of her. "–Fuck up the world! And you've left it up to people like me to get drek done! *We're* the ones who have to go out into the world, risk our lives every damned day, and fix the shit you and your types frag up!"

"And just who are 'my types?'"

"Corpers? Sell-outs? 'The Man,'" Emilia said.

Frostburn snorted. "Honey, you are *so* confused—"

"Over here!" A voice shouted from outside the container.

Emilia and Frostburn both jumped, startled. Frostburn readied herself to counter spells. She reached for her Ceska, just in case.

Gloved hands began to pull open the doors. From behind her came a sizzling sound, an awful stench, and smoke began to fill the box. She glanced back, expecting to find a smoke grenade in their midst, but instead found Emilia, panting, with a smirk on her face and holding her hands up like a game show star demonstrating that the power of magic could do nearly anything, such as melt a hole clean through a metal wall. Which she had just done.

Frostburn stared at the hole, then at her cousin. "Nice," she grudgingly admitted, and the two of them jumped out just as the guards were throwing open the doors from the other side.

The women jumped behind cover on either side of an open lane between the stacks of containers, barely dodging the bullets the guards slung in their direction.

Frostburn leaned out and popped off a burst toward the guards, who had jumped down and leaped behind cover of their own.

"How am I confused?" Emilia said.

"You really don't know?" Frostburn said, then ducked as bullets popped over their heads.

"Enlighten me," Emilia said.

Frostburn remained behind cover and pointed her gun over to blind-fire another burst at the enemy. To Emilia, she said, "I've been running the shadows for a while now. Got a team and everything."

"Good for you. You're still an asshole."

"What's your fraggin' problem, anyway? I know you're Awakened. I think that's incredibly awesome, and I'm *really* sorry I wasn't here to help you through it. But you have working hands, and you know my commcode. Or at least your mom does. You could have called me."

"Why would I do that?" Emilia said, popped around cover, and launched an Acid Stream spell at the guards. She fell back as they fired bullets back at her. "Call the big, bad corporate mage who couldn't get enough attention and money? I don't want your help!"

"Can we just give the attitude a rest? I don't need to be the bad guy," Frostburn said, scowling at Emilia. She waited for the burst fire from the guards to subside, then shot back rounds of her own.

"No!" Emilia said with a hitch in her voice, "You don't get to be the injured party here! You're the one who *left*! You left me *behind*!"

Frostburn glanced over at her cousin, shocked, and saw light reflect off the tear tracks down her cheeks. Emilia scrubbed the tears off angrily and turned away.

"I—I didn't mean to..." Frostburn said, and winced at the weakness of the reply. Bullets pinged off the walls of the shipping containers and whizzed overhead.

"Yeah," Emilia said with a sneer. "Well, a lot of good *that* did me. Do you have any idea what it was like? My best friend took off and left me behind in Redmond because everyone was fawning all over her. Then you buy a house, and oh, isn't she wonderful? But it's in fragging Snohomish. Do you have any idea how awful it is there? What assholes those hick humans can be to people like us?" Emilia's eyes flashed. "Then I Awakened? And I didn't tell a soul! Because I'll be damned if I'm going to become a sellout like you! I refuse!"

"I didn't know," Frostburn repeated helplessly. Emilia's words cut her to the quick, and the weight of responsibility for seemingly everything exhausted her: Emilia's attitude, her acting out, everything. "I—" She stammered. "I didn't know it was that bad out here, I just knew it was better than Redmond. I was just a kid!" She sighed, then frowned in confusion. "Wait a minute, what exactly were you doing here, anyway?"

"Running the shadows," Emilia said, mockingly saying the words as though she were an old trid announcer. "At least, I thought we were," She trailed off and a flush turned her cheeks pink. Her jaw worked as she ground her teeth together. "But I see the guy who pretended to be our fixer only had his eye on you. I'm sure you're thrilled."

"Oh for frag's sake, knock it off! That asshole was out to kill me *and* my team! He targeted you as a way to lure me out, because he heard somewhere that I cared a whole lot about you, okay?" Frostburn was shouting now, but she didn't care; the guards knew where they were, and her nerves were shot. "I'm not out for attention! I just want to keep people alive!" Her own voice hitched.

Bullets zinged through the air, seemingly to punctuate her point, and she whipped around the corner and emptied the rest of her magazine. She fell back under cover, chest heaving, and reloaded.

The guards, for their part, responded in kind. They fired dozens of shots, and through the din, Frostburn distinctly heard someone shout an order to move in.

"New plan: we gotta get out of here—Go! Jump the wall, get to the car!" Frostburn shouted at Emilia, as she laid down the best representation of suppressive fire she could muster.

"Plans are overrated, I'm telling you," Emilia said, but obeyed her cousin's order and bolted for the wall. Once Emilia was out of the line of fire, Frostburn launched a Mass Confusion spell in the direction of the guards and ran after Emilia, heedless to whether the spell worked on any of them or not.

As Frostburn rounded the corner and dashed for the wall, Emilia pulled herself over the top and disappeared on the other side of the wall. Frostburn tried to follow suit, but over twenty-four hours' worth of stress, drain, and fatigue made her muscles only shake as she tried to leap up and catch the top of the wall. Her fingernails scraped stone, and she dropped back onto her feet on the Ingersoll side of the wall.

She heard the footfalls of the guards before they rounded the corner and she bolted. There were only two of them, she saw, and they lifted their guns toward her. Frostburn ran. Her lungs burned and her legs felt like she'd worn iron boots all day. She dodged for the cover of the corner of the building and popped off another burst in their direction before running further. She holstered her pistol and dug in her pockets as she ran, and found one of the stim patches she'd packed.

No time like the present, she told herself. If she dropped from the crash of this thing in the half-hour or so the drug was effective, it was game over for her anyway. Maybe her brother, sometimes professional contact, and fellow ne'er-do-well-type Jules would get the news to her team.

She slapped the patch on her upper arm and gasped as the shiver of stimulant drugs hit her bloodstream instantaneously and flooded through her system.

With the hiss of rejuvenation, she bared her teeth. She was *done* with this drek. She stopped, rounded on her pursuers, and summoned a spirit of fire, then summoned a spirit of water, and *then* called forth her spirit of kin, which still owed her a service after finding Emilia. *Go big or go home*, she thought, managing to avoid the majority of the drain from each of the three summonings. She sicced them all on the guards.

Poof, poof, poof. Each in turn, the three spirits materialized into the physical plane. The spirit of fire took on the appearance of a humanoid shape made of orange flames. The spirit of kin was still the old-timey farmer, and the spirit of water took on the shape of a massive fish made entirely of water. The three soared forward just as the guards rounded the corner. Frostburn watched, amused in a wicked way, as the guards' eyes widened in shock. One brought a rifle up and started firing. The other turned and ran in the opposite direction.

Frostburn sidled away and cast a Levitate spell on herself. She grunted as a dose of drain washed through her and she cursed her luck, because she'd taken care to cast the spell at the minimum power necessary to get her butt off the ground. She was almost, but not quite as bad off as before the stim patch, but she was still up, and the Levitate spell was just strong enough to hoist her up and over the wall.

Boots on the Seattle side of the ground, Frostburn sprinted to her car. Just because she escaped their property didn't mean they'd call off pursuit, and she had a car full of baby runners—she made a mental note to try to avoid calling them that to their faces—that she had to get back home in one piece.

Frostburn reached the street and stopped dead in her tracks.

The elf appeared decidedly less well-dressed than he did the last time Frostburn had seen him. His suit bore scorch marks, his face bore bruises, and a swath of singe cut through his short, neat hair along the side of his head. He stood just next to Frostburn's car. His boot was on the small of Emilia's back, and his pistol was aimed at the back of her head.

"Don't try anything. Drop your weapon on the ground. I *will* kill her," he said with a sneer. Whatever cheerful talkativeness had ensnared him earlier seemed to have bled away.

"Okay, you got a deal." Frostburn slowly removed her pistol from its holster and held it loosely out in front of her. "The deal is, I disarm myself. You let her go." She locked eyes with the elf as she took a half-step forward, crouched ever so slowly to the ground, and set her pistol down gently. Frostburn backed away a step and rose to her full height again, her hands held out before her where he could see them.

Emilia's voice regained some of its customary strength, though it was muffled. "Don't you talk about me like I'm not here!"

The elf shook his head, holding Frostburn's stare like a viper and completely ignoring Emilia. "I don't think so. We can deal right here and now, with my little bargaining chip."

"No way. This is between us, and you and I can deal like adults. You only involved her to lure me out here, but we don't have to do things this way."

The elf scoffed. "I shouldn't have even bothered—they're more trouble than they're worth."

"*Frag you!*" Emilia shouted and a Power Ball exploded around her with a crack like thunder.

Frostburn fell backward as the air around Emilia and the elf seemed to break apart, the seams crackling like lightning scorching the atmosphere. The elf convulsed like he was suffering a seizure and dropped his pistol. Blood bubbled from his nose. Emilia was barely visible within the center of the maelstrom of spell-effect that raged around her. And just as abruptly as it had appeared, the spell ended.

The elf ran wobbily around to the other side of the car, using it as cover. Frostburn took cover behind a tree. Emilia rolled across the ground in front of the car and sat on the ground.

"You all right?" Frostburn called from her cover.

Emilia grunted something in the affirmative.

A snarl came from the direction of the elf, and he popped up just enough to launch a Lightning Bolt at Frostburn. Frostburn ducked behind the tree just in time, and the spell cracked through the air and hit the trunk, leaving a jagged scorch mark and sending bits of bark flying in every direction.

Frostburn darted around cover and tried to assess the situation. Her car was maybe ten to twelve meters away. She couldn't see details inside, but she could see vague silhouettes that told her that Emilia's friends had listened to her and were inside. She hoped that none of them tried to play hero. She did *not* need them trying to interfere. It would just get them killed.

Emilia sat on the ground on Frostburn's side, her back up against the rear passenger door, and, Frostburn just noticed, her Ceska Black Scorpion in her hands. She got on her knees, then popped up, and fired a wild burst in the direction of the elf.

"Stop that!" Frostburn shouted. "You'll hit the others!"

The elf ducked, then rose, his own pistol in his hand, and fired back at Emilia. "Yes, Emilia, stop shooting!" he said. "You wouldn't want to hurt your friends."

"Come on, drekface!" Frostburn said. "Who uses kids as meat shields, anyway? Grow up, get away from there, and fight like a professional!"

The elf laughed. "I don't think that would be in my best interest," he said, and squeezed off a three-round burst at Frostburn. Bullets chewed up more of the tree.

"I'll bet HTR is on its way by now," the elf said. "Or Knight Errant. Or both! I don't really care who kills you. Just so long as someone gets the job done."

Emilia crawled on her hands and knees around the back end of the car. Frostburn noticed her and suppressed the urge to tell her to stop, to knock it off, that she was going to get herself killed, to just—What? To get away? This was her fight, too.

Frostburn instead started talking some more, with a few bursts over the hood for emphasis, in an attempt to distract the elf from whatever Emilia was planning. "You really screwed up, didn't you?

Look at us: all three of us trying to get big-time work done all by ourselves. Except now I have help, and you still don't have anyone to back you up. You know, of course, that any high threat response teams showing up here won't show you any leniency. You're just as culpable as us. You ready to die at the hands of farm guards?"

She couldn't make out just what Emilia was doing: she stopped crawling and sat on her butt at the back end of the car. Another burst of gunfire from the elf made Frostburn pop her head back behind her tree and fully distracted her from wondering about Emilia.

"The day is still young," the elf said. "Perhaps I jumped the gun, but that's only because I was excited to get the job done. I would get all I needed out of you, and then kill you. Then, I'd collect my paycheck. Or maybe I could go help off the rest of your team. Either way, I'm satisfied. And through it all, I probably would have kept the respect of my team of baby runners. I probably could have kept using them to do jobs for me. It's a shame, really. This could have been so much less messy."

Something hard tapped at Frostburn's shin. She jumped in surprise and looked down in shock. Her Ceska Black Scorpion floated in the air next to her leg. Frostburn scowled in alarm and momentary confusion, then glanced over at Emilia. Emilia wore a look of intense concentration, and the machine pistol floated gently down to the grass, where it lay next to Frostburn's foot.

Frostburn looked back up and met Emilia's eyes. Emilia looked pale and sweaty, as well as somewhat scorched from her Power Ball, but she shot Frostburn a grin and waggled her fingers. Frostburn allowed a small smile of her own and carefully bent down to pick up the pistol without exposing herself to the elf.

She rested her back against the tree and slid back up to standing. She checked the magazine. Six rounds left. The rest of her ammunition was in her car. For whatever reason—stupidity, adrenaline, distraction... hell, all of the above—she hadn't grabbed more than one spare mag when she'd raided her car for supplies earlier. Whatever the case, she had to put an end to this.She wracked her brain, trying to come up with a plan. The kids were in trouble, in the line of fire as they were, but the elf so far seemed to regard them as a complete non-issue. Emilia was another matter. Her cousin's eyelids fluttered, she swayed, and her eyes looked glassy. A thin line of blood ran down her face from her nostril.

Frostburn looked for the elf, and spotted the top of his head poking out from behind the front end of her car. She scanned the area, looking for a better angle on him, and made a break for a tree a short distance away. He must have been ready for her, though, and a full auto burst split the air, sending a confetti of bark flying all around her.

Suddenly, it felt like someone took a ball-peen hammer to her leg, and it simply gave out underneath her. She stumbled and just managed to grab the tree she was headed toward. She fell to the ground beside it and dragged herself through the grass to a sitting position behind it. She'd been shot. Air blew through a crisp hole in her pant leg, but blood soon soaked the fabric, sticking it to her skin. Frostburn's respiration accelerated, and she caught herself before a panic response could set in. She concentrated, placed her hands around the bullet hole in her leg, and cast a Heal spell. Icy tendrils of magic set in and around the wound with a rush not much less painful than the original gunshot itself, but the pain in her leg soon subsided as the bullet was squeezed out of her wound and fell out onto the grass. However, the pain in her head redoubled as the drain from the spell washed away whatever advantage she had left remaining after the stim patch. Once she could see straight, a quick examination showed the skin of her leg had knit itself back together. She poked experimentally at the spot, found it functional again, and clambered laboriously back up onto her feet.

She peered around the corner. She still wasn't at the right angle to prevent the elf from using her car as cover, but he had less room to move. Emilia was visible, still near the rear of the car, but under cover from the elf. She could see movement inside the car. *Stay inside, stay inside.* She willed the thoughts to reach inside their stubborn child heads and keep them the hell there.

Emilia leaned over and did something in the direction of the elf. Frostburn could hear a sizzling sound and saw acrid smoke tendrils rise from his direction. She suspected it was another Acid Stream and hoped she wasn't trying to melt more metal. The elf did not seem to react; maybe she missed him? But then Frostburn saw motion: Emilia sagged, barely holding herself up off the ground by one bent arm, and heaved with her heavy breathing.

A whirlwind of white smoke curled into being beside Emilia, and grew, spinning like a small tornado. After a moment, the whirlwind had formed a vaguely person-like shape—a spirit of air—teetered over, and fell on top of and around Emilia's now prone form.

The elf called out from behind the car. "Enough!" he said. "I've got Emilia. Give up, and I'll let her go. Keep fighting me, and I'll order my spirit to kill her."

Frostburn experienced a strange kind of calm. Normally, her thoughts might have seized up at a time like this, desperately scrabbling for a plan. Instead, she was frosty. She stepped out from behind the tree and walked directly toward the elf until she had a clear view of him.For a moment, the look on his face was one of victory. He'd done his homework; anyone who knew anything about Frostburn knew that she needed a plan. She insisted on plans. A moment like this would spell defeat, or at least a need to regroup to give oneself time to come up with a new plan.

A loud honk burst out from Frostburn's car—a helping hand from Emilia's friends inside—and the elf leaped to his feet in shock.

Frostburn marched straight at the elf without missing a beat, lifted her arm in a smooth motion, and fired off a three-round burst directly into his face.

She caught his expression just before the rounds hit. His look creased into an expression of surprise before the stick-and-shock rounds slammed into his cheeks and forehead. Then his visage lit up like a lightning storm. He screamed, his eyes rolled back into his head, showing only the whites, he brought his hands jerkily to his head, convulsed violently, and fell down to the pavement in a smoking heap.

The spirit of air unraveled about Emilia and dissipated as though blasted by a strong wind.

Frostburn ran to her side and rolled her over. Emilia's eyes cracked open just a touch as the car doors opened and her friends poured out.

"You okay?" Frostburn said, worriedly scanning and prodding her cousin in her attempt to check her over.

"I'm good," Emilia croaked and managed a half-grin before clutching her stomach with a groan. "At least, I will be."

"Help Emilia and get in the car. We've got to get out of here." Frostburn barked at the others. Even now, she could hear sirens in the far distance.

She dashed over to the elf and checked him for any signs of life. She found none. Patting his body down, she found his pistol and remaining ammo, a handful of patches, her commlink, and *his* commlink.

"This will almost certainly be useful," she said, pocketing the prizes, then she hopped in the car and sped away.

Frostburn drove, and everyone else in the car remained silent. It was a tense drive, and she didn't want to rely on GridGuide at this particular juncture, just in case anyone caught her license plate and called it in to Knight Errant. She wasn't an experienced driver, and it took all of her attention to drive as casually as she could while still putting as much distance as possible between them and the mess they left behind.

She zigged and zagged through residential neighborhoods, moving directly away from where they'd come, yet keeping to less populated roads as often as possible. It was a full ten minutes before Frostburn relaxed enough to allow GridGuide to resume control of her car and drive them in a roundabout route back to her aunt's house.

It was a full five minutes after that before anyone broke the silence. Five minutes passed before anyone said anything. Emilia broke the silence. "Thanks for getting us out of there," she muttered.

"You're welcome," Frostburn said without much feeling.

Silence surrounded them all once again. The four kids Frostburn had rescued first were crammed in a row into the back seat. Their faces betrayed a multitude of feelings, but they kept them to themselves.

After a period of time that ensured whatever she said would be awkward, Frostburn said, "Thanks for the help back there."

"You're welcome," the dwarf boy said cheerfully.

"Okay, you know, no. This is not okay," Frostburn said and spun around in her seat to face them. "What the hell were you guys thinking, going out there? You don't just go into a corporate facility for your introductory job. At least, not without a decent plan. Or equipment. Or backup!"

"Just like you, I suppose," Emilia said, but without much venom in her voice.

Frostburn sagged and only shook her head. "Yeah, I suppose I'm a shit example, aren't I?"

"And I told you spontaneity was superior to plans, and you didn't believe me. So, I told you so," Emilia said.

"No. No, what *you* said was something like: something, something, something, fragging plans are boring, something, something."

Emilia snorted. "You just don't want to admit you were wrong," she said at the same time the red-haired ork girl said, "So you planned that shot to his face? That was impressive!"

Frostburn glowered. "Okay, fine, *sometimes* plans aren't the be-all, end-all. You happy?"

"Oh, it's okay. I get it. You've got a reputation to maintain," Emilia said breezily.

"For crying out loud, I'm not trying to maintain a reputation!"

"Sure, sure." Emilia pretended to be distracted by the passing cityscape. "You wanna tell my friends what you really do to pay the rent?"

The kids in the backseat blinked and listened attentively.

Frostburn pretended to be involved with driving the car. "Not particularly, but I think you have an idea."

"Yeah," Emilia said matter-of-factly. "You're in insurance."

Frostburn's mouth quirked.

"Oh, we saw the whole thing," the sandy-haired ork said. "You're *obviously* an experienced runner." At Frostburn's silence, he added, "Aren't you?"

Frostburn pursed her lips and heaved a sigh. "Okay. You got me. Fine, yes, I'm an experienced runner, and have been for a while now."

The kids grinned at one another.

"But that doesn't mean *you're* ready to go out and do the same kind of stuff! What I do—what *we* do—it's a big deal. People get hurt, sometimes innocent people that don't have anything to do with the job. People die. You have to be ready to deal with that kind of thing. It takes a toll on you."

Frostburn trailed off, remembering the tolls she'd collected over the years.

"But just because you're a runner doesn't mean you can't get the job done and *not* kill people," the dwarf boy offered.

Frostburn sighed again, which broke into a yawn. Her jaw creaked with the strength of it. "Yeah," she acquiesced, "you can certainly try. But even then, if you aren't prepared, if you let your emotions get the better of you, you might still want to bring the hammer down. And you'll have no one to blame for the psychic fallout other than yourself."

She looked over the kids, whose expressions had all turned somber.

"But everyone's gotta make that choice for themselves. Sometimes it's enough to put down the bad guys and *not* kill them. Sometimes it's not. It all depends."

"Well," Emilia said, and draped her arms over the shoulders of her friends in the backseat, "We're all adults here. And like it or not, we're in the business, too. We're in a good position to do things better next time—thanks to you," she added and nodded at Frostburn. "I mean, isn't it nice to know there's more of us out there? That you're not the only one raging against the shit in this sometimes-drekky world? I know it makes me feel better."

Frostburn considered this. All the pressure, all the risk, all the pain, was it really all worth it just to fight the good fight? She allowed herself a small smile and nodded. "Yeah, I suppose it is nice to know. But it'll be even better to know that you idiots aren't running around out there half-cocked while you try to scrub the world clean of assholes."

"Well, yeah, of course," Emilia said. "So the next time we find ourselves with a big job to do, we'll just give our big, tough, *former* corporate security mage buddy a call and let her whip up a nice, safe plan for us. Right?"

Frostburn snorted. "Or you can learn to make up plans on your own, maybe."

"I already told you, plans are overrated," Emilia said airily, and laughed.

An hour later, Frostburn got out of her car and dragged her feet into her team's meeting. She barely noticed or cared about the topic of conversation when she shuffled heavily into the room. Approaching her team's decker, Zipfile, Frostburn dropped the elf assassin's commlink into the dwarf's lap. "I think you'll find something useful on that," she told her and plopped down into an empty chair. "I gotta get some sleep. I think taking time away from work nearly killed me."

Epilogue, One Year Later

Emilia crouched in the shadows of the alleyway, waiting for her signal.

The signal came over their comms, and Emilia made her move. Leading with her favorite non-lethal option, she launched a Blast spell into the group of Humanis thugs who had thought they were going to enjoy a nice, quiet evening at their clubhouse. The effect boomed, cutting through the night air.

The alleyway echoed with the rest of her team's followup attacks. Digger, the blond dwarf, popped out from behind a dumpster kitty-corner from Emilia, and took down the two thugs nearest him with his shotgun full of gel shot. Nexus, the red-haired ork, fired a stream of industrial glue into the middle of the thugs, tripping and sticking up the rest. And the human, Volt, fired his taser into the last thug left standing, dropping him to the ground.

After a few seconds, all of the Humanis goons lay in a sticky heap in the middle of the alleyway. Emilia grinned at her teammates. She spoke into her commlink. "You make the call?"

The team's decker responded. "Yeah, KE's on the way. Time to go."

Emilia nodded. The others jogged back to their van, but Emilia stepped over to the only conscious thug in the bunch. The human moaned and writhed on the ground, trying to figure out just what had happened to him.

Emilia stared down at him, a sneer around her tusks, and said, before she caught up to join her team and get the hell out of Dodge, "This is *our* town. And we have a plan. We're not putting up with your bulldrek anymore."

ZIPFILE

JASON SCHMETZER

Inside her own custom host, which was safely nestled in one of her commlinks, Zipfile stood in front of her murderboard and hummed, eyes darting back and forth between images, text strings, Matrix IDs, a hundred other data points she was putting together.

To her, the room looked like a blank white wall with pictures and folders and string, an image familiar to a century of police procedural fans the world over. In reality, the host system was amalgamating databases of information that she'd gathered. All of this was digital. None of it was real in the meatspace sense of the world, but Zipfile knew it was real.

To her, *eish*, the Matrix was more real than the real.

She chuckled.

It was a shame it was all going to have to go someday. The system was going to have to be broken. She believed that in her heart even more than she believed that the Matrix was real. The system has as much chances as a rookie shooting the puck against a twenty-year veteran goalie. Miracles happen, sure.

But experience almost always wins out in the end.

Simon Dennis' face glared at Zipfile from the center of her murderboard. It was a stillframe capture from Rip Current's security system of him leaving the corp the last time he was there. Zip knew if she tapped the image it would expand into a kaleidoscope of everything she had learned about Dennis so far. She'd already tapped it a bunch of times. Too many.

Which wasn't a great deal.

The Telestrian Johnson had given them the key piece, though.

They knew where he *was*.

But that wasn't enough to get the run done. Not and get away.

Not when the true target was Renraku.

Zipfile looked along one virtual string. AVR Optronics. The company the Telestrian Johnson had given them. A Renraku subsidiary. Maybe a future acquisition. Many times Zip had seen an AA or AAA corp farming out some work to test a smaller company's chops. If they failed the task given them, no worries—that company would never be a threat or a target. Let some other corp waste its time and resources worrying about them.

But a successful little corp...better to gobble them up in acquisition, or ruin them to make sure they never became a challenge to the megacorp's sovereignty. Those kind of jobs—the non-public ones—were the bread-and-butter work of teams like Zipfile's.

That was one of the things she'd have to find out. Renraku would respond much differently if they owned AVR outright than they would if they had just paid the company to do some work.

Zip shrugged. *May as well pay 'em a little visit.* She looked around her private host and then thought about the door.

A moment later she was on PubGrid, looking at the giant Renraku Okoku grid on the virtual horizon. She could go inside—anyone could, since Renraku granted visitor passes to anyone for a short time—and poke around, but she wasn't sure that's where she wanted to go. There was almost no chance anyone legal would give her the answers she was looking for, and doing in a run in the Okoku was never something to take lightly.

Renraku's demiGODs were very often AIs. They were the frontline security of the Grid Overwatch Division, the overarching security system of the Matrix. After hostile deckers, GOD was a hacker's main enemy.

That was trouble Zipfile didn't need.

Instead, she turned her head and found the plain, corporate host-front of AVR Optronics. It was vanilla, out of the box code. Obviously no one there cared a great deal about being found in the Matrix.

Still, they were a known Renraku associate. Maybe a wholly-owned subsidiary. What the box looked like on the outside might mask a great deal of security on the inside.

Zip frowned. She looked down at her persona. She was an ork today, on this commlink.

"Should be safe," she murmured. Then she stepped inside.

This was one of her favorite parts of the Matrix. In meatspace, she'd have to climb into a car running GridGuide and waste the time away while a machine drove her across town. In the Matrix, everywhere was right here. She could connect to the public hosts in Pretoria from here, if she wanted to.

AVR's Matrix lobby looked just like the outside. Gleaming gray walls, no decorations, and a faceless generic persona that probably wasn't even a person sitting at a desk. The persona's smooth face smiled pleasantly, waiting.

Zip suppressed a chuckle.

For real, out of the box.

She had just entered this host through its public portal, but she hadn't taken any further actions. She hadn't, as they said in meatspace, taken the next step. Base personas like this one were programmed to wait until the potential consumer expressed a minimum of interest, to ensure it didn't waste processing power on people who were just poking their head inside to see what was on the other side of the portal. The Matrix equivalent of window-shopping.

Zip stepped forward.

"Good day, welcome to AVR Optronics, may I help you?"

"Who owns this company?" Zipfile asked, curious to hear the answer.

"Our chairman is–" the person began, but Zipfile cut it off.

"That's not what I asked."

"AVR Optronics is owned by its shareholders," the persona said. A real person—a metahuman jacked in—would have said that in a peevish tone, but the persona didn't have the range. *"As all corporations are,"* it added.

Not smugly, as a corp wageslave would have. Especially one with stock options. Any wageslave would want to make sure anyone who heard that statement understood that the wageslave knew corp life was the best life. The only life. Just in case it was a manager masquerading as a nobody to check on their staff.

The persona made it just a statement. It was just a machine, and not a very smart one at that.

Zipfile regarded the persona. "Can I get a list of all your shareholders?"

"I'm afraid that information is proprietary," the persona said. It paused, fake mouth half-open. It was only for an infinitesimal instant, but Zipfile saw it.

She'd been waiting for it.

"Why do you ask?" the persona said, but Zip knew.

The robot was gone. That persona was now a person beneath the mask. Her questions had earned her a metahuman's interest. She was careful not to move or react, being as she was in a borrowed commlink and not running her deck, but she knew if she had been, and she'd taken a closer look around, there'd be more eyes on her that she couldn't see. There was probably patrol IC behind the walls right now, just in case. Maybe even a spider. Or three.

Eish, this could be Renraku; there could be a full-blown AI picking through her commlink without her even knowing it.

But the smart money was on a metahuman.

She was running security for AVR, there certainly would be. Maybe not a troubleshooter, but someone who'd know how to ask the questions from the script labeled "how to tell evildoers from innocent consumers of the corp." This would be a Renraku-trained operator. Maybe a young one, maybe not that good, but still Renraku-trained. And Zipfile had no illusions that she was better than Renraku.

"I'm interested in purchasing stock," she said.

"Our stock is traded on the exchange," she was told.

"Then I'll go there," Zip said, and jacked out. It might be rude— not saying goodbye, not trading pleasantries—but it got her out of there and reset her commlink. Just in case.

Besides, whether it was paranoia or not, it felt like the walls were closing in.

In a blink, she was back in the real. She was in her rack in the safehouse with the rest of the team, but she was alone. She lay there for a second, adjusting to the sensations of her real, dwarf body instead of the virtual reality of being a hapless ork in the Matrix. The commlink she used to jack that persona lay next to her, all hard plastic and plates.

"*Eish*," she whispered.

The Matrix just felt more *real.*

Turning her head, Zip looked at the wall. She closed her eyes and thought of the distance between where she was and where she needed to be.

The actual, physical location of AVR Optronics.

"Frag."

Just for kicks, she picked up the commlink and checked the log. Sure enough, some IC she hadn't even noticed while she was playing it safe had gotten a mark on her. She isolated the code and saved it for later, but she was sure it was a usual first-level tracker any hacker knew about.

Heck, defeating that simple code was one of the first things a baby hacker learned to deal with.

Which gave her an idea.

"Say that again," Yu said. "Slowly."

The elf sat on the small sofa in their safehouse, one heel up on the opposite knee and his arm thrown back across the back of the sofa. Taking up as much space as possible. Unconsciously putting his body in a position that said *I can have all the space I want because I'm better than you. You get to be in the space I leave for you.*

Except...

You forget I'm older than you, bru, Zipfile thought. She didn't let the internal smile get to her face. Dominance games were something she'd learned about as a kid back in the zone.

No shiny elf was going to crowd her out. No way, no day.

Came to it, she had the whole Matrix to go away into, and that sucker was endless.

"I want to hire someone to take a run at AVR," she said.

Slowly, he'd said.

"Can you say ay-vee-are?" Zip added, grinning. "I know you can. Come on. Sound out the letters—"

"You want to tip them off we're coming?"

"No, I want to see how hard they're protected."

"By tipping them off that we're coming."

Zipfile breathed in through her nose, and held it. She reached up and tapped her fingertips against the ports along the side of her shaved head. It helped her think. She would have ruffled her pink mohawk, but she'd just styled it, and that was work she didn't want to do twice before she went out.

And they were going out.

Even if Yu didn't know it yet.

If nothing else, she was tired of being cooped up in this farmhouse. She'd already had a bucket of fun out with Emu. She'd almost gotten to shoot her gun.

"You're supposed to be the strategic thinker," she told Yu. "Think it through."

"I thought I had," he replied. Zip heard the tone. High testy elf.

"AVR is Renraku."

"We don't know that for sure," Yu said.

"Part of my point," Zipfile said. "Now be quiet. Let the adult talk."

"Uh-huh," the eloquent elf said.

"Renraku is somewhat proficient at Matrix security," Zipfile said. "You'll agree with me there?"

"I'd put that statement on par with 'Dunkelzahn liked secrets,' yes," Yu allowed. "But—"

Zip cut him off. "Shh. Still talking." She clasped her hands in her lap, as if she were speaking to a small child and wanted to stay nonthreatening. "We're going to have to go in there soon, yes?"

"Yes."

"More precisely, *you all* are going to have to go in there. I'll probably be along the wall, hiding out, doing what?"

Yu rolled his eyes. "Defeating their Matrix security."

"Whose Matrix security?"

"Renraku," he growled. "If it *is* Renraku. Listen—"

"Still not done."

Yu glared at her, but gestured for her to continue.

"Now. I'm pretty good, but I do better if I know what I'm going into. Hence the need for what the soldier-boys call a recce."

Yu snorted. "A recce is a failure if they get caught," he told her. "Those boys and girls sneak around in the weeds and the mud and then crawl out and no one knows they were ever there."

Zip smiled. "I chose the wrong analogy," she said placatingly.

"It's a good idea," Yu said just as placatingly.

"Except..." Zip said, setting the hook.

"Except what?"

Got you, bru, she thought. It was the same when they bet on the games. Get Yu to a certain point of ego, and he was yours. If the Johnsons ever figured out to how to play him like she could, it'd go hard on them.

"What about this thing I heard Rude talking about? A Trojan Horse?"

Yu rolled his eyes again. "Zip..."

Zip knew when to drop the teasing and press. It was time.

"I need to know what I'm up against before you guys go in there," she said. "It's a subsidiary, yes. They make Renraku parts, yes. It could be they're on their own, and their security is so crap that even Emu could hack her way in and get what you need." She spread her hands. "In which case you can all blow the building to kingdom come and I'll stay here and catch a game."

"But what if it's not?"

Yu sighed and set his foot down. He leaned forward, elbows on knees, and regarded her. She pretended not to notice that he shot the cuffs of his jacket when he did so. There'd be a next time, and she could razz him then. "Yeah. What if it's not?"

Zip couldn't help her grin. "Toldja."

Yu glared at her. "How would we do this?"

"You're the dealmaker. Haven't you ever hired a shadowrunner before?"

"You want to set some dumb slob up to be taken down by Renraku?"

Zip shrugged. "We'll pay them."

"*You'll* pay them, you mean," Yu said.

"If I have to," she said, and meant it. "I don't want someone too good. I want someone dumb and cheap, who thinks they can make their first big score and get noticed by the corps."

"A kid, you mean."

"Maybe. Be better if it's some wageslave trying to get out from under the corp. Extra credit if they work for one of Renraku's competitors in the real. So when they get caught, the heat goes there instead of on us."

"Mm-hmm," Yu said. He was looking at her, but his eyes were unfocused as he thought. Zip had seen him do this before. He was running through his mental tally of people he knew. The only problem with that...

"I don't want to burn a friend," Yu said.

...was that. Zip grinned again.

"No worries, chummer," she told him. "I posted the job before I came in here."

Yu's glare came back.

"You did *what?*"

"Sounds easy," the samurai said.

Zipfile was wearing her ork in the Matrix again. Next to her on the virtual barstool was Yu in one of her backups, a SINless dwarf with a scarring case of acne and a half-shaved head. She hadn't been able to hide her chuckle when she gave him the commlink and wired it to mask his real SIN.

They were sitting in a virtual bar on PubGrid. Zip had forgotten the name as soon as they walked in. It was the kind of place where wageslaves gathered at the end of their day to complain quietly about their bosses, their husbands and wives, their kids, whatever wageslaves complained about.

For all Zip knew, they complained about the same system she wanted to bring down one day.

She liked these kinds of places. She knew about a score of them; most of the big corps had favorite haunts, both inside their grid and outside on PubGrid. The internal ones the wageslaves visited to be seen by their managers, paying the social dues necessary to secure promotion in the office politics dance.

The bars on PubGrid they came to in order to be invisible, where they could complain about those same bosses.

Out the window—because she kept thinking about it—was the pagoda of the Renraku Okoku grid. The Matrix knew what you wanted sometimes before you did. Across the small table from them sat a plain-vanilla Renraku commlink samurai—Dieter, the guy they'd come to hire.

He'd been the first one to answer her ad with the minimum level of competence. It was a low bar, but the bar was there. She didn't want to send in a raw kid to get ICed.

But she didn't need a real peer, either.

"You're sure," Yu's persona said. "We told you who we think they're owned by."

The samurai looked down, at himself, then gestured at his persona. "Do I look like I need an introduction to Renraku?"

"Lots of people buy their commlinks," Zipfile said. Anyone who'd ever shopped for a commlink knew the default setting for a Renraku device was the exact samurai sitting in front of them. Most people did at least a little personalizing.

Not Dieter.

"It's mine," Dieter said.

"You think you can do it, then?" Yu asked.

Zipfile had to hand it to him. Yu knew how to play a part. They'd switched roles, since Zip knew the lingo. She would act as the face, and he would be the nervous Johnson. Yu had transferred just enough nuyen to set up the meeting—another newb sign, who would pay just to talk to someone this green?—and then let her do the talking.

"I know Renraku," Dieter said, as if that explained it all.

"What about a test?" Zip asked.

Dieter shrugged. "Sure. You bought the hour."

"We put our own hacker on this, but she got caught right off," Zipfile said. She slid a small specimen jar across the tabletop. "She got tagged by this."

The samurai regarded the jar. It wasn't actually a jar, of course. They were in the Matrix. The jar was how the host rendered the locked down box Zip had hid the code for the mark she'd gained when she went into AVR's Matrix lobby. Unless the fool took the whole lid off, which would be the code equivalent of unlocking all the safeguards, it was completely safe to look inside.

Dieter touched the lid, lifted it slightly, then closed it. A glance was all he needed.

The Matrix was fast.

Eish, *it's faster than real life,* Zip told herself.

"That's Renraku all right," Dieter said.

"Frag," Yu muttered. He really was a great actor. "Can you beat it?"

Dieter sniffed. "Not for free," he said smugly.

"How much?" Yu asked. "We have to check your skills, after all."

Zip let Yu haggle with the supposed hacker. Inside she smiled. This guy was perfect. He'd seen too many runner shows on trid, and thought he knew how to play it. That he didn't laugh in their face told her all she needed to know.

If she'd been Rude and was looking for a new shooter, asking if he could hack a simple locator mark was like asking a shooter if she knew where to put the magazine in a pistol.

"I think we'll take your word for it," Yu said. "I want to keep our cash ready for the job."

<*How much did he want?*> she commed.

<*Fifty.*> Yu sent back.

She snorted. Sorting that code wasn't worth a *fifth* of that.

"Suit yourself," Dieter said. "Renraku doesn't mess around. Your own runner found that out."

"She sure did," Zip said drily.

She gave him a time and a place to meet. It was in just a few hours. "You can be ready by then?"

"No sweat," he told her. He stood. "One more thing."

"Yeah?"

"I'll be bringing my own security," he said. "I need someone to watch me while I'm in the Matrix."

"But we're in the Matrix now," Yu said.

"We'll need to be closer to the building," Dieter said, as if explaining it to a child. "The things you'll want, you can't just get to from here."

"Oh," Yu said. Dumbly.

"How much security?" Zip asked.

"One guy," Dieter said. "You won't want to mess with him."

"Fair enough," Zip told him. "We won't even come near you."

"See you then," the samurai said. He blinked out as the hacker jacked out.

"Please tell me I don't sound like that when I talk," Zip said as soon as they'd both also jacked out.

Yu snorted and thrust the borrowed commlink at her. "Only when you're peevish."

"I'm never peevish."

"You don't know what peevish is, do you?"

"'Course I do," Zip said. Then, "Frag."

"Gotcha."

"I'm gonna remember that the next time you try and run me up on a game," Zip said, shaking a stubby finger at him.

"I'm sure," Yu said. He looked around, but none of the others were around. "What do you want to tell the others?"

"Nothing," Zipfile said, standing up. "Except Emu. We need a driver."

"So that's the place," Emu said.

She sat in the front of the Ford Americar she'd lifted for the job. The blue paint was chipped and peeling. The ceiling liner dropped and kept rubbing against Zipfile's mohawk. It felt like a bug in her hair, but she made herself stop swiping at it every time she shifted her weight in the backseat.

"Looks like," Yu said. Zip just grunted.

AVR Optronics looked just like the small factory it was, deep in a decrepit industrial park. High wire fences with ten-meter concrete guard towers like squat turrets every hundred meters or so, lots of dead ground between the fence and the factory walls.

In other words, not laid out by a moron, but not a fortress, either.

If Zip put on her glasses, she knew her AR would be full of warnings and dire messages to keep away on pain of pain or worse. It was all meant to keep the idle away, and impress on anyone else the terrifying majesty of the power of the corp.

Or something.

Zip knew from experience there were at least four easy approaches in plain sight.

"We know how this street meat's gonna do it?" Emu asked.

"Not yet," Zip told him. "I expect a message any time."

"Amateurs," Yu muttered.

"Better him than us," Zipfile said.

"I know," Yu said, but there was something in his voice.

Emu looked over her shoulder at Zipfile, eyebrow raised. Zip shook her head. She touched controls on her deck—she had work to do shortly.

"She's right, you know, mate," Emu told Yu.

"I know," he repeated.

"For real," Emu insisted. "Sending her in blind would be like asking you to go into a meet with no research, no planning." She chuckled. "In other words, without doing all the stuff she does for you before you go into places. Be like you walking in buck naked without that fancy clobber."

"I just don't like risking tipping them off," Yu said.

Emu snorted. "You're thinking 'bout it wrong." She glanced back. "Zip?"

"Yeah?"

"How many times you think someone's hit this place in the Matrix tonight?"

Zip looked up at the building, eyes unfocused, thinking. "Off-site, you mean?"

"Yes."

Zip shrugged. "Ballpark it around fifteen or twenty times since midday. Serious ones that demand attention, at least. Not just kids lobbing data spikes at the firewalls and running away from the trackers."

Yu looked back and forth between them. "You're joking."

"Whole world's on the Matrix," Zip reminded him. "And we ain't the only runners."

"Yes, but—"

"No buts." Emu pointed out the window. "There's a good chance there's a whole other team out there tonight, doing their own run right now. That's if your rented idiots show up and can even get through the fence."

"Maybe not here," Zip interjected.

"Still," Emu said. "Point is, we're not priming the trap, doing this. Places like this get hit all the time. Security is always chasing something. And besides—" she grinned, "—could be these morons show us something we didn't think of."

"Speaking of," Zip said, holding up one end of a cable. "Your babies done yet?"

"Just," Emu said after a second of communing with her drones. "Try it now."

Zip plugged the cable into her deck and waited for a telltale to glow green. When it did, she smiled and leaned back into her chair. She had a connection to the main data trunk that served the building. That would give her an excellent access point for the portal into the factory's systems. One of Emu's drones had run the other end of the cable out and spliced it in.

A nice piece of work. Not that Zip would ever admit it to Emu.

"Any real chance these blokes *aren't* Renraku?" Emu asked.

"Not really," Yu said. "There's no paperwork we can find, but they make deck components. Not commlinks—*decks*. That too much money, too much tech, too much *risk* for Renraku to let too far outside the family."

"Didn't figure so," Emu said.

Zipfile opened her mouth to contribute, but a shitty little Nissan pulled past them and continued down the street. It was a ubiquitous choice, as invisible as the Americar they were waiting in. A dozen just like in varying paint jobs were parked along the street. Several had driven by, but this one was different.

This one pulled over—on the same side of the street as the factory—and stopped near one of the guard towers.

"You've gotta be kidding me," Emu said.

Zip blinked as an AR ping popped up. *On-site.*

"That's them."

"Smooth," Yu said.

Zip leaned forward, one hand on each of the seats in front of her, trying to see. Two men stepped out of the car, in full view of guards, God, and radar. One was short, dressed all in black, and carrying a small case. The other was taller, bulkier, wearing a large black leather duster. The handle of something jutted up over his shoulder.

"Is that a sword?" Yu asked.

"I think so," Emu said. She squinted. "Is that jacket red, or are my eyes barmy?"

"It's red," Zipfile told them.

"Does he think he's a Red Samurai?" Emu scoffed.

"I think he does," Zip said. The three of them shared a look. "They weren't expensive," she said to Emu.

The rigger shook her head and laughed.

If you ignored the sword, the two looked like they were taking a nonchalant stroll down a sidewalk. They walked along until they were beneath the concrete buttress of the guard tower, then stopped.

"They're doing it there," Emu said, *sotto voce.*

Zip just watched.

The ersatz Samurai pulled a pistol out of his jacket and looked up. They were beneath the lip of the platform atop the tower, which meant if it was manned they were out of sight. Zip knew from her initial recon the towers weren't manned. They were there for intimidation and to host sensors. One decker in the building could monitor a whole wall of cameras for a lot less investment than a platoon of security strung out along the wall.

The big guy fired. Dust chipped off the wall near a camera. The small guy cowered and held his case over his head.

"Missed," Yu muttered.

The big guy fired again, this time fragging the camera that looked down on them.

The little guy—Dieter—sat down and opened his case.

Right there.

On the sidewalk.

"Dunkelzahn's balls," Zip muttered. She sat back. "They're really doing it right there." She put her deck in her lap and wriggled to get a good dent in the Americar's cheap upholstery. "Be right back."

She didn't wait to see if Yu and Emu answered through their laughter.

A millisecond later, she was looking at the portal to AVR through the cable Emu's drone had placed. She slid closer, readying the custom SIN she'd ginned up across the afternoon. It would be good enough to get her into the AVR network.

She exhaled. The AVR host showed itself as a guardpost where she had to swipe a card. She did so, trying not to hold her breath. This was an easy hack, one she'd done a thousand times, just as she had to get Yu through the door into Telestrian a few days ago on Denny Way. But she never lost that thrill.

The door panel clicked green.

Got ya, she thought with a grin.

She patted the wall outside the portal and a small camera appeared: a repeater feed that would show her the portal wherever she was, through her deck.

She entered the AVR host and stopped to look around. The host presented itself as the inside of the factory. A lot of corps did that, on the theory that it made the Matrix presence of a facility as easy to navigate as the live one. Personas walked the halls as if they were people, going about the Matrix tasks of any business. Still, there were differences.

Where a meatspace building would have metahuman security, the Matrix had intrusion countermeasures. Shining black spiders stood in artificially large corners bent counter to the laws of physics so they fit. Floating eyes of tracker IC meandered along the hallways.

Because she knew what to look for, Zip felt the presence of even more dangerous IC floating behind the walls.

A few seconds inside, and already she knew her plan had been smart.

There was some heavyweight security inside AVR.

Still, lots left to learn.

"Map," she said, and one appeared in front of her. Her hacked persona had the right permissions for a basic map. It wouldn't show her the really meaty parts of the building. She hadn't set up that senior of an AVR employee. But it would show her departments. That was enough.

No corp manager wanted their wageslaves to have trouble getting to where their work needed to be done. Maps were usually available. *Eish*, Zipfile had spent many a quiet morning hacking into the public maps of little corps all across Seattle, changing map destinations and reassigning offices just for fun. The time she'd put corporate new hire training in the CEO's private washroom still made her laugh. And wonder why the CEO had a camera in his water closet.

Besides. This map was more than she had before she came in.

This run already had a little paydata.

She blinked, and the map disappeared, ingested into her AR and persona. She thought about security and felt the right way to go, so she went. The office she wanted was two floors up in the same quadrant of the building.

Grinning, she focused on that.

And she was there.

Stairs were for meatspace.

Two spiders hulked outside the glowing portal for the main security office. She ignored them and turned down the hallway, looking for an empty office. Empty offices were everywhere in the Matrix.

A cube warrior in the real could have a corner office in the Matrix. And corps had a lot of work that could only be done while jacked in, corps that worked with AAAs like Renraku more than most. It didn't cost the corp any more to have a wageslave with a cubic meter of meatspace workspace have as much in the Matrix as they wanted.

And just like in the real, one of the perks of having an office was ducking out of it.

The third door she tried was open—her persona was keyed to recognize locked doors as occupied rooms—and she went in. It was a pretty basic Matrix workspace: the apparent size of a football field, opulent beyond belief, and completely impossible in the real.

Zipfile sighed.

This was the kind of nonsense the system produced. This was why the system had to go.

But not today.

Today she walked over to the wall and wiped it with her sleeve. The wall flickered, but stayed opaque. Frowning, Zipfile wiped it again. This time a window appeared, showing her the office on the other side.

The security office.

An endless wall of monitors stretched off as far as she could see. Row after row of blank personas watched them as if their silicon gods were going to appear through them: agents, designed to notice anything untoward in the camera feed.

Zipfile lowered her arm and tapped her finger against the wall. The office scene shimmered and reformed as if she were looking over one of the persona's shoulders.

<*I'm in,*> she commed Yu. <*What's going on?*>

<*You can't see?*>

<*Patience.*>

Zipfile's fingertips danced. She flickered between a dozen views before realizing how stupid she was being. There was no need to go looking at every view. The idiot samurai wannabe had already shot out a camera.

Her thumb tapped her index finger. The image steadied on a persona waving its arm. Static filled the screen in front of it.

Zip snapped her fingers.

Suddenly the window had sound.

"Report," a woman's voice said.

"Camera East Bravo Seven nonresponsive," the agent replied.

"Show me the nearest feeds," the troubleshooter said.

Zipfile rubbed her ring finger against her pinky. The image of a shaven-headed ork with silver-tipped tusks appeared. The troubleshooter sat inside a ring of panels, her hand resting on the giant eyeball of a tracker IC as if it were a pet. It was all Zipfile could do not to laugh at the image.

A panoramic view appeared in front of the ork. It showed the tower from a distance—the next guard tower, obviously—and Zip could barely make out the shapes of the two men squatting near it.

<*Looks like our friend is going in,*> Yu sent.

"Good," Zipfile murmured. She touched her middle-finger to her thumb; her deck began recording every feed into it. Then she winked her left eye. A new window opened in her vision, fed from her deck from the camera she'd left outside the portal.

A persona stood there in blacked-out ninja attire. He held the chains of a *kusarigama* loosely in his hands.

"You've gotta be kidding me," Zip muttered.

The ninja stalked forward, swinging the chain-sickle. He swung it around just like the heroes did in the trid shows that were so popular.

"Don't..." Zipfile said.

He struck the scanner with his weapon.

"Drekhead," she murmured.

The box sparked and sputtered, but the light turned green and the ninja stalked through the portal, into AVR proper.

<This is gonna be fast,> Zip sent.

<We're ready,> Yu replied.

<Emu, get a camera on him and run me a feed,> she ordered.

<Two seconds,> the rigger said

Zipfile looked back at the window into the security office. The troubleshooter ork was leaning forward, looking at a new screen. It showed the ninja in the same digital lobby Zipfile had come through.

"Not very smart," the ork said.

"Get him," she ordered, and her voice echoed through the entire Matrix building.

A third window opened up in front of Zipfile; a view of the real world, showing a camera feed from one of Emu's drones. The wannabe hacker, Dieter, sat slumped against the side of the building. The big guy in the coat stood in front of him, slowly looking back and forth up and down the sidewalk. They couldn't be any more obvious if they tried.

Zip touched the wall near her window and then swiped down at her waist, tethering the window to her persona. Then she thought about the lobby. This was going to be a show she didn't want to miss.

She got there just in time to see the first spider step off the wall and go toward the ninja. Several normal AVR personas were standing there like rubberneckers, pointing at the black-clad ninja and private-comming back and forth.

"Sure," she whispered. No one could hear her words. "just barge in like you own the place." She snorted. "'I know Renraku,'" she parroted.

The ninja set his feet and spun his *kusarigama*.

"Stupid," Zipfile mutterered.

The spider attacked, the host presenting its attack as actual bullets. It fired a burst that stitched across the ninja's chest before he could unleash his own weapon. Zipfile concentrated on trying to watch three streams of actions at once.

In front of her, the ninja flew backward, not dead but hurt. He crashed against the wall, arms wrapped around his chest. His chain-sickle lay on the floor near him.

In the security room, the silver-toothed ork grinned.

In the real, the slumped-over hacker's meatspace body flinched as if it had been kicked.

The spider was using hard biofeedback.

This was black IC.

Zipfile jacked out.

"I've seen enough," she said to Yu and Emu. A twisted thought brought the video feed from Emu's drone up on her AR. The big guy was still looking both ways.

While she watched, Dieter's body flinched again.

Harder.

"How bad is it?" Yu asked.

Zip sat forward. "Save it." She slapped Emu on the shoulder. "Get us over there." The rigger stared at her. "Now!"

The ork didn't hesitate; she turned around, put the Americar in gear, and stepped on the accelerator. The Ford wasn't a sports car—it didn't have much in the way of giddyup—but they were moving.

"What are we doing?" Yu asked calmly.

"He's in over his head."

"Wasn't that quite the point?"

"Shut up."

The big fake Red Samurai saw them coming. He turned to face them, reaching up to pull the sword down from over his shoulder. He held it out in front of him as if it were a baseball bat.

"A sword," Emu said, laughing. "I don't know whether to shake my head or give him kudos for balls." She leaned over the steering wheel. "We're in a car, mate!"

Emu put the car half up on the curb in front of the duo. Zip slid over in her seat, closing the AR video feed, and triggering the window down. She leaned out as much as she could.

Americars weren't built for dwarfs.

"Move along," the fake samurai said menacingly, or tried to.

Anyone who'd dealt with Rude when he was pissed off knew what menace was. This guy didn't hold a candle to that.

"Save it!" Zip shouted. "Get your friend out of there!"

"We're here on Renraku business," the guy said. He was an ork, or pretending to be one. Zip didn't want to look at his yellowed tusks too close. A lot of big guys pretended to be something they weren't.

"Hitting a Renraku building," Yu said, rolling his window down. "Seriously."

"I said move along," the protector said.

For a moment Zipfile why he wasn't brandishing the pistol he'd used to shoot the camera out.

Behind him, the hacker flinched worse than before and fell over. His commlink fell off his lap. Zipfile stared at it; no wonder he hadn't shown any finesse—he wasn't even using a cyberdeck.

"Look at your buddy," she said, pointing.

"Like I'm gonna fall for that."

"Dragon's blood," Zipfile heard Emu mutter before the driver's door opened. Emu stepped out. A *thump* on the roof had to be her elbow hitting the metal. The loose liner shook, and Zipfile felt particles of decayed adhesive fall on her shaved head.

The ersatz samurai now had at least one pistol pointed at him.

"Look at your mate," Emu ordered, "or else I'll pop you where you stand."

The big guy stared at her, then glanced over his shoulder.

"Dieter!?" he lowered the sword and spun around, kneeling beside his friend. "You okay? Wake up!"

Zip frowned. "Is he breathing?"

"What?" The big guy looked up. Why wouldn't he be breathing?"

"He went up against a spider," Zipfile said.

"How do you know that?"

"For frag's sake, we're your Johnson!" Yu shouted.

"My what?"

Emu sat down and closed the door. "Okay. I'm done. These yokels are on their own."

Behind the duo, a siren spun up on the main building.

Zipfile resisted the urge to agree with Emu. Instead, she shouted to get the big guy's attention. "Hold up his commlink," she said, when she had his attention. He fumbled with it for a minute, then held it up.

"So I can see the panel," she told him patiently.

He turned it. It was black. None of the telltales were lit, not even the power indicator. Zipfile probed for it in her AR and came up blank.

"It's a brick," she said. "You need to run."

"I'm not leaving him."

"That's nice and all, but he's a vegetable," she told him. "Best case, he dies before security gets here." She shrugged. "Worst case, you're still here when they do."

"Could be locals," Yu put in. "Or it could be Knight Errant." He lowered his voice. "They came after us a couple nights ago. We barely made it out."

The big guy looked at the elf, then back down at his friend, then at Zipfile. She nodded at him. "It hurts. But he wouldn't want you to get caught."

He set the dead commlink back down, then stood. He looked at the sword still in his hand. Then turned and threw it down the sidewalk.

The blade broke when it landed.

"Figures," Zipfile heard him mutter.

Then he took off, lumbering toward the car they came in.

Yu, Emu, and Zipfile watched him go.

"Betcha that's actually *his* car," Emu said. "He didn't bother to lift a clean one."

"No bet," Zipfile and Yu chorused.

The little Nissan tore out with a squeak of tires and was gone a moment later. Emu put the Americar in gear and looked over his shoulder at Zipfile. "We got what we needed?"

Zip nodded.

Emu pulled away.

Yu twisted around in his seat so he could look directly at her. "So? How bad is it?"

Zip shook her head.

"It's bad."

"It's Renraku for sure," she said about thirty minutes later, as they watched the Americar go up in flames. They were in Redmond, near the Barrens, leaning against Emu's Commodore. "A little corp like AVR would never use black IC that quick without a big corp to back them up."

"It wasn't just that Dieter was that clueless?" Yu pressed.

"He was clueless," Zipfile said. She saw the spider firing again in her mind. "But they could have kicked him with a simple reboot; he was running on a commlink." She stared at the fire and relished the knowledge that the ceiling liner would never touch her head again.

"So the Johnson was telling the truth." Yu stood, arms crossed, watching the flames.

"Looks that way," Zip said.

"Bloody hell," Emu muttered.

"Exactly."

After a moment, Yu looked down at her. "Can you do this?"

Zipfile looked back up at him. "It won't be easy."

"That's not what I asked."

"I know."

Yu stared at her for another moment, then looked away. Zipfile was glad he did. She was scared. Excited, too, yes—it's hard to be scared in the abstract of a corp, even an AAA giant like Renraku, when your whole life's plan was to smash the system that enabled them to exist.

But she saw that spider tearing into Dieter.

She saw his body on the sidewalk.

Empty. Drooling.

Alone.

Where she'd left it.

It wasn't that he was dead that bothered her. She'd sent a lot of people to their end, back in Pretoria and here since. It wasn't pleasant, and she'd always have the nightmares, but it was necessary. Bringing down the system would cause a die-off on a scale she couldn't imagine. She wasn't naïve enough to not realize that. The very corps she wanted to kill kept the lights on, kept food in the stores, and the tranquilizing stupidity of trid on the air.

But knowing all those people would suffer wasn't the same thing as watching them die on the sidewalk in front of you.

Or having sent them there, personally, herself.

"Let me work on it," she told them. She turned and palmed the door to the Commodore. "Let's get back."

No one spoke the whole ride back to the safehouse.

"Can't believe ya did that without me," Rude said, rumbling.

"You wouldn't fit in the Americar," Emu put in, chuckling.

The troll looked at the rigger and then back at Zipfile. "We coulda shared a seat. She don't take up much room."

Zip laughed and ignored the quip. "So that's where we stand so far."

"Nothing about magic you saw?" Frostburn asked.

"No, but I'm not sure it'd have been obvious," Zip said. She raised an eyebrow at their mage. "Would it?"

"Probably not," Frostburn allowed. "I can drive by, see if I can get a sense of anything."

"I'll drive," Emu said. "I need to get some new cars anyway."

"Ya leave a drone to keep an eye on the place?" Rude rumbled.

"No," Emu told him. "We didn't think of it."

"Shame," Rude said. "Be interestin' to see who came ta collect the poor sap."

"Be less interesting to have whoever it was find our drone and track us back here," Yu pointed out. "We've already been burned once. Literally."

"Yeah, yeah," the troll said, waving a hand.

"That doesn't get us closer to getting in the building," Frostburn said.

"Getting in the building isn't the problem," Zipfile said. "I can get us in. I was just in there." She looked each of them in the eye for a long moment. "The problem is it's gonna be hard as Rude's head once we get in there."

Rude chuckled. "That's pretty damn hard."

"Fine," Frostburn said, glaring. "It doesn't get us any closer to getting the job done."

"No," Yu said, "it doesn't."

No one spoke for a long moment.

"So what do we do?" Emu asked.

"We could put out feelers," Yu said.

"From way the hell out here?" Frostburn asked. She gestured out the window, toward the Snohomish River. "It'd take a month for these supposed feelers to even get near the city."

"No one's bothering us, are they?" Emu snapped. She'd been the one to find the safehouse, after all. "We'll see anyone coming for kilometers, won't we?"

"That's a few klicks more'n I need," Rude said, patting his holster.

"Careful with that," Yu said. "Might be loaded."

Rude grinned. "It's always loaded," he said, and grabbed his crotch. "Jus' like this is."

"Nice," Yu muttered. "But really—what next? The Johnson isn't going to give us forever to get this run done."

"We're going to need something to make that building go boom," Zipfile said. When everyone else stared down at her she shrugged. "What? That's not my thing, sure, but *eish*, it's a big damn building."

"She's not kidding," Emu said. "It is a big damn building."

"It's not the size of the building—" Rude began, but the whole rest of the team chorused to interrupt him.

"Shut up!"

"We can't just disrupt production," Zipfile put in. "The Johnson said—"

Yu cut her off. "The Johnson said destroy it and make it obvious it was intentional." He frowned and looked into the middle distance. "That's not enough, though."

"Did you miss the part where it's a big damn building?" Emu asked. She stalked out of the room and into the small kitchenette and rummaged around in the chiller. "Seems like enough to me."

"He's right," Rude put in.

"You feeling okay?" Frostburn asked, staring at the troll. "You just said Yu was right about something."

"He is," Rude said. "This time." He looked around, then shook his head. "The Johnson—the other Johnson, Dennis. He made us look like fools. Nearly got Elfy-pants here killed." Two big, meaty fists rubbed against each other. "I know I want payback."

"I do, too," Yu murmured.

"Me, too," Zipfile put in.

"We all do," Emu said from the kitchen. "But how do we get to him?"

"He'll be in the building," Rude said, shrugging. "We do the job. Bring the sucker down. He'll pop like a tick with a building on top of him."

"No," Yu said. "I want to see his face. I want him to know we did it."

"That's harder," Zipfile said.

Yu looked down at her with the same expression he wore when his team was losing and losing stupidly. "You're arguing?"

Zipfile shook her head. "Nope. Just telling you it'll be harder."

Harder didn't mean impossible. It just meant more moving pieces. Zipfile was a hacker. She knew all about moving pieces. "So how do we do it?"

Rude snuffed and sat down on the couch. It creaked dangerously, and from the way the center already almost touched the floor, it wasn't the first time he'd done so. "I figure we blow the place up," he said, waving his hand at the others. "Y'all figure out the rest."

Zipfile rolled her eyes.

Yu breathed deep and shook his head. "Emu, you and Frostburn go see if there's anything magical at AVR. If there is, we'll figure out how to deal with that, and if there's not, well...we win one."

"That'd be a nice change," Frostburn said.

"Rude." Yu said. "Blowing up the building?"

"Can do."

"How?"

"Explosives, Elfy-pants?"

Zipfile watched Yu control himself. "Yes. How much, where is it, and how will we get it on-site?"

Rude frowned. "Oh."

"Yes, 'oh.'"

"I know a guy."

"Go talk to him?"

"I get a ride?" Rude asked, looking at Emu.

Emu traded looks with Frostburn. "Guess we're not taking the Commodore." She looked back at Rude. "Sure, come on. We'll steal something big enough for you."

Zipfile looked up at Yu. "What about you?"

Yu swallowed. "I'm going to go see if the triads can help us find Simon Dennis."

"You sure about that?" Zipfile asked. "You've...asked a lot of them lately." She was still a little amazed the gang had just let them into the crash room before they found this safehouse.

"I'll be careful," he told her. "What about you?"

"I'll stay here and try and run down some leads."

Yu looked at the others. "We ready then?"

"Waitin' on you," Rude said, from right next to him.

Yu closed his eyes and breathed out, slowly. "Let's go."

A moment later the safehouse was quiet, and Zipfile was alone. She looked around, then giggled. They were a crazy bunch, but they were family. She wouldn't trade them for anyone, not even her brother standing here right next to her.

She rubbed her hands against her head. Her mohawk drooped against her fingers.

First thing, she decided.

A shower.

A long one.

When Zipfile got out of the bathroom, she decided to run a thought experiment. What if Dennis wasn't Renraku? The odds were pretty good he was. Why else be working in a Renraku factory? Zipfile snapped a hash into the AR projection in front of her and bit her lower lip.

The target was Telestrian. Who hated Telestrian enough to send them on that first run?

"*Eish*, that's a dumb question," she muttered.

Everyone hated Telestrian that much. Rival corps, UCAS, even lower-middle management inside Telestrian itself. She'd seen any number of cases of runners sent to ruin a boss in the way of a promotion. It was one of the things that drove her so mad about the system: these parasites cannibalized each other every day.

"Got to go," she whispered, the old words. *The system. It got to go.*

From her pocket she pulled a datachip, a copy of the one Dennis had given them before that first, fateful Telestrian job. Of course she'd made a copy, not that she'd told the others.

Unless she had to.

Data like this you don't just throw away.

She slid the chip into a dedicated, air-gapped non-PAN chipreader. It displayed the result in a holo separate from her AR. The copy she'd made had carried over the base read-only memory of the chip itself, manufacturer data and such. It wasn't much, but it was a start.

It was manufactured by the third-largest chip distributor in Seattle.

"Great odds," she muttered.

She was looking for a needle in a stack of haystacks. Whatever the hell that meant. Seattle slang was weird. These people said the weirdest drek.

Clicking the chipreader off, Zipfile sighed. She picked up a commlink from the coffee table and slid it over her head, careful to keep from pressing down the back of her mohawk. It was hell to reshape after the gel set, especially when it was still damp. She snuggled back against her couch cushions and keyed her commlink.

An eyeblink later, she was on the grid.

The worldscape of the Matrix appeared before her. She looked down at her hand—and it did look like her hand, since she'd long since made this commlink's persona look just like herself. She stood on the PubGrid again, with the worlds of the global nets around her. She regarded them, thinking, then shrugged and looked at Shiawase Central. A thought, a tug at her mind, and she was there.

It was a moment's thought to get to Tapper's, a Matrix dive bar where bored Shiawase wageslaves went to complain about the day and ogle the odd bit of the wider world that came to visit. Zipfile knew it well; she watched games in the off-season with a couple guys who ran a quadrant of the Seattle city power grid.

One of them was there now; she recognized the basic meta-link personal slouched at the bar, nursing a drink. She walked over and sat down next to him. This was the Matrix, so the barstool seemed low enough for her to climb on naturally. If she'd been on her deck, in a different persona, it might have seemed normal metahuman height.

"Jobber," she said, nodding. She tapped her fingers two times against the bar and a glass appeared in front of her. "Rough day?"

"Same day," Jobber said. He looked at her, smiled, and nodded. "Just like all the others. Keeping the lights on."

"It's good work," she said. She didn't mean it. Shiawase did more work than anyone keeping the system alive. She'd like nothing better than to stay on this grid all day, mucking things up and pointing out flaws in the grids. The millions of wageslaves only let the system run because they were too comfortable and complacent to care. Turn off the lights, shake up the system a little, and they'd see the flaws right off.

Maybe they'd help her bring it all down.

But that was a job for another day.

"Doesn't pay too well," Jobber grumbled. He held up his drink. In a blink it changed to ice alone in the glass. He shook it. The sound was like coins in a glass.

Zipfile grinned. This was an old dance.

"Got to make ends meet," she said. "Tough world, even when you're not betting on the losing team."

Jobber nodded sagely.

Zipfile smirked. She loved this part. Here she was, on a simple meta-link running nothing more complicated than a basic masker. Jobber was doing the same. This wasn't the hacking of story and legend. This was just two people, sitting in a bar somewhere in an invisible but very real sea of ones and zeroes, making a deal. Getting some of their own where they could.

It was endemic in the system.

It got to go.

But not today.

"Turns out I got some extra nuyen," Zipfile said. "Maybe we could have a friendly wager."

Jobber grunted. "No harm in that."

"I got a serial number," she told him. "From a chip your people make."

"We make a lot," Jobber agreed. "Which brand?"

Zipfile told him.

Jobber gave a Gallic shrug that would have done Napoleon proud. "Not my department. But I know people."

"I might guess who bought this chip. I guess right, I keep my money. I guess wrong, you tell me the right answer and win some cash." She glanced around, but the Tapper was almost empty. Besides, who would object to a friendly wager?

Jobber rubbed his chin. "Depends on the bet."

"Four hundred."

Jobber shrugged. "Deal."

Zipfile sent him the serial number. "Find out who bought this, so you'll know if you win?"

"Two seconds," Jobber said. His persona froze while he sent his attention elsewhere. Zipfile dipped her fingertip in the glass in front of her. It was cold, and she once again marveled at the technology that could make her believe her finger was in cold liquid. They could do so much in this world.

It was so *real*.

All that power. All that capacity.

And still the system persisted.

Go to go.

Eish.

Not today.

Jobber's persona flickered as he came back. "Got it." He pressed his fingertip against the bar and a slip of paper appeared.

Zipfile grinned. "You sure? You remember what happened when you bet against me at that last game?"

"Luck's gotta change sometime."

"Okay." Zipfile sniffed. "John Smith bought that chip."

Jobber crowed. "Wrong!" He slapped the bar with his free hand. "Pay up!"

Zipfile grinned and transferred the money. Then she held out her hand. "Your turn?"

Jobber slid the paper across the bar. "All yours."

Zipfile picked up the slip of paper and slid the name into a cache file. She didn't even look at it. Instead, she picked up her glass and drained it in one pull. Her mind tried to convince her it was good Russian vodka. She knew better than to believe it.

"I'll get it back next time," she said, standing up.

Jobber spun on his barstool and eyed her. "Why pay for that, friend?" he asked. "You could've gotten it yourself with about five minutes' effort."

Zipfile just grinned. "Gotta help a friend out now and then," she said, and meant it. It was a waste of her skills to hack into Shiawase sales records. Kids did that sort of thing in school to prove each other cool. She could do it, sure.

Eish, she could do it in her sleep.

But it also paid to keep connections open. Someday the system would come down, and all anyone would have would be themselves and the relationships they'd built. Keeping her currency up with people like Jobber was expensive, but worth it.

Two birds and all that.

Someone had double-crossed her team. Her family, the people she was closest to in the world outside her brother.

It was worth the cash to find out who burned them.

Worth more than the cash.

She waved to Jobber and left the bar.

Back on the PubGrid, she looked at the name.

Henrik Gould. There was a SIN.

"What the hell kind of name is Henrik Gould?"

Zipfile groaned and slipped out of the Matrix. She needed a snack before she started into this.

Henrik Gould was nobody.

Literally nobody.

His SIN was fake.

"I don't have time for this," Zipfile muttered. She stood in the kitchen, looked at the data displayed on her AR while her microwave ran. On the counter across from her was the empty can from whatever noxious crap Emu had swigged down before taking off with the others.

While she waited, Zipfile queued up a search agent and sent it into the public Matrix, looking for anything else fake Henrik Gould might have bought. It was a long shot, but every once in a while long shots paid off.

She'd lost money on one half-court shot before realizing the truth of that statement.

In the meantime, she decided to come at it from another angle.

"Rip Current Sea Lanes," she muttered.

The company she'd found that owned the warehouse Yu had wanted hit, the job that had started all of this, might be a good place to start. It was a Renraku shell company according to Yu, but Zipfile wanted to test if that story held water.

Earlier she'd assumed it because it made thinking about the whole thing easier, but what if it wasn't true. And if it wasn't true, how would she prove it? She knew from checking security scans the office was already empty, as if it had been unoccupied the whole time.

Her microwave *ding*ed done, but she ignored it. Instead, she stepped out of the small kitchen and looked at the chipreader still sitting on the couch. Jobber had put her onto who might have bought the chip, but that road was cold.

She still had the code.

When Yu had first shown her the drive, she hadn't looked any deeper than the installer. It hadn't seemed prudent, and having seen the effect it'd had on the Telestrian servers, she wasn't sure she wanted it open anywhere near her own network. There could be all kinds of viruses on that little chip.

Eish.

But she had to find out.

And it wasn't getting near her network.

Which meant she was going to have *read code.*

Eish.

Anything was simpler.

Zipfile knew she was a good hacker. She knew it. Her peers knew it. She could run the Matrix and come back with the paydata every day of the week. It was her against the system on those runs, and the system got to go.

So she won.

But she hated reading other peoples' code.

Hated. It.

Forgetting her food, she went into her bedroom, under the bed, and got out an old flatscreen 'puter.

Reading code.

In the *real.*

With her *eyes.*

"*Eish.*"

A couple hours later, she knew two things.

First, whoever wrote this code needed to go back to school.

It was sloppy drek.

And second, she'd just wasted a couple of hours.

The code was stupid.

Eyes burning, Zipfile learned forward and ran her stubby finger down the screen, muttering the code logic out loud as she went.

"Load, check, send notification, destruct."

It was a glorified ping.

This file, once you got past the encryption, sent a notification to another file that basically announced "Hey *bru*, I'm here now. Do your thing."

Zip swiped the flatscreen closed and leaned back in her chair.

None of what had happened to Yu inside Telestrian had been driven directly by this file. All the lights, all the noise, it had come from something else. Whatever Dennis had paid them to plant hadn't been the real target.

The whole run had been one of those things: a distraction, or else the final piece of something else.

"*Eish.*"

She scrolled through the code again and looked at the destination file. It was just a hash, not even a real location. The code didn't even give an identifier. Dunkelzahn's balls, she'd have to crawl the whole Matrix to find another bit of code like it.

She sighed. Hard.

Not she, herself.

She leaned back and jacked in, dipping into the Matrix. She came up on her local network, above and separate from the flat unreal plane of PubGrid. It was a virtual recreation of her apartment, here in the unreal.

Zipfile whistled. A small dog appeared—a search agent—and she fed it the hash code from the Telestrian file. It sniffed, yipped twice, and vanished. Just like the agent out looking for signs of Henrik Gould, this one would sniff around for that hash code.

It wasn't a long shot.

Not by a mile.

It was a light-year shot.

Which meant it wasn't enough.

Zipfile stepped out the door to her apartment. A blink later she was on the PubGrid. She looked around, her mind considering and discarding options, before she settled on one. A sign for the place she was thinking of appeared in front of her.

Joe's.

Freaking *Joe's*.

She hadn't been back to Joe's since her first week in Seattle. The guide download she'd skimmed told it was the center of Seattle's Matrix life, so she wanted to see what that was like. Even in Pretoria she'd heard of Seattle. She'd walked through the doors, on a meta-link with her own actual SIN running, spent four minutes there—virtual, not real—and never gone back.

The whole freaking newb world came to Joe's.

The. Whole. World.

Every kid on the Matrix for the first time showed up at Joe's. Every day. It was a Matrix bar, so it would hold as many people as would log in, but the virtual bar's actual bar disappeared into the horizon as if it extended the entire length of PubGrid.

For the next month after her first visit to Joe's, Zipfile had spent almost every moment removing unwanted spam from her AR. It got into every part of her PAN. At one point her dishwasher was trying to sell her a luxury vacation to Singapore.

This time, she went in ready.

This time her commlink was a Renraku. Felt like poetic justice. She knew, if she asked to look, that her persona would be a kimono-clad samurai. Even before she closed the door to Joe's behind her, she whispered a single word.

"Mute."

Then she grinned.

Joe's was coded to announce you when you entered, as if everyone in the bar turned and shouted your name. The first time she'd visited, what felt like a million people had shouted *"ZIPFILE!"*

This time, there was only blessed silence.

Her network was smart enough to block all the shouts. There was no real sound on the Matrix, after all. The shouts carried the spam.

Instead, she sauntered up to a clear spot at the bar—there was always a clear spot, right by where you entered—and tapped a terminal. In the old days this would have been a chat room, and there'd have been a bar to type text. Flatscreen visitors to Joe's saw the same thing today.

<Who wants to make 50 nuyen?> she sent.

Within a second, there were 47,323 hands raised.

<It's agent work,> she added. In a real shadowrunner den that would cut the pool by 99%. Only newbs wanted agent work. But this wasn't a den.

This was Joe's.

54,983 hands raised.

Zipfile put the hash code and a throwaway commlink code into the terminal.

<Two hours. This code. Location, text-only.> Then she stood up and walked out of Joe's. A moment later, she was back inside her virtual apartment.

She opened a window to look at that commlink code. There were already 68,295 messages.

"Delete all," she said, and called up two more agents.

The first was a Doberman as tall as she was in the real world. This one she showed the original hash to, and then pointed to the open commlink window. "Bite anyone who doesn't match." The Doberman growled and disappeared.

Zipfile chuckled.

It was the Matrix. The agent wasn't a real dog, and it couldn't really bite people, but she'd given it enough teeth that if someone was jacked in full VR, they'd get a jolt of feedback. The second one, a Bernese Mountain Dog, sat patiently. Zipfile showed it the same hash, then waved a finger under its nose. "When he lets someone through, you check," she told it. Then she toggled back out to the real.

Back on the couch, Zipfile chuckled. She loved using dogs for agents in the Matrix. She'd never had a pet, but in the Matrix she had as many as she wanted, and they were all trained.

The flatscreen with the chip's code was still sitting open. Zipfile regarded it for a moment, then realized she never finished her snack.

She left it there, with alerts ready and waiting on her AR if any of her agents found anything, and went back to the kitchen.

Zipfile had zoned out with a forkful of fried rice halfway to her mouth when her AR barked at her. She started. The food fell off the fork and onto her shirt. She cursed and set the fork down, then wiped the rice off her shirt and onto the floor.

Then she stared at the rice on the floor.

"Now I gotta clean that up…"

The AR barked again.

"Fine," she said, stepping over the mess and going back to the living room. "I'll do it later."

In the Matrix, she found the Bernese Mountain Dog waiting for her, a stick in its mouth, tail wagging. She took the stick—it was a data packet, obviously—and gave the dog a treat. It wagged a little more and vanished, back to watching.

Zipfile regarded the stick.

First, it changed into a data readout—in this case, an old-style book, because her PAN knew that's how she preferred to read her text in the Matrix. She sat down on her couch—the same couch that was in her apartment, except cleaner—and flipped through the pages.

She stopped when she saw something familiar.

"*Eish*," she muttered.

She opened a comm window.

<*The elf chick at the warehouse office,*> she sent to Yu <*What was her name?*>

It was only a couple seconds.

<*Melanie*>

<*Think she'd talk to you again?*>

Yu had tracked her down just after the safehouse had been burned, but come away confident she didn't know anything. She was pretty, but so was furniture, was what he had told Zipfile.

<*I'm pretty sure I got what she knows, and no—we didn't end on the best of terms*> Yu sounded peeved. <*You got something?*>

<*Maybe…*> she sent back, and closed the window.

Melanie. She was beautiful, but all those elf bitches were. Zipfile felt her lip curl, and didn't try to fight it. The only difference between this Melanie and any of the Zulu harridans who'd made her childhood such a nightmare was skin color.

Zipfile turned another page. It was an address.

"She can't be that stupid," she muttered.

Getting up, Zipfile put the book down on her virtual coffee table and stepped out onto the PubGrid. The Shiawase sun was right there, and a moment later she was. This wasn't even going to take a serious run. She thought for a second, and sent herself toward Seattle utilities.

In a blink, she stood in front of a modern building whose roof stretched toward the black Matrix sky. Icons for electricity and water and sewer glowed on the walls. She thought herself toward the electricity.

"How can I help you?" a bland agent asked.

"New service," Zipfile said.

"Commercial or residential?"

"Residential?"

"Hold please," the agent said. There was a flicker, and the walls and agent were different.

"Are you a new customer or do you need to transfer service?"

"Transfer."

"Please provide the address," the agent said, and motioned to a slot in the desk. Zipfile looked at a neatly stacked collection of chits on the desktop, imprinted Melanie's supposed address on it, and deposited it in the slot. The agent smiled.

"Thank you," it said, *"but there is already a tenant at that location."*

"Interesting," Zipfile said. She put her hands on the desktop and leaned over it.

It was the Matrix. She could do that here.

Security in a utilities desk was pretty minimal. Zipfile had that code down pat. Once she had caused the sewers of a whole district to back up by leaving a virtual sandwich on the supervisor's desk. Sneaking a basic query in was nothing.

A window popped up behind the agent, though invisible to it. It was a mirror. It showed the back of the faceless agent's bald head, and data on a screen as if it appeared to the agent behind the desk.

Zipfile winked, sealing a copy into her memory, and lifted her hands. The mirror disappeared.

"I must have the wrong address," she told the agent. "I'll return when I'm sure."

The agent blinked out.

Zipfile grinned and jacked out.

Back on the couch in the real, she grinned the same grin.

"*Eish*. What a moron."

She actually lived there. Or at least paid the bill.

<Rude. Meet me.> she sent, and appended an address.

It was time to try a different tack with Melanie.

Melanie the elf lived in a right-on-the-edge of affluent clutch of condos just outside the city. Despite having to come from the other direction, Zipfile found herself still waiting on Rude.

<Dude. Seriously?>
<Relax. Do some laps. Take little steps.> Rude sent back.

If I didn't need him, Zip thought. She sat down on a bench, opened an ARO, and pinged Rude's commlink. It appeared on a map display, just a couple minutes away. She considered hacking into whatever service he was using and screwing with his bill just to mess with him, but it wasn't worth the effort.

Instead, she used the time examining Melanie's building, slicing in security exemptions for she and Rude so they could get where they were going with a minimal amount of alarms. The systems weren't overly complex; good enough to keep the riffraff out, in Zipfile's expert opinion.

Rude finally appeared in some kind of private ride service, driven by a teenage ork with a shocking purple reverse-mohawk. He climbed out of the back of the small van, where normal-sized people would put their luggage. He walked up to the driver's door and high-fived the ork, then ambled over to where Zipfile sat.

"What'm I doin' here, small one?"

Zipfile looked up at him, closing down her commlink. "You're the muscle."

"Always," Rude said with a toothy grin. He belched, and looked up at the building. "Who lives here?"

"Simon Dennis' former assistant," Zipfile said.

Rude whistled. "That cute bit Elfy-pants tried ta get together with?"

"That's her."

"Thought he said she didn't know anything."

Zipfile wriggled until she could slide forward off the too-high bench. It was a lifetime habit; she didn't even realize she did it anymore, except when she had the mountainous bulk of Rude standing in front of her.

She came up to mid-thigh on him.

She sighed.

"Maybe she doesn't," Zipfile told him. "But she's still spending on the same account that bought the chip Yu carried into Telestrian the other day. So either she's embezzling from her former boss, or they're still connected."

Rude's eyes narrowed. He looked down at her with a hungry look. "So she might know a way ta get to him."

"I hope so."

The troll smiled again, this time hungrily. "Me, too."

Zipfile led him toward the building. The low-slung line of two-story condos was behind a two-meter wall with razor wire across the stop. The gate was actually pretty sturdy. Rude eyed it as they walked up and laughed.

"Watch this," he said, raising a foot.

Zip held up a hand. "Hang on." She activated her AR, pinged a preset, and the gate unlatched with a metallic *ping*.

Rude frowned. "That's no fun."

"I had extra time," she told him. "Next time be here when I say, and you can kick the gate clean off its hinges."

Rude grunted, but followed her into the tiny courtyard.

Zipfile pointed to her left. "That's her unit."

Rude looked down at her. "Do I get ta do this door, or do ya have more little AR magic to do?"

Zipfile gestured ahead of herself. "All yours."

Rude grinned. "And once we get inside?"

"Secure the place, secure the girl, and wait for me." Zip raised a stubby finger. "Don't kill her, Rude. I need her talking."

"Uh-huh," the troll said. "Anyone in there with her?"

"Not that I could see," Zipfile told him.

A moment later Rude grunted, kicked, and the thick security door flew off its hinges.

"Knight Errant!" he shouted, and charged inside.

Zipfile snort-laughed and followed him inside.

Zipfile hadn't been hands-on in too many breaking-and-enterings for more years than she wanted to think about. It had been way back in the day, before she left the old country. Since coming to Seattle she had focused on hacking. There were other, larger people to deal with the difficult things like kicking in doors and subduing screaming elf scrags.

Other, larger people like Rude.

Before the door had even hit the ground Rude was through it and still shouting his stupid Knight Errant call. Zipfile had to admit it made a little bit of sense; KE broke into a lot of homes every day, and if there were any recording devices she had missed, they'd get the shouting.

As she stepped over the broken door, Zip shook her head.

Rude probably also got a kick out of pretending to be the assholes who'd hit them up the other night.

Inside the condo, a woman started shouting.

Rude was already around the corner of the entryway and into the main room. Zip followed, her smaller steps giving her the natural patience to wait and see what happened. If the elf produced a gun and started shooting, after all, better for Rude to deal with that too.

Trolls were good at sponging up punishment.

Still... Zipfile brought up her AR. There were precautions to take.

The elf's home was as smart as any other, but she was ready for that. An agent that pretended to the building's own zipped around Melanie's system, locking out Matrix access and other communications. It automatically quashed the in-home security alarm which—Zip grinned as she read the code—would have called Knight Errant on her behalf.

"Oh for the good old days of Lone Star," she muttered. The previous contractor for city police hadn't been quite the same as KE.

Inside the main room, Rude had Melanie pushed down on the couch, one of his big pistols leveled. She was wearing athletic clothes; behind her the trid was frozen on a popular workout video. The elf's attention was clearly fixed on the big troll, so Zipfile hung back, in the cusp of the hallway, content to let Rude take the lead for a second.

"Anybody in the other rooms?" he growled.

Zipfile automatically checked both her own and Melanie's AR and found no other icons.

"Go to hell," Melanie said. "You're not Knight Errant."

"Oh?"

"Look at how you're dressed," the elf said, her disdain sharp as a knife.

Zipfile stifled a chuckle.

<She's got you there,> she commed.

"Ever hear a' undercover?"

Melanie sneered at him. "You couldn't pretend to be a log."

Rude shook his head. "I don't get paid enough for this." He turned and looked back at Zipfile. "You got questions for this elf 'fore I shoot her?"

When the troll spoke, Melanie looked and saw Zipfile. Too many years and too many elves had taught Zipfile exactly what to look for, and she saw the usual disdain for dwarves flash across Melanie's face.

That was enough to erase any lingering doubts that Zip felt about breaking into the woman's house.

Not that she'd had all that many in the first place.

Zipfile stepped fully into the room. She held up her cyberdeck on its sling. "You know what this is?"

"Illegal," Melanie said.

"Then you know no one is coming to help you," Zip said. "Tell us about Simon Dennis."

"Who?"

Zipfile grinned. She walked over and pulled a barstool almost as tall as she was away from the high table and climbed up on it. She settled her deck on her lap and stared at the elf.

"Simon Dennis," Zipfile repeated. "Chief operations officer at AVR Optronics."

"Never heard of it," Melanie said. She looked back up at Rude. "You sure you amateurs got the right place?"

Zipfile thought about the way Yu had described Melanie to him, as if she'd done very well at finishing school. Professional, buttoned up. That didn't match the woman in front of him. She was haughty, braggadocious. As if she knew there was nothing she or Rude could do to her.

<*Be ready,*> she sent to Rude.

<*Always.*>

"I think you called him Mr. Miller," Zip said.

Melanie glared at her. Then, without a single betraying motion, leaped up from the sofa and tried to get past Rude.

The troll was ready. He snatched her out of the air by the arm and slammed her back down on the couch with a roar. She twisted like an eel on the cushions, trying to get across the back, but he grabbed her shoulder, flipped her over, and hammered a quick jab into her solar plexus. She fell forward, alternately wheezing and retching.

"Where'd ya think yer going?" Rude asked. He chuckled. "Youse elfs are all the same."

It took Melanie a minute to catch her breath. Zip spent that minute engrossed in her AR, digging deeper into Melanie's home network. She had a spotlight program running, which would highlight the icon of any device trying to hide itself in the Matrix. So far, nothing, but...

"I'm escaping," the elf wheezed. "You broke in here. Gods only know what you're going to do to me." She looked at Zipfile with teary eyes, but Zip knew that was just the physical reaction to getting punched by a troll. Melanie was not a woman to let her emotions get the best of her.

"Exactly when I mentioned Miller," Zip prodded. "Funny that."

"I don't know who that is, either," Melanie said.

"I don't believe you," Rude rumbled.

Zipfile's AR pinged. She checked the notification, then shut it down. "Doesn't matter," she told both of them. "I found what I was looking for."

Rude laughed, but Melanie said nothing. She watched Zipfile go into her kitchen, to the tray beneath the over. Zip reached down—it wasn't that low for her—and pulled it open. The rack screeched. Inside were the usual pans that no one ever really used.

"You bakin' somethin' in there?" Rude called.

"Not quite," Zip replied. She reached beneath the pans and pulled out an Ares commlink. She held it up so it was visible over the countertop. She kept her hand up until she came back out of the kitchen and could see Melanie's face.

"You don't know Miller or Dennis," Zipfile said. "I've only got one more name."

Melanie glared at her. If looks could be venomous Zip would be convulsing on the floor.

"How about Henrik Gould?"

Zipfile held Melanie's stare until the elf looked away. *Gotcha*, she thought. For the first time since the Telestrian job, Zipfile felt like she was starting to understand what was happening.

Right up until the first gunshot.

The first bullet took Rude in the shoulder. Zip heard the sound and saw him lurch forward at the same time. She stood there, a little bit away from him, still brandishing the commlink.

He fell across the couch, crushing Melanie beneath him, roaring with pain and defiance. Before Zip had time to even process what was happening he was back up on his knee, firing the big pistol in his hand back toward the hallway Zipfile had entered through.

She looked that way.

Black shapes in body armor filled the hallway. Bulbous full-head helmets hid their features, and they carried short subguns with long, thick sound suppressors. The lead attacker fired again, the *crack* of the bullets loud in the small space of the condo, but probably inaudible outside the building.

"*Eish!*" she shouted and dropped to the floor. She didn't even think of drawing her own revolver. This was more than she could process at once. This wasn't like fighting the drones with Emu. That had felt more like a game.

This was real.

It was right here.

<*Who the frag's this!?*> Rude sent.

<*I have no idea!*>

<*Find out!*>

Rude found something heavier than his pistol, either a subgun from one of the attackers or a long gun he'd had under his coat this whole time. A line of shots stitched up the front of the lead black-clad gunner until the last one tore out his throat. He fell to the floor, thrashing, both hands wrapped around the ruin of his neck as his life's blood pumped out faster and faster as panic drove his heartrate up. Behind him, the trid was still frozen in the workout program and in a disgusting caricature the performer on the screen was stuck in a similar post.

Zipfile stared at the bleeding man, horrified.

This was her fault.

She was supposed to know what was going on.

How had these guys snuck up on them? How had they even known she and Rude were here? She wanted to dive into the Matrix and go back through the video logs, to see where they'd come from. If this were a normal run and the team had been surprised, that's just what she'd do.

But here, now...here she was in the middle of it.

Movement distracted Zipfile. She looked toward the overturned couch and saw Melanie crouched there, a look of determination painted on her fine features. She eyed the next commando in line. Zipfile looked back and forth between them. Then the commando's subgun ran dry and the magazine fell free.

Melanie scurried across the floor toward the kitchen while the man reloading blocked the fire of the bad guys behind him. Zipfile twisted on the floor and watched where Melanie went but she vanished behind a cabinet island.

The commando got his subgun reloaded and ripped a burst at where Rude was hiding, but the troll wasn't there. He'd shimmied across the floor and was crouched against a wall, out of the hallway's line of sight. He was watching Zipfile. When she met his gaze, he raised his hands and mouthed *well?* silently.

He's right, Zipfile realized. *I need to get in this fight.*

Pushing with her hands, Zip slid backward until she was in the kitchen. She realized she was behind the same island as Melanie when she bumped the elf's foot. The former secretary turned and snarled at her with a ferocity that would have made Rude proud.

Zip rolled her eyes.

Popping up her AR, she looked for the icons of the attackers. They didn't want to show up, but Zipfile had code for that. It was the work of a couple seconds to get insight into what tech they had that was broadcasting.

"You don't have much time," Melanie whispered.

Zip looked at her. "What?"

"In a second they'll realize I'm not in there with your friend. And then they'll come this way."

"What?"

"Never mind," Melanie said.

Zipfile went back to her work. The subguns were smartguns, all networked into the shooters' PANs. Zip picked at the code, using attacks she'd perfected before. Telltales over each smartgun glowed red, until one blinked yellow.

<*Get ready,*> she told Rude, and fed him a tag for the failing smartgun.

A moment later the icon blinked green.

The subgun noise stopped. Zifpfile heard muffled cursing from the commando. She rolled around the corner of the island enough to see what was happening.

To his credit, the shooter didn't waste more than a second pulling the trigger of his subgun to no effect. He dropped it and reached for a pistol at his waist.

But even that second was too long.

Cued by the icon, Rude leaned around and put a bullet through his throat. It was a surer hit than the helmet; there was no guarantee the round would penetrate the armor. He fell to the floor, rolling through the spreading pool of blood left by his teammate, hands around his neck, desperately trying to hold off the inevitable.

Zipfile slid back and checked her AR.

"Three left," she told Melanie.

The elf sneered at her. "That's two more than they need."

The three remaining commandos seemed to come to the same decision. Zipfile watched them on her AR; one leaned against the wall and started firing short, timed bursts toward Rude's position.

The other two broke into a run toward the island where Melanie and Zipfile huddled.

"*Eish*," she said, and clawed for the pistol at the small of her back.

Melanie must have realized what was going on. She chopped Zipfile in the side of the head and reached for the revolver. It was her long fingers, not Zipfile's short ones, that wrapped around the butt of the pistol and raised it.

Zipfile lolled, disorientated. It was as though she was watching all this on the trid. She really, really wished she *was* watching this on trid.

The gaping back maw of a suppressor appeared over the island. A moment later a black helmet appeared; the commando was sliding across the island, thinking they were deeper in the kitchen.

Melanie put the muzzle of Zipfile's pistol against the faceplate and pulled the trigger three quick times. The commando spasmed and fell across them. Zipfile felt the man's dead weight hit her. It knocked the breath from her chest.

The other commando stuck his subgun over the island and held the trigger down.

Bullets tore into the body covering Zipfile. She felt the shocks through the corpse, but the man's ballistic cloth clothing stopped the rounds from penetrating. She was fine, but fear tore through her sense of shock like being drenched in icy water.

Blood splashed as the bullets struck Melanie, who didn't have a dead man to hide beneath. Shouts of pain Zip was sure were involuntary filled the room.

Zipfile thrashed, ignoring her burning lungs. Any moment the shooter would realize he hadn't hurt one of his targets.

The black maw of the subgun barrel shifted toward her.

And then it was gone.

A roaring filled its place.

Zip worked her way out from beneath the dead man. Melanie lay next to her, revolver forgotten, both hands clutched against the bloody mess that was her stomach.

Zip climbed to her knees and then to her feet. She crouched and peeked over the countertop.

Rude was literally beating one of the commandos to death with the other.

He held one by the boots and roared, swinging him like a board, slamming him down on top of the other. At the apex of one swing the black helmet flew off, revealing the bleeding, black-skinned face of an ork Zipfile didn't recognize.

After a few more swings Rude dropped the body and stood there, panting. He looked at Zipfile and said something, but she didn't hear him. She was looking down at Melanie's body.

The elf was pale and still atop a spreading pool of blood and other fluids. She'd released her stomach with one hand and was reaching toward a drawer. Bloody prints showed where she'd tried to get the drawer open.

"You okay?" Rude said. He was standing next to her.

Zipfile didn't realize he had moved.

Her ears rang. Even Rude's gravelly bass sounded somewhat tinny.

"Zip?"

"I'm okay," she said, or tried to.

"Ya okay?" He repeated. "Ya hit?"

"I'm okay," she repeated, louder this time.

"What the hell just happened?" the troll asked. "I mean, we got lit up, but why? Who was that, and what'd they want with us?"

Zipfile didn't answer. She just looked down at Melanie's body.

"I'll get us a ride," Rude said.

Zipfile bent down and pulled open the drawer Melanie had been reaching for. It was filled with dish towels. Zip frowned and looked down at the dead woman. Her eyes were fixed on the drawer. Her blood was brushed across it. Had she just been trying to get a towel to staunch the blood flow?

Eish. *I get shot up, I'm not reaching for the bleeding towels!*

Zip looked down and saw her revolver. She picked it up. The grips were tacky with Melanie's blood. The elf had used it to kill the first gunman to come for them. The one that had fallen on Zipfile.

Melanie had saved Zipfile's life with those shots.

They'll realize I'm not in there with your friend, she had said.

I'm not in there.

"They were here to kill her," Zipfile whispered. She looked up at Rude, who was holding a hand to his temple while he commed with someone. Emu, probably, to get a ride before KE or someone else came down on them. "Rude."

"What?" The troll blinked. "Ya trackin' now? 'Cause our ride'll be here in ten. Emu called in a favor."

"They were here to kill *her*." She put her revolver back in its holster. "There weren't here for us."

"What're you talking about?"

Zipfile pointed down at the body. "Her. These guys—" she kicked the body next to her, "—were here to kill Melanie. We were just in the way."

"The hell you say," Rude said. He looked around the room. "Why would anyone want to whack that elf?" He shrugged. "I mean, we were gonna, sure, but we had reasons."

Zipfile leaned back over the drawer. She started picking towels out, running her hands across them. She found what she was looking for in the fourth one. There was a bump along the seam. She squeezed it gently through the fabric, feeling the shape.

"It's a datachip," she told Rude.

"It's a towel," Rude said, "but let's go with whatever gets you movin', okay?"

"Inside the towel, idiot," Zipfile said. She stuffed it in a pocket. "Whatever's on it, it was the last thing Melanie thought about before she died."

"Whatever," Rude said.

"You said ten minutes," Zip asked.

"Yeah."

"Then let's take this place apart as much as we can in that time," Zipfile told him. "Whatever else happened, Melanie was the last person we know of who dealt with Simon Dennis. She was buying things on his behalf. Maybe it was harmless, maybe it wasn't."

"She didn't act harmless," Rude muttered.

"No," Zipfile agreed, "she didn't."

Rude reached down and pulled the helmet off the man Melanie had shot. They learned two things.

First, the man was a woman. She had been blond.

Second...

"I know this woman," Rude said. "From somewhere..."

Zip very carefully didn't roll her eyes. Rude's memory was spotty to say the least. He might think he remembered her because he saw a blond woman on the sidewalk earlier. Or she might have been his boon companion for years.

In Rude's fractured head, those were sometimes the same thing.

"She's a shooter," he went on.

Zipfile carefully didn't say *obviously*.

"I know her..."

There was a chirp on Zipfile's AR. "Ride's a couple minutes out," she told Rude.

Rude snapped his fingers. It sounded like tree branches breaking. "Saroyan. Jesse, or Jamie, or something like that."

"Great," Zip told him. "Car's still coming. Go check the other rooms."

Rude flipped her the bird and wandered off. His giant boots made squelching noises in the blood on the floor.

Zipfile looked down at Melanie.

"Thank you," she whispered. She rubbed the pocket she'd stuffed the towel with the hidden datachip into.

Then she went to look for more.

"She worked for Wuxing," Yu said a couple hours later.

When Zip stared up at him blankly, he went on. "Jenny Saroyan. She was a runner, did a lot of business with Wuxing, according to Myth."

"That doesn't make any sense," Zip said.

"No shit."

Zip crossed her arms and thought. *Why would a Wuxing runner want to stop Melanie? Had Miller or Dennis or whatever name he'd been using when he ran Rip Current Sea Lanes done something to piss Wuxing off?* She said as much.

"No idea," Yu said. "You get anything off that chip?"

"Nothing," Zipfile told him.

"Maybe take a break," the elf said. "You've had a day."

Zipfile looked down at the deck in her lap. Melanie's chip was inserted. She was using the power of her cyberdeck to try and force her way through the chip's encryption. It was running fine without her. "Maybe you're right."

"I'm actually right a lot," Yu said.

Zip patted his hand. "Of course you are."

"Seriously, Z," Yu said, after a moment. "You okay?"

"I thought I was going to die," Zipfile whispered. She set her deck aside and rubbed her hands together. Her palms felt dry and wet at the same time. She'd showered, and washed her hands a dozen times since they got back, but she still felt the tacky sensation of Melanie's blood on her skin.

"That never feels good," Yu agreed. He sat down next to her, dapper as always. He leaned in and bumped her shoulder. "But you're still here. Bad guys aren't."

"Thanks to Rude."

"Thanks to you, too," Yu said.

"It was more Melanie than me." When she closed her eyes, she saw the black suppressor swinging toward her. She saw Melanie shooting her gun. She heard the *tick* of the barrel hitting the helmet, then the *blam blam blam* of the shots. She felt the weight of the dead shooter.

She shivered.

"It's going to be a hard couple nights," Yu said. Zip looked at him but he was looking at the floor. "If you're lucky, only a couple of nights." He glanced at her and forced a grin. "If it helps, you did the right thing."

Zip closed her eyes and focused on her breathing for a long moment. When she opened them, she told herself it was time to be someone else for a while.

"What'd you guys find out?" she asked.

"Well, Frostburn says there's *probably* not *too much* magic at AVR," Yu said, grinning.

"Probably," Zipfile deadpanned.

"Right," Yu replied. "Not too much."

Zipfile chuckled. "Mages. Always deal in absolutes."

"Every time," Yu said. "Rude got a line on the explosives before he ran off to meet you. Emu's out picking them up right now, but Rude's contacts aren't the most stable, so Frostburn went with her."

Zip snorted. "And you? Anything from the triads?"

"You were right. I've reached my limit for a while." There was a catch in his voice.

"Everything okay?"

"It will be," he said, and left it there. Then he slapped his knees and stood up, turning to look back down at her. "I'll let you get back to it," he said. "I asked Myth, when I was asking her about Rude's friend, to see if she could get us a better plan set for AVR. If we're supposed to do the snatch on the schematics before we blow the place up, we'll need better maps."

Zip frowned. "I should be doing that." That sort of work was *literally* her job on the team.

Yu grinned. "Maybe you'll get there before Myth's people," he told her. "I told her I put fifty on you beating her hackers."

"You son of a slitch," Zipfile said. She felt herself smile in spite of everything else. Yu knew her well, knew a job and a bit of competition would get her going again. "Get out of here."

Yu raised his hands and backed to the door, then closed it behind him.

Zip looked at her clean palms, rubbed them together, then ignored the phantom tackiness and jacked into the Matrix.

Back in her own private host, Zip stood again in front of her murderboard and thought. The system automatically added in the new data and updated itself. Melanie's picture was now covered with a big red X. Simon Dennis still glared at her.

And way off to the side, in the unknown box, was Wuxing's corporate logo.

Behind her, an old-style coffee percolator sat on the counter, burbling away. This was how her host represented the cyberdeck chewing its way through the encryption on Melanie's drive. It would burble until the coffee was ready; until she could read the chip's data.

Until then...there was the question of AVR.

She called up the map she'd captured during the Dieter raid. She didn't think too hard about where it had come from. Instead, she worked for a short time annotating what she knew about it. Several areas were clearly marked.

What wasn't marked was structural plans. They'd need those to know where to place Rude's explosives. You couldn't just put a stick of dynamite against a wall and hope the whole building came down.

And before that, they needed to hit the central memory.

Black spiders flashed in her memory.

There were two ways they could approach that. The first was for Zipfile to hack in during the run and download the data. She didn't like that idea; she'd seen firsthand the level of black IC running in AVR, and there was always the omnipresent threat of a Renraku demiGOD being just around the corner. She'd take the risk if she had to, but... the other way was to just have someone go inside and grab it.

And since they had to go inside *anyway*...

But to do that, she had to be able to tell them where to go.

Which meant a run or a hack.

She didn't have time for that.

Which meant spending some nuyen. She closed her eyes and sighed.

<*Yu*> she commed, from inside the Matrix.

<*Z?*>

<*I don't have time to dig up construction plans for AVR,*> she sent. <*We need to buy them. Juggler should have someone.*>

<*That won't be cheap.*>

<*Nothing ever is.*>

<*Okay, I'll reach out.*>

That dealt with, Zipfile went back to her murderboard. She'd chased down Melanie testing the assumption that Renraku owned Rip Current Sea Lanes, the company that had hired them to infiltrate Telestrian. What she'd gotten from Melanie so far didn't help or hurt that theory, but the basis of evidence was on Renraku.

If for no other reason than Telestrian had hired them to get revenge on Renraku. Why would a hungry corp like Telestrian take the chance of pissing off Renraku if they weren't sure who hit them? Telestrian had a hundred deckers like Zipfile, she knew. They had the code Yu had put in their own servers. They could read it just as fast as she had, and they likely had all the other snippets that fed whatever the hell had happened when Yu had been inside.

So they should know.

Zipfile frowned.

Something felt off. But she couldn't put her finger on it. Her eyes shifted to the Wuxing logo. What was their involvement? Why kill Melanie? Had it just been coincidence that they had struck while Rude and Zipfile were there, or had their visit been the trigger?

Zipfile sat down—a chair appeared from her host—and cupped her chin. The collar of her Han-style jacket tickled her chin, but she ignored that. It always happened.

Fact: Simon Dennis had appeared to run Rip Current Sea Lanes. Now he was a Renraku executive. Or at least a subsidiary executive.

Fact: Melanie had been his assistant. She had the SIN and commlink that had purchased the chip Yu had carried into Telestrian. She had been assassinated by runners likely hired by Wuxing.

Zip frowned. Runners were freelancers. Even if Wuxing hired Saroyan often, she probably freelanced. They all did. So maybe it wasn't Wuxing that had hit the elf.

Fact: Telestrian Industries believed that Renraku employed Dennis. They believed Renraku needed retribution.

Zip closed her eyes and jacked out.

It was all too much, and she was missing something.

Zipfile had just put the teabag in her mug when her AR pinged her. She called the alert up. It showed a coffee pot shooting steam. Her deck was done with Melanie's data. She took her tea to the couch and jacked in. A new frame hung on her murderboard, flashing. She toggled the data open and began to read.

A minute later she flashed the whole group.

<Got news. Common room. Right now.>

She jacked out.

By the time Rude appeared, yawning, everyone else was present, and Zipfile's tea had steeped. Emu and Frostburn were on the couch. Yu perched on the arm next to Emu, arms folded. He hadn't said anything about the AVR map, so he must not have heard back from Juggler yet. Rude looked around the room, shrugged, and sat down against the wall. His horns scratched parallel lines in the drywall when he put his head back.

"I've got him," she told the group.

"Got who?" Frostburn asked.

"Simon Dennis."

"Got him where," Emu asked with a grin. "Like, locked in your room?"

"I've got his address," she said. "I've got his GridGuide routes to and from AVR. I've got his office number." For proof, she put up an AR holo, and pulsed an office in the executive offices at the assembly plant.

"Where'd you get this?" Yu asked.

"Melanie's chip."

Rude snorted. "That elf bit? She had all this?"

Zipfile nodded. "She didn't trust her boss. And she wasn't what she seemed."

"What's that mean?" Frostburn asked.

"She was setting up to blackmail him," Zip said. "She wanted to be a runner."

Rude burst out laughing. "You're joking."

"She wanted to be a face, I think. She had gathered all this data on Dennis and hidden it on this chip. A couple of the notes are addressed to "Lou," but I don't know who that is."

"A partner?" Yu put in.

Zipfile shrugged. "It could be. Or it could be a boss, or a cutout, or her imaginary friend. I don't know." She spread her hands. "The important thing is, we can grab Dennis if we want. Anytime." She switched the AR display to a map, where a gold icon pulsed. "There he is."

Yu stood up. "You got his SIN. His real one."

"The one he's using right now, at least."

The whole group stared at the map for a quiet moment. Zipfile knew what they were feeling. She felt the same thing. A sense of satisfaction. They had what they needed, almost.

They could do this.

"What else is on there?" Emu asked.

"I'm still going through it," Zip admitted. "There's a lot."

"Don't matter," Rude put in. "Let's just go grab the scummer."

"Maybe," Yu said.

"Whaddaya mean, maybe?" Rude asked. He pointed a gnarly finger at the map. "He's right there!"

"He's only half the job," Yu said, "and not the half that pays."

Zipfile drifted into the only empty chair. "The building. The factory."

"Yeah."

"You get the map?"

"It's coming," Yu said, not looking at her. "Myth said Juggler has a line on it. He's getting me a price."

"This job is really starting to cost," Frostburn muttered.

Zipfile looked at her, surprised. "They went after your family," she said. "You want out?" Someone went after her brother, that someone was dead. Zip didn't care if it cost her a few bucks or the freaking moon.

Dead.

Frostburn glared at her. "Not even a little. But cash is cash."

"I can cover it," Yu said diffidently. "And we need it."

"Okay," Emu said. "We have Dennis. We know the building. We're about to have a map. We have some explosives." She looked around the room. "So what's next?"

Zipfile cleared her throat when no one else spoke.

"Let's figure out how we do this," she told the others.

RETRIBUTION
JASON M. HARDY

THE JOB

YU

The elf at the bar was drinking gin and ignoring a half-dozen unfriendly glares. He stood instead of sat, his back to the bartender, looking out at the sparse clientele with a neutral expression. He considered his tan jacket, black pants, brown shirt combo to be business casual, but in this setting it might as well have been a tux. The lighting was dim, the tables splintered, and the cleanliness of the glasses was questionable.

Finally, an ork in one of the darkest corners spoke. "You're not wanted here."

Yu smiled. "I get that a lot."

The ork rose to his feet. His stance was unsteady. The table in front of him ground on the concrete floor as it edged forward. "We know who you are. Your people killed Saroyan."

Yu shook his head ruefully. "No. The target did that. Not us."

"Your people were there."

"And unaware of the hit. It caught them off guard." He sipped his gin. "The target, though, was prepared."

The ork shoved the table out of his way. "You think Saroyan was unprepared? Bad at her job?"

"To be completely honest, I don't know enough about her to form any opinion."

The ork weaved closer. His jeans were ripped, and his Concrete Dreams t-shirt was frayed. The cloud of alcohol around him could have overwhelmed a barghest.

Yu, though, was built of sterner stuff. He refused to wilt.

The ork jabbed a thick finger at him. "We're mourning here, drekhead, and you're playing like Mr. Smooth, Mr. Ice, or whatever. Get out."

Yu stood up straight and wiped any trace of irony of his face. "Look, I know how this is. I'm one of you. We're all out here together. We've all lost people." He leaned forward, barely. "And we know what we need to do after we lose them."

"I don't need you telling me how to do anything," the ork growled. But he didn't push Yu away, and he didn't take a swing.

"I'm not going to tell you how to do anything. I'm just going to help you do what you want to do."

Later that night, Yu was in another bar. Fortunately, he trusted the kitchen in this one more, because he couldn't keep drinking on an empty stomach. The surfaces were light speckled stone, the accents were warm wood. This time he had a table, and he perched on a high stool nibbling pieces of a veggie platter. Didn't make the fingers messy, didn't have lettuce that could get stuck in the teeth, didn't weigh him down with carbs. The stool was the biggest challenge— looking dignified without slouching over on one of those things was difficult.

Then his target returned from the bathroom. He smiled as the human woman walked by and tilted his glass toward her, and she smiled back. They'd exchanged a few light pleasantries and shared a laugh. The harder part was coming up.

<She didn't text or message anyone while she was gone,> Zipfile messaged. <You haven't raised any alarms yet.>

<Night's not over,> he sent back.

The next move was easy. She was between him and the bar. He could plausibly walk by while getting another drink. So after waiting for a few minutes, that's what he did. He planned the interaction carefully. If he was too playful, he'd seem flirty, and that was the wrong tone. So he focused where he needed the talk to go.

"Remind me how many drinks before negotiation powers slip? Is it ten?"

"Sounds like you're trying to negotiate with yourself," the woman said. "And failing. You may have already hit your limit."

"Then I might as well keep drinking, if it's already a lost cause!"

She smiled, and he continued on his way.

Zipfile reached out to him as he ordered his drink. <You finally made an impact. She's looking up who you are. That smile she gave you? She was taking your picture.>

<I would have turned to my better side if she'd just asked.>

<You already did that when you walked away.>

Yu was honestly not sure how to take that. So he just plunged ahead.

<*What's she finding?*>

<*What she's supposed to. You're Johnny Tsing, Maersk troubleshooter. She's asking a friend if she knows anything about you. The friend, of course, does not.*>

<*How long until the flyover?*>

<*About a minute and a half.*>

<*Okay, I'll slow walk it.*>

He enjoyed a sip of his next gin at the bar, letting it swirl around his mouth, soak into his tongue. He wasn't sure if he liked the taste or just found it reassuring, but then he wasn't sure if there was a difference between the two.

Then he heard the plane. The roar grew, and he started walking. It was loud as he passed the woman, so he had to raise his voice. "11:40 to L.A."

"Really?"

"Absolutely." He tilted his head. "Sounds like it's carrying... commlinks. Lots of commlinks. And some Snohomish Farms cheese. Probably cheddar. No wait—Gouda."

"You have an amazing ear for shipping," the woman said.

"It's my life's work."

"I'm so sorry."

He stopped in his tracks and pointed at her. "You're in it, too. I heard it in your voice. You are a fellow laborer in the field of moving drek around the world."

She raised her hands. "You got me. Wuxing."

"Maersk." He pointed to a chair. "May I sit?"

She swept her right hand to indicate acceptance. He sat.

"So!" he said.

"So," she responded.

He leaned forward. "I'd introduce myself, but I don't have to. You know my name. You knew I was Maersk before I walked over here."

This was the moment where he either pulled it off or blew it. She stared at him levelly, the nearly straight line of her brown eyebrows not betraying anything about her thoughts. He didn't know which way this was going to go until she spoke.

"And you probably knew I was Wuxing when you walked into the bar."

"Isn't it a shame that two people can't just meet randomly in this world any more?"

"This is the world we have."

"Yep. Where people are commodities." He grinned—rakishly, he hoped. "So. Want to exploit each other?"

The conversation took a while—it was past 1 a.m. when he left the bar. Downtown still showed sparks of life here and there—the office buildings were empty, mostly, but people walked in and out of the restaurants and bars attached to hotels, and Jitnees prowled, waiting for anyone looking for a ride. Occasionally someone yelled something into the streets, the actual words lost in echoes off the steel, glass, and concrete all around.

Yu had one more task to take care of tonight, and it wouldn't get done here. He had to get out to Redmond, to the glamorous confines of the Novelty Hill Sleep & Eat. No Jitnee or cab would be willing to take him out there at this time of night, and Emu had expressed clear disdain for ferrying Yu around, especially after what had happened last time. So he was left to trudge back to the American she'd lifted for him.

It seemed like she had access to an unending supply of these things. He had asked her about it once. She'd just shrugged and said, "It's always easy to find things people need but don't really like. Like tampons, or factory workers."

He had been unable to craft a reply to that.

The current stolen American was two years old, silver-grey, and dented on the passenger side in multiple spots, indicating that the driver saw it as disposable transportation anyway. It would definitely be that—like the others, it would be trashed once the evening's work was done. Right now, though, he had a date with the 520.

Traffic was light out of Downtown and into Touristville. It was always a weird drive, as you essentially watched the trappings of civilization melt away outside your windshield. Gleaming skyrakers became luxury residences became plain apartments became ramshackle slums became decaying buildings became rubble. And he had to get through some of the rubble to get to his destination. He wasn't just going to Redmond—he was going to *East* Redmond. The only good thing was that he wasn't traversing the entire district the long way.

The 520 became Novelty Hill Road, and the road became a collection of potholes loosely connected by asphalt. He had neither GridGuide nor a need for great speed, so he drove at an easy pace. He didn't need the car to last long, but he also didn't want to shatter his suspension before he was back at the safehouse,

He chatted over his comm with Zipfile as he got closer, going with voice since he didn't have to worry about being overheard.

"I'm glad you're still up."

"Of course I am. This is hacker primetime."

"Any messages from the contact?"

"Not to me. He's been chatting with a few friends, looking for any background on you."

"And finding?"

"*The truth, or at least the part we want him to know. Nothing you don't want him to see.*"

"Is he bringing backup?"

"*Of course!*"

"Then why aren't I?"

"*What do you think I am?*"

"I think you're not physically here."

"*Well, sorry you're feeling skittish. Wanna wake up Rude, see if he's in a mood to join you?*"

Yu considered that for almost half a second. "Maybe not."

"*Okay then. So what's the easiest way to not get shot?*"

"Don't give them a reason to shoot you."

"*Right. Behave yourself.*"

And with that, the warehouse that held the Novelty Hill Sleep & Eat came into view.

The Sixth World was built on a simple principle, namely: How little can we give people and still make them willing to pay for what they get? (With its corollary, how little can we pay people and still keep them willing to work?) The Novelty Hill Sleep & Eat was one of the clearest expressions of this principle. The name was a statement of purpose, since you could sleep there, and you could eat there, and not much else. The rooms were little more than a pod. The food was little more than soypaste (or, often, *exactly* soypaste). The Matrix in the area sucked. Recreation didn't exist. Death awaited outside if you were foolish enough to make any conspicuous display of wealth.

The good thing was, few people who saw you in the area thought you were up to anything big, because if you were up to something big, you wouldn't be at Novelty Hill.

The biggest trick was privacy. The "eat" part of Sleep & Eat happened in an entirely charm-free cafeteria, with bench seating for up to 150 weary souls. There were no backrooms, no private rooms. You could have a confidential discussion there, but you had to do it quietly, and it helped if you knew some of the slang Barrens rats liked to sling around. Or made up new slang, so you could keep things secret even from the rats.

This meeting would be all business, since there was no reason to soak in the atmosphere. The only small talk would be there for reasons of keeping up appearances.

Yu left his jacket in the car as he walked in. Once inside, he pushed the buttons to get a bowl of soy spiked with an Uncle Charleez' Smoky Backwoods Maple flavor pack. The bowl was in his hands in seconds, the steam carrying the fine scent of a maple-wood campfire that also happened to be burning a handful of moldy dishrags.

He saw his target quickly. It helped that there were only three other people in the cafeteria. One was an elf in fishnet stockings who gave him an inquiring look as he entered, another was a dwarf with a hunched back and a vacant stare, facing the wall and seeing nothing.

The third person was a human, dressed simply in t-shirt and jeans. Spellcaster. That made Yu extra nervous about meeting him alone, because who knew how mages' minds worked? Like Frostburn, who managed to be both a mother hen and an insane ball of destruction. Tough to pin people like that down. Anyway, he had to hope the references—including, eventually, the ork in the first bar of the night—would do their work.

"Can I sit here?"

The human shrugged and did not look up. "Sit where you want."

Yu sat down and heaved an exaggerated sigh. He grabbed his spork and began spooning up paste. The taste wasn't any better than the smell.

"Long day?" the human said.

"Very long," Yu said. "Felt like two days. Started at ten in the morning and didn't let up."

"Ten's not that early."

"Still long when you work until midnight."

"Yeah, but you gotta do it, right? Gotta bring in the nuyen."

"Barely any. Figure I should make a grand for what I did. I didn't get anywhere near that."

"Maybe you need better skills."

"Tell me about it. You know who gets paid? Mages. Spellcasters. The ones who can shoot lightning and hit a commlink half a kilometer away or something."

"Yeah, it takes a good cast to do that. But it's doable."

"They just need someone to tell them what to hit, right?"

"If that someone knows what they're doing."

Yu slurped the rest of his soy. "I tell you, spellcasters. They do it right, they got the world by the tail."

The man looked up with a frown and creased forehead. "It's not always easy as all that, you know."

Yu stood and patted the man on the shoulder. "It's all a step on the journey."

The man grunted.

Yu walked away. Just like that, he had a spellcaster who would hit a commlink with a lightning bolt from half a kilometer away at 10 a.m. in two days. All Yu had to do was get him the location.

Smooth and easy. All the pieces were in place. At least, all the ones he could put in place tonight.

Time to report back. Then sleep.

Back at the safehouse, Zipfile was still up, of course. Rude and Frostburn were sleeping. Emu was up, too, messing with a drone.

She looked up as he came in. "Results?"

"As good as can be expected. Zipfile had it down. The pieces are arranged like she thought."

To Emu's right, Zipfile nodded in quiet pride.

Yu settled into the vinyl easy chair that had become his preferred seat while here, even though it squeaked when he moved.

"What worries me is we're trying to read a lot of people to get this to work right. We read someone wrong, then we get unpredictability." He paused. "I'd really like to be done with unpredictability."

Emu twisted the wrench she was holding, then dropped it to look at her handiwork. "In the wrong line of work then, ain'tcha? And aren't a lot of these *your* reads? You doubting yourself?"

Shift. Squeak. "...Maybe."

She turned on the drone and watched it drift leisurely toward the ceiling while making remarkably little noise. "Don't do that."

Sure, he thought. *I made the reads. I know what we're doing. This will work.*

Still, he didn't drift off until the sun finally started rising.

FROSTBURN

By the time she'd run through all the messages that had accumulated overnight, Frostburn felt she was mostly up to date. The most important information she had was the timeline—one day and change. One more day, and they might all be able to go home.

It's not that she didn't like being with the other members of the team, though stepping over Emu's drone pieces every morning was something she could do without. It wasn't just that some of those grease stains would never come out of the carpet. Living with the people you work with made life feel like work; every hour, every day. She missed her not-work life.

But it was now barely more than a day. That, she could get through. Especially since there was plenty to do in that time.

Emu was still up and tinkering, so Frostburn grabbed some 'kaf and sat on the couch reasonably close to the rigger's impromptu workstation. She knew she was about to make Emu's morning.

"Let's talk about cars."

The conversation with Emu was helpful, but also frustrating. It underlined the fact that there was a perfect mage for this job—and she wasn't it. This job demanded subtlety, finesse, and sneakiness. Sure, Frostburn could be stealthy, but mainly for the purpose of sneaking up on people and throwing a fireball or ice spear in their face. The job she had in front of her was better suited to a conjurer, or a manipulator, or something. But she was the tool the team had, and she was what would have to work—blunt as she was.

Zipfile made a persuasive argument why this wasn't going to be in her department. "Yeah, I could make the car not work for a little. But most of the things I can do remotely can be fixed easily, unless I try to fry the whole circuitry. Which is hard, because most people don't leave that on when they're not driving, so my access is limited. And if I do it while he's driving, it defeats the whole purpose of having the breakdown sneak up on him. Plus, do you know how many places my fingerprints are going to be when this is over? I have enough on my plate. You can do this. Figure it out."

So, with help from Emu, she figured it out. Maybe. Then Emu drove her and Zipfile to what was going to be the scene of the crime.

Simon Dennis, the Mr. Johnson formerly known as Mr. Miller (Frostburn had learned long ago that working the shadows meant being comfortable with lots of names and shifting identities), had a nice home in a safe part of Renton. Just east of the 405 was a cluster of a few dozen houses spread around a perimeter road with another single road cutting through the middle of it. The trees surrounding the development were mostly natural, with a few artificial models for power generation or surveillance thrown in.

"This is why I'm not gonna be helpful here," Zipfile said, watching the trees. "The people living here have money, tech resources, and a mountain of paranoia. There's a lot of corp facilities that'll be less guarded than this mess, at least Matrix-wise. They won't have Black IC—probably—because the corps can be touchy about letting that into the wild, but they'll have enough alerts set to get both GOD and Knight Errant to the scene in short order. Which is bad for the low profile we want to keep."

"But I'm just going to coast?" Frostburn asked.

"Do you know how paranoid someone has to be to keep a mage or spirit on retainer?" Emu asked.

"Shadowrunners do it all the time."

"Exactly. But you know how neighborhoods like this treat spirits—they don't trust 'em. Unauthorized summoning will get you cracked down on, hard. It's way worse than unauthorized spellcasting, since from what I hear, most of the times they don't know what people are casting anyway, so they don't scrutinize auras too closely. But spirits of any kind just make 'em nervous. From what I hear, it's best not to test 'em."

They didn't go into the subdivision itself, as both Emu and Zipfile assured her that they would be tracked as soon as they did so. But a drive around revealed a rather plain five-story hotel just west of the development. Zipfile made a quick render of the building and its environs and found that the top floor would be slightly too low to get a view over the trees—but the roof would be just right,

"This will work great," Frostburn said. "I'll get a room, set up shop here."

"Do you want company?"

Frostburn bit her tongue to keep herself from saying, "No, that's okay" too quickly. In the end, backup was more important than solitude. Solitude would come soon enough. "Yeah, having someone here would be good. And we should be coordinating anyway. Do you have a SIN we could use here?"

Zipfile rolled her eyes. "I could check in here with a drawing I made of my kitty in grade R."

There were about 200,000 hotel rooms in Seattle. A lot of them were Downtown, and were nicer than this, and tens of thousands were sleeping tubes, or something close to it. But about twenty thousand were like this—same full-size bed, same chipboard desk, same pay-for-play trid player. Twenty thousand identical rooms.

Frostburn couldn't decide whether that made her feel comfortably anonymous or entirely like a nonentity, a person to be overlooked and disregarded.

But like solitude, existential questions could wait a day or two.

When she did this for real, she'd need to be up on the roof herself, but for planning purposes, a drone was sufficient. Emu wasn't there anymore, but she'd left a crawler behind, and even entrusted Zipfile to run it herself. The dwarf took to it like a kid with a new remote-controlled car on Christmas.

"Forward...backward! Forward...backward! Now side to side!"

Frostburn glanced at the ARO Zipfile shared with her showing what the drone was seeing. It was moving in accordance with Zipfile's description. She returned to the car schematics Emu had referred her to.

"You better hope no one's paying attention to the roof."

"Oh, someone is. The two other kids who have drones up here are watching it all." She paused. "I think we're gonna race."

"I know tomorrow seems like it's a long way away, but maybe we should focus?"

After a single race around the roof—which she won handily, thanks in part to a cornering algorithm she whipped up on the fly—Zipfile set the drone to work.

The fates were smiling on this job enough that Frostburn was beginning to get suspicious. Sooner or later, she was going to have to pay for it. She just hoped fate could wait.

The garage of Dennis's house was where her focus would be, and it was perfect. The yard had a colorful array of bushes and native flowers—Zipfile's drone caught a glimpse of the gardening drone wandering through the branches and leaves—which partially obscured the front of the house. The driveway was broad and bright, leading up to a white garage door. She had a clear shot. She could even see the release for the opening mechanism inside a window above the door.

It was too perfect.

Even the car schematics she was looking up were making sense—the parts she had to target were things she already knew.

Zipfile kept the drone moving and taking pictures so Frostburn would have a virtual model of what they were seeing. Content that the dwarf knew what she was doing, Frostburn turned back to her AROs. She closed the car schematics and instead focused on the spell formula she had picked up—thanks for a referral from Emilia, of all things.

Food would come in ninety minutes. The sun would set in three hours. She'd probably wait three or four hours after that. Then, there would be no more sitting around.

At one o'clock in the morning, Simon Dennis was safe at home—in bed, judging by how the lights in his house had gone off a few hours ago. Zipfile was in the hotel room, hacking a Jitnee driver's profile while pacing the drone across the roof to keep an eye on things around Frostburn.

Frostburn, of course, was on the roof.

She wished she had been able to levitate herself from the floor of the room right out the window, but she had trouble steering through the angles when airborne. Instead, she had to step out the window and give herself a jolt as she fell and then caught herself. And then slowly drift upward.

They had put themselves on the top floor, so there was no other window to worry about passing. It was a short trip until her feet were on something solid. She scurried backward reflexively, moving away from the edge. Behind her, cars passed every few moments on the 405. None gave any indication of seeing her, primarily because she'd made herself invisible before stepping out of the window. This wasn't amateur hour.

Before she did anything, she scanned the area for auras—mages, spirits, anything that might throw a challenge her way. A few houses in the subdivision had mana barriers around them—*good for them,* Frostburn thought. Good to see people actually paying attention to the world. But it was even better to see that Dennis's home was not one of these. And none of the magical auras she saw looked like an entity—nothing that would see her or interfere with her. At 1 a.m. in this part of Renton, all the good mages were home in bed.

From the rooftop to the garage was about 120 meters. She had to make three shots from her perch. All of them would be hard.

Actually, the first shot itself wouldn't be difficult—*seeing* it would. The lights in the house were out. There were no lights in the garage. The only nearby lights were street lights, and their glare off the garage windows only made the task harder.

<Get the drone next to me,> Frostburn messaged Zipfile. <Focus on the top of the garage.>

The drone's camera zoomed in, and the earlier images they had taken during the day came in handy. They could match up the daytime images with the nighttime ones to see which line or which shadow she was seeing was the item she wanted.

Zipfile went to work. Once the drone had found what should be the handle they were looking for, she programmed an ARO to paint it in Frostburn's field of vision, so that her AR glasses painted a line over where the handle should be. The success of the spell depended on its accuracy.

She reached out. Normally this would just mean reaching out with mana, but Frostburn unconsciously reached out with her hand, too, as if it could stretch 120 meters to the garage. The spell she had learned was sort of like levitate, but with a downward pull instead of an upward lift.

She couldn't be sure if it worked. She couldn't even be sure if she had actually cast it. If she had done it, the only effect was a small bit of movement and a *click,* which she couldn't hear at this distance. There would be only one way to know.

This time it was a straightforward levitate spell, but slow. She let the mana ooze forward, almost crawling toward the bottom of the garage. It slowly reduced gravity's pull on the door, allowing it to creep up its rolling track.

Except it didn't. She had let out enough mana to make the whole thing go up—more than enough, by her estimation—and the door did not move.

The first spell hadn't worked.

She panted. She'd accomplished practically nothing, and she felt an edge of weariness. She really, really wanted to blow something up now.

She took a breath. Back to square one. Focus on the ARO. Picture where the handle would be. Imagine its reality. *Feel* its reality.

Her hand was out again. Her fingers opened and closed, then clenched. Then moved down.

Again, no sign of anything. So she let mana flow into the bottom of the garage door.

Slowly, it raised.

She did not cry out in triumph, but she allowed herself a little dance. Dancing while invisible was the easiest way to dance like no one was watching.

She let it get most of the way up, then paused it. If she let it get all the way up, she'd have to contrive a way to get it back down. This way, she'd just be able to let it go when she was done with it—gently, of course.

That meant she'd be sustaining two spells for the rest of the job. Not optimal.

At least targeting would be easier. The car had been backed in so that the charging port was easily accessible, and she could easily see the familiar green glow of the port reflected on the cable. This shot would be a piece of cake.

Except for the two spells she was already sustaining.

The spear she was going to make had to be small but sharp. It couldn't make much noise when it hit.

And it had to hit a target less than a centimeter wide.

But she could do this. She hadn't been ice darts champion three years running at the Sewer View Tavern for nothing.

She put her left hand on her hip, then pointed with her right in a quick flicking motion. A sharp, gleaming dart shot out of her index finger and traveled straight for the garage.

The reflected light of the charging port went out. Perfect shot. Triple-20.

Almost there. One more spell. A long one.

Or maybe several consecutive spells. Depended on how you counted. Either way, it would be exhausting. And her legs were already wobbly.

It was another ice spear, or series of spears. She made the ice loose and chunky, so it broke apart as it flew. By the time it arrived at the car, it hit the windshield with a splat—hopefully not too loud of a splat—and what was now slushy ice slid down toward the hood. Then another. And another. And another.

She kept it up as long as she could. Probably too long. Her legs buckled as she threw another one, her vision swam, and before she knew what was going on, she was looking down and the ground was moving toward her.

She dropped. Her head was past the edge of the roof, as were her shoulders. The rest of her, though, was held up. The roof was tilted, but not so much that she was in danger of falling.

She lay there, the roofing rough through her clothes. She probably wasn't invisible anymore. The garage door was probably down. She didn't know if there were any lights on in the house. She couldn't move her head to look. She also didn't want to move any body parts to compose and send a message. So she just spoke.

"Any sign Dennis is awake?"

Zipfile heard her over the comm. *"No. No neighbors, either. Wealthy people and their white noise machines are a great blessing in our line of work. And since you unlatched the garage from the inside, no automated systems thought you were breaking in."*

"Next week, everyone on the block will have their alarms looking out for unauthorized ice."

"Yeah, but that'll be next week."

Frostburn didn't reply.

"So, you coming back down?"

Blood was flowing to Frostburn's head, since it was lower than her feet. It wasn't comfortable, but it also wasn't enough to make her want to move.

"In a minute," she said. "I'm just gonna lie here. For a sec."

It was approaching two in the morning. It felt like she had done her part here. There was more to do before sunrise, though. Zipfile, below, was hacking away. She'd ask how it was going when she felt like talking.

RUDE

The whole world wants to get out of the way of a determined troll.

That was a central fact of Rude's life, and he was more than willing to lean into it. Gaze straight ahead. Raise the shoulders and lean forward a little. Then stomp. And watch how crowds of people part.

It didn't work everywhere, of course. Some of your more sophisticated audiences recognized the tactic for what it was, and all it did was made them more alert.

All the more reason to use it while he could.

He stomped through Glow City. Nothing in this place felt all that stable to begin with, and more than one person looked fearfully at the concrete walls as Rude passed by, ready to see cracks appearing and spreading. He watched them out of the corner of his eye, because he loved to see their panic.

Glow City didn't have any official protocol. People set up stalls and tried not to step on each other's toes. Some of the few intact rooms were held, by common consent, by a few of the top sellers, people who had a knack for bringing valuables in each and every night. If you wanted electronics, from commlinks to trid players to even cyberdecks, you came here.

The serious hardware—the stuff Rude was looking for—was harder to find. There was nothing official about this protocol; it was more like instinct. People knew certain classes of goods should be difficult to find. They should only be sold to the people willing to work to find them. These sellers never were in the more easily accessible areas, and they avoided setting up in the same place twice.

The auxiliary building was a good place to start—it was out of the way and dark, so few people wandered into it by accident. Rude pulled open a flare as he walked in and held it over his head, announcing his presence. He wouldn't have any trouble seeing in the dark, but the flare was to let him be seen.

This wasn't the right place today, though. The auxiliary building was mostly empty, and the few people there were selling pop-culture drek—vinyl albums and the like. Nothing Rude needed.

Building 4 was another good option, as it had developed into a warren of warehouse shelves, but it, too, was a bust for the night (though there were some ammo dealers he would have liked to talk to if he could spare a minute). That left perhaps Rude's least favorite option.

The Sixth World had a particular affection for architecture that shouldn't exist but did, due to a combination of magic and necessity being the mother of invention. The interior of the cooling tower of Glow City had a ramshackle staircase winding around the inside of it, giving access to a variety of pods and platforms constructed into the wall. There shouldn't be a good way of holding some of these structures up, but most of them had some magical help in becoming what they were. The questions that were always on Rude's mind, though, were one, did these spellcasters actually know anything about architecture, or were they just winging it; and two, did they ever plan on having trolls walk on their projects? The staircase and the places it led did not feel at all safe to him. But if that was where he was going to find what he needed, that's where he needed to go.

The first set of stairs were nice, solid stone that caused Rude no worries whatsoever, and the wooden stairs that followed them after the first stone platform were solidly built. Then you had to step over this weird pod that was only accessible through a trap door (that wasn't troll-sized, so ghost help Rude if what he needed was in there), and from that point on the stairs got a little dicey. They were mostly wooden up past that platform, and some had clearly been built without the assistance of a spellcaster, or even a competent carpenter. Stairs that creaked when you stepped on them were one thing—stairs that noticeably sagged a few centimeters were another. And stairs that dangled by a single nail were an even larger warning that something here was wrong, and maybe someone troll-sized shouldn't be taking this route.

But someone troll-sized was.

Rude almost danced up the stairs, each step carefully flowing to the next, sometimes with a hop or twist put in to help him hit the part of the steps that looked the safest. He stopped on platforms that looked promising, or sometimes on one that would give him a break and a chance to survey the next part of his climb. The first platform had a batch of home-brewed *hurlg* that he might have to check out later. The second platform made him feel like he was on the right track—they had a fine collection of street drugs on display, awaiting the pleasure of the user. None of the harder stuff (novacoke users would have to look elsewhere), but deep weed, psyche, and long haul were all available. That made Rude feel like he was getting closer to the right kind of criminals. He continued up past Awakened reagents and a grenade collection, which just increased the feeling he was getting closer.

Then he arrived at another pod that was only accessible by trapdoor. He would have loved to pass by this one, but the vibe it was giving off made him stop. A couple bangers sat on top, perched casually, doing nothing to try to convince passers-by that they were dangerous. Which meant they weren't to be taken lightly.

Rude stopped dancing and assumed an unhurried walk for the few steps to the pod's trapdoor. "Youse ain't gonna make me go down there, are ya?"

One of bangers, a male ork, shrugged. "You don't gotta go nowhere you don't wanna go."

"But ya got the stuff."

The ork shook his head. "Stop fishing, *omae*. You think you shouldn't be here, just don't be here. You want something, ask."

"Gotta blow somethin' up," Rude said.

"Then get in the pod."

Rude pointed at the trapdoor. "In there? How?"

The other banger, a female human, whipped the door open. A sharp wooden *clap* echoed in the cooling tower.

"Drop your head in, tough guy."

Rude shook his head and grumbled, but he stepped forward, dropped to his knees, then stuck his head through the trapdoor.

The pod was almost a cube, four by four by five. Two people sat inside, a female elf and a male human. The elf was carefully cleaning an assault rifle, while the human, who had cheekbones like polished marble, leaned back in his folding chair and looked pretty. Behind them were crates covered by canvas drop cloths.

The elf did not glance up from her rifle as Rude's head dropped in. "What?"

"I wanna blow stuff up."

She snorted and still did not look up. "What are you, twelve?"

"I need 100 kilos of 60-weight dynamite and ten blocks of Semtex."

That finally got the elf to look up. "Well, look who knows someone who knows something about explosives!"

"Yeah, blood's rushing t'my head here. Can we do this, or what?"

"You're not just walking out of here with a hundred kilos of dynamite, pal. Even if you could carry it."

"I'll bring this whole pod to the ground if it means ending this conversation."

The elf shook her head. "You're why people hate working retail. Smile for the camera."

Before Rude could react to that, the human had pulled out his commlink and snapped a picture of Rude's head. Then he turned the screen toward the elf. "His face is upside-down."

The elf guffawed.

"Oh, youse're hilarious," Rude said. "We doing business or not?"

"Be patient," the elf said. "I know you have a few guns in that part of your body we haven't seen yet. Do you loan them out to just anyone?"

"No."

"Why not?"

"'Cause they're mine."

"Sure, but if I promise to give 'em right back, why not let me hold one for a minute?"

"You? 'Cause I think ya might just pop me in the head."

"There you go. You get it. We have to make sure you're not just going to take our stuff and blow up something we care about."

"Tell me whatcha care about, and I'll let ya know if I'm goin' after it."

"Yeah, no. Nice try. Now *shhh*. Let the databases work."

Actually, Rude wouldn't mind letting the databases work if they showed him something about his past that would fill in the gaps, but he didn't think the elf was going to share her findings. Unless she saw something that made her order the bangers on the roof to put a bullet in the back of his skull.

They wouldn't. Probably. One reason he came all the way out to Glow City was he didn't have any ongoing beefs with the people who operated here.

But in case things went wrong, he'd applied a little extra armor to the back of his skull.

A few minutes went by. The elf cleaned her gun. The human glowered prettily. Then she looked up.

"Well, look at that! The system says we can do business! How nice for us. Just one more question—how do you plan on transporting the items you've requested."

Rude twitched his head toward his back. "Backpack."

Both elf and human stared humorlessly.

"Fine. Car trunk lined with flame-retardant material, suspension inspection performed just today by a vehicular expert. But whaddaya care if I blow myself up?"

The elf let a hint of a smile show. "What do I care indeed? All right, get your head out of here. My associates up top will tell you what to do."

Relieved, Rude pulled his head out of the trap door.

"Here's what you do—" the ork banger started.

Rude held up his hand. "Wait'll I hear something 'sides my own pulse." Just because you're a tough street samurai doesn't mean your circulatory system likes prolonged inversion.

He had to endure an entire drive of Emu on the comm saying, *"Don't hit a pothole don't hit a pothole don't hit a pothole"* before he arrived at the designated parking garage.

The trunk of the Hyundai Shin-HyungT (The last "T" is for "troll") was not only wrapped in flame retardant material, but also a fabric to prevent chem sniffers from detecting anything, which helped Rude get as far as he had. Now, though, he'd gotten as far as he could on his own. Being a troll with attitude gets you a lot of places, but one place it won't get you is inside a building in the middle of the night while carrying a case of dynamite. He'd need help on this, which was bad enough—what made it worse was where the help would come from.

An American pulled in shortly after he did, and a familiar form dressed in casual black stepped out.

"Alright, Elfy-pants, ready ta show me how ta blend inta the shadows?"

Yu shook his head. "We can't count on the shadows always being large enough. I brought help." He jerked a thumb at the car's backseat, where Frostburn was sprawled across the back seats, sleeping.

"Oh yeah, she'll definitely save the day."

"She's had a long night, but she'll be okay. It'll be better than making you crawl through the whole building, don't you think?"

Rude couldn't help but agree. "How are we gonna wake her?"

Yu smiled his smug smile, the one that made his face extra-punchable. "I learned a trick." He walked over to the car, opened the door, stuck his head in, and said, in a conversational tone, "Emilia's in trouble."

Frostburn's head jerked up, and she looked around for two seconds, startled, before figuring out what was going on.

"Drek-for-brains," she said. "You keep abusing that, it's going to stop working."

"Worked this time," Yu said. "That's all I needed."

Frostburn stretched as much as she could in the backseat, then sat up and got out. "Let's go find a place to disappear."

While they looked for a place where they could conveniently disappear from view, an additional reason for the mage to be along came up.

"They've got a spirit," Frostburn told them as they circled the building. "Just a watcher, but it'll see the invisibility spell easily, and it'll raise an alarm."

"Which means?"

"Watchers are pretty dumb. They're usually set into a routine, I'll learn the routine, and we'll go from there."

Learning the routine took only about ten minutes, because spirits covered a lot of ground quickly, so in that time period it covered the entire building five times.

"Two minutes," Frostburn said. "That's what you have between spirit passes."

"So whadawe do?" Rude said. "Not like we can just duck inna broom closet or something while it goes back. If we're in the building, it'll see us, right?"

"We just have to be watching the clock at all times, and we have to use the stairs—down. It's going from bottom to top, right?"

Frostburn nodded.

"So every time the spirit's coming near, we go downstairs, let it pass, then get back to work."

Rude didn't like it, but he also didn't have an alternative. "That's what we'll do."

The whole time he was getting ready for this, Rude didn't think he'd like it. It was too contained. Too small. Too quiet. He liked big, loud statements. Big, loud action. He was going to feel stifled. Boxed in.

Then it started. And he loved it.

It was high-wire tension. Focus in every movement. A sort of grace.

Zipfile had gotten them a map of the key pillars of the building. In an ideal world, they'd drill holes in each pillar and insert the explosives with precision. But this was nothing close to ideal. The work would be done in bursts of about one hundred seconds, and they couldn't come close to the noise that drilling through steel—and whatever was covering it—would make.

They had to go clumsy, but they also couldn't just be obvious, since leaving dynamite strapped to the outside of the columns would be noticed by even the dimmest office drones—and possibly even the watcher spirit. The cladding around the support columns had a gap of about four centimeters at the base. That, plus the SnatcherSnake toy robot arm they had picked up, would help them get the explosives in place.

Each stick had a fuse that would be triggered by a detonator that had to be within five centimeters of the fuse. The signal wouldn't travel farther than that. The detonators would be placed with the dynamite and then left off until, hopefully, it was too late.

Yu had provided some tips on moving silently, but Rude surprised himself by not really needing them. When they snuck through a door closing behind a night janitor, he moved like silk feels. Or like water. He *flowed* through the door. Even though he was carrying about fifty kilos of gear (he'd damn well made Frostburn and Elfy-pants carry some of it, and while the ork held her own, who was gonna ask an elf to carry anything close to what a troll hauled?). He knew the joy he was having in movement meant something, probably something about his past, but he was too enthralled with it to think about it carefully.

The janitor, deep in the thrall of whatever was pumping through his ear buds, didn't even flinch as they slipped in.

The timer had already started. Two minutes. First column. Pull out dynamite, spray adhesive, slip it under, adhere it. Keep fuse down. Check timer. Repeat if possible.

They got three sticks on the column. Then moved. Forward, right, through a door, down stairs. Wait. Watch timer. Then back up. Frostburn first, looking on two levels, astral and physical, but not doing much else because she was keeping three people invisible.

The watcher spirit wasn't the only obstacle. Physical guards made occasional rounds and watched the hallways with cameras. The invisibility spell was there to hinder their efforts, but that didn't mean they could make noise, or move things too much with their invisible hands.

They kept moving, column to column. Pull out, spray, slip in, adhere. Check fuse. Check timer. Get out of sight. Over and over.

Then Frostburn tripped.

They were on their way up after getting out of the watcher's way. The ork caught her toe on the top step, then stumbled forward.

The floor was a metal sheet. It rang like a bell on early Sunday morning.

All three of them said nothing. They didn't stand still. They went down, as quickly as quiet steps could manage. Rude used the handrail to support his weight so his feet made only glancing contact with the surface of the stairs. The building was built to modern standards, so it had a reinforced handrail at troll height—Rude mentally added the architects of the place to the small list of corporate people he maybe didn't entirely hate.

It almost made him feel a touch bad about what he was doing to their work.

At the bottom of the stairs, the door opened, smooth and silent. That was Yu, who clearly had some secret art to opening doors stealthily. Rude went through, not knowing where Frostburn was.

Above, footsteps hit the landing they had just left. Two of them. Voices, too.

"See anything?"

"Scuff mark, maybe. But I sure heard something."

"Yeah. Camera mics picked the sound up, too."

"But they didn't see anything?"

"No."

Rude mentally patted Frostburn on the back. Keeping her focus while tripping was good work. Of course, he wouldn't actually *tell* her that. He assumed she knew.

"Watcher's going up, so it will see anything above. Let's check down."

They had to coordinate and move quickly, and they had to do it without commlinks. They had all their electronics off to avoid giving an observant spider anything to notice. They couldn't signal to each other, because they couldn't see each other. But they were ready for this.

A sticky note appeared on a wall in front of Rude, out of nowhere. He moved to the left side of it. He might have heard Frostburn to his right. The note said: "*R, 30m st, R dr, up, back.*"

He stared at it until it vanished again. Then he counted to three to give Frostburn time to move, and then turned right to follow the directions Rude had written.

He went straight about thirty meters and saw a door opening to his right. Behind him, the two guards had entered the hallway and were looking around. The door swung into the stairwell—the guards might see it from their angle, they might not. Either way, no sense in waiting around. Frostburn should have already gone through, so Rude followed.

He slipped up the stairs as the door closed silently behind him. Did Yu have to study lots of different door types to know how to move them quietly? Was it instinctual?

Had Rude studied how to move quietly? Had someone taught him? Who? When? Why? No time for misty memories right now. Focus.

Rude waited for the door at the top of the stairs to open, then slid through it. They returned to the column they had been working on, but they didn't get back to work. They slunk into dark corners and waited, watched. When the timer told them the watcher was coming, they went back to where Frostburn had tripped in the first place. The guards had moved on.

So much of these movements had been worked out the day before. The system of communicating by sticky notes. How Rude, Yu, and Frostburn should position themselves relative to each other. They'd even gone up and down some stairs in Frostburn's hotel with blindfolds on to get some practice in moving together without seeing each other. One or two passers-by had seen them practicing, but it was probably far from the weirdest thing they'd see that day, so they didn't seem to care.

Rude had grumbled a lot during the planning and practice, but that was mainly out of habit. He knew it would be valuable, and the last couple of minutes had made that clear.

They went back to the work of preparing for the building's destruction.

Frostburn's stumble must have been a sort of wake-up call, because the rest of the night went smoothly—if slowly, as the even distribution of 100 kilos of dynamite while avoiding a watcher spirit was time consuming. All told, it wasn't terrible. When they were done, the early arrivers to the building were still a few hours off, and early morning traffic might allow them to get back to the safehouse and get a small amount of sleep. Frostburn made some halfhearted remarks about maybe she could just go back to her hotel, but Yu brushed her off, and Rude ignored the two of them. They'd done their part, he'd done his. The pieces were in place, the plans had been made.

Tomorrow, it would all go off.

That mean Rude might not sleep. The high-wire grace he'd felt while they made their way through AVR was leaving, but he could feel adrenaline building to replace it. There were moments in the next day he was looking forward to—*really* looking forward to—and he wasn't sure he'd be able to chase the visions of them out of his head to allow sleep. Yeah, he was tired, but he knew how to push through that—adrenaline, determination, and street drugs were a powerful cocktail.

So while Frostburn and Yu immediately disappeared to sleep when they hit the safehouse (having re-appeared, physically, back at the parking garage when they left), Rude sat down next to Zipfile, who of course was awake and working.

"Ya know we been out riskin' our hoops while ya sit here playin' in the Matrix, right?"

Zipfile didn't look at him. "I know."

"All the risk, right in our shoulders. While you sat here."

"Go tell Dieter there's no risk on my end."

"Who?"

"A guy. Who died doing what I'm doing."

"What happened, he choke on a Frito?"

Zipfile finally looked up. "If you're so bored, you could go find an alley cat to kick or something."

"But then I'd havta move."

"Lazy rudeness is the worst rudeness."

"'S all I got right now."

"Lucky me."

Rude disappointed himself by letting several minutes go by without another comment. But then he thought of one. "Ya know how much of this we're *not* being paid to do?"

"Some." Her hands wiggled for a few moments on Matrix tasks Rude couldn't see. "Consider it an investment in ourselves."

"Yeah. 'Cause we're the only ones really investin' in us."

"For now."

Something was tickling at his head. It had been different once. He thought it had. He had been sought out. A desired commodity. Then the big blur, the big grey in his head that separated *then* from *now*. And separated the people who wanted something from him from the person he was now.

He couldn't, though, remember what it was they wanted from him.

That thought occupied him so much that he might have fallen asleep while wrestling with it.

ZIPFILE

Plate spinning and juggling are two different tasks, even though they're sometimes used to describe the same things. Juggling is more controlled. It's difficult, sure, but the art to it is that you control the velocity and trajectory of each item you throw. You just need deft hands. That's easier said than done, but it's all in your control. If you do it right, you can stand in one spot and let the items fall to you.

Plate spinning is different. Yes, you touch each plate, but you have to go to them. They won't come to you. And your movement adds more variables, like a tremor in the ground or the breeze of your passing. And you do not reach a point of equilibrium or calm, you just keep moving.

The vast majority of times, Matrix runs were plate spinning, not juggling. This one was not just plate spinning, it was plate spinning in a crowd of people who actively wanted the dishes to break.

Dieter had shown her of the challenge of making a frontal attack on any part of AVR's Matrix. She wasn't going to walk in there and just bend the system to her will. But she still had a big role to play.

She'd like to just stay remote and keep all the plates spinning from some bunker, but the job would be tough enough without adding Matrix noise to the challenge. Plus, it gave her the chance to let Yu think his little speech earlier had worked.

Around six in the morning, when the team was assembled and ready to go out and get the job done, Yu stood between them and the door.

"We've been running in five different directions lately. We've helped each other, sure. But we've been scattered. There's good reason for that, but now we're together. We're a team. We're going to make a statement today."

"Yeah, RIP," Rude said.

Yu ignored that, of course. "We're all in this together. Let's give 'em hell."

"Wasn't that from *Chase: Errant Knight*?" Emu said.

"I thought it was from *Blood Runners*," Zipfile said.

"Maybe it was a compilation," Frostburn said. "A greatest hits collection of sappy speeches."

Yu turned to let them all go out the door, looking a little disconsolate. Rude clapped him on the shoulder as he passed. "Lookit how ya brought everyone together to mock ya. Good job."

Then they went out.

It took two vehicles. Yu drove Emu's Bulldog step-van; Emu drove her GMC Commodore, freshly detailed and made to look like a Jitnee car, with both real-world and AR light-up logos. Zipfile rode in the Commodore, with everyone else in the Bulldog.

Zipfile had already set up everything she'd have to monitor. That list was:

- Maintain the hack making Emu's car an authorized Jitnee;
- Make sure no one's fake SIN was blown;
- Monitor what was happening at AVR without doing anything that might make their ID grumpy;
- Ensure every dynamite detonator came online and stayed there;
- Ensure the blocks she had put on nearby emergency services were intact;
- Maintain the master detonator; and of course

- Make sure the approximately two billion cameras in the area saw what they were supposed to see and didn't see what they shouldn't see.

All the plates needed to stay up—right up until the big boom, when she'd happily let a few of them drop.

This meant she wasn't great conversation on the drive. She was going to have to do this on the move when they got there, so she spent the drive training her brain how to see all these things at once, making part of the background noise of her thought process. Lungs breathed, heart beat, and brain watched the Matrix.

Traffic had picked up beyond middle-of-the-night level, but it had not yet reached why-aren't-we-moving-what-is-wrong-with-everyone level. It was one of those Seattle mornings where the sun didn't so much as rise as make the cloud cover incrementally lighter shades of grey. Rain spat intermittently as if the clouds, like much of the population of the sprawl, were just really having trouble getting going this morning.

The Commodore stopped before Zipfile knew they were getting close. They were further away from the building than the Bulldog, since Emu would need to be able to drive up when the time came. They were in a Soybucks parking lot. Zipfile would be here long enough to grab a soykaf, then she'd be off to fill the anticipated ride request from Simon Dennis, who was about to find out his car battery was entirely drained.

Emu reached into the back, grabbed a case, and handed them to Zipfile. "You got four in there. I assume you know how to activate them?"

"Are you asking if I know how to turn on a drone? Really?"

"Okay, fine. Take them. Go."

Zipfile turned and looked at the passenger-side door and stared. "What are you waiting for?"

The dwarf glanced back over her shoulder. "I'm not a rigger, so I'm just not sure how to open one of your fancy car doors!"

"Get the hell out of here."

Zipfile grinned and opened the door, getting a shove on her shoulder from Emu to help her get out. She turned and looked back at the rigger before walking away. One advantage of being a dwarf is you didn't have to bend awkwardly to talk to someone inside a car.

"Do it right," she said. "Make him see you."

Emu nodded, and Zipfile headed off to AVR.

Zipfile wore a white blazer over blue-and-black vertically striped pants. Frostburn had a white tank top over a short plaid skirt and long black leather boots, giving her a kind of business punk vibe that worked with her hair. Yu was Yu, his dark suit and skinny red tie making him look like someone who could walk into any office in the world.

Rude—well, Rude looked like hired muscle. Zipfile didn't think he could look like anything else. Black trench coat, jeans, white t-shirt. Basic and simple. And they wouldn't be the first business people traveling with muscle, so he'd be fine.

Of course, they weren't supposed to be together, so Rude was assigned to someone—specifically, to Zipfile. She hoped it would be a blessing, not an obstacle.

Two blocks away, they stopped. Zipfile reviewed the status of the fake SINs, and Yu reviewed who should go in when and what they should do when they got there.

Then Zipfile and Rude walked away, since they were going in first. It was underway.

She wanted to have a kind of laid-back stride, but that wouldn't be possible if she was going to keep pace with Rude, so she went with business brisk instead. Rude, of course, got to walk as lazily as he pleased without fear of falling behind.

It was just before eight. Worker drones were all over, flooding into 'kaf shops and offices. Wireless devices weren't really a problem now, since there would be so many that a security spider wouldn't be alerted by seeing one. They'd only look for something threatening, so one of Zipfile's jobs was to keep that from happening.

The most immediate concern was looking like she fit in inside an office building without actually doing anything.

They approached reception for the day's first test.

A female elf—corporations of a certain size seemed to have a bottomless supply of attractive elves to stock their front desks—smiled at her as she approached. "Can I help you?"

"Yes, thanks! I'm Lesedi Kriege, I have a ten o'clock with Suelyn Briggs." She smiled as the receptionist started to speak. "I know, I know, I'm early. Very early. Traffic delays never hit when you expect, right? But it's spitting rain out there, and all the 'kaf spots are crowded, and wandering around the city isn't going to work in these heels. I won't bother Ms. Briggs early, but if there's a water cooler near any sort of horizontal surface, I'll plant myself there and won't even be noticeable."

The receptionist nodded, partially because Zipfile's fake SIN had been cleared, and because the appointment (phoned in by Yu yesterday) had been verified. "Of course, Ms. Kriege. There's a lunchroom through those doors, down the hall, and on the right. No one will be eating yet, so you can be there and barely be noticed!"

"Perfect! Thank you. I'll make sure my associate—" she jerked her head backward, "—doesn't break anything."

Rude, whose SIN had also cleared, squinted menacingly at the receptionist as he passed. Zipfile wasn't sure if he was playing a role or just acting on his mood.

They were in. She watched the ARO with information on the SINs carefully, looking for signs of any alerts, any double checking, any alarm.

She saw none.

Time to get some crappy workplace soykaf.

She led Rude to the lunchroom—she full well knew where it was, of course, even if the receptionist hadn't directed her—and walked inside. It was empty. Rude filled up the doorway, letting her have the room all to herself for at least a few seconds.

She opened Emu's case, took out the small crawler drones, and turned them on. They followed their programming and immediately scurried to dark corners of the cafeteria.

She checked their signals. Her programming had held—they looked like commlinks. Four commlinks, moving around the building like commlinks on the hips of office workers do.

<Drones are green,> she messaged.

They scurried off. Zipfile had volunteered to program them for the job they needed to do, and Emu had shot her a look somewhere between incredulity and murderous rage. So they were in her hands now.

Once the drones were moving, Rude cleared the doorway and sat down. There was not a troll-sized chair in the room, and his feelings about it were clear on his face. He put two chairs next to each other and perched on them. Awkwardly.

"One hundred minutes until my bathroom trip," he said. "Got a deck of cards?"

"I'm so glad this is leisure time for you." Emu was going to control the drones, but Zipfile sure as hell was going to watch them move. Four more plates added to her show.

They sat quietly for ten minutes. Then Frostburn sent a message that she had what she needed, and was ready to come in.

"All right, get up. Time to find a commlink. An Erika Elite, specifically. I caught a signal from what looks like one about two offices away."

Rude stood and followed her out. Zipfile walked past the designated office. The name on it was Anita Ibarra.

They split up, Zipfile moving toward the office door, Rude moving to the end of the hallway. Zipfile knocked gently on the door frame, since the door was open.

"Hi, you're Anita, right?"

The woman inside, who had dark hair tucked into a sensible bun, nodded.

"Hi, I'm Lesedi Kriege with Cartwright. I'm here early for a meeting with Suelyn Briggs, and my commlink and your public host simply are not getting along. Any chance you could help me see where I'm going wrong?"

Anita smiled and walked to the office doorway. "Share some AROs with me, and I'll see what I can do."

The nice thing about the first floor was that most of them reported to Suelyn Briggs. Which made them willing to help her, since it meant helping their boss.

Anita flipped through the AROs Zipfile shared. The public file transfer center was nowhere to be found—since Zipfile had gone to a decent amount of trouble to edit it out. That was another spinning plate.

"You're right, it's not there. That's the darnedest thing!" Anita said. "The Matrix—who knows what it'll spit out, right?"

Zipfile grinned in shared commiseration. "I swear it's become sentient. And is a total ass."

"Here, let me share my view, I can at least show you where it is." Anita made a few gestures, and some AROs appeared to Zipfile, showing her what she had seen before she had deliberately screwed things up.

"Yep, that's definitely different than what I'm seeing. You've got a square building with the columns, and an x-shaped building. Which one should I be looking for?"

Anita raised her arm to point to one of the hovering buildings. That was when Rude came crashing into the doorway.

Sweeping Zipfile out of the way, he knocked Anita to the ground. The troll stood over her menacingly for a second, then stepped back, suddenly looking confused.

"Uh-oh," he said.

"What the *hell?*" Anita said. "You—clumsy *drekhead!*"

"Max, you *idiot.*" Zipfile said at about the same time. "What do you think you're doing?"

"I...I thought I saw something," he mumbled. "I thought she was making a move. A threat."

"Let me help you up, Anita." Extending a hand, Zipfile rolled her eyes as she pulled the corp exec to her feet. "I am *so* sorry about this. Our higher-ups just started sending bodyguards on some trips—" She glared at Rude, who managed to look suitably abashed. "—but I don't think they screened them very carefully."

Anita frowned as she dusted herself off. "I'd get rid of him if I were you. Fast. Before he gets arrested for assault."

"I will take that under advisement," Zipfile replied. "but more importantly, are you all right?"

Anita straightened her skirt and checked herself over one last time. "I'm okay, but...where's my commlink?"

Zipfile looked over to where it lay in the hallway floor. "There. Is it okay?"

Anita gingerly picked it up, but the shattered glass and other parts falling off it made it clear that it was not, in fact, okay.

It helped that Rude, in his charge, had made certain to hit it with a small glass punch he had been holding.

"Oh no," Zipfile said. "Oh no, I'm so sorry. That's unacceptable. That's—that looks like an Erika, right? An Elite? Hold on." She made a show of typing things on her commlink. "Okay, I'm having a replacement couriered over, on us. We'll have you back up and running before you know it. The messenger will be here soon."

Anita still looked upset, but nodded.

"She'll be one of our people—with Cartwright." She smiled wanly. "If we know anything, it's how to move things quickly."

"Fine. I appreciate you taking care of this, but I really need to get back to work. Excuse me." She walked away. Zipfile didn't blame her for being angry. But once the rest of this morning's events were done, Anita would likely have forgotten all about this commlink incident.

Zipfile returned to the lunchroom and set about activating the new 'link Frostburn had just boosted. Frostburn arrived about ten minutes later, posing as Lisa the courier, and the receptionist sent her back to Anita's office, and Zipfile made sure everything was working properly. Anita seemed content. And Frostburn was in the building.

Yu came a few minutes later. He had arranged an appointment for himself like he had for Zipfile, and his SIN held up.

They were all in.

They only met up at the lunchroom long enough to nod at each other. Emu's drones had been busy in the meantime, connecting fuses and turning on detonators. The team followed their work as best they could, strolling around the floor and looking at the bottom of support columns as much as they could without looking stupid or obvious.

Then it was 9:30. Frostburn nodded to the others.

"See you later, Lisa," Zipfile said, and passed her a commlink. One that, if it were hit with some outside electrical force, would set off everything. Frostburn took it and left.

"Positions," Yu muttered. "Stay safe."

They split up.

Zipfile walked to a west stairwell, Yu to one on the east. Rude went to the bathroom.

There were four bathrooms on the first floor. Zipfile watched a feed from Rude's 'link as he went into every one, just long enough to drop something in the wastebaskets—though in two cases, he crumpled up some extra paper, filling the baskets more.

There was no wireless capacity on these devices. Just a timer, set so they all went off at the same time.

Four trash fires started in four separate bathrooms. The packages Rude dropped in had a little extra material to make sure they didn't just burn out in seconds.

Fire alarms went off.

The building's alarm system triggered sprinklers in the bathroom, but the sprinklers had been bent the night before. They didn't spread the water right. The fires burned. People poked curious heads out of offices, and some of them saw smoke.

Voices grew louder. Some people ran to the bathrooms and saw smoke and flames. They immediately pulled manual alarms, even though alarms were already going off. This mainly served to make more noise.

Then the floor captains kicked in. The loudspeakers came to life. Thank heavens for corporate training.

"AVR employees, please exit the building now. Please follow established emergency drill procedures. Exit the building now."

Well-trained staff should be able to leave a building like this in less than five minutes. Ideally, the fire department would be here before then—if the alarm had contacted them. Zipfile didn't want to break into the AVR host, but the underfunded Seattle Fire Department was another matter. The nearest station, a mere three kilometers away, currently had no idea that alarms were going off. And they had been disconnected from the emergency alert system, too. Help was on the way, but not from the closest possible place.

Zipfile had helpfully positioned herself near an exit, and she directed people out, making sure they didn't stop to think if it was really a serious enough fire. She also scanned the crowd for the face of Simon Dennis.

She caught glimpses of Rude dashing through the hallways. Most people were out of the first floor, so Rude had pretty much a free run of the place. He found a few papers to add to one of the fires, then got ambitious with the legs of some chairs.

It was enough. It would burn as long as they needed it to.

<*Any sign?*> Zipfile sent to Yu.

<*Not yet,*> he returned, but as soon as he did, it didn't matter. Because there he was, grey hair, tailored suit, and all. Simon Dennis didn't look pleased, but he also didn't look like he knew what was in store.

It wasn't Zipfile's job to let him know. Not yet. She stepped out of stairwell to make sure he didn't see her, just to be on the safe side. She still had a view of him as he stopped, looked around briefly before leaving, then exited the building.

He was out. Since he was on her side of the building, it was her job to follow him. She did, messaging Yu and Rude as she did so.

<*I'm on him.*>

The traffic behind her seemed to be pretty light. Most of the building was out. For their sake, she hoped they all were out.

One minute.

Most of the workers were across the street. Zipfile went a little further away, just to be sure, but she couldn't be too far from Dennis. She had a role to play. She edged near him. He exchanged a few words with other workers, but nothing sustained. He stared at the building, puzzled.

Forty-five seconds.

Maybe he was beginning to figure it out. Maybe something odd about the morning was tickling the back of his brain. He was looking around with increasing purpose, like he was seeking something specific. It was almost time to give him something to see.

Thirty seconds.

Zipfile had been using shadows and her shortness to keep out of sight. But now she stepped into the gray daylight, stood up straight, perching herself fully on top of her high heels. The street closest to her rose uphill, so she took a few steps back to gain elevation.

Fifteen seconds.

"Dennis," she said. There was a lot of noise on the street, but she spoke it loud and clear.

He looked at her. He didn't know, at first. But then she saw it register.

"You should get out of here," she said.

Confusion on his face became a sneer. "What do you think—"

Somewhere, a half-kilometer away, a mage cast a lightning bolt at a commlink because he had been paid to do so. The commlink blew up, as commlinks struck by lightning tended to do. That set off another reaction.

There was a *crack* from the building, sharp and piercing. Then another, and another. They piled on each other, building a physical sense of concussion as they repeated, with a growing *thud* rumbling under the crack. The noises traveled around the building.

Then, for an agonizing moment, the building was still. Some dust drifted out broken first-floor windows. She thought they had failed, that they had not done enough—until the side of the building nearest her sagged. That sag rolled the edge of the building like a collapsing wave. The weakened first floor couldn't hold, and it went down, and the lack of support pulled the other floors. They all started coming down, pancaking into each other as dust billowed and encompassed the lot. It built into a combined puff and pillar, and everyone knew that when it cleared, there would be no building left.

Dennis paled. His brow creased, his body tensed, and he looked ready to attack. But he looked over his shoulder, then looked ahead. Then he ran.

"You be safe," Zipfile called after him. "You find somewhere safe to go."

She felt pretty confident that wherever Dennis wanted to go, he wouldn't want to walk far.

Luckily, a ride would be ready for him.

EMU

as. The entire building where he worked—that he had been in charge of—had just collapsed in a heap. He might be curious about what was going on, except he had seen someone he very much had a problem with right by the building. And she had delivered something that sounded like a threat. He would want to get away, but there was one small problem—he'd left his car at home, thanks to a drained battery. So what now?

He needed a ride. That would be fine. Rides were everywhere. He just needed to signal a Jitnee. Someone would take him out of—hey, wasn't that his Jitnee rider from this morning? Great. She definitely could get him somewhere else.

That was the situation they'd set up this morning. Zipfile had found out that when Dennis used a ride share, he used Jitnee, and then she made sure that his next request would be routed to Emu. After dropping Zipfile off in the morning, Emu sped away from the AVR building to Dennis's house so that when the call came, she could be there in minutes. And she was.

Dennis had not met Emu in person, but he knew what she looked like. That meant a disguise had been needed. Nothing fancy. Her hair was pulled back, and some nanopaste and makeup made her face rounder and her cheeks bigger. The fact that she was dressed in a normal, boring blouse-and-pants combo didn't help—the floral pattern of the blouse was so non-rigger that she had to actively fight nausea when she put it on.

It was far from the only distasteful part of this ride, because she not only had to earn a five-star rating—she had to be *liked.* The very worst, most humiliating part of this job was the time she had spent reading articles on likability. She had some notion that that wasn't something you should have to learn, but she also had a notion that without help, she wasn't going to make the connection she needed to make.

Fortunately, she wasn't trying to sleep with Dennis or anything, so there were some lengths she would not have to go to. But she also wasn't going to get by just turning in pleasant music and shutting up.

In the end, it was both simple and incredibly difficult. The simple part was that all she had to do was ask him about himself and keep the conversation on topics he clearly wanted to talk about. He was a sport shooter, and could have spent the entire ride talking about it. He nearly did. The tough part was she couldn't just turn around and scream, "Shut up shut up shut up *shut up!*" at him, even though she really, *really* wanted to about a half-dozen times. As a plus, she learned about three different shooting ranges she didn't know about (and probably couldn't afford), as well as something called the Shooting Stance Controversy of 2079 that, if she heard any more about it, might just force her to steer her car right into a building.

It seemed like it worked. He made a point of showing her that he was giving her a five-star review when he left, and he gave her a warm smile.

When he got in her car that afternoon, trap shooting was far from his mind.

"Drek. Drek drek drek drek drek *drek*!"

"You okay, mate?"

"*No*! I'm *not* okay! *Drek*! I should stay. People will be looking for me. Police. Police will be coming. Do I need to talk to them? What do I tell them?"

"Tell 'em the truth, mate. You tell them it was shadowrunners."

He started to respond. "But if I tell them that, I'll have to tell them—" Then he started to understand.

Emu helped him out by peeling the nanopaste off her face, then turning around and smiling at him the next time the car stopped. By the expression on his face, he'd already guessed.

"You're—you're psychotic," he said.

"Naw. If that were true, you and all your employees would be lying under a heap of rubble. Do you know how much trouble we went through to keep you all alive?" She shook her head. "Work of art, really. What we did here."

There was rapid movement in the back seat, then a sharp *snap*, a cry of pain, and a *thud*. She glanced at the rear view to see Dennis clutching his right hand in pain.

"You leave that gun where it fell," Emu said. "Understand where you are now. You're in a rigger's car. Worse than being in a spider's web. You don't want to try anything that makes my machines angry."

"What do you want from me?"

Emu pointed to the Jitnee logo glowing in her car. "I want to take you where you're going and get a five-star review! The same thing every hardworking person of the world wants."

"You want money? Is that it?"

"Why do you think we're doing this? You keep your money to yourself. We got paid for this. No worries."

He leaned forward, coming close to getting himself another shock from one of her hidden devices. "Are you going to kill me? Is that what this is?"

"We could have killed you last night, at your house. I could have killed you when I picked you up this morning. We could have left you in the building when we blew it up. I could have killed you when I picked you up again. You should be happy. We clearly want you alive."

"Then what the *hell* do you want from me?"

"I already told you, mate. Your building was hit by shadowrunners. That's what you're going to tell anyone who asks. The investigators will be able to find out some information about them, but here's a big clue—the detonation was set off by a lightning bolt hitting a commlink. Some astral investigators should look at that, fast. It will be good for them to know that."

"And that's it?"

"That's mostly it. There's just one more thing: You should remember the list of times I gave you when we could have killed you."

She pulled the car to the side of the road and stopped. She had circled enough that they were only four blocks from AVR. Streets were being blocked off, and crowds were gathering. It was time to get far from here.

"We're not coming after you, because we're done with you. Unless you decide you're not done with us. Are you done?"

Dennis nodded twice, but then his eyes widened as he heard a voice coming through a police loudspeaker.

"GMC Commodore! All occupants please exit the car with your hands visible!"

She turned and glared at him.

"PanicButton. I hit it as soon as I recognized you. We hadn't...we hadn't come to an understanding."

"You get one freebie. But we're done. Get out."

He couldn't exit the car fast enough—with his hands up, as the cops demanded.

Emu rubbed the steering wheel of the Commodore. When she got up this morning, she wasn't sure if she'd get to outrun Knight Errant. The day was looking up.

"This is your last warning! Exit the car!"

They wanted to open fire. They were unnerved by the explosion and probably jumpy as hell. She couldn't count on them to be contained at all.

Time to jump in.

The adjustments she made to the vehicle were instinctual and almost instantaneous. Tighten suspension. Turn off traction control. Switch off the things the designers put in to protect people who didn't know how to drive.

When you're meat driving, you think of mechanics and processes—depress brake, lightly press gas, then go off brake and floor it.

Jumped in? You surge. You leap. You pounce. You just *go*.

Business-district streets feel great, both smooth and grippy. Very little rubble. The Commodore leaped to life. A few anxious, quick-fingered cops fired several rounds, which felt like pebbles hitting her back. They didn't come close to anything vital. She fishtailed a little peeling out from her parking space, but she figured that just made her look cool. Then she was off.

She had modified the Commodore, but it was still a Commodore, meaning it wasn't going to beat too many cars off the line. But it could corner.

Job one was getting away from the cops behind her. Job two was getting away from the AVR site. That meant turning right.

The cops were prepared. Two prowlers, closing the gap right in front of her. Making a V that pointed away from her. Which was a mistake.

She hit the bottom of that V at a good clip. Both cars spun away from her. The crash on her front felt like her shoulders caving in. But not breaking. She lunged ahead, felt more bullets hit her, and was past.

Keep turning. Don't be predictable. Main streets would be blocked. Find something else.

She went the wrong way down a one-way street. Crossed over a curb and some grass meant to keep two streets from connecting. Raced down a diagonal street, saw a cop coming to cut her off, drifted sideways into a park with a broad sidewalk and then used that to cut across the whole park. People scurried away, but they would have been safer staying put. Emu would only hit what she wanted to.

She could feel the damage, scrapes all over her body. No deep pain, though. Everything still worked.

Mentally, she could do this forever, run and keep running. But physically, cars needed fuel, people needed food. She'd have to stop at some point. She needed an endgame.

The car was toast. Its description and identification were everywhere. She'd never be able to drive it in Seattle again. So she had to figure out where its last hurrah would leave her.

Then she saw an H in a circle, and she knew. She knew this place. She knew what would work. She darted off a quick message as she approached a horrendous intersection—the street she was on was ending, intersecting with a north-south street that had just had a piece of it branch off, curving southeast. Then there was another north-south street about a half-block away. There wasn't enough space between these roads for any buildings, so the spots were paved over, left as parking spaces or just empty plascrete.

It was also a lot of pavement to play with.

Police cars were heading up the curved street to cut her off. She hard turned left, then right as soon as she got any traction, taking her in a tight S. The police cars had gone straight, so they missed her.

She kept the right turn going and shot down the curved street they had taken. She had another two on her tail, cars that had chased her pretty much since she started moving. More were probably coming up the curved road. She shot down it and saw those other pursuers, but she was going to beat them to her spot, which was barely more than a dirt road. It was short, a driveway really, leading behind a utility building. Cop cars squared behind her to follow. She only stayed on the road for thirty meters, then she bumped over a thin divider of ground separating the driveway from a half-full parking lot.

Two cop cars came after her. Two others anticipated her, shooting ahead to try to cut her off. She skirted the edge of the parking lot and then turned onto a connector road. She was in front of a hospital complex, a half-dozen buildings with walkways between them and a drive leading through the heart of them. The connecting road took her to the drive—the cops cutting her off had gone straight up it. They had broader roads and fewer turns. It would be close.

She cut her turn on the left side of the road. She would have slammed into any cars going the opposite way of her, but there were none.

She careened down the drive. It was pretty fresh, light-colored plascrete, smooth and easy. Cool, even. But two hundred meters away, it would end in a cul-de-sac around a fountain.

The cops knew. Two of them stopped, blocking the road with a V set up in the right direction.

Too bad she wouldn't have the chance to try to crash through them.

She barreled toward the cul-de-sac. This next move was going to hurt.

One arc of the cul-de-sac was separated from a broad plaza by a set of concrete bollards. She aimed the car so the bollards didn't line up with the tires, and gunned it.

It was like twin baseball bats straight to her head. She couldn't see after the impact. She knew bad things had happened to the axle, but it was still rolling. It just wouldn't do anything fancy now.

It was straight for a few seconds, then she had to pivot around a crescent-moon garden. Then pivot back to hit some blessedly regular road.

She'd carved a path for anyone to follow, but she had the advantage of surprise. The first car pursuing her hadn't anticipated the turn, and had reacted too slow to follow her, but the second careened through at a high speed—too high to steer clear of the crescent-moon garden. It went into the garden and didn't come out.

The drive she was on was short, ending by intersecting another small road that ran along the back of the hospital.

She didn't intend to use that road.

On the other side of the road was a chain-link fence. Her car was hobbled, but it could still handle chain-link. She crashed through.

She was driving on grass. Barely. She was hobbling. Limping. But still moving. The grass was mostly dead with a few lively green circles—it had been a golf course, but it had fallen into disuse. The heavily watered former greens were the last signs of life.

Three trees were in front of her, a whole stand to her right, with a small gap between them. She pointed the car at the gap. She patted the dashboard, moved to the passenger side, opened the door a crack—as small a crack as she could—and rolled out as the car pulled even with the cluster of trees. She swiped out with her hand as she fell, making contact with the door and closing it. She rolled into the trees and lay flat.

The Commodore kept rolling, taking a nice slow drive toward the fourteenth hole. A police car followed it almost immediately, then another.

Emu dropped her connection with the car. At this point, it was a relief, because she didn't have to feel the wounds that the car had collected anymore. She stayed low, crawling on elbows and knees back toward the hospital. The car would stop soon, and the cops would find out she wasn't in it.

There was another copse of trees twenty meters to the east. She looked toward where the Commodore had gone. It had stopped. The police officers were out of their cars, approaching it slowly. She stayed low, using bushes for cover, and made it to the next copse. It was thicker than the first, stretching all along the fence. She followed it, making it to the corner of the old course. Some other interlopers had pried open the fence here. She shimmied through it.

She looked to her left. A car was parked, with a familiar logo glowing in the windshield. The driver poked his head out of the window.

"Are you Carol?"

She smiled. "Sure am!"

She jogged to the car and slid in the back seat of the Jitnee she had called when she first entered the complex intersection a few blocks away.

"Where to?"

Emu sat back, smiled, and got away.

THE UNWANTED

YU

Yu got away easily, Frostburn and Rude with him. They were at the Bulldog when the mage Yu had hired sent his lightning bolt, and the car was already moving as the building fell. Plenty of cars were in the street, and they moved faster once the booms started, so there was no cause to notice the van. If any security footage was sent offsite so it still existed, it would show them entering the building, but separately, and not suspiciously. There was little any law enforcement authorities would gather that would implicate them.

Not that law enforcement would lack for things to look at. That was part of the point of the whole exercise.

ZIPFILE

Zipfile had a little more difficulty getting away. Since she was the one who saw Dennis, she had to be present when the building fell, which meant she was caught up in the panic of people running, screaming, and surging into the street. She had no travel options besides feet, and she didn't want to do anything that would draw any attention. She turned everything off besides a commlink, which she used to monitor police chatter. She hated it—she felt like she was walking around with her head cut off—but she didn't hear anything targeting her.

She wasn't eager to leave any sort of Matrix trail or burn another SIM (Lesedi Kriege was likely gone forever; maybe she'd show up in Neo-Tokyo or something if she wanted to throw investigators a curveball). She also didn't want to walk all the way to the safehouse, but she didn't want to reach out to the other team members, either. In short, she liked none of her options.

But the worst decision would be staying around and waiting for Dennis to catch sight of her again. She opted to walk a few more blocks, then hail a cab the old-fashioned way, with a raised arm and a ready credstick.

Everyone was waiting for her at the safehouse, even Emu. Rude was sleeping on the sofa, Emu and Yu were drinking something cold, and Frostburn was packing. The mood was good, but not yet relaxed. They still had a final meeting to get through.

YU

Yu had sent a message to Mr. Johnson signaling their availability for a meeting at any time. It might not have been necessary—if he was paying any attention to the world, the news of the AVR building's collapse would have reached him—but Yu figured it never hurt to let Mr. Johnson know they were still alive.

The lack of an immediate response was not surprising. Like a popular kid in high school, Mr. Johnson usually knew the importance of not appearing overeager. Even after a couple of hours, not hearing anything was not alarming. But as the normal workday was ending and the sun was lowering, Yu started to find the lack of a response alarming.

He did the things you always do. He turned his commlink on and off. He refreshed his message window several times. He sent himself a few messages to make sure the functions were working right. Everything told him that the reason he hadn't gotten a message from Mr. Johnson yet was simply that Mr. Johnson hadn't sent one.

He didn't like that. At all.

Honestly, the barest case scenario was that something had happened to Mr. Johnson and he was dead. Sure, they'd be out some cash and wouldn't have the chance to settle things, but it also meant Mr. Johnson wouldn't be coming after them because he was dead. There were worse possibilities.

Then the message came. <*Midnight, Vasa Park, lot 12.*>

That was it. No "Great!" No "Nice job!" Yu didn't like it at all.

He walked from the kitchen to the living room.

"I don't like this at all."

He shared the message with the team.

"What's wrong with it?"

"You want a list? It came late. It's too laconic. He wants us in Bellevue, in a dark area, by a lake. At night." He paused. "I think he wants to kill us."

Everyone was silent for a moment.

"Duh," said Rude.

"Seriously," said Zipfile. "Haven't you been paying attention to what we've been doing?"

"No, I know, but this is confirmation," Yu said.

"This is confirmation," Zipfile said.

"Yes."

"Of what we already believe."

"Yes."

"And have been planning for this whole time."

"Yeah."

"Shocker."

Yu shifted uncomfortably. "But there's a difference between knowing...and *knowing*."

"If you say so. So, we've got a site. Let's make it work."

It was tough for Yu to focus. He knew their status. When one Mr. Johnson tries to kill you, you have a clear picture of your value.

When you think a second is trending the same way, then you really feel unwanted.

The word played in his head. *Unwanted.* He didn't like it, but then he did. It wasn't a pleasant label, but it had a ring of truth.

FROSTBURN

One thing shadowrunners think about that normal people don't is exactly how someone might be planning to kill them. Your average corp drone, bless their heart, doesn't even think about people trying to kill them. Like, at all. While a shadowrunner knows three different ways someone might kill them when they're grabbing a burger at McHugh's.

After a little conversation, they agreed Mr. Johnson would want the job done quickly. He wasn't going to talk. He wasn't going to take the time to monologue or anything, unspooling his genius plan to the runners. They'd served their purpose, so he could take them out. The team's job was harder—not just survive, but give Mr. Johnson a reason to keep them alive indefinitely.

In short, Mr. Johnson didn't need to talk. They did.

They'd had an outline of a plan from the beginning. They spent the next hour putting some specifics to it. Then they went out again.

EMU

The situation was screwed. It would be difficult. Some of them might die.

But she was going to get to drive something she hadn't driven recently, so it was okay.

She drove the whole team to Weowna Park by 11:15. They split up immediately. Most of them were heading south. Emu would be soon, but first, she had to go east, to the lake.

She had about fifteen minutes to find someone careless. She wouldn't have the chance to look at every watercraft she saw (and that would be suspicious anyway). She'd have to follow her instincts.

There were docks off every house here, but to see them you had to walk on the shore, which was private property. If anyone saw her, they might yell at her, which was fine. Or shoot her, which was less good. The main goal was to move casually, smoothly, like someone just wandering on a nice evening, so if anyone saw her, they'd just think she was aimless, but not dangerous.

Still, it would be best if she took care of things quickly.

She had a few guidelines. If it was too shiny, pass it by. If it was covered nice and snug, pass it by. If the nearby house was too bright, pass it by.

Those guidelines carried her by eight houses. She saw an uncovered jet ski and gave it a quick search, but no key was in sight, and the craft was firmly locked to the pier. She moved on. She passed four more piers.

Then she saw it. Covered by a tarp, but sloppily. Drifting far enough from the pier that it was clear it wasn't firmly locked, or even well tied. Definitely worth a shot.

The tarp provided great cover. She slipped under it and climbed on the jet ski. Now she could rummage around while being out of sight.

Her hand reached for the underseat compartment, opening it and reaching in. Sure enough, she felt the coil of the cord attached to the key. She took it out but didn't insert it. She untied the craft, then slid off the back, standing knee-high in the water. She pushed it out from under its tarp, then pulled herself up some, but left her legs dangling off the back.

She started frog kicking, slowly moving the jet ski ahead. She had a good distance to cover in a short time.

FROSTBURN

Frostburn was one hundred percent acting on the assumption that Mr. Johnson would have someone on astral overwatch. But that was not a reason not to use magic.

She made Zipfile invisible. Frostburn was pretty sure that in her heart, Zipfile knew she was being a decoy, but she was still excited about what she had to do. Even if it meant drawing fire.

Once they had separated from Emu, Frostburn took a round about route to the south side of the park. Zipfile was to the north.

She hoped their first reaction would not be a fireball to her face. But she was ready if it was.

RUDE

Rude stewed as he ran. Had they not seen him at AVR last night? How smoothly he moved, how calmly he performed?

Okay, he'd been invisible. No one had seen it. But still, didn't they know? He had a lot of things he could do, a lot to bring to the table. Instead of looking at those options, they'd fallen back on the basic troll tank strategy. Did they really think he *liked* causing mayhem and destruction?

Okay, he did. And in a campsite full of RVs? Some of those things folded like tissue paper. He was really going to have a chance to tear some things up.

What was he mad about again?

Typecasting was only bad when you're sick of playing that type. Rude just realized he was still very much into this sort of work, so they could typecast away.

Still, this would go better if he was angry at someone.

Oh, yeah. Mr. Johnson. Who was probably preparing to kill them.

The guns weren't out yet, but Rude jogged on, now ready to fully perform his part.

YU

Yu walked along Squibbs Creek, worrying that he wouldn't be shot at.

The whole plan was based on the assumption that Mr. Johnson wanted them dead, and that he had people who would take them out as soon as they appeared. If that happened, his team had a plan. If it didn't?

He wasn't sure what they'd do. So it would be nice to be shot at.

Not that he'd be the first one targeted. That was the job of the people with magic auras. His job was to see who did the firing.

The trees and bushes lining the lazy creek provided lots of cover—regular eyes would have trouble seeing him, thermographic eyes might have trouble picking him out if they didn't concentrate, and assensing mages might lose him in the middle of the auras of all the living things around him. That allowed him to draw close to the park—and his eyes had an advantage in the dark.

He didn't have weapons out yet. He was about to cross a road, and there was no point in alarming any locals who might be nearby. People in Bellevue could be sensitive about such things.

He'd checked the location of lot 12. It was near the water, which was good for Emu, bad for him. He wouldn't be able to rely on cover from the creek bed all the way. He'd need to improvise.

It was 11:55. He had two minutes to get in position.

ZIPFILE

"They'll see two magic auras," Frostburn had said. "If they're any good, they'll see that one is a spellcaster, one is not. So, who does street wisdom tell us they'll go for first?" She pointed to herself. "That's right. The first shot's coming to me."

Zipfile wasn't so sure. Maybe they'd take her out instead, figuring that she was relying too much on invisibility to get her where she needed to go, and she was overconfident and not well defended. In any encounter, going one shot, one kill to start things off was the exact right way to do things. Yes, Frostburn was a larger target, but would they notice that if they were looking at auras? She was worried they wouldn't care.

The bullet that hit her shoulder at 11:57 told her she had been right to worry.

She felt it before she heard it. It spun her, and she let it take her down. She'd been bracing for it the whole walk, but it still surprised the air right out of her lungs. And hurt.

Anyone who had seen her aura in the first place would know at a glance that she wasn't dead. They might even know that she wasn't that hurt. But she hoped they wouldn't be able to focus on her for long.

YU

There it was. First shot. With a quick message from Zipfile.

<Hit. Fine, armor absorbed. Gonna lie down for a few.>

He was in Vasa Park now. It was small, only a handful of acres and a dozen or so places to put an RV. About half of those spaces were right on the lake. Lot 12 was one of them, near the beach. There was a playground, a basketball court, a bathroom building—that sort of thing.

He'd come in from the north, while Zipfile had been just northwest of the site, walking along the nearest road. He had climbed a hedge row separating the park from residences and wound his way through a parking lot. There were two people perched on top of a bathroom building just south of him. One of them had just shot Zipfile.

He heard two beeps. That was a message from Frostburn.

It meant the one on his right was the mage. And should be his target.

His gun was out now. Just a pistol, but he'd gotten close enough.

He squeezed off three shots. The silencer turned them into a barking wind—the other guy on the roof would have trouble locating the shots.

The first guy would have more trouble, because he had just been shot in the head.

Yu moved, back and away from the deceased mage and his friend. He looked for movement. He knew those two wouldn't be everyone. He just didn't know how big of a force he'd have to deal with.

The shooter was looking in his direction, but not firing. Then he moved his arm toward Yu.

Directing people.

Yu moved backward, faster.

Then the bathroom building erupted into fire.

FROSTBURN

You don't always have to hit people. The flammable thing they're standing on will do just fine, especially if it's bigger than they are.

They had seen her. She knew they had. They would have been going for her next, except Yu had geeked the mage. It was good shooting. So she did her part. She was just south of the main entrance to the park, and now she was watching. Seeing what the fire attracted.

They had numbers. More than she thought. Four near the RVs by the lake. Two on the beach. Two about fifty meters to her right, close to the beach. Two pairs of two north of her. And who knows how many in the RV with Mr. Johnson.

It was a gauntlet.

She waved an arm toward the closer of the pair north of her, sending darts of ice flying at the through the woods. She doubted they would do much damage. But they'd get attention.

She ran southeast, along the edge of the park. Action would be moving to the lake soon enough.

EMU

The sound of gunfire was like music to Emu. The building that erupted into fire was a symphony.

No more damned paddling. She pulled herself onto the jet ski, started the engine, and shot forward.

She hadn't been able to bring her assault rifle. It just wasn't concealable enough, so she had to settle for pulling out a Colt America. But it wasn't time to fire it yet.

No, the cavalry would provide the bullets.

The three Roto-Drones drifting over the lake didn't actually play "Ride of the Valkyries" as they approached, but she still heard the music in her soul. They were high up, hard to see against the dark of the night sky. They weren't loud yet, but they were getting louder.

If Mr. Johnson's people were on their game, they'd have noticed them.

She had them heading toward the beach. Frostburn told her two people were on the beach, two more close by. She'd see how they reacted.

When the drones were within a quarter-kilometer of the beach, she opened fire. The mounted Ingram Smartguns weren't terribly accurate at that range. But bullets in the air still had an effect.

The guns clattered, the bullets thumped the sand. She saw silhouettes on the beach turn, look up, take a shot.

She revved. They reacted. One of them was smart, moving toward a small beach house for cover. The other experienced decision paralysis.

She squeezed off shots to make sure he never got the chance to decide. He fell.

She wheeled the jet ski around. Out of the corner of her eye, she saw one of her Roto-Drones falling. It hit the lake with a splash.

It was going on Mr. Johnson's tab.

<Active hacker,> she sent. *<Stop them.>*

ZIPFILE

She was still lying on the ground when Emu's message came. Break was over.

A good hacker can find any icon and charge into it, sometimes punching through it, other times at least occupying its attention so it can't do anything but play defense. You go with a flurry of blows so strong, so fast that anyone, no matter who they are, has to struggle to keep up.

A great hacker doesn't have to do that.

She'd met Mr. Johnson already. Been in the presence of his gear. So she had done what any quality hacker would do—she broke into it. Quietly, smoothly. And left herself a backdoor.

Which she walked through now.

First vital piece of information: Mr. Johnson was not in the RV in lot 12. He was two away, in lot 10. Not surprising, but good to confirm. The decker was in there with him, and Mr. Johnson's commlink was slaved to the decker's cyberdeck.

So her backdoor let her right in to the cyberdeck. When she had a moment to reflect, she might laugh herself into hysterics about this, but she had too much to do now. She sent a data spike to the heart of the cyberdeck, amped up by her Overclock program. Then she sent another for good measure.

She'd love to be in VR to see what was happening to the deck's icon. She imagined smoke, flames, and general disintegration. It would have been really satisfying.

That wasn't the only hack she needed. The next one wouldn't be as easy, because it wasn't part of the decker's network. But it was vital. So she set to it.

YU

The gunfire from the beach pushed people inland, but the chaos near the bathroom made them pull back toward the RVs. Job one was protect Mr. Johnson. Killing Yu and the rest of the team was at best job two.

Yu encouraged them with his gunfire from the parked cars. He alternated between shots aimed directly at them and shots a little to the west. Any little influence pushing them east was good.

Behind him, lights suddenly went on. He turned.

The neighbors were awake.

Mr. Johnson definitely hadn't called the cops, but the neighbors surely would. Time was now very short.

There was another small shed not far from the burning bathroom. Yu fired a few shots toward the backing-up forces, then ran to it and climbed on the roof.

EMU

It was a great few minutes sweeping up and down the shore, firing at anything that moved, but then the messages came that told her it was time to get serious. Regretfully, she steered the jet ski south and let the Roto-Drones go on autopilot. Right now, all they needed to be was a perimeter guard.

Just south of the park, the road curved to a few meters away from the lake. A driveway was even closer. She moved toward it.

RUDE

It was time. Finally.

He had been on the outskirts, taking potshots, but as Mr. Johnson's people regrouped, he charged. He was going in with twin Predators. And grenades on the belt and a sword on his back.

He led with a flash-bang to put them on their heels, then a scream to unnerve them. Then bullets to put them in the ground.

There was smoke and dust, and blood was spattering. He was pretty sure only a little of it was his, but he could worry about later. His arm hurt. It was okay. It should

As he approached the RVs, he holstered a Predator and got out his sword. It wouldn't get into the guts of the RVs like bullets might, but it would scratch them up real nice.

Each swing brought sparks and deep gouges. He fired the gun occasionally, but the sword was way more satisfying, a test to see if he could bury it so deep in the vehicles that even he couldn't pull it out.

He didn't succeed, but it was fun trying.

The opposition was using the RVs as cover. After the initial shock, they might have been rallying. He looked for a big group to charge.

Then one of the RVs came to life. The electrical motor hummed rather than revved, and the tires spit gravel forward. Then it moved.

Mr. Johnson's people went after it as soon as it started rolling. Rude occupied himself cutting them down from behind.

FROSTBURN

Frostburn sprinted. She was not where she was supposed to be.

The people near the beach had been a problem. They must have had fire-retardant clothing—she thought she had smoked them a few times, but they didn't go down, and they kept firing back. They finally retreated toward lot 12, and she realized she was behind schedule.

She was running past a playground when she heard tires throwing gravel. It was happening. She was supposed to be on the other side of the road.

There was the RV, moving down the road. Zipfile had control. Some lackey was leaning out the front window, firing a pistol while fruitlessly working the steering wheel.

She went with an ice spear on him. It hit his head, and he sagged.

She was too slow. And on the wrong side. It was passing her.

She put on a burst as the RV passed and lunged for the ladder on the back. The vehicle wasn't moving too fast, but grabbing the ladder still nearly ripped her arm off. Her feet dragged on the ground, rocks cutting her shins. She pulled, hard, and got her other arm on the ladder, then raised herself on to the ladder entirely.

There was a *thud* on the roof. She stepped up a rung and looked. Yu had just jumped aboard.

There was a window next to the ladder. An ice spear shattered it, and a nice light fireball chaser let everyone inside the RV know that she meant business. She swung her legs up and over the edge of the window and climbed in.

Mr. Johnson was there, pistol out. He fired, one into the wall, one into her neck. She grasped her neck with one hand, and threw an ice chunk at him with the other. It hit his shoulder and sent him spinning.

She ran forward. She was not a street fighter, but she was still a damned ork. She lowered her shoulder into Mr. Johnson and sent him flying. She stepped over him, ran to the front door, and opened it while her hand on her neck channeled healing mana.

Yu swung down into the vehicle. He dashed right to Mr. Johnson and slapped restraints on his wrists.

"Cast it," he said.

A mana barrier went up that covered the whole interior of the RV. It wouldn't keep out bullets, but there were fewer and fewer of those as they pulled away from Mr. Johnson's people. She took a breath.

Yu helped pull Mr. Johnson into a seat at the RV's table, then sat across from him.

"Let's talk."

YU

They swung by the point where Emu was waiting, and Frostburn let her pass through the barrier. Emu took control, and the RV puttered along like a normal vehicle. A normal vehicle with bullet holes and large sword gouges on it.

"You don't even have to talk," Yu said. "Just listen. Look, we understand. Tying up loose ends. This was a mess to begin with, and messes need to be cleaned up. I get it. I just want you to understand who we are." He shared an ARO with Mr. Johnson that had a snippet of a newscast about the AVR explosion.

"Our sources inside Knight Errant indicate that the explosion, while itself not magical in nature, was triggered magically," the reporter said. *"A tip led them to investigate the signature of the spell used, and an off-the-record source told me it had 'known connections to Maersk operations.'"*

Mr. Johnson looked at the area where the image had been for a few moments after it closed. Then he looked at Yu. It was difficult to read anything in his expression other than weariness and pain.

"Look, you know and I know Maersk won't suffer anything from this. They'll have to occupy themselves cleaning this up, making themselves look nice and innocent, paying some bribes, all the usual. In the end, they'll be fine. But will this occupy them for a little? Distract them?"

Mr. Johnson sat still. Then he nodded.

"You have three of us here. But Rude and Zipfile, they're out there. No matter what you do to us, they're out there. So here's the real question—how are you going to put them, and us, to use?"

Finally—finally—Mr. Johnson cracked a hint of a smile.

FROSTBURN

It was three a.m. She was home.

The lights responded to her pre-set gestures. The speakers played Maria Mercurial for her. The kitchen was already making tea. And no one else was making noise, or worse, trying to talk to her.

Her neck was a little sore, but it could have been much worse. She was healthy and alive. Was she safe? Who knew? What were the promises of a Mr. Johnson worth? But he'd let them go. He'd even paid them. For now, that was enough.

They'd shown they could play the game. They never directly revealed all the information Yu had uncovered in his night of legwork, but they made it clear that they understood Mr. Johnson was connected to Wuxing. And rather than threatening exposure, they showed that they understood. They got a runner who could fake a Maersk signature to light up the commlink that blew the building up, and they pointed the police investigation at one of Wuxing's biggest rivals.

It was a simple message: *We know how to play the game. We can do more than you think. What do you want to do with us?*

Throughout this whole mess, they had been a team no one wanted. A team set up to fail. A team that not even all of the members were sure they wanted to be on sometimes. But they'd gone up against both Renraku and Wuxing, and they were still alive, paid, and about to sleep in their own beds.

Tomorrow, they might be the target of either or both corps. They might be hunted. But tonight was peace. Tonight, they were unwanted, and that was the right thing to be.

SNEAK PEEK:
TOWER OF THE SCORPION
A SHADOWRUN NOVELLA BY MEL ODOM
COMING SOON

Rashida bint Tariq bin Feroze al-Nazari steals through the deadliest shadows in the world: Dubai, in the Caliphate of Arabia. In a merciless land policed by the Caliphate Guard, under a government that exacts harsh penalties against any shadowrunner, she must break into the Saqr Tower and get out with the intel she's getting paid to retrieve.

Hired to steal a black op software package from Raqmu Enterprises, Rashida calls on her team of shadowrunners to help with the smash-and-grab. And this run isn't just for the nuyen. The people behind Raqmu Enterprises killed Rashida's family. Failure isn't an option.

But death doesn't scare Rashida. A Scorpion shaman, she fights for her life every day against the spirit that grants her the power to destroy her enemies, but ultimately seeks to consume her very essence. Amid treacherous desert sands and a city as deadly as a viper, Rashida must battle enemies both within and without if she is going to survive...

Preparing to take a man's life is much different than boosting data or intel.

Rashida bint Tariq bin Feroze al-Nazari admitted the difference as soon as she'd taken up her observation post over the porta-buildings and popup storefronts collected in the desert valley below. Thoughts of killing the man down there had been in her mind for years, but she'd never gotten this close to acting on them.

Tonight...was different.

Killing another person wasn't new. The first time she'd taken a life, the act hadn't been planned. It had come as a result of need and training, to protect a teammate. Afterward, she'd been sick. But those feelings had dissipated quickly, chased off by thoughts of saving her friend. She'd lost a few of those over the last few years as well. A career in the shadows wasn't based in longevity.

This death, however, was coldly planned, part of the total package. It wasn't paid for by the Mr. Johnson who had hired her. Rather, the promised death was part of the payment the anonymous corp exec had enticed her with. She'd willingly agreed.

Quiet as a gentle sigh, Rashida rose from the sand dune where she'd lain in hiding for the last seventy-six minutes under a gibbous moon. She strode toward the night market wrapped in a neon bubble at the foot of the hill and her target, thinking only of tearing the life from the man she had pursued for so long. Dry desert wind carried the sharp teeth of the chill that would bite deepest before the morning sun returned.

"Whipstrike." Khadija's concern came through the encrypted commlink.

"I'm here," Rashida responded. Whipstrike was her street name. Khadija was called Optivor because the decker saw many things with her hacking skills.

"I know you're there, sister. No problem with the connection." The decker monitored Rashida's progress from an out-of-the-way jackpoint in Algiers. The country had a long history of piracy, and that infamous tradition continued with smuggling and illegal jackpoints. Khadija lived in Marrakesh, but she made it a point never to do business there.

Rashida had never conducted a run inside Arabia for the same reason. Since the nations in the Arabian Peninsula had joined to form the Caliphate of Arabia in 2055, the Caliphate Guard units made very public examples of shadowrunners who got caught—unless the Caliphate had employed them. In that case, the shadowrunners simply disappeared—just as dead—because failures weren't allowed to come to light.

"Your bio signs spiked a minute ago," Khadija said.

Rashida cursed softly. She wasn't a novice. She'd been a runner since her university days six years ago. She was a professional. Blowing out her breath, she slowed her heart.

"Got sand in my eyes," she told the decker. "Null sheen."

"All good now. Reading five by five. Anything you want to talk about?"

That wasn't good. Even though Rashida's pulse rate was down, Khadija wasn't buying the excuse. They had been friends since university, and had gotten bloody together on their first run that went sideways when the rest of their team betrayed them.

"Not now," Rashida answered. "Later."

"I'll hold you to that."

For a moment, Rashida stood still as the breeze riffled her *hajib,* cooling her head beneath the material and her piled mass of black hair. She thought about how close she was to Eberhard Beuys. Her breath puffed against the *niqab* covering her nose and lower face, but she controlled her heartbeat, dialing back her anticipation along with her anxiety.

At the bottom of the tall dune, in the center of a crossroads marked by ATV treads and camel tracks a hundred meters below, the Rub al Khali Souk shot neon spears into the black, star-studded night from dozens of tents and fabricated buildings, as well as from bright, multi-colored lanterns strung around the marketplace's perimeter. A trio of buildings jerked erect along the outer fringe of the traveling market as late-arriving proprietors hastily set up shop. The whine of servos juking the ceilings up and popping the walls into place carried over the shifting sand. As soon as the structures locked into place, the interior lighting came on.

The marketplace was named after the Rub al Khali of Bedouin legend, the dream place where djinn, spirits, devils, and monsters roamed. The shapeshifting Ghoul and the Hanash serpent were also the stuff of nightmares. But it could be a place of learning as well; Muqarribun, the Arabic magicians, had gone there seeking knowledge.

In a way, that was where Rashida had found Scorpion, her totem spirit.

The sight of the marketplace took her back to her childhood, to an innocence she could scarcely remember. Her father had carried her on his broad shoulders, putting her up high enough so she could take in all the technological and magical wonders spread out for shoppers to see. She'd always felt like she was watching a fairy tale filled with djinns and spirits taking shape before her eyes, but they were mages and Awakened creatures made more mysterious through cyberware and magic.

Her father and her brother had been drawn to the decks and the software designers. They had loved technology, sharing interests and skills Rashida never had.

Her talents lay in another field, one that was not so innocent. For a moment, she closed her eyes and relived those memories. Her father had been strong and warm, a large man with a big laugh and sparkling eyes. He'd bought sweets for her, telling her they could never let her mother find out. Rashida's thoughts wandered rebelliously to an image of her father bleeding out on the thirsty sand. Only a short distance away, Qasim was a crumpled knot of pain, torn beyond recognition.

She banished the memories and opened her eyes.

You can't undo the past, she told herself. *But you can avenge it.*

Amid the neon beams and 3D holo advertisements for Saeder-Krupp, Evo, Wuxing, a couple dozen local and out-of-country corps hopeful of creating market inroads warred in vain against the true commerce lords. Lofwyr's stylized dragon head, Saeder-Krupp's trademark, slowly spun high in the sky, warring for attention against Wuxing's restless flames and Evo's helix gears. The small businesses' holos struggled to gain a toehold against the massive projections of the AAA megacorps, but their efforts were dwarfed by comparison. Sound bites in a dozen different languages and canned music threaded through the noise of the market hawkers.

Holographic yellow and red fires danced in giant rectangular braziers marking the souk's four entrances at the cardinal points. Men and women wearing white Kevlar with Ifrit Services Security badges on their shoulders, chests, and backs patrolled the gates. ISS was the largest protective arm in the Caliphate.

ISS drones hovered over the *souk* as well, mixing in with the holo projectors and news gathering craft piloted by local and international journalists. The *souk* was technically illegal, but no law enforcement agency ever "found" it if the proper bribes were in place, and if found, only the "right" people were arrested. Still, the marketplace was news, and news was free advertisement for biz. Distortionware would make sure no one was identified, of course. The drones' presence increased the risk Rashida faced, but they also added to the overwhelming sensory onslaught attendees weathered. Ultimately, they provided necessary cover.

"You must kill your enemies..."

The dry voice of Scorpion whispered in the dark recesses of Rashida's mind, as it had since she'd accepted the totem spirit's guidance only a few years after the deaths of her father and brother.

"Our enemies must not be suffered to live..."

That was only one of Scorpion's many lies. The spirit wouldn't just give her power to defeat her enemies. If it was permitted to, Scorpion would consume her, erase all that was her, and take over her body as a host. Then it would seek to destroy all human and metahuman life, not just the people Rashida hunted tonight. The shaman who had introduced her to the spirit had warned about that, but Scorpion held an affinity for her, and the spirit was the only one from whom she could claim the power to make herself strong enough to exact her vengeance.

Even after years of practice, putting away Scorpion's lethal hungers required dedicated resolution. Control over the insect spirit balanced on a knife blade, and the fact that Rashida's current goal touched on that old anger regarding her father's and brother's deaths tipped the scales in Scorpion's favor.

Rashida's hands darted over her body, finding her weapons under the loose *chador* she wore over a Kevlar blouse and pants. Imperceptible slits in the gown rendered those weapons instantly available.

"Chummer." Khadija's voice was gentle over the commlink. *"You're not moving."*

"I'm putting my mask on." Tapping into her power, Rashida wove a layer of astral energy over her face. The spell was one she'd used before. It was expertly crafted and familiar, almost a ready-made thing because she knew it so well.

Observers who weren't cybered or didn't work in the astral plane wouldn't notice anything unusual about her face. They would see someone unfamiliar and nonthreatening, someone they wouldn't be able to describe later. Those who were augmented in some way or were mages would see bits and pieces of her face, but never all of it. Only directed, focused attention could tear the spell away.

"That's funny." Khadija laughed. "All anyone can see of you is your eyes."

"I want anyone who notices me to remember someone else's eyes." Rashida had memorable eyes, amber shot through with topaz, like her father's. She also wanted potential witnesses to remember someone else's height and size. The market lights wavered for a moment, and she knew the spell had taken effect.

Scorpion chittered in the back of her mind, anxious now, feeding off the volatile mix of emotions whirling through her.

Calmly, Rashida walked down the dune. Her boots sank deep enough into the sand that the calf-high tops threatened to fill. Several groups and stragglers, all Bedouin as she was, dressed in gowns and headwear, rode camels or ATVs or walked toward the souk.

The mechanical clatter of the ATV engines warred against the crescendo of riotous music spilling from PA systems around the marketplace. Middle Eastern zither chords melded with Jamaican drumming and guitars shredding Western metal. The party atmosphere was carefully cultivated. Daytime visitation centered mainly on biz, but the nights specialized in off-grid tech work and mage spells the Caliphate wouldn't sanction publicly, and only tolerated because if those wants weren't met, more unrest would run through the Kingdom. For the right price, tech docs secretly chipped or augmented followers of Islam so that no one in their family or corp would know unless those secrets were shared or revealed by the bearer.

Adult fare became available after dark, too. Several of the tents and RVs specialized in metahuman sex shows. The Caliphate opposed nonhumans as a general rule, reluctantly tolerating them in strictly defined areas. Elves, dwarfs, trolls, and orks were more accepted in Arabian neighborhoods that depended on tourism, but they were never truly welcome everywhere. Allah had designed men to be men, and no one could change that in the eyes of hardcore believers.

At the east gate, Rashida stepped into the line of people waiting to enter the souk. The Ifrit secmen studied screens attached to decks running facial recognition software. The program databases didn't identify visitors; no one would want that in a black market. But it did serve to keep out known terrorists and corp spies. Getting attendees blown up in an attack or having wares stolen from vendors or their cred accounts hacked while in attendance would be bad for biz.

In spite of her shadowrunning experience, Rashida remained a cipher, invisible. The secwoman who scanned her did a thorough job in short order, then waved her on through.

"Enjoy the bazaar," the guard said. "Lots of good deals. Plenty of great food." She handed over a pair of disposable eyewear for visitors who weren't chipped or didn't have cybereyes.

Passing into the *souk*'s main area, Rashida pulled on the black plastic glasses. Powered by solar cells charged earlier, the glasses juiced and sprang to life. Instantly, information opened up when she gazed at a 3D holo in front of a shop. The default language was English, but Arabic, Chinese, and other languages could be selected at the tap of a button on the eyeglasses arm.

"I've got eyes on the prize." Khadija's voice turned brittle, indicating her tension.

Rashida felt guilty for just a moment. Khadija was her best friend, and she didn't like risking her on a personal mission like this. But more than anything, she wanted this face-to-face with Eberhard Beuys to balance the scales between them. Someone had to pay for the murders of her father and brother. Even if Mr. Johnson hadn't been paying for the run, she would have wanted to know about the man.

The real trick would be getting out of here after that meeting without getting caught. Especially if, at the end of Mr. Johnson's biz, she killed Beuys as she planned.

"Go to the right, around the Lebanese street vendor," Khadija directed. She sighed wistfully. *"You wouldn't believe how much I'd give for some* shawarma *and* badem tatlisi *right now."*

After the decker mentioned the pita sandwich and almond cake, Rashida immediately noticed the spicy and sweet smells. She glanced at the small grill set up with transplas shelving that supported pots, pans, and disposable serving dishes. Rashida stopped in front of the vendor long enough to purchase an order of *kebbe*.

"You got kebbe*?"* Khadija made the act sound scandalous.

"For cover." Rashida bit into one of the stuffed meatballs and took up the trail again. Her stomach recoiled because of the tension she was feeling, but she kept the morsel down.

"I hate you."

Despite the stress she was under, Rashida smiled at her friend's mock venom. "Once this is finished, I'll take you to dinner, anywhere you want." Mr. Johnson paid well for success.

"Deal, and you're throwing in dessert."

"But of course." Rashida flowed through the crowd, all of the people hunting bargains as they negotiated prices in loud, rapid voices. Barkers standing in foldout kiosks and popup storefronts hailed the steady stream of passersby.

Cyberware replacements for limbs as well as internal organs rotated in holos above a large, ornate Shiawase Biotech shop. Three attendants, two young women and one young man, strutted around out front. Each wore an x-ray overlay suit that showed their various cyberware for anyone who wanted to see. Not much of their flesh was left to the imagination either, so they drew plenty of momentary attention. A neon crawler advertised: *DOCTORS ON CALL. GET YOUR UPGRADE TODAY!*

Next door to the Shiawase shop was a kiosk featuring Mitsuhama Computer Technologies decks. The gleaming units looked sleek and lethal. In the right hands, with the right software, they would be. Khadija was proof of that.

The decker sniffed in disdain, her dismissal carrying over the commlink. *"Showpiece drek. Use-and-lose hardware for the uninitiated. But they probably have some good stuff in the back. Maybe you could take a minute–"*

"Not going to happen," Rashida responded. Behind the *niqab*, no one could see her lips move.

"Spoilsport. And there you sit eating your kebbe.*"*

"We take care of the run first, Mr. Johnson's payment second, and then we party and shop somewhere far from here."

Closing in on her quarry, Rashida popped the last meatball into her mouth and dropped the serving dish into the nearest bin, which promptly incinerated it. No one wanted fingerprints or DNA collected later. Rashida wore thin gloves to prevent those possibilities as well.

Still pretending to be a gawker, she walked slowly, throttling her impulse to race to Eberhard Beuys. For her and Mr. Johnson, Beuys was only the beginning.

A few minutes later, Khadija said softly, *"Heads up. He's in the kiosk next to the Horizon booth. I verified his DNA with a spyfly."*

Rashida's pulse quickened, but she knew Khadija would ignore that. Under the circumstances, the change was expected.

The Horizon popup storefront rolled footage from two just-released megahit vids in full-on surround sound that thundered over the market. Across the top, a scene from *BattleThumpers* broadcast a martial arts spectacle set in Thailand's jungles, showing mercs in high-tech gear attacking an enclave of giant creatures that resembled hornets. Autofire mingled with hoarse curses and thrumming wings.

In the back of Rashida's mind, Scorpion stirred, its hunger peaking and demanding release again.

The lower half of the screen showed armored soldiers fighting through floating jellyfish-looking aliens with long tentacles in the bowels of a radiated starship as red warning lights blinked along the steel corridor. A crawler ran at the bottom: Ares Space Marines!

"Wow," Khadija said. *"I gotta check out* Marines. *Looks totally wiz. Is that a game or a vid?"*

"Less focus on pop culture," Rashida said as she walked past the Horizon kiosk. "More focus on biz."

"Momentary lapse. I got you. Don't worry about me."

Rashida trusted her friend. Khadija had always been there for her, but the woman often tended toward ADHD.

The Gateway of Dreams kiosk advertised simsense rigs and software. Rashida assumed the popup offered illegal sensies as well as the travelogues advertised in digital bursts on the transplas windows. The current selection presented snowscapes and beautiful beaches too generic to place.

"May I help you?" A large ork in his forties stood behind a small counter. Like most of his kind, he was beefy, with heavy jowls and fierce tusks jutting up from his massive jaw. His suit concealed at least one weapon—Rashida knew that from the way he held himself. He wore a headset commlink behind his right ear that glinted as he turned to face her. His right eye sparkled unnaturally in the light, letting her know it wasn't organic.

"External commlink," Khadija said. *"Old Erika Elite model before Novatech became NeoNET. Means the guy's piss-poor, or he's a mage of some kind, maybe."*

Rashida took her friend's words to heart. Beneath the *niqab*, she smiled, knowing the sales rep couldn't see her face, but he'd still notice the way her eyes changed. Even though they weren't really her eyes.

"I hope so." Rashida spoke in a demure tone as she stepped over to the counter. "I'm trying to persuade my husband to take me to London on holiday. I love Sherlock Holmes. I thought maybe a sensie showing the city might entice him."

No one else was in the shop. That meant either the illegal wares were by appointment only, or Beuys was using the popup to spy on other vendors here.

The rep smiled around his tusks. "Sherlock Holmes, eh?" His smugness told her he wasn't impressed with her choice.

"Sherlock Holmes?" Khadija snorted. *"Seriously? Why didn't you just go up to this slot and tell him to shoot you in the face?"*

"Not helping." Rashida hadn't really thought about her answer. Her father had read Sherlock Holmes stories to her and Qasim when they were small, sharing his love of the Great Detective and Victorian London. He'd spent his time actually reading to them instead of parking them in front of a trid. Trying to hang onto the memories of him was why she'd gone to university at London when she was old enough. He'd attended Oxford, and had paid his own way.

She had paid her way too, but not in a manner her father would have approved of. With effort, she shoved the memories away and remained focused. Her hand hung loosely, but her fingertips were bare centimeters from the *karambit* at her hip. The crescent-shaped knife, curved like a sabretooth's fang, was the weapon her father had trained her to use to defend herself.

"I...may have something suitable here." The rep tapped his monitor. "Got *The Wedding of Princess Diana, The Whitechapel Murders*— right time period, but probably a little gruesome for romance...ah.

How about this? *Arthur Conan Doyle's London.* Didn't even know we had that one." He tapped the monitor again and a vid of what was probably a busy 19th century London street took shape in front of him.

As it coalesced into holographic reality, Rashida stepped forward and delivered a throat strike to the rep, shutting off his wind, but not killing him. He probably wasn't an innocent, but she wasn't supposed to kill unless she had to.

Mr. Johnson would just have to get over Beuys's death.

The ork stumbled back and shook his head in mingled pain and surprise. He struggled to clear his throat, making more sound than Rashida expected. As a metahuman, he was physically tougher than a human, and she hadn't adjusted for that.

Sloppy, she admonished herself, knowing her old *silat* teacher wouldn't have approved. Advancing on him because the Indonesian martial art was an aggressive style, she chambered her leg and fired a kick into the ork's face, drawing the *karambit* in the same motion.

Her opponent's forehead was a slab of bone, and the impact jarred her. He tried to yell again, but only wheezed while struggling to raise his arms to defend himself. She followed up with the *karambit*, reversing it to slam the thick finger ring into his temple with a meaty *thud*.

Instantly, the ork's eyes rolled back into his head and his large jaw went slack. The padded temporary flooring laid over the desert sand muffled the impact of his fall.

Rashida had the *karambit* against her opponent's throat before his body settled. Trembling, she waited for any sign of resistance. Even though she preferred not to, she wouldn't hesitate to kill him. Nothing was going to prevent her from reaching Beuys tonight.

Thankfully, the ork remained unconscious.

Kill! Scorpion ordered, and Rashida felt the spirit at the back of her mind struggling to be free. Her hand pressed down, and the blade's edge bit into the ork's neck, unleashing a thin trickle of blood. *Kill!*

LOOKING FOR MORE SHADOWRUN FICTION, CHUMMER?

WE'LL HOOK YOU UP!

Catalyst Game Labs brings you the very best in *Shadowrun* fiction, available at most ebook retailers, including Amazon, Apple Books, Kobo, Barnes & Noble, and more!

NOVELS

1. *Never Deal with a Dragon* (Secrets of Power #1)
   by Robert N. Charrette
2. *Choose Your Enemies Carefully* (Secrets of Power #2)
   by Robert N. Charrette
3. *Find Your Own Truth* (Secrets of Power #3)
   by Robert N. Charrette
4. *2XS* by Nigel Findley
5. *Changeling* by Chris Kubasik
6. *Never Trust an Elf* by Robert N. Charrette
7. *Shadowplay* by Nigel Findley
8. *Night's Pawn* by Tom Dowd
9. *Striper Assassin* by Nyx Smith
10. *Lone Wolf* by Nigel Findley
11. *Fade to Black* by Nyx Smith
12. *Burning Bright* by Tom Dowd
13. *Who Hunts the Hunter* by Nyx Smith
14. *House of the Sun* by Nigel Findley
15. *Worlds Without End* by Caroline Spector
16. *Just Compensation* by Robert N. Charrette
17. *Preying for Keeps* by Mel Odom
18. *Dead Air* by Jak Koke
19. *The Lucifer Deck* by Lisa Smedman
20. *Steel Rain* by Nyx Smith
21. *Shadowboxer* by Nicholas Pollotta
22. *Stranger Souls* (Dragon Heart Saga #1) by Jak Koke
23. *Headhunters* by Mel Odom
24. *Clockwork Asylum* (Dragon Heart Saga #2) by Jak Koke
25. *Blood Sport* by Lisa Smedman
26. *Beyond the Pale* (Dragon Heart Saga #3) by Jak Koke
27. *Technobabel* by Stephen Kenson
28. *Psychotrope* by Lisa Smedman
29. *Run Hard, Die Fast* by Mel Odom

ANTHOLOGIES

NOVELLAS

SHADOWRUN SPRAWL OPS

In the year 2079, shadowrunners do the jobs no one else wants. There's plenty of work to do, and plenty of obstacles to overcome. Backstabbing corporate pawns, aggressive law enforcement, and other shadowrunners angling for your payday can get in your way. Your job is to beat them to the punch and make the big score before they can stop you.

Shadowrun: Sprawl Ops puts players in control of their own team of shadowrunners, selecting who they'll hire and then building up the cash, gear, and abilities the runners need to survive the streets. Only one team will complete the final mission that scores a huge payday and wins the game. Do you have the guts, wiles, and treachery it will take to make it to the top? Time to find out.

Topps

CATALYST game labs

WWW.CATALYSTGAMELABS.COM/SHADOWRUN
©2018 The Topps Company, Inc. All Rights Reserved.

Shadowrun fiction is back. Over 40 titles available now in popular ePub formats. Immerse yourself in exciting action, intrigue, and drama. Visit the Catalyst Game Labs store to download your next adventure!

STORE.CATALYSTGAMELABS.COM

©2018 All Rights Reserved.
Catalyst Game Labs and the Catalyst Game Labs logo are trademarks or registered trademarks of InMediaRes Productions, LLC.